Abby Malone

A Novel by
Shelley Peterson

Abby Malone

ILLUSTRATIONS BY MARYBETH DRAKE

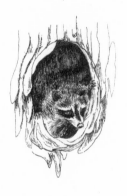

The Porcupine's Quill

CANADIAN CATALOGUING IN PUBLICATION DATA

Peterson, Shelley, 1952–
Abby Malone

Young adult.
ISBN 0-88984-207-8

I. Drake, Marybeth. II. Title.

PS8581.E8417A72 1999   jC813'.54   C99-931660-5
PZ7.P47Ab 1999

Canadä

Published by The Porcupine's Quill, Inc., 68 Main Street, Erin, Ontario
NOB 1TO. Readied for the press by John Metcalf. Copy edited by Doris
Cowan. Typeset in Ehrhardt, printed on Zephyr Antique laid, and bound at
the Porcupine's Quill Inc.

Represented in Canada by the Literary Press Group.
Trade orders are available from General Distribution Services.

We acknowledge the support of the Canada Council for the Arts
for our publishing programme. The support of the Ontario Arts Council
and the Department of Canadian Heritage through the Book and Periodical
Industry Development programme is also gratefully acknowledged.

7   8   9   ·   07

To Clarence and Marie Peterson,
who inspire and uplift everyone they meet

Contents

Chapter One
Merry Fields

And, though she be but little, she is fierce.
– Shakespeare, *A Midsummer Night's Dream*, III, ii

IT WAS HOT. Muggy and hot. Abby's skinny legs sweated in her jeans, and she squirmed in an effort to get comfortable. The supply teacher, Miss Smithers, droned on in a monotone punctuated with peevish sighs about English grammar, and how few people bothered with the finer points any more. No one in the class had any idea what she was talking about because her subject had been off the curriculum for years. She'd been going on for hours, it seemed to Abby, as the classroom baked in the heat of this Thursday afternoon in June.

Abby had a difficult time tuning in.

'And so the categorizing of subject and predicate is not only … *blah blah blah* … when parsing a sentence, but … *blah blah blah* … between the topic of the phrase and what is being observed about it …'

Blah, blah, blah. Abby's mind continued to drift. She idly observed her fellow grade-eight classmates.

Her best friend, Leslie Morris, looked almost bug-eyed in her effort to appear interested. Abby smiled affectionately. She knew Leslie wouldn't want to hurt anybody's feelings, however boring the person was. Her golden-brown skin glowed with sweat and her black hair was even curlier than usual from the humidity. Leslie was sensitive and kind, the only kid in the class who didn't ridicule Abby about her father.

Leo Rodrigues, the self-declared class bully, slept on his desk and occasionally uttered a short snort that sounded very much like a hog, the animal that Abby thought he most resembled. His side-kick, Larry Lloyd, was carving something for Pam's amusement on the inside of his desk. Pam Masters, sitting next to him, was more interested in her nails and whether Tommy Singh was watching her. Tommy couldn't care less about Pam's nails, and was finishing off a sketch of what he thought Annie Payne would look like in the nude. Abby turned her head to assess Annie, and decided that Tommy had a vivid imagination. All this time the teacher's voice drifted in and out of Abby's consciousness.

'Most educational institutions today are returning to the complete parsing of the sentence after experimenting unsuccessfully with other ... *blah blah blah*. May I have your attention, now, while I ... *blah blah* ... the various usages of the Subjunctive ... *blah blah blah*....'

Abby gazed out the window of the one-level yellow brick school and sighed. There were so many things in her life that were troubling her. So many things she was confused about. So many things more important than this interminable grammar lesson. She studied the day outside.

The sky over the fresh green pastures was a Mediterranean blue, and the little wisps of cirrus clouds flitting over the tree-tops made Abby think of ocean spray at sea. New corn was growing in the field next to the school, and wild spring flowers shot vivid colour into unexpected places along the fence line. Past the fence Mr Pierson's Hereford cows grazed calmly, watched over by the huge chestnut-and-white bull.

Their farm was called 'Merry Fields' in honour of Maryfield, Saskatchewan, the town where Mr Pierson grew up. Mr and Mrs Pierson, both in their mid-seventies, were her friends. Ever since she was small, they had always been glad to see her whenever she dropped in to ask advice about keeping little homeless animals alive. They'd remained stalwart supporters of her family throughout the long and very public trial. The view of Merry Fields out her classroom window comforted and cheered her.

Abby's eyes travelled hopefully across the road. There she was, the most beautiful horse that Abby could imagine. The little mare was silky and fine-boned, with long legs and an intelligent, pretty little face. Her mane, tail and legs were jet black and her healthy, glossy coat was dark brown; a true bay. Abby often watched her from her desk by the window, wishing more than anything to have a chance to ride her someday.

She could picture herself on the mare's back. Racing over fields, splashing through rivers, jumping huge hurdles effortlessly. This horse, with her elegant action and smooth gaits, would feel as if she was gliding instead of trotting. Abby was sure they'd be a great team, maybe almost as good as Hilary James on the famous Dancer, who'd won countless competitions and was the toast of Caledon. Abby sighed, imagining herself winning the Caledon steeplechase, and having the red ribbon pinned on the bay mare's bridle by Hilary James herself. Hilary, exclaiming what a brilliant rider Abby was. Hilary, smiling in admiration. Dancer bowing his famous bow, nose touching the ground, just for her. Abby was happy now, deep in her favourite daydream.

From the time she was little, she'd loved horses. Her Irish father, Liam, was an experienced horseman who'd been raised just south of Galway, the home of the Galway Blazers. Over the years, he'd entertained Abby with countless stories of the famous hunt and the courage of the Irish horses. He'd ridden ponies before he could walk, and had won many prizes for his riding skills. His most treasured memory was winning the first-place ribbon in the Limerick steeplechase when he was just her age.

When she was seven years old, he'd given her a little Welsh palomino pony named Goldie. Abby had ridden her all over the countryside, sometimes spending all day in the saddle. Often, she'd simply catch Goldie in the field, hop on her back and off they'd go. She loved that pony. They jumped fences, raced down the back roads, and won ribbons jumping at county fairs. Liam often said that Goldie was her best teacher. Abby had thought of her more as a friend, but she'd learned how to understand the animal's emotions as well as how to master the required technical skill.

When they had needed the money to pay the lawyers, her mother had sold Goldie. Abby's legs were starting to hang too low to the ground anyway, but the loss of Goldie had left her feeling empty, especially so soon after her father's departure to jail. She hadn't had a chance to ride since then, and she missed it. Right now she yearned for school to let out so she could give the carrot in her pocket to that little mare across the road. Abby could daydream and watch this particular horse forever.

A little wren sitting on the branch beside the open window suddenly chirped his cheerful message and startled her. Abby gasped out loud, jolting the sleepy classroom.

'Miss! With the blond ponytail and red shirt. Stand up.'

Abby turned quickly to the front. Did the supply teacher mean her? What was she wearing today? Oh. A red shirt. She rose slowly.

'Do you have a comment to make on the subject matter, or do you have something to share with the class?'

'Abby doesn't *have* anything,' Larry snickered, 'so how could she *share* it?' The class started to rouse itself from its sleepiness. Some of the kids joined in laughing.

'Is your name Abby?' the teacher asked.

'Yes.'

'Abby, what is your last name?'

'Malone.'

'Maloney baloney, your daddy's a phoney!' Larry hooted, made confident by the class reaction to his previous remark.

Not stopping to think of the consequences, Abby spun around and threw her pen directly at Larry. It hit him squarely on the forehead. Larry leapt to his feet howling with rage, and lunged for her. The loyal Leslie stuck out her foot and tripped him, and he fell hard onto the floor in the aisle.

'Class! Class! Enough!' Miss Smithers, knowing things were already out of control, rang the bell frantically. She was hoping to get the attention of the principal, Mr Edwards. The classroom erupted into a full-scale battleground, everyone out of their seats and happy to be relieved of their boredom. The noise level rose to playground pitch.

The only one not screaming and laughing was Abby. She felt mortified. What Larry had said about her father was a low blow. Abby turned her face to the window to hide her deep crimson colour.

What was this? With unbelieving eyes, she saw that Mr Pierson's Herefords had broken down their fence to eat the young corn in the next field. She blinked and stared.

Probably thirty head or more were devouring corn. They had to be put back. They'd get sick from eating too much corn, and the crop would be ruined. And Mr and Mrs Pierson were always doing nice things for her. She wanted to help, and it had to be now. Abby quickly thought of a plan.

Unnoticed in the commotion of the classroom, Abby quietly opened the window just enough to slip out, and dropped down onto the grass a few feet below.

She ran as fast as she could to the field across the road where the pretty young quarter-horse mare was grazing. Abby'd been told that the breed had been named 'quarter' horse because they can run the quarter mile faster than any other breed of horse, even beating out thoroughbreds for that distance. They tend to run in bursts of speed, tire, then speed again.

As she ran, she pulled the piece of binder twine that she used as a belt from her jeans belt loops. She grabbed the fence post with both hands and vaulted over the fence. She always had carrots in her pocket to give the mare a treat on the way to and from school, and now she was very glad she did. Normally this habit only caused problems in the laundry.

Abby gently called to the mare, trying to disguise her urgency. 'Come on. Come on, pretty thing.' She held out her hand, offering the carrot as she walked closer, repeating soothingly: 'Come on, come on, pretty thing.'

The little mare looked up from the business of munching grass and watched the girl approach. She was pleased to see her. This person brought her treats. She tilted her ears toward Abby and came to meet her and take the carrot.

'Good girl.' Abby was beside her now, and the young mare snatched carefully at the carrot with her teeth. Abby held the binder twine ready in her left hand. As the mare stretched her neck to get the carrot, Abby grabbed her leather halter, popped the middle point of the twine into the horse's mouth and threaded it through the halter on both sides for reins. She'd ridden this way on Goldie.

'Abby Malone!' Abby faintly heard her name being called. She could see the supply teacher outside the school, waving her skinny arms, skirt billowing in the breeze and hair flattened on her head. Abby pretended not to notice and leapt onto the mare's back, pulling herself up and throwing her right leg over. The mare felt just right. It was thrilling to be on a horse again.

'We have a job to do for Mr Pierson,' she said in as reassuring a voice as she could muster. 'What do you think of cows?'

The mare wasn't at all convinced that she liked what was happening. She'd been in her field, grazing, and now the girl who brought her carrots was on her back. She gave a couple of tentative bucks, and when her passenger stayed on, she decided to see what the girl wanted.

Abby put her into a trot and looked for a way out of the field. There wasn't a gate in sight, only split-rail fencing. She cursed under her breath for not thinking about this before now. 'Think before you act!' she muttered. *Everybody always tells me that. Why don't I learn?*

Miss Smithers was now accompanied by the principal and two other teachers. They were heading in her direction. The entire class was straining to see the action, heads and arms and even legs sticking out of the windows. They were all yelling and hooting.

The cows were becoming excited by all the screaming and were extremely restless. The outer cows began circling the inner ones, and the inner cows wanted out of the circle. And the bull was watching the group of teachers with what looked to Abby, even from a distance, like extreme bad temper. The teachers didn't know the danger they were in.

Abby felt the blood pounding in her veins. Her palms were sweaty. 'What have I done?' she asked the mare. It occurred to Abby to quit now, but the thought of sick, bloated cows and Mr Pierson's distress solidified her resolve. The mare started dancing, wanting action.

'Okay, okay. So we jump out.' She headed the mare toward the lowest part of the fence-line, legs tightly guiding and preparing her for the leap. Just as they took off into the air, Abby realized that the ground was much lower on the other side of the fence, beside the road. Then she saw the drainage ditch. And then the pickup truck, coming fast.

[14]

'Holy Hannah!' she said under her breath as they landed hard on the lower ground. They leapt again over the ditch, Abby sliding uneasily on the silky coat of the mare. She grabbed the mare's neck and squeezed her legs around the mare's belly with all her strength in an effort to stay on.

'BBBBLLLLLLAAAAHHHH' – the truck sped past, full weight on the horn.

The mare reared in fright, then turned to go back to her field where it was safe and there were no big scary trucks. 'Steady, girl,' said Abby firmly. She was trembling, but sure of where she wanted to go. She took a deep breath and spoke to herself as much as the mare. 'Calm down. C-a-l-m d-o-w-n.' The little quarter horse allowed herself to be guided across the road.

Facing west toward the scene, Abby assessed the situation. The cows were in the field of young corn, between the school on the south and the pasture on the north, from which they'd escaped. The fence was broken but passable, if Abby could persuade them to go back. Then she'd have to prop up the fence to keep them in until it could be properly repaired. The Piersons' house and front field and driveway sat beside the cows' pasture. She noticed that their truck wasn't there. The pasture continued behind the house and extended to the north. Further north was another large field, and to the north of that was the busy highway.

The cows were now racing in a wide, ever-faster circle, and the bull was leading the action at the outer rim, eyeing the teachers every time he came around and faced them. The corn field was now damaged badly, but at least the cows were too busy to eat. Abby wasn't at all sure about the best course of action.

The little quarter horse knew what to do. With sure instincts carried in her genes for generations, she began to circle with the cows at full speed, neck to neck. With each round, she had them running in a smaller and smaller circle until they had nowhere to run. They simply stopped in confusion, gasping for air, sweating and bewildered. Abby grinned and patted her horse. The muscles in her legs were so weak from exertion and tension that they felt like spaghetti.

'Good work! Now we lead them back through the hole in the

fence.' The quarter horse knew to face them toward home and steer them quietly in from behind. Abby sat back and let her do her work.

The herd seemed relieved and quite ready to go back home. Abby rode just behind them on the east and the bull kept order on the west. The cows were going back easily, finished with their big adventure. Abby now considered the problem of how to secure the fence after she got them through.

She heard yelling from behind. She turned to look, and to her horror, the teachers, all four of them, were running at the herd waving sticks in a misguided effort to send them home.

Abby put up her hand in a 'stop' gesture, but still they came.

'Stop! It's okay now!' she hollered.

The teachers, confident that they knew better, spread out like a fan and charged the herd, banging their sticks.

The cows bolted. Terrified by the running people and the waving sticks and the noise, they went berserk.

The cows kicked and bucked then stampeded along the fence, turned onto the road and galloped northward toward the highway. The little mare shot off after them in a desperate effort to head them off. Abby glanced back and saw that the bull had stopped to face the principal. He was pawing and waving his tail in warning. Mr Edwards backed off, hands up in surrender.

She held on for dear life. This was bad. No saddle, hands rubbed raw from the twine, surrounded by stampeding cows headed for certain destruction on the open highway. Abby could see transport trucks and cars ahead.

The mare swung to the outside of the herd and began to squeeze them over to the west side of the road. The open gate was just ahead on the left.

'Good girl. You're a smart mare.' Abby could only hang on to her mane and pray.

Just as it seemed that the cows were about to cause the greatest traffic accident the county had ever seen, they made a sharp left and headed down the farm lane, never altering their speed. The quarter horse positioned herself to the north of the lane to block any runaway cows from reaching the highway.

From this vantage point, Abby could see the bullfight that was being played out in the cornfield. Mr Edwards had dropped his stick and was backing away from the bull. Miss Smithers, the supply teacher, was clinging on to another teacher, Mr Perser, who was trying to look brave and scare the bull by roaring like a lion. This was causing the bull to become confused about which one of them to gore. The other teacher, Miss Mayou, was walking backwards towards the school, taking tiny steps and flapping her hands ineffectively at the bull, like someone shooing flies.

Abby rode through the herd that had huddled at the end of the lane and opened the gate to the field. As soon as every last cow was safely in, Abby kicked it shut, and thanked her stars when she heard the click of the latch. She hoped they wouldn't go directly back through the hole in the fence, but she could only do one thing at a time. And there was still the problem of the bull.

The teachers, she thought, should know better. It would serve them right if she left them to face their predicament alone. But she couldn't leave Mr Pierson's prize Hereford bull out in the corn field. Patting the drenched flanks of the heaving mare, she urged her toward the bull.

'Help!' cried the supply teacher weakly.

'Don't run, or even move,' ordered Abby firmly. 'We're coming between you and the bull. For heaven's sake, don't do or say anything.' The teachers nodded dumbly, faces stricken with fear. Abby didn't know if she could pull off this manoeuvre. She was banking heavily on the weariness of the bull and the comfort a horse gives to a cow. But she knew enough about bulls to understand that an angry, confused bull is an extremely dangerous and unpredictable animal.

Abby guided the mare beside the bull with trembling legs. Every one of her muscles was spent. She was taking a big risk and she was scared.

She looked down at his massive skull and said in a low, calm voice, 'Now, now, it's all right.' The clever little horse nudged the surprised bull with her side to get him moving. When he decided to comply, she walked beside him toward the hole in the fence. Abby was amazed. This was working. She wondered if the mare had ever done this before.

The cows had come around the barn and were standing in a row, staring. They looked comical with their identical expressions and posture. Very quietly, the little mare guided the subdued bull into the pasture without incident.

Extremely grateful, Abby slid to the ground, saying, 'Thank you, little mare. You saved the day.' She was immensely relieved. She wanted to lie down in the green grass and rest, but she couldn't stop now. She propped up the fence with a sturdy fallen branch, anchoring it as best she could with a big rock. 'This should hold until I tell Mr Pierson,' Abby muttered to herself.

The mare stood panting, chest heaving. Abby knew she'd have to cool her down before putting her back in her field.

'Come with me, young lady! You've got a lot of explaining to do!'

Abby turned around. Wide-eyed and totally amazed, she faced an angry Mr Edwards. Fury had replaced fear rather quickly, Abby thought.

By the time she'd left a note on Mr Pierson's door about the fence and put the little quarterhorse mare back in the field, her mother had arrived at the principal's office. She looked tired and worried. Abby ran to her mother's arms.

'I didn't mean to do anything wrong, Mom. Mr Pierson's cows got out and I had to do something....'

'This sort of thing happens much, much too often, Mrs Malone,' Mr Edwards interrupted, 'Abby is constantly in trouble. According to my records, this is the ninth time I've had to call you in since September. I realize that things aren't hunky-dory at home, but even so, we are educators, not disciplinarians.' His jaw jutted out when he was mad, noted Abby.

'Abby defied Miss Smithers by jumping out the window and running away. She then made use of someone else's property to corral cows. She'll be suspended for a day to think over her conduct. I will decide on the appropriate discipline.' The principal hadn't stopped pacing the whole time he talked.

'Mr Edwards,' interrupted Mrs Malone, 'I'm sorry you've been inconvenienced, but I'd like to hear Abby's side of the story too.'

'I'm a very busy man. Make it quick, Abby.'

Abby looked long and hard at Mr Edwards. He'd made up his mind. There was no use in protesting her innocence, and her whole body was aching from the hard riding she'd done.

'I'll tell you in the truck, okay, Mom? Can we go now, Mr Edwards?'

'Yes. You are dismissed. But on Monday morning I want you to hand in a full-page apology to Miss Smithers. And it is *very* important that you alter your behaviour for the rest of the year, *if* you are permitted to stay. Do you understand?'

'Yes, Mr Edwards.'

Mother and daughter left the school side by side. An observer would have had no doubt of their relationship. Both were tall and slender, with blond hair and fine features, but the resemblance ended there. Abby was graceful and coltish, and she moved with a light step. Her mother walked with rounded shoulders and slug-gish feet. Where Abby's face showed strength and vitality, her mother's was weary and spent, puffy and prematurely lined.

They climbed into the old farm truck.

'What am I going to do with you, Abby?' asked Fiona Malone wearily as they drove home. The road meandered through the beautiful, rolling hills of Caledon. The green pastures shone like emeralds in the afternoon sun.

'Mom, I'll explain everything. But can we go see Dad tomor-row? I mean now that I don't have to go to school ...'

'We can't. I've got an interview with the bank, and I can't afford to change it again. I'm sorry.' She looked with concerned eyes at her daughter.

'It's okay.' They drove along in silence for a minute. Abby knew her mother would probably miss the interview anyway because of a hangover, but she couldn't say it. She had to think of a way to con-vince her that she could go to Kingston alone. 'Why don't I take the train? I can do that. Remember, I took it home once before.'

'It's a long way. I'd rather you didn't, honey ...'

'But Mom, it's important to me. He's lonely there, you know that. It would surprise him, and cheer him up. Dad gets so bored in jail.'

'Okay, Abby. But you have to be very, very careful, and don't talk to strangers and …'

'Great! Thanks so much, Mom! I love you.'

'I love you, too, Abby.' Abby didn't see the tears welling up in her mother's eyes.

They turned into their farm. The old Ontario red brick house stood neglected but proud among the overgrown shrubbery and weedy gardens that Fiona had once tended so fondly. They'd done a lot of work on it over the years, and now were in danger of losing it. Abby's father, Liam Malone, had been convicted of embezzlement after a lengthy court battle, and they were coming very close to the end of their savings, after paying hugh legal fees. Abby was steadfast in her belief that he was innocent. She trusted that one day the truth would come out, and that he would be released with his honour intact. Fiona was equally convinced of this. But if it didn't happen soon, there would be no home for him to return to.

Liam had been a partner in the law firm Malone and Curry, a small, respected, and successful practice in Brampton. Colonel Kenneth Bradley, the retired multimillionaire heir to the Bosco Windows and Doors fortune, accused the law firm of stealing from him. Five million dollars was missing from a trust fund his late father had set up. Liam Malone and his partner Terence Curry had been in charge of the fund, and they came under suspicion. The money had never been found and since only Liam's signature was on an incriminating cheque, he was convicted while his partner was exonerated. Terence Curry had turned the offices upside down looking for anything that would prove his partner's innocence, but some important papers had disappeared. Liam insisted that he was innocent, but he was sentenced to three years, and sent to Millhaven Prison in Kingston for assessment. Terence Curry had been keeping the practice going as best he could, but people's faith in the firm had diminished and there wasn't as much business any more. He kept in close touch with Fiona and Abby, visited Liam in jail as often as he could, and continued to offer the family financial support, which their pride would not allow them to accept. His loyalty and friendship meant a great deal to the Malones.

A dark grey streak disappeared behind the large oak on the front lawn. Penetrating, anxious eyes peered around the trunk to observe the occupants of the truck. Only when there was adequate proof that no stranger was present did the young coyote gleefully spring through the truck's open door into Abby's lap, and joyfully lick her face all over.

'Abby! Can't you train him not to do that? He gives me a heart attack!'

'Mom, he can't help it, it's just the way he is.' Abby and the coyote cuddled together happily.

'I don't know what we'll do with him if we have to move.'

'What do you mean, Mom? He'll come with us! He's got nowhere else to go. He thinks I'm his mother.'

'We can't take him anywhere civilized. He lives outside and comes and goes at will. He's not a dog, you know.'

'Of course I know. But he's my best friend. Where I go, he goes.'

'Abby, Abby, Abby. Whatever will become of you? You must stop picking up every stray creature that comes along. We have a full-fledged menagerie already, and there's no assurance that we can stay on the farm.'

'I can't just leave things to die.' Abby swung her legs out the door and the two youthful occupants scrambled down.

'Cody, come help me feed the babies!' Abby called, as they ran leaping and skipping to the barn.

Fiona stood and watched. Her heart was aching. The bank manager, although a reasonable person, would have no choice but to decline to approve another loan. She knew that. They had no income and the house was fully mortgaged. They'd have to move. It was only a matter of time. She needed a drink. Her first of the day. She'd promised herself that she'd quit today, but she'd only have one little drink to help her through. Tomorrow, she thought. Tomorrow she'd give up drinking entirely.

Abby, with Cody following adoringly along at her heels, opened the barn door to be greeted by a variety of sounds. Scratching, scurrying, chuckling, cackling, all from the raccoon cage. Abby turned her attention first to a small, very quiet cage.

Reddy, a young red squirrel with a broken leg, wasn't doing so well. Mr Pierson had set his leg last week, and wanted to see him again to check if it was healing properly. The little fellow looked very weak to Abby, and she vowed to visit Mr Pierson that afternoon.

The two raccoon kittens, Rook and Rascal, looked out at her from their spacious dwelling, and stuck their tiny leathery hands out of the bars, asking for release.

'Okay, okay. Just for a while. But don't get into trouble. Ha!' Abby chuckled with pleasure at the sight of their little round bellies and curious faces. They hurriedly waddled out of their enclosure and immediately began investigating everything in sight, starting with Abby's shoelaces. Bored once the laces were untied, Rook rolled onto his back, tangling himself in binder twine. Rascal jumped on top of his brother in a rescue attempt that struck Abby as hilarious. She laughed aloud.

The raccoons' mother had been shot by an angry farmer who'd spotted her foraging in his garbage. They would've starved to death like most other wild orphans, had Abby not heard them squeaking feebly in the big oak tree.

Abby carefully opened the drawer under the heat lamp where she'd put the tiny young rabbit she'd found that morning. She feared the worst, because the creature had been very scared. Most wild rabbits can't survive shock, even if their injuries aren't severe. She took a look. Sure enough, the small brown furry body was lifeless. Gently Abby picked him up with the cloth underneath, wrapped him with it, and put him in a small box.

'We'll have a funeral this afternoon,' said Abby. Cody watched her sadly, reflecting her every emotion. If Abby was sad, Cody was sadder.

'We'd better feed the beasties and get in the house before Mom starts drinking. I'll ask her to the funeral and maybe she'll drive me over to Mr Pierson's with Reddy. Then she won't drink till later.' Cody cocked his head and narrowed his eyes, trying hard to understand.

As it happened, Fiona couldn't make it to the funeral. And

when Abby asked for a ride over to Mr Pierson's, she didn't mean it. She knew her mother wasn't fit to drive, but she didn't want her mother to know she knew.

'You just go on ahead, dear. I'm not feeling up to it.' And her head dropped back down onto her folded arms on the kitchen table. The kitchen was a smelly mess. Dirty dishes, spoiled food, unswept floor. Abby made a note that she'd clean up before bed. And the laundry needed doing. She'd get that done, too.

Abby left the house and got on her bike after carefully making sure that the little squirrel was safe in its box and secured to her fender.

They travelled back down the road toward the school. Abby carefully drove her bike around each pot hole and bump to avoid discomfort for the squirrel, followed by a devoted and attentive coyote.

Abby was greeted at the door of the Piersons' farmhouse with the delicious aroma of cooking. She sniffed before knocking. Chicken stew. Apple brown betty. Fresh bread. Her mouth watered. Her stomach growled. She hadn't eaten since her stale peanut butter sandwich for breakfast, many hours earlier. She knocked.

'Coming! Coming!' Abby heard quick footsteps approaching the door.

'Abby, my dear, dear girl! Come in! Where's that coyote of yours? Would he like to come in, too?' Mrs Pierson, with great kindness showing in her sparkling, intelligent eyes, welcomed her into the house. She was a tiny woman, with soft-spun platinum hair that was neatly controlled by her hairdresser once a week, but more usually crumpled and slightly wild, mirroring her zesty personality.

'Thank you, Mrs Pierson, but Cody likes to stay outside. Is Mr Pierson home? I want to ask him to look at Reddy.'

'The dear little squirrel? Oh, my, he doesn't look too perky, does he?' Mrs Pierson had opened the box to take a peek. 'Mr Pierson will be in shortly. He's fixing the fence that the cows broke down. We're so grateful to you for bringing them home, Abby. My! You do so many things! Can I get you something to eat?

You look famished.'

'No, thank you. I've just eaten. My mother absolutely stuffs me as soon as I get home from school.' Abby didn't want anyone to guess that all was not well at home.

'Whatever you say, dear, but I've baked far too many cookies again, and nobody here eats cookies. I don't know why I do that. And I have an abundance of milk. We only end up giving it to the barn cats when it starts to go off. Couldn't you help me out?' Mrs Pierson wasn't fooled by Abby's words. She could see by her pinched face and dull eyes that she was hungry.

'Well, if the cookies are going to waste ...'

'Oh yes! We'll probably throw them out. And the milk ...'

'No, don't throw out the milk, either. I think I could manage to drink a little.'

'Oh, good. Abby, you're such a help.' Laura Pierson watched the skinny teenager gulp down the milk and gobble the cookies, and felt a deep pang of sympathy. She was such a nice girl, and so bright. And too young to be dealing with all the problems at home.

'Where's my friend Abby?' a big voice boomed. 'Her coyote is watching the house, and I'm danged lucky he let me in!' Big Pete Pierson entered the kitchen after removing his dirty boots in the hall. Even though he was past seventy and had lost most of his hair, his bearing was ramrod-straight and he obviously didn't consider slowing down an option. He walked over to the sink and vigorously scrubbed his hands. 'I want to hear the whole story of the cows and the bull escaping, Abby. You rounded them up on that wild quarter horse of George Farrow's? My, my, what a girl.' He dried his hands on the towel on the counter.

'It was the only thing I could think of, Mr Pierson. And I guess it was also an excuse to ride her. She's the prettiest thing I've ever seen.' Abby's face lit up as she talked about the mare.

'Well, well! Is that so?' Pete loved horses, too, and understood her pleasure.

'I brought Reddy. He's not doing so well.' She brought the box to the sink.

'No? Let me have a look at him.' Mr Pierson gently lifted the lid. 'You're right. He's too still, and doesn't react to me touching him. He might not make it, Abby. You know by now they mostly don't. But his leg's set straight.'

'What should I do? Can you think of anything? I've kept him under the heat lamp, I've fed him corn syrup and milk from the eye-dropper, I've cuddled him just enough and not too much. I can't think of anything else to do.' Abby looked forlorn as she set the box on the floor beside the kitchen table.

Pete Pierson scratched his head. 'Can't think of anything, either. You've done your best, Abby. That's far more than most people could do. You've got a knack with animals.'

Cody uncharacteristically started scratching at the door.

Abby leapt to the door and started to turn the handle. 'Oh. Is it okay for Cody to come in?'

'Of course, dear,' exclaimed Laura. 'This is an honour! Any friend of yours is welcome here.'

As soon as Abby opened the door, the coyote slunk in and sat quickly beside Reddy's box, nervously looking around. Abby sat on the floor beside him, to reassure him in this new environment.

'Why do you think he wanted in, Abby?' asked Pete. 'He's never done that before.'

'No, he hasn't. It must be important.' Abby rubbed his ears, and Cody gave her a quick lick on the cheek. But that wasn't why he'd wanted in. Purposefully he nudged opened the cardboard flap of Reddy's box with his nose, and stuck his head in.

'Oh, Pete! He'll hurt the squirrel!' Laura became very agitated, and flapped her arms in distress.

'Don't worry, Mrs Pierson, Cody loves little animals. At least the ones that we rescue. He won't hurt him.'

'Just watch, Mother, and stay very quiet,' Pete said firmly. Laura slapped her hands over her mouth and watched.

Cody lifted Reddy out of the box very carefully with his mouth, and carried him over to the old mat by the door. Gently, gently, he began licking him. First the little belly, then the tiny legs, excepting the bandaged one, and then the back and finally the head of the little red squirrel. Reddy began to squirm. He rolled over to be licked again on his belly.

Abby and the Piersons were transfixed. The coyote was

bringing the little squirrel back to life. Cody shot a quick glance at Abby, asking for approval.

'Good boy, Cody. Good boy.'

'Well, I'll be,' said Pete quietly. 'He's doing the job of a mother; stimulating Reddy's blood flow and warming him up.'

Cody went back to work, licking until the baby squirrel curled up and went to sleep, nestled safely between Cody's front paws, next to his warm fur.

'Well, I never!' said Laura.

'Amazing. I've never seen anything like it. He's a special creature, that Cody.' Pete shook his head and quietly got up. 'I think it's best to leave them alone for a while.'

He walked over to the stove and checked the oven. 'What's cooking, Mother? I'm hungry.'

'Don't call me that. I'm not your mother,' she chuckled at their old joke. 'It's chicken and potatoes and carrots in a stew. Just how you like it.'

'I won't eat it unless Abby stays for dinner.'

'Pete! That's no way to invite a young lady to dinner.'

'Abby, may we request the pleasure of your company for this evening's repast?' Pete made a sweeping bow that caused his arthritic back considerable trouble. 'Ouch!' He clutched his hip and with an effort managed to straighten up.

'Old fool!' Laura cackled. 'I love ya!' She danced over and gave him a big kiss.

'Thank you both, but my mother's waiting for me. And she's been cooking up a storm. She'd be disappointed if I didn't come home to eat.'

'Why don't I call her and see if she'll join us?' asked Pete, hospitably.

'No!' Abby's reaction startled everyone, even Cody. 'I mean, thank you, but maybe another time.' She felt embarrassed and wanted to leave. 'I really have to go.' Her face was beet red.

Laura knew that something was terribly wrong. She knew that food didn't cure problems, but it certainly helped. And the look of Abby's skinny body was too much for her.

'Dear, I made far, far too much dinner for just Pete and me. I still make enough for all the boys, but they're long gone with families of their own. Do me a big favour and take home a doggy bag. You can eat it for lunch tomorrow, or for a snack. I won't take no for an answer. You've had such a big day, rounding up the cows for Father. What a brave girl you are, to do that for him. We can't thank you enough.'

While she talked, she shovelled steaming stew into a large container, stuffed fresh bread into a plastic bag, and apple brown betty into a jar for good measure. With cookies on top. All wrapped and tucked into a box and presented to Abby in a way that she couldn't refuse.

Abby blinked away a tear. 'You're so nice to me. Thank you.'

'Nonsense. We're lucky to have a young lady like you coming to visit.' Pete tucked the sleeping squirrel back in its box, and started for the door. 'I'll give you a hand. Mother foists all this food on you, and never considers how you'll get it home.' He winked proudly at his wife as he passed her. Abby gave her a shy, grateful smile and walked out the door, arms laden with food and followed by her coyote.

Pete secured the squirrel box and the food containers onto Abby's front and back fenders, and sent them down the road with a hearty wave.

'Come back soon with Reddy. I want to see how he's doing. And thanks again for getting the cows today!'

Abby didn't answer. Her throat was choked up with emotion. What great people, she thought. And Mom will have a delicious hot meal.

Chapter Two

Millhaven

This above all: to thine own self be true ...
– Shakespeare, *Hamlet*, i, iii

VERY EARLY the next morning, Abby was up and fed and show-ered, ready to visit her father in jail. She'd cleaned the house until late the night before, after eating her share of Mrs Pierson's hot dinner. Her mother hadn't been hungry, so Abby had put the rest in the refrigerator. Maybe her mom would eat it today, when she woke up.

She looked around. Everything was neat and clean, and the last load of laundry was in the dryer. It was time to go. Abby would have been grateful for a ride to the train station, but her mother was still sleeping, and Abby knew not to expect her to awaken until the early afternoon.

She took enough for her trip out of the money pot in the cup-board, and carefully closed the door behind her. 'See you later, Mom. I'll give Dad a hug from you,' she whispered. She headed for the barn to feed her little charges.

The raccoon twins rattled their cage noisily, clambering up and down their wooden posts and chattering bossily.

Cody was cuddled up with Reddy, who was much improved, and looked up at Abby proudly. He was happy to have a job to do for his beloved mistress. Abby sat down on the straw with them.

'You look after Reddy today, Cody. I'm going to see my dad.' She stroked him and smiled fondly, remembering how she'd found him. Someone had run over a coyote the previous spring. Abby had come across it on her way to school, and could see from her enlarged teats that she'd been a nursing female. After school, she'd searched high and low for the den, to no avail. Dejected, she'd given up hope for the litter's survival. But the thought of starving pups had nagged at her, and early the next morning she started her search again. No luck. At school that day, the teacher asked them to sketch a still life of a wild spring flower, and it was in her search of a suitable model that Abby at last found the den with four badly malnourished pups.

'I should've called you "Art",' she said chuckling, 'or "Crocus".' Three pups hadn't made it. Two were already dead and one died within hours of his rescue. Only Cody had been lucky enough to survive his ordeal.

'I'm so glad you lived, Cody. You're the best friend I've ever had. And the best nurse.'

She fed Cody, Reddy, and the raccoons and was on her way.

As she rode her bike south along Highway 10, she felt very lucky about a lot of things. She compiled a list of blessings in her head. One, that she was going to see her dad. Two, that she had a companion like Cody. Three, that Reddy was looking better. Four, that she didn't have school today. Five, that the Piersons were such good friends to her.

But her mind kept going back to the beautiful little mare, and how exciting it was to ride her. Like the wind. Abby would love to ride her again. Should she ask the farmer? Would he mind? She'd never met him, but she'd heard he was rather cross with kids. He didn't like them going near his fence. Abby rather reluctantly came to the conclusion that the farmer would probably say no to a scruffy kid like her, coming knocking on his door. In fact, she decided, he'd be furious with her if he knew what she'd done. But she smiled as she relived the exciting time she'd had rounding up Mr Pierson's cows.

Her musings passed the time, and the long bike ride to the Brampton Go station seemed remarkably short. She bought her return ticket to Union Station in Toronto, and then counted her change. She had just enough for the connecting train to Kingston, a juice to drink with her packed lunch, bus fare in Kingston, and a snack on the way back. That would tide her over until she got home, and then she could maybe make some scrambled eggs and toast for herself and her mom. She'd brought along a book to read on the train, and she was looking forward to the day's adventure.

* * *

The train pulled into the station at Kingston two hours later. Abby had read contentedly, and dozed for a while after lunch. She woke with a start, fearing that she'd missed her stop. With relief she read 'Kingston' on the big sign, and prepared to get off the train.

A friendly lady sitting across from her kindly asked where she was going.

'Millhaven Penitentiary,' Abby replied.

The lady looked shocked, muttered a feeble, 'Oh,' and busied herself in her handbag to avoid further conversation.

'Does that upset you?' Abby muttered under her breath. 'I'm sorry. Next time I'll answer "Queen's University. Faculty of Engineering".' She wished she had the nerve to say it aloud. She hated the way people reacted to any reference to jail.

The passengers disembarked, and Abby made her way to the bus that would carry her through the beautiful old city of Kingston, Ontario, to one of the toughest Canadian prisons.

The looming grey walls reminded Abby painfully of how her father was living. Locked up. She imagined with a shudder the horror of steel doors clanging shut, and echoes of guards' boots disappearing into the silence of bare concrete. Abby swallowed hard. The unfairness of it came flooding back, along with her enormous love of the man who'd stood by her through all her waywardness. She seemed to be in trouble more than not, but her dad helped her understand that she wasn't bad, just independent. Not rebellious, as the school claimed, but creative and instinctive. 'I must be difficult to raise,' Abby thought, not for the first time.

She missed him terribly. He was a very important part of her life. Things were so much worse when he wasn't around. A handsome and charming man, Liam Malone made any place livelier just by his presence. He was good and decent, with a heart big enough to contain the world, it seemed to his daughter.

The bus stopped, and Abby got out. She made her way to the first visitors' gate, which looked similar to security gates at the airport. She noticed the world-weariness of the faces around her. Prison saps people's energy, she thought. The visitors seemed as joyless as the guards at their postings. It was depressing. She thought of her dad, so close now. She stepped up to the gatehouse.

The guard asked to see her pass.

'I'm here to visit my father, Liam Malone.'

'You need a pass. Is anyone with you?' He looked down at this skinny, pale teenager, idly thinking that she needed a mother.

'No. But it's visiting hours, and I want to surprise my dad. He doesn't know I'm here. Can you tell me how to find him?'

'Look, young lady, you need to have an adult with you, and a pass. We couldn't run this place if we let in everyone who had a story. Go home, get your mother, get a pass, then come back. But not before.'

'My mother lives north of Toronto. I came on the train. It took all day till now to get here,' she checked her watch, 'and it's two-thirty, and I left my house at six this morning.'

'Don't waste my time. Next.' The guard turned his attention to the weaselly-looking man behind her. He had a pass. She had no choice but to step aside.

She fought back the tears, not wanting to look like a baby. How disappointing, to come all this way ... but the gate was opening for the weasel, and Abby saw her chance.

She made a dash and slipped in through the gate.

'Hey! You little bitch!' The guard was thrown out of his lassitude, sputtering and angry. He raised the alarm and ear-piercing bells blasted loudly. 'The bitch ran through! Grab her!' Guards seemed to appear from nowhere. Abby put her head down and ran.

She ran smack into a short, round, middle-aged gentleman wearing a suit and tie.

'Steady on!' he said, as they untangled themselves. He held her shoulders firmly, and looked her directly in the eye.

'Where's the fire?' He spoke with stern authority.

Abby was caught. At least she'd tried. She hung her head.

'Where's the pass is the problem.'

Just as she spoke, two young guards, a man and a woman, came stomping noisily up to them, huffing importantly. The woman spoke.

'Sir! The girl has no pass. She entered this institution illegally.

I'll escort her to the main gate for questioning.'

The gentleman looked at Abby, then turned back to the guard who'd spoken. 'Frisk her.'

The guard checked her for smuggled items, then stood back. 'Appears to be clean,' she said. 'Should I take her away?'

'That won't be necessary. I'll handle it personally. And for crissakes stop the bells.'

'Yes, sir!' The two young guards nodded curtly and went back the way they'd come.

The man turned back to Abby and assessed her carefully. 'You have some explaining to do. I'm not sure you understand how serious this is.' He paused. 'I was getting some coffee. Hot chocolate?'

Abby's head jerked up. She was astonished by his kindly tone. 'Thank you.'

They were waved through the second gate and the man guided her down the long corridor towards the cafeteria. Abby was puzzled. 'Who are you?' she asked.

'I'm the warden. I'll ask you the same thing after we get something to eat.'

She told her story as they sat together in the staff cafeteria. The warden, whose name she learned was Jim Price, filled her tray with all the things he knew a young person would like; hot chocolate, french fries with gravy, a hot dog, and a big glass of milk.

He set it down in front of her, and chuckled at the amazement in Abby's eyes.

After she'd eaten her fill, Abby carefully wiped her mouth with the napkin, and set it down beside her plate.

'What are you going to do with me?' she asked, very solemnly.

'Take you to see your father, of course. I'm inclined to believe what you've told me. Don't let me down.' He rose from his chair. 'I'll escort you to the visitors' area. Your father's a lucky man to have a daughter who'd travel all this way to see him.' He chuckled again. 'It's gratifying to have someone finally break *into* my jail.' The warden thought a lot of his joke, and Abby laughed with him. Suddenly she fell silent as she realized the seriousness of what she'd done.

Abby sat nervously where the warden had left her. A guard went to get her father, and Abby was fidgety with anticipation.

He appeared through the doorway with the guard.

'Daddy!' Abby blurted out.

'Abby!' They raced to the glass window that separated them.

Liam wanted to pick his daughter up in his arms and spin her around.

'What a wonderful surprise!' he said. 'You look as beautiful to me as the dawn of a summer's day.' He wiped the tears out of his eyes. 'What a surprise! Thank you for coming, Abby. I've missed you so much.'

Abby couldn't help it. She sobbed as she smiled. It was so good to see him. She wanted to take him home. Things would be so much better if he were there. Her mom would be so much happier.

'Now then Abby, did you come here to cry, or to have a visit with your old man?' Liam regained his composure.

She started to laugh through her tears. 'I came to cry.' They laughed together.

'Come now, how are things, and I want the truth.' Her father looked at her earnestly. 'Starting with why you took the day off school.'

'It's a long story, and a bit of a bore.'

'I've got all the time in the world to listen. Unless it takes longer than three years.' He grinned at her and winked.

Abby started talking. She told him about Mr Pierson's cows, and how the teachers had reacted. She told him about Cody and Reddy, about the raccoon kittens, the young rabbit that died, the Piersons being so nice, and as much news as she could remember. She told him how her greatest dream was to ride the beautiful quarter-horse mare again. Liam was very interested in talk about horses. They were a great source of joy in his life, a joy that he loved to share with his daughter. They chatted and gossiped and laughed.

'Have you told me everything?' Liam asked.

'Everything I can think of,' she answered, carefully.

'Then why have you not breathed a word about your mother,

Abby? Is she well?'

She didn't want her father to worry. He could do nothing from prison.

'Mom's just fine, Dad. Honest. She makes me all kinds of food, and keeps the house so clean it squeaks, and does all the laundry, and makes me do my homework and, gosh, I don't know how she finds time for it all!' Abby smiled at him with big eyes, willing him to believe her, and trying to look honest. She wanted this joyful mood between them to go on forever.

Liam looked down at his hands. 'That bad, is it?'

'What do you mean? Everything's perfect!'

'My little angel. If everything was perfect, you wouldn't need to list all the things that Mom does. You're doing those things, aren't you, now? Cooking, cleaning, laundry?'

Abby looked down at her worn sneakers. 'Yes. But I can't do it all the time. The house gets dirty.'

'Is she into the booze?'

Abby still couldn't look at him. She whispered, 'I don't know.'

'Abby, I love your mother with all my heart, you know that. But I know she has a weakness for the drink. Tell me, Abby. I can't be happy if I don't hear everything. I'll imagine it worse than the truth.'

Abby reluctantly opted for truth. 'Yes, Dad. She's drinking. But we're managing fine. I'm not a baby any more. I've grown up a lot since you were home.'

Liam blinked and swallowed hard. Abby had unwittingly touched a number of nerves. He hated missing her childhood. He hated that he couldn't be home to help his wife with her drinking problem. He needed to solve the mortgage crisis, but there was no money left and nowhere to turn. He wanted so much to carry his responsibilities as a father, a husband and a breadwinner. He felt a frustrated failure at all three.

Abby changed the subject. 'Dad, how long will you be here?'

'Well, it's up to the powers that be, but I'll probably be moved in another month, when my classification is complete.'

'Where will you go?'

'I'm hoping for Beaver Creek. It's the nicest. It's an old air force base near Bracebridge, and I'd live in a chalet. It's even got golf, so the rumour goes! The time will fly by.' Liam tried to sound enthusiastic for Abby's sake.

'And is there glass between the prisoners and their visitors?'

'No. We'll give each other a big hug.' Liam longed to do just that. His little girl needed a hug, he could see. He worried about her. He'd been in Millhaven for only two months, and already things at home were falling apart.

'Abby. Tell your mother that I'll be calling her tomorrow morning.'

'Dad, it's better if you call in the early afternoon.'

Liam looked dejected. 'That bad, is it?' He stood and began to pace. 'I can only make calls in the morning, Abby, so that's when I'll call. She'll have to get a grip on herself. I'll have to make that happen, somehow.' He sat down again. 'The Piersons. They've been good friends to you?'

'Yes, Dad, the best.'

Liam nodded several times, thinking.

The guard cleared his throat. 'Visitation's over.'

Liam looked strongly into Abby's eyes. 'I didn't do it, Abby. I need you to hear me say it. I'm innocent.'

Abby blinked. 'I know that, Dad.'

'I love you, Abby. More than you can ever, ever know. Thanks for coming.'

'I'll come as often as I can, Dad. I believe you. You know that, don't you?'

'Yes, yes, I do. I'm grateful for that, Abby. Stay strong.'

Liam put his big hand on the glass, and Abby reached out with hers. She slowly placed it on her side of the glass, and noticed how much smaller her hand was.

The guard coughed. 'Time to go.' He took Liam by the arm.

The warden arrived at that moment and stood next to Abby. 'One moment, guard.'

The guard dropped Liam's arm in surprise and stepped back. Liam's eyes widened.

'Did your daughter tell you how we bumped into each other?' the warden asked Liam.

'No, sir, she didn't.'

'First reverse jailbreak in my long tenure.' He escorted Abby out.

Liam wondered what had happened. Then he smiled. Abby would be just fine.

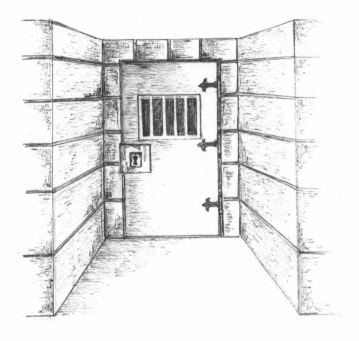

Chapter Three
Moonlight Sonata

A horse! a horse! my kingdom for a horse!
– Shakespeare, *Richard III*, v, iv

MONDAY MORNING was drizzly and dark. Abby lay in bed watching the drops of rain trickle down her deep-silled window. The last thing she wanted to do today was to face school. She'd quickly dashed off a letter of apology to Miss Smithers the day before, and it fairly dripped with insincerity. Just right, Abby thought.

She lay in her snug bed, letting her mind wander over the events of the weekend.

She'd slept most of the way back from Kingston, her book unread. She transferred to the Go train at Union Station, and returned to Brampton, where she was relieved to find her bike still locked onto the rack. By the time she got home, an hour and a bit later, the sky was pitch black. Once the animals were fed and watered, she tumbled into bed, snug in the cosiness of her room.

The next day was Saturday, and she awoke to beautiful weekend weather. Sunny and warm, and rich with the scents of spring blossoms. The old viburnum filled the air around the house with the deep, rich perfume of another era. Like lilac, but denser and more haunting. And there was a letter from Leslie waiting for her in their secret mailing spot in the oak tree. It was a funny letter describing Miss Smithers and Mr Edwards running after the cows and the bull. Her friend's clever parody made Abby laugh.

That afternoon, Abby had biked down to visit the quarter-horse mare. Mr Pierson spied her across the road, and together they stood for over an hour, leaning on the fence and chatting about horses.

She hadn't known about Mr Pierson's childhood. He'd grown up with horses on a farm out west. He told her all about Carl, the

Wonder Horse, his favourite horse of all time. Carl became famous in Maryfield when he and Pete beat out all the professional jockeys on their fiery mounts in a race that was open to all contenders. Mr Pierson had been a gangly teenager of thirteen when he entered the big-time county race. Everyone in town had laughed at the small black horse ridden by the raggedy, dirty-faced jockey. Not one person put a nickel on him. But the scrappy little fighter Carl never gave up until his nose broke across the finish line first. Pete had been proud to bursting as he picked up the purse of thirty newly minted dollar coins, which he brought home to his mother for groceries.

When Mrs Pierson saw Abby and her husband talking at the fence, she ran across the road with a bright pink scarf flapping on her head and insisted that Abby take home a chocolate date cake she'd baked that morning. Abby was thrilled.

Sunday morning her dad called and had a long talk with her mother. Abby made herself scarce for the rest of the day, long after she knew her mother would be too drunk to talk to her. Abby didn't know how Fiona had reacted to her husband's lecture; she hadn't wanted to know. So the day was spent with Cody and Reddy and the coons, the animals foraging in the woods and Abby daydreaming.

Which brought her to today. Dreary, miserable, rainy Monday. School. Miss Smithers. Leo and Larry. Ugh. When is Mrs Singh coming back, she wondered? How long does it take to cure pneumonia, anyway? At least she could look forward to seeing Leslie, whose mother only let her spend time with Abby at school. And Mrs Morris wasn't too happy about them seeing each other at school, either. She suspected Abby was a bad influence.

Abby recalled the cheerful letter in the tree, and she smiled. The thought of seeing her friend motivated her just enough to stumble out of bed and into the shower.

Duties done, breakfast bolted, animals tended, Abby biked the muddy road to school in the rain.

'Abby!' Leslie whispered, as the students shook the rain off at their lockers.

'Why are you whispering?' asked Abby loudly, with a smile, 'We're not in class.'

'Because there's a man here, looking for you. He was here on Friday. He owns the horse you rode to round up the cows. Abby, you were so brave! How did you know how to do that? Everybody says that you're brave, Abby, not just me.' Her friend looked at Abby with genuine pride.

Abby frowned. 'The owner of the horse? Looking for me?'

'Yes. He asked around on Friday, then went home when people said you weren't at school. He's here again today.'

'Does he know my name? Is he mad at me?'

'He knows it now because Miss Smithers told him, but I couldn't tell if he was mad.' Leslie finished collecting her books, and clicked the padlock shut on her locker door. She straightened and stared down the hall.

'Abby, there he is! At the end of the hall!'

Abby didn't wait to find out if the man was angry. She assumed he'd likely strangle her for kidnapping his horse right out of the field. She darted into the girls' washroom and pulled the cubicle door shut, then hopped onto the toilet seat so her feet would not be seen.

Abby waited. While she crouched on the toilet seat, she thought, I'm dead if I'm late for class. And I'm totally dead if the man catches me. What are my options? This is not good.

Just then, she heard the bathroom door open. She held her breath.

'Abby? It's me, Leslie. He's gone, but he left a letter for you with the principal.'

Abby hopped off the seat and opened the cubicle door. 'A letter? What does it say?'

'How am I supposed to know? Isn't it enough that I followed him to the office and listened at the door? Come on, we're almost late.'

They rushed down the hall and barely made it to their desks before the bell rang.

Miss Smithers looked directly at Abby. 'Do we have some

unfinished business from last week, Miss Malone?'

Abby stood. 'Yes, Miss Smithers.' She pulled the apology out of her knapsack and walked to the front of the class. She handed it to the teacher. 'I hope this is adequate. I'm deeply sorry for my behaviour last Friday.'

'Don't let it happen again,' Miss Smithers sniffed.

As Abby turned to go back to her seat, she tried hard to keep a totally straight face, but couldn't help a discreet eye-roll for Leslie's benefit. Some of the class tittered.

'Abby Malone. What did you do? Did you make a face at me behind my back?'

'No, Miss Smithers. I...I've got something in my eye.'

The class howled with laughter.

'Abby Malone, go directly to the principal's office. I will not countenance such behaviour. Get out of my class!'

Abby wasn't sure why this was happening. Why was she always, always, always in trouble? She walked very slowly towards the office, dreading the encounter with Mr Edwards. Why could she not have resisted the urge to roll her eyes? He was sure to expel her. Her stomach twisted with fear. Her eyes filled with tears. She didn't mean to be bad. She didn't feel like a bad kid. But she must be.

She turned the corner in the hall, and then stepped back. *Get a grip*, she told herself. Mr Edwards shouldn't see her crying. She took a deep breath, held her head up high, and started around the corner again, heading straight through the door and into the office.

She was so busy looking composed that she didn't see Mr Pierson sitting on the chair inside the door of the office waiting room.

'Sweetie!' he said.

Abby jumped. 'Mr Pierson! What are you doing here?'

'Neighbour business. In fact, I came over to tell Mr Edwards how grateful I am that one of his students saved my herd last Friday.' He winked at her with a conspiratorial nod of his head.

'You'd do that? For me?' All of Abby's composure fell away, and she found tears brimming in her eyes.

'Now, now, don't cry.' Mr Pierson looked helpless, as he searched his pockets for a handkerchief. He found one and handed it to Abby, who wiped her eyes and smiled at him in thanks.

The office door opened and Mr Edwards looked out.

'Mr Pierson! How may I help you?' The principal strode into the waiting room and shook Mr Pierson's hand. 'This is indeed a pleasure.'

'Perhaps you should see to this young lady, first.'

'Abby?' Mr Edwards gave a dismissive flip of his hand. 'She can wait.'

Pete's eyes took on a steely edge. 'Perhaps you should see to the young lady. I have time to wait. She has classes.'

Mr Edwards misread Pete's eyes. He joked, 'Oh, Abby's here more than not. What can I do for you?'

Pete looked thoughtfully at Abby , who was burning up with shame, then spoke to the principal. 'I came to commend the school for quick action in capturing and returning my valuable Herefords. Since it must have been one of your students who broke my fence in the first place, I'm sure you felt it was only proper. If the cows had remained in the corn field, I would have suffered severe losses, and I might have had to recoup them in court. As things stand now, however, due to the quick thinking of one of your pupils, there will be no need for me to take action against the school.'

Mr Edwards was stunned. His mouth hung open as he tried to think of what to say. 'Well. Yes. We – uh – we moved fast. Yes indeed. Yes. We saw this as a first priority. Yes, indeed.'

Abby realized what Mr Pierson was up to, and she timidly joined in the game. 'But, Mr Edwards, wasn't I being punished for rounding up the cows?'

'Abby! Heh, heh. I don't know how you got that impression!' He smiled obsequiously at Mr Pierson. 'A misunderstanding, no doubt.'

'Is this the girl who saved my herd?' Pete asked, indicating Abby.

'Well, yes, but the teachers and I had the initiative. I gathered up the brave souls who were prepared to risk their lives and ...'

Pete interrupted. 'The girl's action was heroic. She should be commended.'

'Of course.' Mr Edwards' smile was forced. 'We'll do that.'

'I'll walk her back to class while you think of a way to thank her. And let me know what you'll be doing for her. You will let me know?'

'Yes, yes.' Mr Edwards was distinctly unhappy about all this, but in the face of Pete's powerful personality, he was helpless.

Then he remembered the letter from the owner of the horse Abby had ridden. It was sure to be nasty, maybe even the threat of a lawsuit. Mr Edwards smiled smugly. 'Oh, Abby, before you go, I have a letter for you.' He ducked into his office and returned with an envelope.

'Thank you, Mr Edwards,' Abby said politely, as she took it from him. 'Um, Miss Smithers asked me to see you. Did she call?'

'Oh, yes. It was nothing. Nothing important.' Mr Edwards usually looked forward to heaping humiliation on Abby, but not with Mr Pierson there. He hoped that the contents of the letter would make up for it.

Abby and Mr Pierson walked together down the hall.

'Thank you,' said Abby.

'It was nothing,' answered Pete.

'It was something to me. You were very clever, the way you made it look like I'd saved the school from a big lawsuit!'

Pete chuckled. 'It was fun. By the way, what's the letter about?'

Abby's face darkened. 'I don't want to open it. It's from the man who owns the quarter horse across the road. He's been look-ing for me. I know he'll be furious with me for riding his horse without permission.'

'George Farrow? I can't imagine he'd be furious with a fine girl like you. But, you won't know till you read it.'

'I suppose you're right.'

The two of them sat on a bench in the hall, the tall old man and the young girl. Abby tore open the envelope and slowly pulled out the letter. She unfolded it and read aloud:

Dear Abby Malone,

Please come to my barn after school. I would like to meet you. You are the only person that mare has ever allowed to remain on her back, and I'd like to hire you to train her.

Sincerely,
George Farrow

Abby's eyes were huge with surprise and elation. 'Wow! D'you really think he'd hire me, I mean, pay me *money*, I mean actually *pay* me to ride the most beautiful horse in the entire world?'

Pete started to laugh. He laughed loudly enough that Miss Smithers came rushing out, shushing and grimacing.

'Sh! Sh! There are classes going on!'

'I'm sorry, but this student of yours is the most amusing person I've talked to in ages. I couldn't help it.' Pete stood to face the teacher.

'Abby? Well, I don't know about that.' She turned on Abby. 'What are you doing loitering in the hall? You should have gone straight to the principal's office.'

'I did ...'

'Don't give me a story, young lady.'

'Excuse me,' interrupted Pete. 'Abby was at the office. I was walking her back. And I'll pick her up after school, if that's all right. We have an appointment with her employer.'

Leaving Miss Smithers at a loss for words, Mr Pierson strolled boldly down the hall and out of the school. Abby felt, for the first time since her father went to jail, that she wasn't all alone in the world.

Pete Pierson's face was furrowed and preoccupied as he entered the farm house.

'Hello, lovey!' called Laura, along with piano tinkles. 'I'm just finished practising.'

Laura would have been finished anytime Pete came in, because her whole world revolved around him, and he knew it. 'What's wrong, Pete?'

'Laura, the Malone girl is getting the runaround at school. I'm not sure what to do.'

'You'll do the right thing, you always do.' Laura had perfect confidence in him. 'And speaking to George about her was a great idea. Do you think she'll like the job?'

Pete smiled. 'She's delighted. And not only will she make a little spending money, she'll have somewhere to go after school. Something to do.'

'And we can keep our eye on her.' Laura's face saddened. 'Why would her mother lose herself to alcohol, do you think? With such a lovely child to look after?'

'Laura, we've seen how that works in our own family.'

She had to agree. 'Knowing what drinking does to a family only makes me worry more. Liam was right to call and ask us to look out for her. My, he must worry. Locked away, and feeling useless.'

Pete didn't say anything. He was staring into space, deep in thought.

'What are you thinking, Pete?'

'Mmm,' was all he said for a long while.

A few minutes later Laura was peeling potatoes at the sink when she was startled by his belated answer.

'Liam Malone!' Pete burst out. 'I didn't believe it then and I don't believe it now. He never committed that crime. I'd love to prove it, too.'

'Would they retry him? I mean, if you found some proof or something. Would there be another trial?'

'How the law works,' said Pete, 'is a mystery to me.'

'Wouldn't it be wonderful, though? To prove his innocence?'

Pete let out a sigh. 'Maybe we're just daydreaming.'

'Maybe, Pete, but maybe not.'

Abby thought she was in heaven. She was about to ride the beautiful quarter horse, and this time with the approval of George Farrow, the owner.

Pete Pierson had been waiting for her after school as he'd promised, and together they went across the road to the big red barn. Abby was nervous while being introduced to George

Farrow, a big, tall man with a friendly face and a 'Mundell's Lumber' cap. But his praise was genuine, and she soon relaxed.

The little mare was out in the field. Abby coaxed her with a carrot, and soon had her in her stall, eating a reward of oats. Capably Abby groomed her, careful not to make any sudden movement that might startle her. George helped Abby with the saddle and bridle, and when she was ready they led her out to the riding paddock behind the barn.

'Where did you learn to ride, Abby?' asked George. 'You have a feeling for horses. Nobody has ever done what you did with this mare. Imagine! Rounding up cows!'

'My dad says that Goldie, my pony, taught me, but Dad really did. He rode in Ireland before he could walk. He taught me everything I know, but also that you can't know everything about horses. He said that each horse has something new to teach you.'

Pete and George looked at each other and nodded.

'True words, Abby,' said Pete. 'True words.'

Pete got worried when Abby was about to mount. 'Now you be careful. George says she's a wild one. Maybe we should lunge her first.'

This seemed like a good idea, so they put her on a long rope and had her trot and canter around in a circle without a rider for a good fifteen minutes.

'I had her trained for my granddaughter last summer,' explained George Farrow. 'But she bucked and poor Lucy sprained her wrist first time out. So I had another trainer come and try, but he said she was too much of a handful. Quite honestly I was thinking of selling her and getting something quieter. But after you herded Pete's cows and tamed the bull, I changed my mind. Nothing could please me more than to have the mare ready for Lucy when she comes back this summer.'

'Well, I'll try my best.' Abby stood up on the mounting block, which looked like two stairs going nowhere, and gently slid herself onto the mare's back.

'What's her name, Mr Farrow?' she asked.

'Moonlight Sonata. Her sire was Beethoven, and her dam was Moonmaiden. It seemed logical.' He smiled.

'Moonlight Sonata. What a beautiful name.'

Abby asked George to lead the mare for a few steps, until she was comfortable with the situation. He obliged, leaving the reins to Abby when she asked him to.

Now Abby felt like a queen. They trotted around first to the right, and then to the left. She began figure eights, a continuous series of turns shaped like an eight. The mare responded perfectly.

Abby urged her into a canter. The mare bucked high. Abby flew off, thud, into the mud from the morning rain.

Pete rushed to Abby. George ran and caught the mare.

'Abby! Are you all right?' Pete asked.

Slowly, Abby raised her face from the mud, and started to laugh. She couldn't stop. Her arms and legs and face and hair were covered in mud. The two men looked at the goopy mess and couldn't help but laugh, as well. Only the mare couldn't see the humour. She snorted.

'Oh, wow.' Abby stood up and tried to shake off the mud. 'Okay. I think I see the problem. This one, anyway. She doesn't accept the transition from trot to canter. Let me catch my breath.' Abby got control of herself, and led Moonlight Sonata over to the mounting block. She got on again.

Moonlight took a few steps and piggishly bucked again. Abby was expecting it this time, and turned her sharply to the left before she could buck again. They turned tight circles right and left, slowly widening, and increasing the pace. The mare relaxed after a few rounds, and Abby began putting her through her paces again. Soon, they were cantering calmly and steadily both ways on correct leads.

Abby felt that the lesson had been learned, and that Moonlight had had enough for one day. She dismounted and led her back to the barn.

'Well done, Abby!' said George Farrow. 'You have the magic touch. You're hired.'

Pete Pierson grinned and winked broadly at her. He was pleased.

'When should I start work, Mr Farrow?' asked Abby as she rubbed the mare down.

'You just did. I'll pay you five dollars each day you come to ride. I'd like you to come every day, but suit yourself. The more you ride, the more you earn and the better I like it, but I know you're a busy girl.'

'I'll come every day! Thank you, Mr Farrow.' Abby couldn't believe her luck.

Pete Pierson reflected that Abby Malone seemed to be able to communicate instinctively with animals. And George Farrow knew he had a good deal.

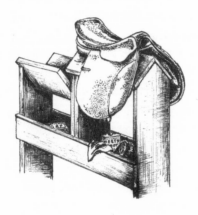

Chapter Four

Fire and Charity

Past and to come seem best; things present worse.
– Shakespeare, *Henry IV*, Part Two, I, iii

ABBY WAS IN high spirits. She sang aloud as her bike skimmed along the road toward home. She had a job! And Mr Farrow said she was good at it! If she went every day after school, and weekends, too, she'd make thirty-five dollars a week. One hundred and forty dollars a month! And riding Moonlight Sonata! Oh, life was good.

A half mile or so from the house, she saw a small dark animal running fast along the road toward her. She tried to focus on it, but it was still too far away. She pedalled faster, a strange feeling growing in her chest that something was wrong. The animal tearing down the road, getting bigger every second, was Cody. She could see his eyes large with fear, and he telegraphed his urgency. She pedalled faster still, until they met. She leapt off her bike and scooped him up into her arms.

He was covered in sticky soot and panting wildly, gulping in the air. His sides were heaving, and his tongue stuck straight out. He smelled strongly of burning hair.

'Cody, Cody, it's all right, boy. Calm down. Cody, good boy.'

Cody squirmed out of her arms and started running toward home. He stopped and looked back, his eyes imploring her to hurry.

Abby ran beside her bike for a few strides and jumped on. She pedalled as fast as she could, fear numbing her brain. Something was very wrong.

Abby could see and smell smoke long before she arrived home. It billowed and drifted, obscuring her vision. She thought her heart would burst from exertion and fear. Was it the house? Was her mother all right? Her legs were screaming with pain, but she pushed herself on, faster still. She turned up the lane and stared.

It was the barn. Only the frame was standing. The rest had been totally devoured by the fire, which was burning furiously, crackling like lightning and roaring like thunder and spitting great cinders. The heat was overwhelming, even from the end of the lane.

Her animals! Abby started pedalling again, but stopped just past the house. Nothing could have survived such intense heat. She put her bike down.

The firefighters were dousing the surrounding trees and ground. They'd given up on the barn. There was nothing left to save. Nothing to do.

Abby's stomach twisted. She felt hollowed out.

A large hand rested on her shoulder. She turned around, and looked up into the kind face of Terence Curry, her father's law partner.

'Abby. What a shame.'

Abby couldn't speak. She knew she'd cry if she opened her mouth, so she just stared up at him. The tall, lanky man had been her father's law partner since before Abby was born. He and his former wife had always been family friends. Abby remembered her father telling her before he went to jail that she could trust Mr Curry with anything. As Abby looked into his sad blue eyes she knew Mr Curry was trying to comfort her, but her loss was too great. Nothing and nobody could comfort her now.

'I dropped in to say hello to your mother, and we both smelled smoke. We looked outside, and the barn was burning. I thought it might be too late, but I called the fire department and they were here within minutes.' He shook his curly grey head sadly. 'It was a fine barn. It'll cost a lot to replace.'

Abby's eyes filled with tears and she turned away.

'Come to the house, Abby. Your mother will be glad to see you.' Terence Curry sensed correctly that Abby wasn't in the mood to talk. He gave her shoulder a sympathetic pat and walked back to the house.

Cody nudged her leg, and jolted her out of her reverie. He took her hand gently in his mouth and pulled her toward the field behind the barn. Abby let him guide her, wondering where he was taking her.

'Hey!' yelled a fireman. 'Get away from there!'

'I'll stay far away from the barn!' hollered Abby and broke into a run to keep up with Cody, who was bounding off into the field. The fireman shrugged. He was too busy to chase her.

Cody checked behind him every few seconds to see whether Abby was still there. At the ridge on the farthest corner of the farm, the coyote stopped. He gave a soft woof and tucked his tail between his legs. Abby ran to catch up, puzzled by his demeanour.

At his feet lay the baby squirrel, badly singed from the fire. He was dead. His tiny mouth gaped open, leaving Abby no doubt that his last breaths had been painful.

'Poor little Reddy. Good boy, Cody. You tried to rescue him,' Abby cooed in a voice breaking with emotion. She knelt over and gently scooped up the small body in both hands. 'Cody, you're a wonderful coyote. You tried your very best.' To get the little squirrel out, he must have run into the burning barn, in the intense heat, blinding smoke and scorching flames. Abby was very thankful that Cody had survived the rescue attempt. They sat on the ground together, tears streaming down Abby's face while Cody cuddled in Abby's lap.

'Don't feel bad about the twins, Cody,' Abby said through her tears. 'There's no way you could've opened their cage without hands.'

'Che che che che,' came a noise from up the tree. 'Che che che che che che.'

Abby looked at her coyote. He gazed up at his mistress. His grey fur was singed black all over. His grey eyes were all bloodshot from the smoke. 'Rook and Rascal! You rescued the twins. Just how, I'll never know.'

She looked up into the maple. She saw one masked raccoon face in the crotch of the tree, peering curiously down at her. Then out popped the other, right above the first.

'You crazy kids!' she shouted, and two sooty raccoons kittens scampered head first down the tree and tumbled into her arms.

'Mom! Mom, wake up. Dad's on the phone. He doesn't have much time.' Abby tried to rouse her mother from a deep sleep. Liam had called to talk to Abby before she left for school. He'd been very upset to hear about the fire in the barn, but relieved that no one was hurt. He was deeply understanding about Abby's sadness over Reddy's death, and she felt much better after talking to him. They'd had a much needed heart-to-heart and now he wanted to speak to her mother. Fiona had fallen asleep on the couch the night before, arm dragging on the carpet next to the drained bottle of Canadian Club whisky. She smells awful, Abby thought. Stinky from the whisky and morning breath. She hadn't changed her clothes in a couple of days.

'Just a minute, Dad, I'll try again,' Abby said into the phone.

'Abby. My darlin' girl.' Liam's voice was flat. He was depressed at his family's state of affairs in his absence. 'Try one more time, and this time shake her hard.'

'Mom! Dad's on the phone!' Abby took her mother's face and patted it hard. She lifted her up by her shoulders and really shook her.

'Stop it,' mumbled Fiona. 'Leave me alone.'

Before Fiona could shift her body into a more comfortable position and fall back to sleep, Abby stuck the receiver to her ear, and yelled, 'Okay, Dad. Shoot!'

'Fiona! Get a hold of yourself! Are you there? Talk to me, girl!'

'Liam? That you?'

'Of course it's me! You all right, love?'

'Never better.' Fiona was struggling to sit upright, clumsily knocking over the coffee table, and with it all the dirty dishes and congealed food. 'Christ.'

'Fiona? What was that?'

'Nothing, Liam, honey. How are you? I miss you ... I love you ... oh, why can't you come home?' Fiona was crying now, huge tears rolling down her face.

'Get a hold of yourself,' Liam repeated. 'Are you looking after Abby?'

'Of course I am! What kind of mother do you think I am?' The tears dried up, and anger replaced sorrow. 'And why do you keep asking about Abby, and telling me to smarten up? I need a little sympathy, too.'

'Abby's just a child, that's why. Now, let's not quarrel, love.'

'Then why did you call? Just go back to your cell and leave us alone. You've been away over two months now, and over two years to go, so you're no use to me or....'

Abby could take no more. She grabbed the phone from her mother's hand and took it as far from her as the cord would stretch.

'Daddy, don't worry. I'm fine, for sure, really. Mom'll feel better later. But I'll be late for school if I don't hurry. I love you, Dad.'

'Abby, you're a wonderful, beautiful, strong girl. I love you more than you'll ever know. If ever you need help, go to the Piersons. I told them you'd call if you need them. They're good people.'

'I know, Dad. Gotta go. Love you.' Abby hung up the phone, and willed herself not to be a baby. She raced out the door as fast as she could, before her mother could stop her.

Cody knew something was wrong. His Abby was unhappy. He understood that he wasn't to follow her when she rode away on her bike. But he was totally devoted to her, and his heart was sad when she was sad. He crept out of his dug-out hole under the porch and stealthily kept her in sight, all the way to school.

Leslie grabbed Abby by the arm as soon as she got to the lockers. Excitedly she pulled her along and then stopped, holding Abby's hands over her eyes.

'Don't look till I say.'

'What lame-brained scam are you pulling this time, Les?'

'Moron! Just wait till you see! You'll eat your words.' Leslie opened her locker with one hand, keeping Abby's back to her with the other. Then she said, 'Okay. Now look.'

Abby opened her eyes. In Leslie's locker was hanging an old white lace gown. It was huge. It had yellowed in patches, and sagged limply on the hanger.

'What's this for?' asked Abby, amazed that Leslie could think this old dress would be such a great surprise.

'It's your graduation dress! Remember you said you couldn't come 'cause you didn't have anything to wear? Well, *voilà!* Isn't it fantastic! My mother wore it to hers, and she put it in the Goodwill box just yesterday. So I snuck it out when she was doing the dishes. Aren't you happy? Now you can come!'

Abby looked at her friend. What a good friend, too, she thought. She smiled, put her arms around Leslie, and together they danced in a lively circle. Abby didn't have the heart to tell her how awful the dress was.

'It'll be perfect! I'll look like a ... a ... well, I'll look just great.'

The two friends linked arms and happily went to class, just as the bell echoed down the halls.

Abby got to her seat with seconds to spare. She organized her books and looked up to see Pam sitting on her desk.

'Pam. Get off my desk.' Abby had no time for Pam. In her opinion, Pam was spoiled and vain and cruel.

'Why, Abby! Don't be so touchy. I just came for a little visit.' Her eyes were totally innocent. 'Miss Smithers was called to the office, so I thought we might have time for, you know, a catch-up chat?'

'A catch-up chat? Right. What exactly did you want to get caught up with, Pam?' Abby looked over in Leslie's direction, hoping for support. But Leslie was busy finishing her math. She seemed to be having trouble with it and was concentrating hard.

'Well, Annie and I think you need help. Your clothes, Abby!'

Abby stood up to meet Pam face to face. 'You know my situation, Pam. You're just being mean.'

'Let me be blunt. You always look so, so, you know, thrown together.'

'Well, you make me throw up.'

'Very mature, Abby. Annie and I are only trying to help.'

'You can help by being a nicer person.'

'No, we have a better idea. We're giving you our, ah, you know, hand-me-downs? My mother's always going on about doing nice things for people, not just thinking about myself, yadda yadda. So, I looked at my clothes, and thought, 'Some of these are so last year, but they'd be a big improvement in Abby's wardrobe.' My mother's buying me new clothes, anyway, and I talked to Annie, who's getting new clothes too, and she agreed, and so we decided to help you out! When you go to your locker, Abby Malone, you'll find a green garbage bag full of beautiful, almost new clothes. Annie put it there just now. What do you say?'

Abby felt a mixture of emotions. She was nonplussed. She really needed clothes, and Pam and Annie were always beautifully dressed. Even their cast-offs were sure to be in good condition. 'So last year' would be a big improvement. But Pam and Annie being nice? Was this a trick? Or were they seriously trying to help? Pam certainly seemed genuinely pleased with herself. Any way Abby looked at it, it was embarrassing to receive a garbage bag full of clothes at school. Plus the horrid graduation dress that Leslie had brought for her, however well-intentioned.

'Well, Pam, I don't know what to say.'

'Well, Abby, wouldn't "thank you" be a good start?'

'Thank you, Pam.' Abby blushed deeply. She sat down again, feeling as small as a mouse. Pam flashed her a triumphant smile and gave Annie a thumbs-up. Annie looked pleased, and glowed at Abby condescendingly.

Abby felt like the class charity case. She *was* the class charity case. All the pleasure she'd shared with Leslie dripped away. She wasn't sure she could stand to stay at school for the whole long day.

Mrs Smithers bustled in. 'Leslie, show me your math homework.'

Leslie gasped. She wasn't finished. Abby groaned to herself.

Recess. Finally. Abby put away her books and went to Leslie's desk. She was still writing out, 'When I need math help, I'll ask for it,' two hundred times. She looked up and said, 'Abby, you go. I have to finish this.'

'How long will it take?'

'All recess. Sorry.'

'That's too bad, Les. See you later.' Abby slowly walked away. She looked back at her friend. Leslie was hard at work, forming her letters with great care. Leslie was dyslexic. This was no easy task for her.

Abby went outside, happy to breathe the fresh air, but friendless without Leslie. Since her dad's well-publicized trial, most of the kids' parents discouraged them from being friendly with her, so they didn't want to be seen with her. And some of them were downright overjoyed to make her life miserable.

'Abby, you sit on something?' Abby turned to face Leo, the person she least wanted to see.

'Pardon me, Leo?' she asked, standing squarely, ready for trouble.

'Pardon me, Leo?' Larry mimicked. He stood beside Leo, grinning stupidly.

'I said,' Leo replied, taking his time, 'you sit on something?'

'I sat on my chair all morning, Leo. Does that answer your question?'

'Well, not quite. Unless there's blood on your chair.'

Abby couldn't breathe. She slowly turned to look at the back of her old white shorts. There was red poster paint all over her behind.

Leo and Larry convulsed with laughter. Larry was on his hands and knees, he was laughing so hard.

'Did you see her face?' Larry screamed.

'Abby had an "accident",' yelled Leo.

'Jailbird is bleeding!'

'You shut up! You did this to embarrass me! And my dad was framed! We'll prove it one day! He's better than all your fathers put together! You ruined my shorts!' Abby's face was crimson with rage and her body was shaking. All the kids in the yard had stopped playing and were staring at her, except Leo and Larry, who were imitating her gestures and roaring with laughter.

Cody could take no more. Out of his secret hiding place he sped. Tossing aside all his survival instincts, he rallied to protect his Abby from these threatening humans. He charged full speed at Leo, teeth bared.

'It's got rabies!' yelled a boy. Some kids screamed, some ran, others were stunned and couldn't move.

Leo's eyes bugged with fear. He stumbled backward, falling hard on his bottom. Quickly, Cody turned to Larry, whose face was wide-eyed and terrified at the sight of a potentially rabid coyote running amok in the schoolyard.

Cody leapt at Larry, who threw himself on the ground, whimpering. Cody stood over him and growled menacingly. Leo had gotten to his feet by now, and came up behind Cody brandishing a stick. He raised the stick over his head and brought it down hard. Cody twisted around, grabbed the stick in his teeth and twisted it out of Leo's hands. The coyote took one step toward Leo, and Leo turned and fled. With the stick in his mouth, Cody chased Leo, dodging and darting around the yard, Leo bellowing for help. While Leo was occupied with Cody, Larry ran into the school and got Mr Edwards. They came out together, the principal's face set in a determined frown.

'Cody!' Abby commanded. 'Drop it!'

Cody froze, and dropped the stick. He looked at Abby for approval.

'Good boy, Cody! Go home!' Cody looked puzzled for a split second, then turned and ran.

Mr Edwards strode quickly in her direction. 'Abby!' he called.

To her relief, Cody had disappeared from sight. Abby felt a pang of disloyalty at sending her rescuer home with his tail between his legs, but she didn't want him caught.

She turned to meet Mr Edwards' fierce gaze.

'You are nothing but trouble, Abby Malone. Leave the premises immediately. And don't return. Ever!' Mr Edwards turned on his heel and stormed away.

Abby couldn't meet anyone's eyes. She'd been completely humiliated, and was acutely aware of the bright red blotch on her shorts. With burning face, blurry eyes, and heavy heart, she got her bike from the bike rack. But then she remembered the graduation dress and bag of clothes at her locker.

The bell rang. All the kids funnelled into the school. Abby waited long enough for them to return to class, then she slipped into the school and softly tiptoed to her locker.

Tucking the big lace dress under her arm, she hoisted the garbage bag onto her back. Then she put them back down and scribbled a note to Leslie explaining what had happened, and tucked it under her locker door. Fully loaded once more, she walked dejectedly out of the school, trying hard not to cry.

She tied the bag onto the bike's front fender, and wrapped the sleeves of the dress around her neck. She got on the bike, and started off down the road. The wind caught the dress like a lacy white sail, and Abby suddenly pictured what she must look like. She started to giggle.

Laura Pierson was hanging her laundry out to dry, and she spotted the unusual sight. She waved to Abby and motioned her to come over. Abby turned her bike into the driveway.

'Well, well! So good to see you, dear! Can you stop for a bite to eat? Mr Pierson's gone to town, and I'd love some company.'

'That would be great,' answered Abby. It would be nice to visit. She loved old Mrs Pierson, and besides, the thought of what she'd probably find at home wasn't too appealing.

'What's on your back, waving in the wind like a musketeer's cape?'

'Oh.' Abby untied the arms and held it so Mrs Pierson could see. 'It was my friend Leslie's mother's graduation dress. She thought I could wear it, but, well, I don't know.' Abby looked at the dress and wrinkled her nose.

Laura assessed it carefully. She rubbed the fabric between her fingers, and spread the skirt out to its fullest.

'It will do splendidly,' she pronounced.

Abby was aghast. 'I'll look ... laughable!' she exclaimed. After her recent dose of kids laughing at her, it was the worst possible thing she could imagine.

'It'll need some work, of course. I'll wash it in just the right powders, and we'll fit it especially to your taste. Why, there's enough yardage here to make two graduation dresses!'

Abby was doubtful, but she didn't want to appear ungrateful. 'You don't have time to do that, Mrs Pierson. But thanks for the offer.'

'Of course I have time. It'll be fun! I never had a daughter, and I love to sew. I'm really very good at it, if I say so myself. And if it doesn't suit you, well, no harm done. All right?'

'All right!' Abby's face broke into a beautiful smile. Mrs Pierson caught a glimpse of the woman Abby was destined to become, and was pleased at what she saw.

'Then come inside, my dear. We have work to do! And let me rinse out those shorts for you.'

A few hours later, Abby was riding homeward, happy thoughts filling her head. Mrs Pierson had fed her a delicious lunch, and had insisted that she take home a bag of sandwiches and cookies and fruit. The red paint in her shorts, which fortunately was water-based, had come out, and they were clean and dry. Mrs Pierson and Abby had taken the seams out of the dress, and together they'd designed something simple and lovely. Abby thought it'd turn out perfectly. For the first time, she looked forward to graduation.

Suddenly she remembered. Oh, no. What if she didn't graduate? Mr Edwards had told her to leave and not come back! What should she tell her mother? And Mrs Pierson, after all that work?

Abby didn't want to worry about it now. She'd come up with something. Right now, she wanted to get home and feed the raccoons, which she'd moved to a new location after the fire. She'd lined the old hole in the oak tree with straw, just like their previous home had been, and now they were free to come and go at will. They would still need to be fed, and they would still need protection for a while longer, but this seemed to be the best arrangement. In fact, she mused, this was probably a good time for them to start gaining their freedom.

As soon as she got home she'd praise her ally Cody for helping her in the schoolyard. He was her loyal and steadfast friend in every situation, and she wanted him to know she appreciated him.

And then she would train the beautiful horse, Moonlight Sonata. She'd ride her every day, rain or shine, and have her ready for Mr Farrow's granddaughter.

Abby could picture it now. She saw herself handing over the

reins to a girl named Lucy, whom she pictured as friendly and beautiful. Lucy, now getting into the saddle and exclaiming about what a perfectly trained horse Moonie was; what a dramatic change from last year; how nobody else could have done such good work; that Abby was a miracle worker. Abby beamed with pride at the daydream. She was going to try her best to make it come true.

Chapter Five

Graduation

A good heart's worth gold.
– Shakespeare, *Henry IV,* Part Two, I, iv

THREE WEEKS LATER, it was the morning of her graduation.
Abby lay in bed awake. Shivers of excitement tingled up her spine
and she hugged herself with anticipation. The dress was beautiful.
Abby had never seen a dress so lovely. Mrs Pierson had done a
perfect job, and seemed genuinely happy to do it. Her generosity
of spirit was a gift that Abby acknowledged with gratitude. A
more tangible gift was the pair of cream shoes that Mrs Pierson
shyly asked her to try on with the dress. Abby had been overwhelmed. They were the exact colour of the dress, and fit just
right. Mrs Pierson had also given her a pair of panty hose to wear
– Abby's first. She felt beautiful, and grown up.

The question of whether she'd be graduating at all was
resolved very simply. By the time Abby got home the day of the
red paint incident, her mother had been alerted and told to send
her back. Apparently the whole story had come out, and Mr
Edwards had realized, grudgingly, that it wasn't totally Abby's
fault. The coyote, however, was *never* to return.

Moonlight Sonata's training was coming along well. Abby had
made it a priority to ride her every day, and the work showed. She
was quite confident that Mr Farrow's granddaughter, Lucy,
would love her as much as she did herself.

Abby got out of bed, had a shower in the rusty tub, and got
dressed for school. She swallowed her pride and picked out a nice
top and pants from the clothes that Pam and Annie had given her.
That gesture still puzzled Abby. Even though the girls were
snobby and wouldn't be caught dead eating lunch with her, they
seemed to like her better than before. Maybe they felt good about

doing something nice, even though it made Abby feel embarrassed and needy. And suspicious. Abby knew she still had a lot to learn about human nature. Animals were much more straightforward.

She took a deep breath, straightened her back, and remembered something that Mr Pierson had said. 'If you take pride in yourself and in what you do, nobody can make you think less of yourself.' And Mrs Pierson had told her, 'Most people are too busy worrying about themselves to worry about you.' That was reassuring. And true, she thought. People are much more likely to think you're looking at their pimple, than to notice yours. She smiled at the thought. And felt stronger.

She took one last lingering look at her graduation dress, and went downstairs for breakfast. To her amazement, her mother was up and cooking breakfast.

'Mom!' she blurted. 'You're up!'

'Good morning, darling.' Fiona smiled warmly.

Abby felt good all over.

'Breakfast, Abby? I've poached you two eggs on toast. Is that okay? I don't know what you usually have.'

'I usually grab a piece of bread and peanut butter! This is fabulous! Thanks, Mom.' Abby sat at the table, incredulous. She had many questions, but didn't want to push her luck.

'Mom, are you, ah, up for a reason? It's great that you are, I mean ...'

'Abby, there's no reason except that I wanted to kiss you goodbye. This is your last day of school. Summer's here, and you're graduating tonight. Isn't that a good reason?'

'Yes, Mom. That's a really good reason.' She tried to eat her eggs, but her throat had constricted.

'My little girl.' Fiona sat beside her, and put her arm around Abby's shoulders. She spoke earnestly. 'I'm going to kick it, honey. I'm never going to drink again. I promised your father, and now I'll promise you. And I never go back on my promises.' She turned her daughter's face to hers, and smiled gently. 'Things will be so much better, Abby. You'll see.'

Abby flung her arms around her mother and said, 'I love you, Mom.'

'You'd better get going, Abby. You'll be late.' Fiona was teary-eyed, and wasn't sure how to handle this situation. She felt guilty and weak for drowning herself in the engulfing, soothing, obliter-ating nothingness of alcohol. It was totally destructive. Holding her child in her arms like this, she hated herself for what she'd put her through. She vowed again never to touch the stuff, and said a little prayer for strength.

Abby wiped her eyes and stood up. 'Mom, thank you. If I can help, I want to do it. Just tell me how.'

'I have to do this myself.' Fiona stood up beside her daughter, and put her hands firmly on Abby's shoulders. 'And I *will* do it. Now, you get to school, and when you come home we'll have a nice dinner that I'll make specially for you. Then we'll pretty you up for the big night. Now what about a dress? I'll go pick something out for you!'

'I have a dress, Mom, that Leslie's mother wore, and Mrs Pier-son sewed for me.'

Fiona was taken aback. She pushed away her jealousy that someone else had had the pleasure of dressing her daughter. 'Good! I'll curl your hair, and maybe show you a little about make-up. Just a little lipstick and a touch of powder; you're too young for more. And I'll paint your nails with my apricot- tinted clear pol-ish. I'll be the proudest momma at the graduation tonight. What do you say?'

Abby couldn't say anything at all, she was so happy. She squeezed her mother tight, then shot out the door before she started to cry.

Abby fed her creatures and took off for school on her bike.

She was halfway down the road when the big silver Lincoln driven by her dad's law partner sped by. Abby turned her head, following the car with her eyes. Where's Terence Curry going, and so fast, she wondered?

School was let out early, and Abby headed right over to George Farrow's farm. She'd brought her riding things to school so she could exercise Moonie before coming home. Home, she thought. I have a real home, now. She was filled with the wonder of her mother's transformation, and thrilled at the prospect of getting to know her again, without the muddling impact of alcohol.

'Abby, my girl,' bellowed Mr Farrow from across the field. He waved jovially as he came closer.

'Hi, Mr Farrow!'

'Great day, eh? Moonie's been waiting for you. Look!'

Moonlight Sonata ran lightly across the pasture toward them, nostrils flaring, feet hardly touching the ground. She gaily kicked up her heels and shook her head, her glossy, healthy black mane shining in the sun.

'Isn't she the most gorgeous thing you ever saw, Mr Farrow?' gasped Abby.

'You bet. You've done an incredible job with her. I can't believe the difference in just a few weeks. You're a talented trainer, Abby Malone. I know my granddaughter Lucy will be glad to be able to ride her.'

'I hope so, Mr Farrow,' replied Abby, blushing with the praise. 'When is she coming?'

'Tonight. For the summer. Her parents are split, sad to say, and things are very difficult at home. Have been for some time. The good news is, she wants to spend the summer with us. I'm pleased, for our sake, that she chose us instead of her other grandfather. We'll do our best to give her a good time.' Mr Farrow certainly looked pleased. His expression changed. 'She made the right choice. Her other grandfather is a very busy man.'

'You mean he doesn't have any time for her?'

George Farrow looked approvingly at Abby. 'I didn't say that, now, did I? But you're close. He's not one for children, I'll put it that way. He doesn't like disruptions.'

Abby nodded. She knew other adults like that and decided that she would have chosen to spend the summer with Mr Farrow, too. She felt sorry for Lucy, having divorced parents.

Abby wanted to meet his granddaughter. They were the same age, they both liked horses, and Abby was usually a little lonely in the summer. Leslie always went to camp, not that she'd be allowed to spend much time with Abby, anyway.

A thought crossed Abby's mind. 'Will you still need me to ride,

Mr Farrow? Now that Lucy's coming?'

George Farrow looked surprised. 'Well now, I hadn't given it any thought.' He rubbed his chin. 'Ride her today, of course. We'll see how it goes. How's that?'

'Fine. You're the boss.' Abby's eyes admired Moonie again and she smiled. 'It sure is fun riding her. Anytime you want me, I'll be here. And you don't have to pay me.'

'You've earned every penny.' Mr Farrow's eyes crinkled with affection for Abby. 'Well, better get to work!'

Abby groomed Moonie, cherishing every brush stroke and soft touch of her coat. This might be the last time. She tacked her up, inhaling the rich smell of leather as she placed the saddle on Moonie's back and slipped on the bridle. She calmly led her out of the barn. Up she went, into the saddle.

Abby always began by walking and trotting her in collected circles. After ten minutes of warm-up, Abby unhooked the gate and took Moonie on a scenic tour of the Farrows' acreage.

As they followed the river path along the valley, Abby became aware that they were not alone. She looked around, but saw nothing. Moonie let out a nicker of recognition, and Abby laughed aloud. Creeping along the ledge over the rise was Cody, having a little fun stalking them.

'Once a coyote, always a coyote.' Abby called to him. 'Sneaky!'

Abby guided Moonie up the embankment and they cantered along the deer path in the meadow. A good-sized tree had fallen across the way. It was far higher and wider than anything she'd jumped before, but Moonie merely lifted her front feet in stride and sailed over as though she'd been jumping large obstacles all her life.

'Hey, Moonie! That was fun. Let's do it again.' They turned around and took it the other way; then cantered a few strides farther before Abby turned the little mare back, for a third time over the big log. This time Moonie really soared, leaving lots of air between herself and the jump.

Abby was excited. 'You've got some talent, little one. Maybe, if I still have a job tomorrow, we can raise those jumps in the paddock!'

Maybe Moonie should compete, thought Abby. If she got the right training, I bet she'd do fine. Show-jumping? Dressage? Cross-country? Eventing? The Caledon steeplechase, for sure. Abby speculated on the spunky little mare's future, and drifted into a wonderful daydream of having ribbons galore pinned to Moonie's bridle. First-place, second-place, third-place ribbons. She'd have so many ribbons that Abby might not even keep the fifth-and sixth-place ones.

As they travelled across the bank of the river, Abby wondered if they could ride cross-country all the way to her house from the Farrows' farm. She called Cody. He'd know the way.

'Cody, let's go home! Home!' The young coyote pricked up his ears at the familiar word and started running. Abby and Moonie followed, cantering behind him along the deer paths through the woods. After slowing to slide down a wide ditch and scramble up the other side, they came up through the trees at the edge of Abby's meadow. There was an old wire fence along the property line, half up and half down. Abby looked carefully for a safe place to get through, and found a spot where dirt and weeds covered the wire on the ground. They walked across without incident.

'Cody, we did it! Good boy! That's my house, Moonie. Let's say hello to Mom!' They trotted through the meadow toward Abby's house, watchful of groundhog holes. Abby walked Moonie around her house.

'This is where I live, Moonie. Mom! Mom!'

The house remained silent. 'Maybe she can't hear me calling because she's having a bath, or something. Or doing laundry. She couldn't hear anything if the water's running.'

They turned to go, and Abby took one last look over her shoulder. She hoped to catch a glimpse of her mother, and prayed she wasn't drinking. She pushed the dark thought away, and they trotted off the same way they had come.

Her hour of freedom and fresh air and companionship passed by too quickly. Reluctantly Abby walked Moonie back to the barn, making sure she was cooled out. She was all too aware that this might be her last ride. She untacked her, curried her, picked the stones out her feet, then led her back to her pasture. Abby turned her to face the gate when she let her off the lead shank, to keep the mare from bolting in her eagerness to run. On the way out, she checked the water bucket, to make sure there was fresh clean water for Moonie to drink. She leaned on the fence for a moment, savouring the familiar smell and sight of this horse, before jumping on her bike and heading home.

Abby knew that Cody was following her, unseen. She always got a good feeling from that. She grinned from ear to ear in anticipation of seeing her mother, and having dinner with her. She could hardly wait to get all dressed up for the graduation, too. It was to start at eight o'clock that evening, but the graduating class was asked to be a half-hour early. Abby looked at her watch. It was after five already. She had no time to spare. Lucky they were driving tonight.

Pedalling hard, Abby flew up the lane and dropped her bike at the back door. 'Mom! I'm home!' she called out.

There was no answer. 'Mom! Are you here?' A small tingly feeling wormed in her stomach. 'Mom?'

On the kitchen table lay an open letter with 'Union Bank, Mortgages and Loans', on the heading. Abby picked it up before she could think whether it was any of her business. It read:

Dear Mr Curry,

We have reviewed your request of the tenth of this month regarding the Malone farm. Unfortunately, the circumstances of the fire that destroyed the barn are not conclusive. We have asked the Caledon Police Department to investigate, and only after consultation with them shall we proceed to determine the settlement. We advise you to counsel your client to look elsewhere for more immediate relief for her mortgage. As she has been cautioned several times in writing, the notice to vacate will take effect by September 1st unless mortgage payments are remitted.

Sincerely,
Ernest Wentworth,
Union Bank, Mortgages & Loans

Abby stood rooted. She was dumbfounded. Had her mother expected insurance money from the barn fire? And the insurance money would save the farm? Had Mr Curry been driving to their farm this morning to give this letter to her mother?

Abby's head pounded as she tried to figure out the importance and the meaning of this letter. Now there was to be a police investigation. And they were going to be evicted. Oh, Lordy. If only her father were home.

Abby put the letter down in the same place as she found it, and cautiously moved into the living room. As she feared, her mother lay in a deep stupor, sprawled on the couch. An empty wine bottle and a semi-finished bottle of gin had dropped to the floor at her side.

'Mom, you need help. You can't kick this drinking habit alone. Nobody can do it alone.' Abby spoke to her mother, knowing that she couldn't hear, but needing to hear herself speak. She felt fairly certain that the news of the police investigation had overtaken her mother's resolve.

Abby stared at her mother. She looked disgusting. Abby was terribly disappointed. Her voice rose in intensity.

'But what about me, Mom? What about me? Don't you ever think of what you're doing to me? You're killing yourself!' Abby crumpled on the floor next to the empty bottles, sobbing. 'You're so selfish! I hate you! I will never, ever, ever, *ever* be like you!' Abby picked up an empty wine bottle and threw it against the fireplace. It shattered. Then she poured the remaining ounces of gin into the potted geranium, and stuck the bottle viciously upside down into the soil.

She ran upstairs, teeth clenched, fists tight, unwanted tears squeezing out of her eyes.

She had a shower, running the cool water over her face and body until she couldn't stand it any more. She got dressed. She brushed her hair. She brushed her teeth. But emptiness and a sense of betrayal dulled her eyes and robbed her of happiness. She no longer cared about her graduation.

It was well past time to leave. She stood over her mother, emotions all tumbled and confused. She whispered, 'I'll see you when

I get home.' But the word, home, had none of the warmth that it had had earlier in the day.

Abby picked up her bike where she'd dropped it, and started pedalling back along the road. Cody made sure he was visible this time. It made the road feel less long and dusty, and she was grateful for his company.

Laura Pierson was washing the dinner dishes at her kitchen sink under the window. Her eye was caught by a white flash on the darkening road. She looked more closely.

'My heavens, Pete! It's Abby Malone. Riding to her graduation on her bike.'

Pete Pierson pulled himself out of his chair with remarkable speed. He joined Laura at the window.

'Get cleaned up, Mother. We're going out.'

Leslie was worrying about her when Abby walked into the classroom. She pulled her friend aside.

'Abby, you're late! Mr Edwards is mad, but I told him that I knew you'd be held up. You're all dirty and sweaty! Come with me, quickly!'

Leslie dragged Abby down the hall to the girls' washroom and tore off armfuls of paper towel.

'You do your face. And here's my hairbrush. I'll get the dust off your legs and shoes.' They worked together in silence.

'Now take off your dress, Abby, and put your armpits under the dryer. Is this my Mom's old dress? It's gorgeous! Just a little dusty.' Leslie shook the artfully restyled dress until dust no longer puffed out.

'Thanks, Leslie. I had to ride my bike. The car wouldn't start, so my Mom can't come. She's waiting for a mechanic.' Abby spoke over the noise of the dryer. She stepped back into her dress.

The baldness of the lie wasn't lost on Leslie. No mechanic would come after hours on a Friday. But she was too kind to call her on it. And she felt very sorry for her brave friend. Leslie was touched, too, by Abby's attempt at family loyalty. Everyone knew that her mother was a drunk.

'Abby, try this lipstick.'

Abby hesitantly applied the soft peachy colour to her lips.

'Oh, yes! Perfect, Abby. You look fabulous.'

Refreshed and cheered considerably, Abby held her head high as she walked into the classroom, Leslie firmly at her side.

'About time!' roared Mr Edwards. 'Get in line, it's time to go into the auditorium. Alphabetically, as rehearsed. Snap to it! We can't hold them up any longer!'

The kids assembled themselves, anxious about the ceremony ahead and conscious that their parents would be watching. They filed out of the room in alphabetical order, tittering and giggling and clattering their dress-up shoes on the hall floor.

Abby was excited. With her perfect cream shoes and her panty hose and the streamlined dress, she knew that she was as well dressed as anyone, including Pam and Annie. 'I feel like a princess,' she thought. She noticed that some of the boys looked admiringly at her. Amazing. Of course, they looked quickly away when she caught their stares, but for the first time she could remember, Abby felt beautiful. She felt feminine, even desirable. This was a lovely new sensation, and Abby allowed herself to luxuriate in it.

She thought of her father, and how proud he'd be to see her looking so fine on her graduation. She wished him a hug and a big hello, and sent it telepathically. She was sure he received it. No use sending her mother one. Abby sighed. Put it out of your head, she ordered herself, and enjoy the evening.

Abby took her seat at the end of the second row on the stage, and gazed out into the audience. This is my last time ever at this school, she thought. I wonder if I'll miss it? The thought of missing Miss Smithers or Mr Edwards caused her to snort.

Mr Edwards gave her a venomous warning look, then proceeded to the microphone.

'Ladies and gentlemen, girls and boys. Welcome to the Caledon Public School graduation. We are here to honour the young people you see before you. They have come a long way from the little four-year-olds who arrived in junior kindergarten, and have a long way to go yet before they are fully educated adults.'

After several minutes of clichés and homilies, Abby found her attention wandering. It was interesting having this different vantage point in the auditorium. Quite nice to watch people watching Mr Edwards. All kinds of people. Mr Lloyd, a fat man with a huge red nose and a tie that seemed much too tight for his fat neck. Mrs Rodrigues, looking worried, with three rumply kids who wouldn't sit still. The haughty old Masters sisters wearing small hats sitting side by side, hands folded primly in their laps. Skinny Mr Payne, whose glasses kept slipping down his nose. Some people were fidgety, others were calm, or bored, or fascinated. All kinds.

Finally Mr Edwards finished his speech. Now the diplomas were to be presented, starting with Alice Arcand, who spoke perfect French. Her mother stood up and clicked a picture of her at the precise moment she received her diploma, light flashing momentarily in the darkened audience. Stephen Aswan, Jeff Baird, Jason Casino, Jenny Chang, and on down the row of chairs.

Larry Lloyd stood when his name was called. He winked at Leo and made a comedy routine about avoiding Abby's chair as he went past her to get his diploma. Holding his breath, and bending away from her, he plugged his nose as if she smelled. Abby blushed to the roots of her hair, and Leo laughed. Several others snickered. Abby closed her eyes and wished she'd die.

'No,' she thought. 'I won't miss this school. One bit.'

'Abby Malone.' Mr Edwards called her name. Abby was glued to her chair, embarrassed to be blushing and frantically willing the colour to fade.

'Abby Malòne!' Mr Edwards barked. He was not pleased to have to repeat her name.

Abby got up from her chair, head down so her hair would cover her face. Leo made a loud farting noise. The suppressed snickers of her classmates turned to loud guffaws. Abby wasn't sure if she could make it all the way over to Mr Edwards. She thought she'd probably faint.

Suddenly, Abby heard loud applause from the audience. Someone was applauding her! Then someone else joined in. She looked out. In the dark she could make out the outlines of two people standing at the back of the room, clapping as hard as they could.

One was tall with a very straight back. The other was small with puffy hair. Mr and Mrs Pierson! Abby took a deep breath. She stood up straight and proudly received her diploma. By now others in the audience had joined the applause, and it continued until Abby had returned to her seat. This was not what Leo and Larry had intended, and Abby was sincerely pleased to observe their sullen glares.

All the diplomas had been given out, and the speeches were over. Abby couldn't wait to find the Piersons. As she rushed through the crowded auditorium, she almost collided with Leslie. She gave her a big hug, and said, 'Isn't it great? We're finished with this school!'

Leslie grinned and answered, 'Never to return!'

'Thanks for your help, Leslie, earlier.'

'No big deal. I can't believe that dress was my mother's! It looks great on you. What did you do with it?'

Abby wasn't listening. Her attention was focused elsewhere. 'Leslie. Who is that person?'

'What person?'

'That person. No, no, don't look, he's looking over here. Okay, now, he's turned away. Who is he?'

'Why do you want to know?'

'Do you know him?'

'Yes, actually. Why?'

'Only because he's the most gorgeous guy I've ever seen in my life.'

'Sam?' Leslie was incredulous.

'That's Sam? Your brother Sam? Impossible!'

Before Abby could recover from this news, Leslie darted off and returned, pulling her brother by the arm.

'Abby, this is Sam. Sam, you remember Abby Malone, my best friend?'

'Of course I do.'

Abby stared, confused and embarrassed. She mumbled, 'Hello,' and turned pink. She looked into his dark brown eyes, intrigued by their sweetness, startled by their twinkle. His skin was the same warm colour as Leslie's, and his hair was dark brown and wavy. He was taller than Abby by a head. She was mesmerized.

'We've met before, Abby, though I see you don't remember.'

'When?' she asked, thinking that she could never have forgotten.

'About a year and a half ago when I came to the school to get Leslie.'

'You were him? I mean, he was you?' Abby couldn't imagine how the short chubby kid with braces had metamorphosed into this ... this ...

Sam laughed. A lovely, sincere laugh. 'Yes, I was him, and he was me.' His eyes appraised her. 'You've changed, too. I might not have recognized you, either.'

'Sam,' Leslie said, 'go keep Mom and Dad busy while I talk to Abby. Please? For just a minute!'

Sam smiled and bowed his head. 'Yes, master. If I must.' Then he turned to Abby. 'It was nice to see you again.'

'Go now, Sam! We're leaving soon.'

'Okay, already! Bye, Abby.'

Abby watched him turn and walk into the crowd. She couldn't help but sigh. When his head disappeared, she turned on Leslie. 'Why did you send him away?'

'So we could talk! What's with you, Abby? He's only my brother.'

'He may only be your brother, but get used to girls falling for him.'

'Abby, don't forget, this was the guy who dumped his insect project in my bed! And hid my good shoes and locked me out of the house!'

'That was ages ago, Leslie! And you filled his boots with cow poop, as I recall!'

'Anyway. Look, will I see you this summer?'

'I'll be around. You know, the usual. But aren't you going to camp?'

'I don't want to, and maybe they won't make me go this year, but ...'

She was about to continue when Abby saw Leslie's mother

approaching. Sam was following her, making a gesture of 'I tried'. She gave Leslie a quick squeeze on the arm, whispered, 'Leave me a message in the tree!' and darted through the crowd toward the Piersons. She knew she'd saved Leslie from another lecture from her mother about how to choose friends.

'Mr Pierson! Mrs Pierson! Over here!'

The Piersons heard Abby and turned in her direction. 'Abby! You look like an angel. What a girl!' Pete gave her a big hug.

Laura was still wiping the tears from her eyes. 'You dear dear dear dear child! We're so proud!'

'Thanks for coming! I didn't know you were here until you started clapping! It's so nice of you to come. And Mrs Pierson, I can't thank you enough for making my dress.'

'You're the prettiest girl here, and you would've been the prettiest even in rags.' Pete smiled with great affection.

'Thanks, really. I know my mom will be so relieved that someone came because she had to wait for the mechanic because the car broke down and so she couldn't drive me and she was so disappointed because she really wanted to come but ...'

'Now don't you worry. Sometimes things can't be helped.' Pete kept his arm firmly tucked into Abby's. 'Why don't we help ourselves to some of these sandwiches and then we'll drive you home.'

Abby panicked. 'No!' She didn't want them to see her mother and find out she'd lied about the mechanic. 'I mean thanks but I've got my bike.'

Pete was undeterred. 'We'll put it in the back of the pick-up. No trouble.' Pete didn't let her arm go. He patted her hand.

'It's far too dark out there to ride a bike, dear. We want to make sure you're home safely,' said Laura. She understood Abby's concern. 'We can't stay and visit, though. We'll have to drop you off and run.'

Abby was relieved. 'Well. Thank you, then, I'd love a ride. Thanks so much.'

The sandwich table was filled to overflowing. The Parent Teacher Association had outdone itself. Abby was suddenly ravenous, and helped herself. She looked around to make sure she was unobserved, then she wrapped four more sandwiches in a napkin and pocketed them.

Pam Masters saw Abby do it and grabbed Annie Payne's arm and hysterically pointed at her. The two girls put their heads together and laughed at her, teeth flashing and faces red with amusement. Abby stared at them and blatantly stuffed another sandwich into her mouth. 'I don't like them, anyway,' she said to herself. Then she smiled sarcastically at them, cheeks bulging with chicken salad on white, no crusts. To her horror, Sam was watching. He seemed to find the whole thing extraordinarily amusing.

As she sheepishly finished her huge mouthful, Abby and the Piersons headed for the door. Abby wheeled her bike over to the truck, and Pete hoisted it onto the flatbed. They climbed into the front seat, Laura insisting that Abby ride between them so they wouldn't have to fight over who'd sit beside her. Abby was thrilled to be so important, and glad to have escaped the embarrassing incident.

Out of the corner of her eye, Abby noticed a sleek, silvery form glide quickly up into the back of the truck and curl up beside the bike. Cody. Abby felt very happy. She liked that feeling.

Chapter Six

Lucy

The eye sees not itself
But by reflection.
– Shakespeare, *Julius Caesar*, I, ii

ABBY LAY LANGUOROUSLY in bed the next morning, sunlight streaming over the white, nubbly bedspread. She listened for a moment to the wrens gaily singing outside her window, and smiled. No school for a whole summer. She'd had a lovely dream about Sam, she couldn't remember what. Maybe she'd find a way to see him again. Sighing with contentment, she lazily stretched her toes. She'd woken up from a dream about Mr Pierson. It was so vivid, she almost could hear his voice. Wait. In the kitchen. That was Mr Pierson, in real life. That was no dream. He was downstairs talking to Mom!

Abby sprang out of bed, pulled on her shorts, and stumbled downstairs. She couldn't let her mom handle this alone. Her mom didn't know that she'd told them that the truck broke down and she had to wait for a mechanic. Abby would look like a liar if her mother told a different story. And Fiona might fall apart if he said anything about missing last night's graduation.

Abby burst into the room, ready for anything. What she saw disarmed her. Her mother and Mr Pierson sat calmly facing each other across the table, steaming mugs of coffee in their hands. They both looked at her, startled by her sudden appearance.

'Good morning, Abby,' said Mr Pierson, warmly.

'Good morning!' replied Abby.

'Hi, honey,' said Fiona. 'Come sit down. Mr Pierson wanted to know if you needed a lift over to exercise Moonie. He wouldn't think of waking you, so we've had a nice visit.'

'Moonie? I didn't think I ... well, Lucy's here, isn't she? The granddaughter...? Did Mr Farrow say ... do I still have a job?'

'Slow down, Abby!' laughed Fiona. 'I guess you do! So grab some breakfast, and get going. I'll feed your creatures. You go now because I'm hoping we can visit your dad today.'

'Holy! Great!' Abby couldn't quite believe her good luck. To ride Moonie again *and* visit her dad, all in one day. She raced upstairs and got into her jeans, then swooped into the kitchen and pocketed one apple for herself and another for Moonie.

'Let's go!' she grinned.

'Not so fast. Here, take this bagel with cream cheese. And give me a kiss!' Fiona reached out to Abby, who hugged her with all her strength, and gave her a kiss.

'Now you can go,' said Fiona happily. 'I'll pick you up in an hour and a half. I'll bring some clean clothes, don't worry.'

'If anything changes, if you don't come, I'll just walk home.' Abby looked squarely at her mother.

'Nothing will change, Abby. I won't touch a drop.'

Abby stared.

Mr Pierson nodded. 'That's good, Fiona. That's the first step. To talk about it openly. You'll make it, yet.'

Abby was amazed. 'Did you know about the ... that?'

'Her drinking? Yes. But your mother and I never talked about it until just this morning. It'll be a lot better now. You'll see.'

On the way to the Farrows', Pete told Abby about his brothers. They'd had varying degrees of problems with alcohol and two had died horribly from it, ruining not only their own lives, but the lives of those around them. It was a lot to think about. Abby sat listening, amazed that Pete had faced this situation, too. She had to conclude that he was an expert. He'd seen it all. If anyone could help her mother it would be Pete, but Abby's hopes had been dashed before. Whatever the outcome, she thought, it sure felt good that she could talk to someone who really understood.

Pete dropped her off at the barn and jauntily waved goodbye. There was nobody there. For a moment she was unsure of what to do. Should she check with Mr Farrow before riding? What if he said it was a mistake, and that Lucy was riding Moonie now? Abby quickly tacked the mare up and hopped on her back. If she was told her job had ended, at least she'd have had a last ride.

She chuckled in glee as they trotted quickly toward the trails at the back, successfully avoiding detection. Mr Edwards was right, she thought. She was a bad kid.

Moonie seemed especially happy to be out. Their spirits were synchronized perfectly. Today, nothing could be anything but perfect. Moonie tossed her head saucily and gave a couple of delighted little bucks to show her eagerness. Abby laughed at her.

'Moonie, stop it!' She squeezed her legs on the mare's sides and Moonie broke into a canter. 'Is that better, little speed demon?' Moonie indicated by her smoother strides that it was much better.

It was a beautiful day. The sun shone through the trees, speckling the bright summer grass with dancing light. The morning sun felt good on Abby's back as they cantered gently down the hill.

Cody joined them out of sight of the barn and they all happily flew over an old rotten fallen tree. *Splish splash splish splash* they went, through a small muddy stream that looked blue with the reflection of the sky until Moonie's hooves disturbed it. They cantered up the daisy-spotted grassy rise and onto the dirt path through the dark woods, jumping any obstacle they could find. Cody came and went, as his nose dictated.

When they got to the river, Abby slowed down to a trot, then walked Moonie into the water. The river was high that day and the current strong, and in one area the water was so deep that Moonie had to swim. Ears forward, head up and legs stretching as far as they could go, Moonie single-mindedly headed for shore. Abby gave her the reins and floated above her. Cody dog-paddled beside them, struggling against the force of the current. Cody got to the other side first and shook off the water. Moonie arrived seconds later, and once out of the water shook herself off, too. Abby laughed as the horse seemed to turn into a giant egg-beater, shaking vigorously from head to toe. Then Moonie thought she'd have a roll in the wonderful mud. Abby kicked her forward in the nick of time, just as her knees were bending, and off they went again.

The hay field at the other side of the river was flat and there was a wide path mowed through it. 'Perfect. Let 'er rip, Moonie!' yelled Abby, and they flew. Moonie stretched her neck and galloped freely. Her strides lengthened rhythmically and the wind rushed past. My, my, thought Abby, she's fast! I bet she could take on a thoroughbred. Abby smiled as they ran, laughter bubbling inside her. She smiled and her teeth dried in the wind.

Any other time Abby would have wished she could stay out all day, but not today. She was going to visit her dad. It would be so good to see him! Her mother would be coming to pick her up soon, so Abby got her bearings and took the short cut back.

She sang aloud as they crested the hill behind Mr Farrow's barn. Cody had magically disappeared. He liked to remain undetected.

Ahead of her were six unlikely-looking hurdles that were set up next to the barn. Abby thought she'd just have time to try the course once, walk Moonie out, untack her and wash her down before Fiona arrived.

Moonie was eager to jump, and willingly paid close attention to Abby's signals. The mare trotted up to the jumping area, then cantered in a small collected circle on her right lead, straightening into the first line of jumps. She arched her neck and tucked her front legs as she lifted off the ground and over a misshapen log. She jumped in perfect form. Landing lightly, she took three strides before jumping over an assembly of old truck tires strung along a pole. She continued on her right lead around the corner and faced a discarded gate propped up with rails. Four strides toward a turtle-shaped wading pool full of water. Moonie didn't like jumping this, but she found her mark and bravely leapt, changing leads to circle back over the in-and-out. Once that was accomplished, Abby slowed her to a walk, praising and patting her. Moonie wanted to jump some more, so she grabbed the bit with her teeth to gain control, and sidled her way back to the first jump, hoping that Abby would let her do it all again.

Abby laughed out loud as she slowed her into a walk. 'Naughty, naughty! We have to cool you out now, but maybe tomorrow we'll jump some more if I still have a job.'

'So, you talk to animals?'

Abby looked around to see where the voice had come from. 'Hello? Who's there?'

'It's me. Lucy.'

Abby couldn't see anyone. Moonie nickered and pointed her ears to the hayloft door. Abby looked to where she pointed and there, in the darkened doorframe, sat a girl with a gleaming white cast on her arm. Abby assumed she must be Lucy, but she couldn't see her face clearly.

'Can you teach me to ride like that?' she asked.

'Sure. No problem. What happened to your arm?'

'That angelic horse you're riding has a split personality. She bucked me off yesterday before I even got my feet in the stirrups and broke my arm. What's worse, the exact same thing happened last year, only I sprained my wrist instead. Can you believe it?'

'Ouch. That's too bad. She bucked me off, too.'

'Come on!'

'Really, she did. But it was muddy, so I didn't get hurt.'

'Grandpa never told me that.'

'It's true. So, is that why I could ride today? Because you can't ride until your arm heals?'

'I'm not riding Moonlight ever again! No way. She's a demon. At least to me. She likes you. Why doesn't she like me? I bring her carrots. It's not fair.'

Abby wanted to get a good look at her. 'Climb down from the barn, Lucy. Why don't you get on Moonie right now, and help walk her out?'

'No! My arm hurts!'

'I'll lead her. She's tired, she'll behave herself.'

Lucy sat for a long moment, then disappeared from view. Abby thought she'd gone to the house, so she started walking Moonie away.

'Where are you going?' Lucy whined. 'I thought I was going to walk her out.'

'There you are! Great.' Abby slid down and faced her. Lucy had a mop of dark brown hair and green eyes. Her face was impish and small, and held an expression of petulance. Abby noticed that they were the same height.

'Hi. My name's Abby.'

'I know. Abby Malone. Grandpa talks about you like you're perfect. I'm Lucy. So. Are you going to help me up?'

Abby led Moonie over to the log. 'Stand on this. I'll keep her still.'

Lucy was able to scramble onto the saddle using her one good arm to pull herself up. 'Don't let her do anything bad,' she demanded.

Abby looked into Moonie's left eye. She silently warned her to behave. Moonie understood. 'Just relax, Lucy. Let's go.'

They walked around and around the jumps, Abby leading on foot, Moonie's head hanging in submissive boredom.

'Well, look at this!' A deep, pleased voice rang out.

Moonie's head shot up, but Abby checked her before she could spook.

'Grandpa, look! I'm riding Moonlight!'

'I can see that. Good girl. I never thought I'd see you on her again!'

'It's easy! Abby said she'd teach me to ride like her.'

'Abby, that's wonderful. Why didn't I think of that myself? If you'd been here last night, she never would've broken her arm.'

Abby smiled. 'Who knows? Horses are unpredictable at the best of times.'

'Yes, but you've got Moonlight Sonata so calm and obedient, I didn't think there'd be any problem. Anyway, when can you start?'

'I guess I already did.'

'By golly, I suppose you did! Oh, Abby, your mother's here. She's in the kitchen talking to Marge. Give me Moonie; you run.'

'Thanks. But can we get Lucy down first? Not that Moonie'll do anything with you here, but I want to be sure....' She was embarrassed to be telling Mr Farrow what to do with his own horse, but she knew that Moonie had a mind of her own.

'You're right. Down you get, my Lucy!' She fell into his strong arms, then landed lightly on the ground. 'Proud of you! Takes guts to get back on a horse that threw you!'

Abby was happy that she still had a job. 'Are you sure it's okay to leave you to untack her and wash her down?'

'Sure. Off you go. Don't keep your mother waiting.'

'Thanks, Mr Farrow. I'll see you tomorrow. What time?'

'Anytime you get here. We've no plans tomorrow.'

'I want to ride a lot!' Lucy told her grandfather.

'A little at a time, until your arm heals,' he responded. 'Right, Abby?'

'Right. You'll be an ace in no time.' Abby searched in her pocket and pulled out the carrot she'd brought for Moonie. Moonie nickered softly, thanking her. With a backward glance, Abby waved goodbye and dashed to the kitchen door.

Before she knocked, she peeked through the window of the kitchen door. She stood for a moment and watched her mother and Mrs Farrow at the table, laughing and talking together. It looked so normal. It made her think that maybe this time, just maybe, everything would work out fine.

Driving to Kingston Abby found herself surprisingly uncommunicative. They had so much to say to each other, so much time to fill in, yet Abby felt almost shy. It troubled her, and she knew her mother was trying the best she could, raising topics of interest and gaily chatting. But Abby was reticent. Her mother had apologized for the graduation, but Abby wasn't sure she realized how much it had hurt her. She guiltily wondered if she was paying her mother back for the heartache she'd caused. Maybe we need more time, she thought. Well, we'll be in the car alone all day.

By the second hour in the car, after a snack at a roadside restaurant, Abby felt happy and relaxed. As the miles passed she was getting more and more excited about seeing her father.

When they finally arrived at the penitentiary, the warden met them at the entrance. 'Good to see you, Abby!'

Fiona was nonplussed. Abby answered, 'Hello, Mr Price. It's nice to see you, too.'

'I asked the gate to inform me of your visits. This must be your mother. How do you do? I'm the warden here, Jim Price.'

'Pleased to meet you, Mr Price. I wasn't aware that you and Abby had met.' Fiona was confused. She looked from the warden to Abby.

'She didn't tell you?' Jim looked at Abby, too.

'I haven't told her yet, Mr Price, but I will. It was nice of you to help me last time, and take me to the cafeteria. This time we have passes.' Abby didn't want the warden to feel that he had to babysit her.

'Oh, I know that. How else would I know you were coming?' Jim Price put his hand on Abby's shoulder. 'I just wanted to be your welcoming committee.' His warm smile left Abby in no doubt of his sincerity.

'Your dad's waiting. Let's go.' The warden led the way down the halls, saying hello to familiar visitors, and nodding pleasantly to staff. When they got to the visitors' area, he sat them down and disappeared through a door. A minute later a guard appeared with Liam.

Liam's eyes took in his family. His bride of twenty years, still beautiful to him. His precious daughter. He swelled up with gratitude.

Abby heard Fiona catch her breath. She looked at her mother and saw the love in her eyes, the strength of the bond between husband and wife. Abby was glad. This was her family.

They all stepped up to the barrier. All three Malones pressed their heads together, Liam on one side, Abby and Fiona on the other. They fervently wished that the glass would disappear and life could be the same as it had been.

While Abby and Fiona were in Kingston visiting Liam, Cody was watching over things at the farm. It had surprised him that his food had smelled of Fiona. She never left food for him. That warned him that something different was happening. He would watch carefully until Abby returned.

Pete was repairing the broken hinge on a gate when he noticed Lucy feeding Moonie a carrot in the field. She stroked Moonie's neck and rubbed the mare's ears with her good arm. Pete thought this was very nice. A car sped down the road behind him as he returned to his work.

***

[82]

Cody heard an engine sound. His head shot up. His keen eyes followed the silver car as it turned up the driveway. As usual, this particular human was driving very fast. He'd been here many times before. From his hiding place, he could see the man get out of his car and go to the door of the house. Something about him made Cody nervous. The man knocked. He was impatient. He knocked again, then tried the door. It didn't open. He turned and started loping up to the ruins of the barn. Cody had to lie very still, as the man's path passed very close to him.

The human stopped, looked around, then pulled a black object that Cody didn't recognize out of a clear bag. He wore clothes on his hands. Using a stick as a poker, the man buried the object in the ashes. When he was finished he stood up straight, and as he backed away from the ashes, he swept away his footsteps with a cedar branch. When he was done, he pulled off his gloves and stuffed them in his pocket. Cody crouched. As the man passed him, Cody shadowed him.

When he was close enough, Cody reached his head up and gently closed his teeth around a glove. He quickly ducked back into the bushes. The man felt the movement and turned around, hands shooting to his pockets. When he realized that he'd lost a glove, he started looking for it. 'Damn. Where is it?' He thrashed around, searching. After a minute of futile effort, he gave up and returned to his car. Cody watched him as he left the property in a cloud of dust.

Pete had finished his repairs on the hinge and was hanging the gate back in place when Terence Curry's silver Lincoln raced past, throwing gravel as it went. That man drives too fast, he thought. The gate hung perfectly. Pete stepped back to admire his work, when something caught his eye.

Lucy was trying to get on Moonlight Sonata. She had her left foot in the stirrup and because Moonie was circling to the right, away from her, she couldn't get the other foot off the ground. Pete worried that her left foot was stuck. He quickly crossed the road, and as best he could, hauled himself over the fence. I'm far too old for this, he muttered to himself.

He quietly walked up and gently grabbed Moonie's bridle, stopping the action.

'My foot's stuck!' she wailed. 'Stupid horse!'

'Here, let me help.' Pete deftly loosened her boot from the stirrup. She dropped to the ground. 'Your foot was jammed in pretty tight.'

'I hate this horse!' Lucy started to cry. She clenched her good fist and swung out at Moonie. Pete caught her arm and held it.

'Now, now, Lucy. You're just frightened.' Her arm relaxed and Pete released his grip. 'Why are you out here alone with her? You've got a broken arm. And I understood that Abby was going to teach you.'

'It's my horse. And she already taught me. It's easy. And it's boring walking around and around in a circle.'

Pete smiled and nodded his head. 'Sure is.'

Lucy looked at him suspiciously. 'What?'

'Boring, walking around in a circle. I bet you weren't bored just now.'

'No, I was terrified!'

'Really? Why's that, do you suppose?'

'Because I didn't know how to make this stupid horse do what I want!'

'And what do you want her to do?'

'I want to go for a ride. I want to run along the river and jump like Abby.'

Pete scratched his chin. 'And she wouldn't do that?'

'No!'

'Maybe she *is* a stupid horse.'

'Well, she did all that for Abby.'

'So maybe she isn't so stupid.'

'Hold on here,' said Lucy haughtily. 'Are you saying that I'm the stupid one?'

Pete smiled. 'No, Lucy, I'm not. But if I spoke only French and you spoke only Spanish, would either of us be stupid if we didn't understand each other?'

'Of course not.' Lucy's brow wrinkled. 'You're saying that I don't know how to make Moonie understand me.'

[84]

'That's right. You have to learn how to signal her with leg, hand and body position. Right now, she doesn't know what you mean. And she'd prefer not to be under the control of someone she doesn't understand.'

'Which makes her very smart.' Lucy smiled. She started to laugh, thinking it over. 'So learning to ride is really learning how to talk to a horse.'

Pete nodded. 'Partly. It's learning to communicate, both ways. You have to learn how to understand what the horse is saying, too.'

They'd been walking toward the barn as they talked. When they got there, Pete showed her how to brush Moonie and pick the dirt and stones out of her feet. He taught her how to take off the saddle and bridle, and put on the halter. They led her out to the field with a lead shank, and let her go.

'Thanks, Mr Pierson. You really helped me, and taught me a lot.'

'It was my pleasure.'

Pete walked across the road humming. It's always nice to do a good deed, he was thinking. And Lucy won't try that again.

Cody waited in his hiding place. It was getting dark, and his Abby wasn't home. He fidgeted slightly and yawned. He would wait.

Abby and Fiona enjoyed each other's company on the way back from Kingston. They'd had a heartwarming visit with Liam, and were feeling both happy and melancholy. Happy to have been together again as a family, and melancholy because Liam stayed while they went home.

Already, Fiona was fighting the desire to have a drink. It was a difficult thing. She prayed for strength, knowing that she must put it behind her. For Liam, for herself, but mostly for her daughter. What a great kid, she thought. A real solid person. Smart, kind, and independent. That thought caught in her throat. Independent because she had no choice. She shook her head and vowed again. This time she would beat it.

'Mom,' asked Abby, her thoughts travelling their own direction, 'if Dad is innocent, why can't we do something to prove it?'

'Oh Abby, we've been over this dozens of times.'

'I know, but what if we could prove he didn't do it?'

'How? Find a signed confession? Abby, sweetheart. Five million dollars disappeared from a trust fund that your dad was looking after. It's never been found. We couldn't prove that he didn't take it.'

'Did they prove that he did?'

'Not to my satisfaction, but the jury concluded that no one else could have done it. There was enough proof to convict him; a cheque with his signature. He said he didn't sign a cheque for that amount. I believe him, but the jury didn't.'

Abby sat in thought. After a while, she quietly spoke. 'If Dad did it, I'll still love him. I wouldn't hate him. You'd tell me if he did it, wouldn't you Mom?'

'Yes, Abby. And I know he didn't.'

'How do you know?'

'I just do. Your father doesn't have a crooked bone in his body.'

Abby nodded. To herself she said, *I'm going to find a way to prove it.* She just didn't know how.

Chapter Seven

Fired

The better part of valour is discretion.
– Shakespeare, *Henry IV*, Part One, v, iv

ABBY WAS UP early the next morning. She tiptoed downstairs and got the animals' food ready. Once outside, she couldn't help but sing out loud, 'Oh, what a beautiful morning, oh, what a beautiful day. I've got a … Cody! You crazy coyote!' Cody had bounded out of nowhere and leapt up at her to lick her face.

'Cody, we've got so much to do today. First let me feed you and leave food out for the raccoons. Then help me pick flowers for Mom. She's quit drinking. I'm so proud, Cody, and I want her to wake up to fresh flowers. Then we've got to exercise Moonlight, and give Lucy a lesson. I think she'll turn out to be a good rider, don't you? Then, Cody,' Abby leaned over him as he ate and spoke quietly to him, 'when all our chores are done, we'll solve the mystery of the century.'

Cody looked up with thoughtful eyes. Abby continued, 'The mystery of who took the Colonel's money!'

Cody saw that she was excited, and he reflected her mood. He bounded around, zigging and zagging. Then he stopped. He remembered something. Cody tore off up the hill to the wreck of the barn.

'What's up?' Abby called as she followed him.

Cody was digging at something. The stench of burned-out wood assailed Abby's nostrils. Cody turned to her and presented her with a strange-looking object.

'What have you got, boy? Drop it.' Cody placed it gently on the ground at her feet. As Abby bent down to examine it, Cody shot off again.

Abby had no idea what this thing was. It had frayed wires

coming out, and it looked old and blackened. She thought it had probably been burnt in the fire. Why did Cody want her to see it?

Cody dropped a man's sooty glove beside the strange object.

'Where'd you get this, Cody? What's going on?'

Abby was puzzled. Cody generally didn't bring her things. Was this a new game he'd invented? Was he trying to get some attention because she was away yesterday? Hmm. Abby got up from her squatting position.

'Let's pick some flowers for Mom. We'll figure this out later.'

Abby and Cody strolled across the field behind the barn to the secret meadow. Abby had always called this meadow 'secret' because it was tucked behind a row of trees and out of sight until you were suddenly upon it. This is where the nicest wildflowers grew. They found beautiful bunches of pale violet and vivid purple phlox. They picked brilliant red wild poppies and fresh white daisies with yellow centres. Arms full and heart happy, Abby started back to the house with her faithful Cody at her side.

Cody growled. Abby's head shot up, suddenly alert. 'What is it, Cody?' He growled again, placing himself between her and the burnt-down barn.

Then Abby saw what was going on. There were two police officers looking around the ashes. 'It's okay, Cody.' Cody slunk away into the trees to watch over Abby from a safe distance.

'Hello,' she called.

'Hello.' The two officers looked up. The younger one just glanced at her then resumed his search, but the older one smiled. 'You must be Abby, Fiona and Liam's daughter.'

'Yes, I am. Nice morning.' She wasn't sure how to make conversation with an investigating officer.

'I'm Inspector Murski, and this is Detective Bains. We're here to take a look at the mess.'

'And decide how it happened?'

'Yes. That's about it.'

'Milo, look at this.' The younger policeman was staring at something with great interest. 'Looks like part of a switch for the electrical circuit. And there's a glove beside it.'

Murski turned to see what was there.

'Excuse me, Mr Murski?' Abby thought it might be important. 'This morning my, er, dog showed me that. He dug it up.'

'That explains the scratch marks all around here,' grumbled John Bains. He didn't seem too pleased.

'Clever dog! Could very well be the cause of the fire.' Detective Murski took latex gloves out of his pouch and pulled them on. 'Let's just collect these items and search around.'

'The glove's not burnt, Milo. Just sooty.' John Bains looked pensive.

'You're right, John. Let's see what else is here.'

Abby watched as the two men sifted and sorted through the charred remains of the barn. They worked silently and thoroughly. After a few minutes, Abby remembered that the flowers she'd picked needed to be put in water. She said goodbye to the men and walked down to the house.

As she passed the big maple, a corner of white paper caught her eye. Leslie had left a message in their secret hiding place! Abby carefully set the flowers on the grass and climbed onto the thick lower branch. She pulled the note out of the hole, and read:

Abby – Mom says I have to go to camp even if she has to tie me up to get me there. Too bad. It's getting boring. I've done all the sports. I've made all the crafts. But worse, I'll miss you. I'll try to break a bone or get a horrible disease so I can come home. By the way, Sam wanted to know where you live.

See you eons from now – Leslie

P.S. Write! You have to! care of Camp Kill Me Now (Kilmano) Box 35, Kenora, Ont. P1C 0C0.

Sam wanted to know where she lived? Amazing! Maybe he liked her, open mouthful of chicken salad sandwich or not! Abby sighed. She thought of Leslie at camp. Abby had always wanted to go to camp. She imagined beautiful, rocky northern islands, sunny days of canoeing and sailing with friends, laughing kids, everything happy. But if Leslie didn't want to go, why spend the money? It didn't seem logical. And it would've been fun for Abby to have her friend around for the summer.

She picked up the flowers and entered the kitchen. Oh good, she thought, her mother wasn't up yet. She picked out the nicest tall vase and arranged the flowers in water. She set them in the middle of the table, then stepped back to admire them. They looked perfectly lovely. Her mother would love them.

The police had finished, and Abby watched them drive out the lane.

She ate some toast and jam, then tiptoed up to change into jeans to ride Moonie, and give Lucy her lesson. She was very quiet, and was pleased that she didn't wake her mother. She avoided the third stair from the top and the bottom step because they were squeaky, and gently closed the kitchen door behind her as she left.

Cody stood waiting, under the old maple. He was rigid, nose pointing to a faraway destination. He whined.

'What is it, boy?' Abby asked. Cody whined again. Abby searched the distance for some hint of what he was looking at. Nothing.

'Cody, we've got to get over to Farrows'. Let's go.'

She had just got her leg over her bike, when Cody whined again, this time very urgently. Abby looked again.

'Holy!' Moonlight Sonata was careering across the field, running flat out toward the house. Something was wrong. The mare looked lopsided, somehow. Then she saw the problem.

Abby threw down the bike and started running as fast as she could.

'Hang on, Lucy!' she hollered at the top of her lungs. 'Hang on! I'm coming!'

As she ran, she tried to figure out how to stop Moonie without Lucy falling off. She'd try to stop her gently, but it was going to be difficult to catch the panicking horse. Abby realized that she'd have to play it by ear.

She needn't have worried. Once Moonie recognized her, she whinnied a worried greeting, and slowed to a trot. By the time the mare and Abby met in the middle of the field, Moonie was walking, eyes round and scared. Abby took hold of her bridle and gave her a pat. 'Good girl, Moonie,' she said softly as she pulled the reins through Lucy's fingers to ease the considerable strain on Moonie's mouth. Abby was impressed that the young mare could control her fear so admirably.

Lucy, sideways on the horse and gripping the slipped saddle for all she was worth, started yelling. 'I hate this stupid horse! Get me off!'

Abby let go of the bridle and grabbed Lucy around the waist. She lifted her with all her strength, and ordered her to let go.

'I can't!' Lucy wailed. 'I'll fall!'

'Just let go. I've got you.' Abby was upset at how Lucy had abused this noble horse. She tried to remember that the girl was terrified.

Lucy finally let go, and Abby lowered her to the ground. Lucy was shaking.

'My arm hurts. It's all her fault!' She hauled her leg back to kick the mare, but Abby blocked her.

'Stop it,' she said sternly. 'Take a deep breath. Get a hold of yourself.'

'I never want to see you or this horse again in my life! Moonie ran off on me. And came to *your* house!' Lucy began to sob.

Abby had no sympathy. 'Cry all you like, Lucy. I guess it gets you out of all kinds of trouble, but it doesn't do a thing for me. Why were you on her in the first place? You were supposed to wait for me!'

'It's my horse, not yours! And anyway, I couldn't wait all day!'

'It's only nine o'clock in the morning! And I was coming now!'

Lucy narrowed her teary eyes at Abby. 'You can't yell at me! I can fire you! You can't tell *me* what to do!'

'I won't tell you anything, Lucy, because you don't listen anyway. But I want you to see what you did to your horse.'

Moonie's mouth was dripping blood. The bit had rubbed off a piece of skin from Lucy's rough handling, and Moonie had bitten her tongue.

'So what? She deserved it. She wouldn't do what I told her to!'

Abby stood staring at the girl, amazed at her callousness. She had absolutely no idea how to respond.

'That old man across the road said he thought going in circles was boring, and all I had to do was learn how to talk to horses, and then I could ride like you!'

Abby was stunned. 'Mr Pierson? If he said that, he didn't mean it literally. You don't learn to ride a horse by just talking to it, and you have to do the boring stuff before you jump on and gallop away! And maybe you heard wrong, anyway.'

'I did not! That's what he said! But Moonie won't listen!' She started to cry again, then stopped abruptly when she remembered it wouldn't have the desired effect.

Abby shook her head in disbelief. 'Look, Lucy. I don't want to talk right now. I'm so mad at you I could punch you in the face. You should've waited for me. You risked your life, you could have killed Moonie, and you make no sense at all. Moonie can't understand English.'

'That doesn't make her stupid. Mr Pierson said!'

Abby had no idea what Lucy was talking about. She thought her head would start to ache if she didn't get away.

'Lucy. Listen to me. I'm going to ride Moonie back to your farm. You take my bike. It's on the ground beside the big tree.'

'You shouldn't leave your bike on the ground, Abby.'

'I dropped it to help you, you, you … oh, never mind! I'm outta here.' Abby lithely hopped onto Moonie's back, guiding her back home with her knees. Her mouth was much too sore to touch.

'I don't know the way home!' Lucy lamented. 'I don't know where I am!'

'Turn left out the drive, and ride all the way to your road. Then turn left.' Abby trotted off, knowing her patience was paper-thin. 'And if you get lost, you deserve to be eaten by coyotes!' Abby couldn't resist a parting shot. It made her feel a little better.

Abby and Moonie and Cody took their time on the way back. The day was beautiful; the birds were singing, the flowers brilliantly coloured, and the earth smelled rich. She felt all the tension leaving her body.

'Lucy is a fool. An absolute fool,' she said to Moonie. 'If I could, I'd buy you and ride you all the time. We'd compete together and we'd win all kinds of trophies. But we can't afford you. If I had my way I'd never give her another lesson. Moonie, you'll be sold if you and Lucy don't figure out how to get along. Her grandfather will buy her some slow old plug, and I'll never see you again.' She sighed. 'So be patient, okay? I'll try to teach her fast, so this doesn't happen again. But I want to teach her well, too, so you won't get hurt, and that takes time. Oh, Moonie. I guess we'll just have to do our best.'

They meandered along, Abby enjoying the early summer and chatting away to Moonie. By the time they got to the Farrows' farm, Abby's good spirits were restored and Moonie was completely calm. Cody disappeared, as usual. Abby slid off, landing lightly.

'You're in big trouble, Abby Malone!'

Abby spun around. Lucy, beaming with malicious delight, was fidgeting at the barn door.

'*I'm* in trouble?' asked Abby, incredulously.

'*Big* trouble. I could've been killed! You're fired. Never set foot on this property again.'

'Lucy ...'

'Pleading won't work. It gets you out of all kinds of trouble, but it doesn't do a thing for me!' Lucy mimicked Abby's earlier lecture.

Abby's face darkened with rage. 'Are you blaming me for what happened? Are you crazy?'

Just then, George Farrow appeared at the barn door. 'I'm sorry, Abby. Lucy told me what happened. We simply can't have accidents. I think it's best if we look for a more experienced teacher. Someone older. And a safer horse.' He looked sad but determined.

Abby knew it wouldn't help, but she had to try. For Moonie's sake. 'Mr Farrow, I think I should have a chance to explain.'

'Abby, I'll listen, but I've made up my mind. Lucy tells me you instructed her to ride over to meet you at your farm to save you the trouble of biking over.'

'No, Mr Farrow, that's not how it happened. It was Lucy's idea to take Moonie out on her own. They just showed up at my house when I was getting on my bike to come over to give her a lesson. I would never have let her ride alone, for Moonie's sake.'

'Is this true, Lucy?' George Farrow sternly asked his grand-daughter.

'No. On my honour, I told you the truth.' Lucy's face strained up at her grandfather, eyes wide and earnest. 'Abby's just saying that so she won't get fired. And don't forget what she said! That she'd punch my face and that coyotes should eat me!'

George sighed deeply, then faced Abby. 'Abby, you have to understand I don't blame you for this. You're young. Common sense will come in time.'

'You believe Lucy? You think I told her to ride over?'

'Yes. She's my granddaughter. I have to take her word over yours.'

Abby placed the reins in Mr Farrow's outstretched hand. She gave Moonie a quick hug. Moonie nickered. Abby walked away from the barn, chin up and fighting off the tears. She picked up her bike and rode home.

Things only got worse. There was a white van parked in her driveway, and two women were standing on the lawn. One was her mother, and the other was yelling. Even from a distance, Abby could see that her mother wasn't feeling well. It was in her posture.

The woman had a bunched-up armful of clothes, which threatened to fall on the grass as she waved her fist at Fiona.

'I'll call the police, I swear! That girl of yours will end up like her father!' With that venomous remark, she thrust the clothes into her car, and backed all the way out onto the road. Abby gave her lots of space. The van spun around on the road and squealed off.

'She seems a little miffed at something, Mom?' Abby said, trying to assess the situation. Her mother looked awful. She must've got into the sauce last night, Abby thought.

Fiona ran her fingers through her greying hair. She breathed deeply and tried to stand tall, but she couldn't manage. 'You've got yourself into a mess, young lady. Let's talk about it inside.'

Abby followed her mother into the house. Fiona sank into a chair, and rested her head on her arms. 'I'm not feeling so good, Abby.'

'I can see that, Mom. Drinking last night?' As soon as she said it, she regretted it, but the damage was done.

'Abigail! Don't you speak to me like that!' Fiona barked, grasping the table edges with her hands, and half-standing. 'Don't you ever speak to me like that!' She glared at Abby with bloodshot eyes. 'You stole a girl's clothes! How could you? Isn't it enough that people think your father's a crook?'

Abby's eyes widened. 'I never ever stole anything! What are you talking about?'

'A crook *and* a liar!'

'Mom!' Abby was shocked. Her eyes filled with tears. 'Stop it, Mom! I never stole any clothes, I swear!'

'That woman came here to find stolen clothes. Her daughter told her that you stole more than twenty pieces of clothing over the school year! I didn't believe her, but she searched your room, and they were all there! Clothes I'd never seen before!'

Abby plunked down on the chair across the table. 'And you believed her? Mom, was her daughter named Pam? Or Annie?'

'You stole from Annie, too?'

'So it was Pam. No, Mom, I promise you. Annie and Pam made me their charity case, and gave me a garbage bag of old clothes. That was a few weeks before graduation.'

'Don't make this worse by lying. You never told me anything about it.'

'You were never sober enough to tell after school. Or awake enough before school! When do you think I should've told you? There are lots of things I never told you! Like how Mrs Pierson made Leslie's mother's old rags into a beautiful graduation dress for me. I didn't tell you how lovely I looked at my graduation that you were too drunk to attend. And until now, I never even told you how sad I was that you weren't there!'

Fiona's head had slumped back onto her arms. Her chest was heaving, and Abby couldn't stand listening to her wrenching sobs.

'Mom, you cry. You have a good cry. You go on feeling sorry for yourself, because I'm leaving. I can't take this any more. And thanks for standing up for me with Pam's mother. Thanks for believing in me!'

Abby stormed out of the house and ran past the barn and through the secret meadow. She kept running until she got to a special place that only she and Cody and the raccoons knew about. She climbed into her favourite tree and nestled into her little corner. It was a wide, comfortable tree, branching low to the ground. She'd found this spot when she was small. Here, she could be alone to think.

Hidden in the leafy bosom of this squat giant of an oak, Abby shivered and hugged her knees to her chest. 'Everything's gone wrong.'

The branch beside her rustled. Cody was trying to climb up.

'Oh, Cody, you're a true friend,' she said. She reached down and helped him up. He cuddled beside her, and licked her tears away.

She heard chattering. She looked up, and saw the twin raccoons scrambling down the huge trunk.

'Rascal! Rook! Where've you been for the last couple of weeks? I've missed you both.' The raccoons had grown larger, and were healthy. 'You're eating well, I'm glad to see. And you still let me pat you?' Abby knew that raccoons become totally wild when habituated correctly. It was essential for survival, but right now she was glad they were still tame enough to hug.

'All my problems are with humans,' Abby told them. Three pairs of adoring eyes watched her intently. 'Mom's a drunk and she thinks I'm a thief. Mr Farrow thinks I'm a liar with no judgement who puts his granddaughter in danger. Lucy lies through her teeth to save her hide. Pam frames me by giving me clothes, then says I stole them. My dad's in jail while the real thief goes free. Have I covered everything? Wait, no, I haven't. Mrs Smithers the lunatic supply teacher and Mr Edwards the insane principal blamed me for everything all year. They're crazy! On top of everything else, we're losing our house unless we pay our mortgage by September the first!'

The animals listened hard to her tone of voice. Abby saw their concern and tried to shake off her despair.

'Is this bearable, I ask?' Her attentive audience gave Abby confidence, and she got right into the spirit of it. 'How is a person to go on? What is a person to do?' Her voice took on a decidedly Shakespearean tone. 'Surrounded by insanity, how is a person to remain sane? I ask you, dear animals, nay, I beseech thee, how may I contend with the slings and arrows of outrageous fortune, and win the victor's shield?' Abby's accent and tone and pitch sounded strange to the animals. Their scruffs started to rise.

'It's all right, sillies, it's only me.' She giggled at herself, and felt altogether happier. 'See what spending time with Mr Pierson does to a person? Maybe one day I'll go on the stage.' The ruffs calmed down, and the animals relaxed.

'I think I'll go to Merry Fields and talk to Mr Pierson. He'll know what to do. Thanks for listening.' She rubbed them each on the head and jumped down.

Chapter Eight

Dancer

The fire in the flint
Shows not till it be struck.
– Shakespeare, *Timon of Athens*, I, i

LAURA AND PETE saw Abby ride up their lane on her bike. They noticed the silver streak dash under their porch, too, but only because they were watching for him.

'Pete, that girl needs mothering. She's filthy!'

'Looks more like soot. Maybe she was rooting around at the barn.'

'It's a good thing I've got some cookies in the oven.'

'Laura, you *always* have cookies in the oven!' Pete gave her a good-natured slap on her rump. He loved his wife and all her cosy ways.

Laura opened the kitchen door and called out, 'Come on in, dear! How nice of you to drop around!'

Abby smiled her thanks. She stood at the door. 'I have to talk to you about something.'

'Now, before you say another word, you sit right down here at the table and I'll get you some milk and cookies.' Laura ushered her into a chair.

Pete sat down beside her at the table, and patted her hand. 'Anything at all, Abby, you know that.'

Abby nodded. She knew that.

Laura placed a large cold glass of milk and a plate of warm, freshly made chocolate chip cookies in front of Abby. Abby's stomach growled loudly in anticipation, and she blushed. 'Excuse me!' she said.

'Don't you worry about a little tummy rumble,' reassured Pete. 'Now, "An honest tale speeds best being plainly told." *Richard III*.

What did you want to talk with us about?'

'Pete! Let the girl eat!'

Abby took a long drink of milk, and reached for a cookie. She dropped it back onto the plate. 'They're still too hot, Mrs Pierson. Can I talk first?'

Pete said, 'Don't let my wife boss you around. See what I have to put up with?'

Abby smiled. 'I don't feel sorry for you, Mr Pierson.'

Laura was pleased with that response and sat down with them.

Abby studied the glass of milk for a minute, then spoke, head down. 'I think I need some help. I don't want you to think badly of her, and I know she won't want me to be telling you this after she said she wouldn't do it any more, but ...'

Pete and Laura exchanged concerned looks over Abby's head. Laura said kindly, 'Yes? Go on, dear, don't worry.'

Abby steeled herself. 'My mother is drinking a lot, and I don't know how to help her.'

Laura asked, 'Does your mother think she needs help?'

'I don't know. She told me she was going to quit for sure. I know she hates it. You know, all the ... bad feelings and not remembering and, well, all the mess.' Abby was having a hard time getting her feelings into words.

'We do know, dear,' said Laura. 'We've seen enough of it in our own families to know what you mean.'

'Both your families?' asked Abby.

'Yes.' Pete talked gently. 'If you look, it's probably found in more families than not. Alcohol is a widespread problem. It's hidden most of the time, but it's there all right. So don't feel you're alone, Abby. And we can help.'

Laura had taken Abby's hand in hers. She squeezed it and said to Pete, 'I'm going to take the truck, Pete. Can you manage without me for a while?'

Pete winked at her. 'I can manage without the truck, but never without you. You're okay alone?'

'Better alone this time. Woman to woman. If I go now, I'll keep her sober and ready for the meeting at seven.' She was out the door in a flash.

Abby was confused. 'Where's Mrs Pierson going, and why so fast? What meeting? Is there an emergency?'

'Of sorts. We've talked this over with your father, and we agreed that when the time was right, Laura would take your mother to an Alcoholics Anonymous meeting.'

Abby was stunned. 'But she'll be mad at me! I didn't want you to tell her!' Abby jumped up and ran to the door, but Laura's truck was gone in a cloud of dust.

'Don't worry, Abby. We'll never betray your trust. Mrs Pierson will do this on your father's behalf. Not yours. I've already talked to her about her drinking. She knows that we know. The burden isn't on your shoulders.'

Abby sat down in the same seat. 'I sure hope this is the right thing.'

'Nothing else works for alcoholics, Abby.'

Abby sat silent. She picked up a cookie and ate it. Then another. And another. Pete got her some more milk, and left the jug on the table.

'There's something more, isn't there?'

'Yes.' Abby wiped her mouth on the napkin. 'Actually quite a few things. The most important thing I'll leave for last. I need advice. The first thing is, I've been fired.'

'George fired you? Impossible! You've trained that horse so well.'

'Lucy went for a ride without me. Moonie took off on her and ran to my house. Lucy had a horrible scare and could've been hurt badly. She told Mr Farrow that I told her to meet me there because it was too much trouble for me to ride over on my bike.'

'So you were fired?'

'Yes. Mr Farrow said that he had to believe Lucy over me.'

'Well, she's family.'

'But it's not true! It doesn't do her any favour to be allowed to lie!'

'I know you're telling the truth. And my guess is that George knows, too, and hopes that Lucy will feel so ashamed for getting you fired that she'll confess.'

'Really? Somehow I can't see that. Lucy wasn't ashamed at all.

She looked downright elated.'

'Hmm. Let me talk to George and try to sort it out.'

'But won't he think I've tattled to you?'

'Not at all. Now that I think about it, Lucy tried to ride Moonie alone once before. She got her foot stuck in the stirrup. I helped her, and explained why she shouldn't do that. I thought she understood my reasoning.'

'She didn't.'

'I can see that. But George should know about that incident. Then he'll have to consider that you were telling the truth.'

'Thank you. I feel better already.'

With more cookies and milk, Abby and Pete discussed the stolen clothes fiasco. They decided to put it last on the list of troubles because they couldn't make sense of it, nor could they think of how to resolve it.

On the subject of the barn fire, Pete said he would call Milo Murski to get an update. When they knew what they were up against, they could better decide what to do.

Finally, Abby brought up the subject that was nearest to her heart.

'My father. Do you think he stole the money?'

'That's quite a question.'

'So you do?'

'No! I most certainly do not.'

'If my father is innocent, then someone else is guilty. And that person is free, and he knows who he is. I want to find out who that person is.'

Pete scratched his head. 'Very logical. How do we do that?'

'That's what I want to know.' Abby's brow furrowed. 'That's precisely what I want to know. Will you help?'

'You bet. I have to be honest with you, Abby, I don't know where to start. I've thought about this, myself. We'll keep thinking while we take care of the smaller things. Okay?'

Abby nodded, pleased that Mr Pierson had committed his help.

'Let's find out where we are with the barn fire.'

Abby nodded again.

Pete carefully straightened his painful back as he stood. He got his address book out of the desk drawer and picked up the phone. He dialled.

'Inspector Murski, please.' He covered the mouthpiece, and said to Abby, 'One thing at a time.'

'Hello, Milo! It's Peter Pierson.... How's your father...? Long time, indeed...! Yes, I want to talk to you about the fire at the Malones' barn. Any news on it...? Yes, of course I'll tell you how I became involved. A little girl is sitting here in my kitchen with more problems than a grown-up could deal with ... you don't say ... I understand ... yes, I understand it's classified information ... you'll have to go out there again...? Yes ... hmm....'

Abby watched his reactions closely as he spoke to the inspector. She didn't think it was good news. As soon as he was off the phone, Abby jumped up from her chair.

'What is it, Mr Pierson? Why do you look so worried?'

Pete ran his fingers over his bald scalp. 'Apparently the scorched object that the police took to the lab was planted. It has different ash on it, meaning it was burned somewhere else. And the glove they found at the site; it appears that someone dropped it there after the fire. It wasn't burned. They're holding on to it in case it might lead to the arsonist, if the fire proves not to be accidental.'

'In case it was arson? And the glove was the arsonist's?'

'That's right. But why would someone set fire to your barn, Abby? It doesn't make any sense.'

'Not to me, but I should tell you about the letter.' Abby explained about the letter from the bank. She told him that they were to be evicted, and that there'd been a hope that the insurance on the barn might pay the mortgage.

Pete whistled. 'Very interesting. In other words, there's a motive for arson.' Pete remained thoughtful. 'Inspector Murski just told me something I didn't know. About Colonel Kenneth Bradley's trust fund.'

'The same trust fund that Dad was convicted of embezzling?'

'Yes. The same. It's actually a trust for the Colonel's children, so it's their money that's missing. Apparently the Colonel's father didn't want the Colonel to lay his hands on the family money, so he put it in trust for his grandchildren, the Colonel's children.'

'Why did he do that?'

Pete shook his head sadly and answered, 'Probably because he didn't believe the Colonel would spend it wisely. 'It is a wise father that knows his own child'.'

'Shakespeare, of course?'

'*Merchant of Venice*. The old man knew the Colonel's weaknesses, and thought the money should skip a generation.'

'But the Colonel has lots of money of his own, doesn't he?' Abby asked.

'He certainly appears rich with his cars and horses and houses. But he leverages his money to the hilt, which means he borrows a lot from the bank. He's always in debt.'

'Wow.' Abby considered this for a moment, then continued. 'He hunts with hounds, you know. I watched them gallop past our farm. His horse wouldn't jump over the wall beside the big tree at the road. He whipped his horse hard for stopping. And it wasn't the horse's fault. The Colonel's fat and rides like a sack of potatoes.'

Pete laughed. 'That's the Colonel all right. He never changes. By the way, he's not really a Colonel. He just likes the sound of it, and insists that people use the title. The Canadian Forces will catch on one day and have him drawn and quartered.'

Pete lifted the car keys off their hook, and opened the kitchen door wide.

'Where are we going?' Abby asked.

'To get to the bottom of all these mysteries. After you, Abby.'

They backed the ancient Plymouth sedan out of the shed. The car was a deep indigo blue, but time and dust and pigeon droppings had made that fact indetectable.

'I want to see the barn for myself,' said Pete. 'Or at least what used to be the barn. I want to take a good look at it.'

'There's not much to see, Mr Pierson. It's all ashes.' Abby sat quietly for a moment. 'How do we find out who took the Colonel's money?'

'Abby, we can only do one thing at a time. Don't forget, the police are working on it. Until we think of a new angle or find new proof, we'll have to wait.'

'Waiting's the hardest thing of all,' said Abby sadly. 'Especially when my father is in jail for something he didn't do.'

Abby knew something was wrong the second they turned in their drive. Cody was howling. And visible. He was in plain sight where the barn had stood, baying, head thrown back.

Pete drove right up to the ashes, and that's when they saw him. Terence Curry. He was crouched down, backing away from Cody, hands palms out as if protecting himself from attack. He was shaking, and his face wore a horrified expression.

Abby jumped out of the car. She ran to Cody.

'It's okay, boy! Good boy.' Cody wagged his bushy tail once in acknowledgement but never took his eyes off Terence Curry.

'Terence!' shouted Pete, puffing up the hill.

'The animal is rabid!'

'What's going on here?' asked Pete.

'I came by to visit Fiona, and got attacked by this ... wolf!'

'Cody is a coyote, Mr Curry, you know that.' Abby stroked Cody's back with the intention of calming him down. 'And I can't imagine what got into him. He knows you.'

'Whatever it was that got into him, I hope it's gone. He scared the pants off me.' Terence Curry was upright now, and dusting himself off. He was relieved that help had come and rapidly assumed a more dignified manner. Abby noted how tall he was. He was taller than Pete, who stood over six feet tall.

Pete stroked his chin. 'As long as I've known Cody, he's never exposed himself to humans unless there's a darn good reason.' This was difficult. Pete didn't want to insult him, but he'd just told Abby that they'd get to the bottom of things. He steeled himself and asked, 'If you came to see Fiona, what are you doing up here, Terence?'

'This is ridiculous!' joked Curry. 'You're taking a coyote's word over mine?' He smiled broadly, looking from Pete to Abby and back again.

'I'm just confused,' Pete answered. 'What's got me puzzled is that Cody usually avoids contact with humans. Were you taking a look around the ashes, and Cody took offence?'

'I lost a glove here yesterday when I was assessing the damage. I was searching for it when this wolf, pardon me Abby, coyote, accosted me.' Terence Curry winked at her fondly as she knelt beside Cody.

Abby spoke without thinking, 'A glove? The police found it when they were here this morning.'

Interest showed in Terence Curry's face. 'Really?' He ran his fingers through his hair. 'The police have it, then?'

'Yes, I'm sure they'll be happy to return it,' Pete answered.

'Thanks,' said Curry. 'I'll check with them.' He looked at Cody with trepidation and asked Abby, 'Is it safe for me to go now?'

'Oh yes. Don't worry, Mr Curry.'

Pete and Abby watched as Terence Curry strolled to his car, periodically looking over his shoulder at Cody, to make sure he wasn't being followed. He waved goodbye and drove away.

'Well,' said Abby. 'Could he possibly have planted the false evidence?'

'Be careful of jumping to conclusions, Abby. I'll call Milo Murski about the glove, but let's go slowly and carefully here.'

'But it's Mr Curry's glove. He dropped it here at the barn. Doesn't it make sense that he dropped it while he was planting the burnt switch to cover up arson? And if he was trying to cover it up, then he set the barn on fire, too?'

Pete patted her fondly on the back. 'You're getting carried away. It's probably exactly as he said. He may have simply dropped a glove and come looking for it.'

'In summer? Why would he wear gloves in this heat unless he was trying to avoid leaving fingerprints?' Abby was prepared to be suspicious of everybody, longtime friend or not.

'Abby, we must go slowly and steadily. Come on, let's phone Milo.'

'If it was Mr Curry, it's horrible! He knew my animals were locked inside!'

'Slow down. We merely know he lost a glove. Let's not assume guilt until it's proven.'

'I see what you mean. But he sure made Cody nervous. You saw that.'

Pete nodded thoughtfully.

Abby slept fitfully that night. She woke up several times, tossing and turning, thinking too much, sweating. There were too many things on her mind.

Her mother thought that Alcoholics Anonymous would help, and wanted Mrs Pierson to take her back. This was good news, but time would tell.

She thought up different schemes of how to visit Moonie, realizing with each scenario that it wasn't possible. In one scenario, she crept into the barnyard and rode her bareback through the fields and over the fence and home, the night air whistling past them as they galloped. In another, Mr Farrow begged her to return, vowing never to doubt her again. The best, though, was the one where Mr Farrow caught Lucy red-handed getting on Moonie alone, realized his mistake, and made Lucy apologize.

She worried about Moonie. Moonie needed her. Nobody understood her the way Abby did. And Abby needed Moonie, too. It was her dream to prove to the world that Moonie was the fastest, highest-jumping, most remarkable horse ever born. Abby knew in her heart that only she could bring out the best in the mare.

When she thought of her dad, her heart lurched. He shouldn't be in jail, and she didn't know how she was going to get him out. It was so difficult being patient and letting the police deal with matters. She hoped that she and Mr Pierson would think of some faster way to help.

The barn fire nagged at her. Was Mr Curry responsible? And if he did it to help, shouldn't he admit it, and take his punishment? Surely a judge would go easy on a man trying to help a mother and child at risk of losing their home? There was something she was missing.

She really needed sleep. She tried to chase all her worries away by thinking of Sam. She imagined his handsome face with those sparkling eyes, and for a moment, she relaxed. He was such a good person. Maybe, just maybe, they could see each other. But Abby thought that would never happen. Even if he liked her, his mother disapproved of her friendship with Leslie. What would she think of Sam dating her?

Abby found everything so confusing. She tried lying on her stomach, she rolled on one side then the other. She threw off her covers. She changed her cotton nightie. She couldn't get comfortable. Finally at three o'clock, she got up and went downstairs to get a drink of milk.

She wasn't alone.

Cody slipped through the kitchen window as Abby walked in.

'Cody!' she whispered, surprised, 'What are you doing?'

Cody wasted no time. He took her hand gently in his mouth and pulled her toward the door. Abby followed without question.

Outside, the moon was full and the summer night was rich with earthy aromas. Viburnum, peonies, leaves, soil. Abby inhaled deeply, filling her lungs with the cool humid air and clearing her sleepy head. Cody impatiently tugged at her hand and shot off ahead of her into the night.

Abby hiked up her longwhite cotton nightie and ran after him barefoot.

The moon came from behind a cloud and softly lit the field. Cody streaked ahead, quietly yipping. Abby ran on, wondering what she'd find at the other end of her journey.

Moonie. Half down on the ground at the fence line. Abby ran faster. She blinked, trying to see more clearly. She couldn't tell where the mare's legs were, she was in such an awkward position. Abby swallowed her fear and summoned up all her courage. She prayed as she ran, 'Please let Moonie be all right. Please let there be no broken bones. Please let me know how to help her.'

She got closer. Then she saw. Moonie was dripping with sweat from fear and exertion, her two back legs tangled in the wire fence.

'Easy girl,' she said gently as she knelt beside her, out of breath. 'It's me, your friend Abby. Easy, girl.' Abby talked to Moonie and stroked her neck. At first Moonie's panic was so intense that she didn't respond, but finally she let out a big sigh of relief.

'This is the worst thing for a horse, isn't it? To be helpless and unable to protect yourself or run.' Abby had caught her breath now, and kept talking and soothing and stroking. She slowly worked her hands down to the wire around Moonie's legs.

Moonie's eyes rolled in fear. She tried to jerk away, the rusty old wire creaking eerily with the added tension. Moonie scrabbled with her imprisoned legs and managed to get herself more tangled. Abby began again at her neck, stroking and talking.

'Moonie, you've got yourself in quite a pickle. Were you coming to see me again? A moonlight visit from Moonlight Sonata?' She talked on and on, knowing that her gentle singsong voice was reassuring to the frightened mare. 'Did you forget the safe place to get through? And you didn't see the fence in the dark? Hmm. I guess that you were moving fast, you saw it too late, tried to jump it at the last minute, and got your back legs caught in the wire. And made it worse by struggling. Hmm, how are we going to get you out of this mess?'

As Abby talked on and on to Moonie, she carefully sorted out the wire and slowly began to loosen the strands from around her hooves. First one leg and then the other, until Moonie was completely free of the wire. Abby's hands were raw and covered with dark rust.

'Okay, Moonie, get up.' Abby could hardly breathe, afraid to know how badly Moonie was hurt.

Moonie tried out each foot, and realized the wire was gone. She pushed her hind legs under her, stretched her front legs ahead, and lurched up onto her feet. She looked quite pleased with herself, and happily shook herself off.

'No broken bones. Good girl!' Abby checked her for cuts and swellings, and pronounced her a lucky girl. 'You've got some nicks and scratches and a couple of cuts, but you'll be good as new in no time. Phew!' She hugged the mare's neck tightly, and rubbed her head. Moonie nuzzled her.

'Cody!' Abby called. The coyote appeared instantly. 'You saved Moonie. Good boy. Thanks, Cody.' She knelt down and rubbed his ears. Cody gave her a quick lick on her nose. 'Who knows what shape she'd have been in by morning.' She shuddered at the thought.

'What do we do now, folks? It's the middle of the night. Should I take you to your farm, Moonie?' Moonie snorted. 'Or would you just jump out of your field and come back again?' Moonie pawed the ground. 'Maybe you would. Well, you can stay over tonight, but I'll have to take you back tomorrow.'

Abby, Cody and Moonie started off toward home. It was exhilarating walking barefoot through the meadow in the night with cool dewy wet grass between her toes. The moon threw a yellowish wash over her world, changing the familiar landscape into a place wilder, more magical than it was by day. Warm pungent breezes wafted through her hair and tickled her skin. Abby took a slow, deep breath of midnight air, filling her nostrils and lungs with the soft, balmy night.

Abby laughed when Moonie light-heartedly gave a playful little buck, threw her head saucily and began to cow-hop. Cody dashed beside her, weaving in and out as she swerved and swooped. Moonie reared up lightly and thrashed her front legs. Her dark, glossy coat reflected the soft light of the moon. Then, with an agile leap, she tore off and galloped gracefully around the field as fast as she could go, Cody right on her heels.

Eventually she slowed to a walk, and quietly returned to Abby's side. She nodded her head up and down and nickered in Abby's ear. Abby could feel that the free-spirited cavorting had pleasantly erased Moonie's tensions. She reached up and lovingly patted her neck. 'I'll let you graze on the lawn for the night, Moonie. Mom won't mind.'

Abby ran cool, soothing water from the garden hose over Moonie's long, fine legs for almost ten minutes, which cleansed the cuts and brought down the swelling.

She crawled into bed a little later. Fatigue took over, and she fell immediately into a deep, dreamless slumber.

The next morning, Abby was awoken by a racket on their lawn. She jumped out of bed and looked out her window. She rubbed her eyes and looked again. Hounds. All over the place. Sniffing, howling, racing from one smell to another.

Cody! The hounds must be hunting Cody!

Abby pulled on her jeans and a T-shirt and was downstairs and outside at lightning speed.

'Get out of here! Out! Out! Go away!' Abby picked up a fallen branch and waved it around, hollering at the top of her lungs. The hounds ignored her and, noses to the ground, continued hunting. They were getting closer and closer to where Abby suspected Cody was hiding.

Abby knew Cody's secret hiding place under the porch would be safe from the bigger, clumsier hounds, but she wasn't sure Cody would stay there. If he took off, there'd be trouble. The hounds would chase him and if they caught him, they'd kill him. Abby doubted the hounds would be fast enough to catch him, but she didn't want to take the chance.

She saw wide-eyed Moonie standing under the oak, utterly transfixed. She'd never seen so many hounds so close.

Abby threw a rope around the young mare's neck and jumped on. She snapped a supple shoot from a low-hanging branch of the oak and steered Moonie straight for the centre of the pack.

'Get away!' she screamed, waving the switch among the hounds. She ran at them again, and this time she got their attention. 'Scram! Get out of here!'

Abby looked down at a dozen or more surprised hound dog faces. She yelled again, 'Scram!' They turned tail, and fled.

Abby quietly called to Cody. He very softly yipped; his way of telling her that he was all right.

Relieved, Abby and Moonie tore off down the lane, to chase the hounds far enough away that they wouldn't come back. They turned left out her lane, and Abby followed. 'Go away!' she hollered. 'Get lost!'

The hounds raced down the road and ducked into the trees, Abby in full pursuit. They galloped wildly around bushes and over rocks. Abby ducked to avoid a branch and raced on. Over the crest of a hill, she came to a full stop. She found herself face to face with the whole hunt field. There were close to thirty people on horses, dressed in clean shiny boots and breeches and riding jackets. They all stared at her, amazed at the sudden appearance of twelve terrified hounds followed by a switch-wielding girl.

'Child! What are you doing, disturbing our cub hunt? And what do you think you're doing to the hounds?' a portly older man with a permanent frown bellowed as he huffily rode up to Abby on a tall grey horse.

'Chasing them away from my coyote! That's what!' Abby was mad.

'Your coyote? You own a coyote?' Even his smile seemed to be a frown.

'Yes. Well, sort of. And the hounds were sniffing him out, so I chased them away.' This sounded logical to Abby, but the expressions on the faces of the assembled group remained stunned.

'Do you know who I am? Do you know to whom you are being so impertinent?' The man puffed up his chest and his frown got deeper.

He looked familiar to Abby but she couldn't quite figure out why.

'I'm Colonel Kenneth Bradley, Master of the Foxhounds. I ask you to remove yourself from this place at once.'

It was Abby's turn to be stunned. Colonel Bradley! The trust fund. Abby took a good look at him. He looked old to her, maybe sixty-five or more. His skin was red and veiny around his large, bulbous nose. His teeth were large and yellow, like a very big rat, Abby thought. Pale blue watery eyes peered at her from under bushy grey eyebrows and fatty lids. He had a substantial belly which was threatening to pop off the shiny brass buttons closing his red hunting coat.

'What are you gawking at, child? Leave us this minute.' He flicked his hand dismissively and turned his horse with a sudden jerk. Then he yanked it back around to face Abby again. 'I said, this minute!'

Abby collected her wits and turned Moonie around with her knees. She started for home, confused by all that had happened.

She knew she'd done the right thing. She couldn't let the hounds get Cody! Lucky that Moonie was there. Otherwise it would've been impossible to chase them away.

She was so engrossed in her thoughts that she didn't notice a woman on a tall elegant chestnut stallion ride up beside her.

'Hello.'

Abby started. She looked into the face of a pretty young woman. 'Hello.'

'I didn't mean to startle you, but I wanted to apologize for the Colonel's behaviour.'

'Why? It wasn't you.'

'I know, but I'm hunting with him, and he was rude. He embarrassed me. He embarrassed everyone.'

'Thank you. It's very nice of you to tell me.'

'I wouldn't want you to think we're all like that. We're not.'

'Well, he's certainly scary, isn't he?' Abby started to feel better. She was glad this woman had come along. 'And he didn't believe me about Cody.'

'Cody? Is he your coyote?'

'Yes. I found him when he was only a few days old. His mother was killed on the road.'

'Lucky for Cody that you found him.'

'Yes. And lucky for me. He's my best friend.'

Mousie knew what she meant. Sometimes an animal is the only one that seems to understand. Dancer had been that animal for her.

'What's your name? I'm Hilary James.'

'Hi. I'm Abby Malone. Oh, my gosh. Hilary James? Mousie? That's Dancer? Dancer, is that you?'

The great horse snorted.

Dancer had been a legend in Caledon for years. The unruly stallion had become the greatest jumper the countryside had ever seen. Hilary James, nicknamed Mousie, was the role model for all the young riders for miles around. She was their heroine, and they dreamed of one day finding a horse like Dancer and jumping to fame and glory. Abby was no exception. Mousie was her idol and Dancer her dream horse.

'Oh my gosh. I can't believe it.' Abby knew she was babbling and felt helpless. She blushed.

'Abby, I'm complimented. Dancer is too, aren't you, boy.' She patted his neck. 'I'm impressed with you, Abby. Riding with no saddle, no bridle, as if it's no big deal. And everyone in the hunt secretly applauded you, the way you stood up to Colonel Bradley. Congratulations.'

Abby was glowing. 'Thanks a lot. I didn't want the hounds to catch Cody, that's all.'

'Now that we know there's a tame coyote living here, we'll leave it alone. I'll make sure of that.'

'You will?'

'Absolutely. I don't get back often, but I'll inform the masters and the secretary and all the members to leave your farm alone when we start in the fall. We're very responsible. Funny, most people are grateful to have coyotes chased off their property. Of course, most people don't have them for pets.' Hilary assessed this brave blond girl riding beside her. 'You're quite the person, Abby. You ride beautifully without tack, you have a pet coyote, and you stand up for yourself. I'm glad I met you.'

'Me too. I'm glad I met you, too.'

At that moment, a big bay heavy hunter with a white blaze and four white socks caught up, his handsome rider smiling broadly. 'Well done! You told off the Colonel in no uncertain terms!'

'Sandy, this is Abby Malone. Abby, meet Sandy Casey, my fiancé.'

Sandy pulled his horse to a halt. 'Whoa, Henry. Your fiancé? You'll marry me? Yippee!' Sandy jumped down from Henry and, reins in hand, knelt at Dancer's feet. 'This is the happiest day of my life. I love you, Hilary.'

Abby stared at this drama being played out in front of her. She'd heard of the romance, heard rumours about their being sighted holding hands at the Terra Cotta Inn, or shopping for antiques at Tub Town in Belfountain. The gossips loved snippets of news about Hilary and Sandy and loved embellishing the details even more.

'Sandy, we're embarrassing Abby.' Mousie grabbed Sandy's hand and pulled him to his feet, then playfully kissed his hand. Their eyes locked momentarily and Abby could see how much they cared for each other.

Sandy placed his foot in the stirrup and threw his leg over Henry's saddle. 'Abby, You're the witness. Now she'll have to marry me. We won't let her go back on her word. Deal?'

Abby smiled, thrilled to be included. 'Deal.'

'This is Sandy's idea of a running gag,' said Hilary, smiling broadly. 'I said I'd marry him ages ago.'

'You can never have too many witnesses,' he retorted happily.

The next lane was Abby's farm.

'I live here. It was nice to meet you both. And Dancer.' She was in awe. She'd heard so much about them, and here she was, riding along with them as if it happened every day.

'Nice to meet you, too, Abby,' said Mousie.

'Bye, Abby,' grinned Sandy. 'Don't let me down. You're the witness, remember?'

'I'll remember,' laughed Abby as she rode in her lane. 'How could I ever forget?'

She turned to watch them continue down the road. Tall, handsome Sandy Casey on his dark bay hunter. Beautiful, kind Mousie on the spectacular and athletic Dancer. 'They're really nice,' thought Abby. 'I can't believe it. Mousie and Sandy and Dancer, in real life.'

She shook her head. What a lucky day.

Chapter Nine
Laura's Cow Trouble

Oh, Lord, that lends me life
Lend me a heart replete with thankfulness!
– Shakespeare, *Henry VI*, Part Two, I, i

AS ABBY WALKED Moonie past her house, the front door opened. George Farrow stood at the door frame, glowering. She suddenly realized that she was riding his horse. Abby could see her mother peering anxiously behind him. She knew it looked bad. 'Hello, Mr Farrow, let me explain ...'

'Abby Malone, what in God's name are you doing with that horse?' He was puzzled and furious.

'She came here in the middle of the night and got trapped in the wire fence and Cody brought me to help and ...' Abby tried her best as she slid off the mare.

'Abby, these are the facts. Moonie was in the barn when I went to bed. She was gone this morning. I looked for her all over the country. Lucy suggested I try here. She said maybe you stole her so we couldn't send her away today. I couldn't imagine you'd do something like that.' As George Farrow spoke, he walked up to Moonie and took her by the rope. 'The fellow who wants to buy her came first thing with his trailer. He was very angry, and rightly so, to come all that way for nothing. Now I find her here. Turns out Lucy was right. You had no business taking her, no matter how much you like her. She's my horse, not yours.'

'Mr Farrow, you have to believe me. I didn't steal her. I didn't even know you were selling her! She turned up last night ...'

'Forget it, Abby,' he interrupted. He spoke to Fiona, 'You're going to have to get this child under control. I'm not pressing charges. You have enough problems. I'm taking Moonlight Sonata home and hope the man still wants her. I'll pick up my truck later.'

Abby couldn't stop the tears from coming as she watched Moonie being led away. It was so unfair!

Fiona came up beside her. 'Abby, tell me the truth. What happened?'

Abby faced her mother. She saw a haggard, pasty-white, puffy face and two bloodshot eyes. She guessed that her mother had been sleeping off another binge when Mr Farrow came knocking at the door. Abby felt a great weariness come over her. 'Mom, let's go inside. The light is bothering your eyes.'

Fiona allowed herself to be led into the kitchen. Abby put the kettle on to boil as she explained exactly what had occurred. Finally, she put a steaming cup of coffee in front of Fiona and said, 'So you see, Mom, it wasn't anything like what Mr Farrow thinks.'

Fiona nodded her head, letting the aroma of fresh coffee waft up her nostrils and help to clear her head. 'I believe you, Abby. I thought I heard noises last night, now that you mention it. It all makes sense.'

'Is there anything I can do?' Abby asked.

'I don't think so. Mr Farrow won't likely change his mind about what happened. And he's right, it's his horse and he can sell it if he likes.'

'But she's not just any horse, Mom! She's Moonie! And I care what he thinks. I'm not a thief!' Tears welled up again in Abby's eyes.

'I know, dear. I know.' Fiona put her coffee down and reached over to hug her daughter. 'I wish I could help, honey.'

Laura Pierson was weeding the flowerbed at the front of the farm house under the kitchen window when George Farrow plodded past leading Moonie. She dropped her trowel and brushed herself off.

'Hello, George! Can I get you a cold drink?'

'Well, Laura! I could certainly use one!'

Laura was back with a cool glass of lemonade before George and Moonie were halfway up the drive.

He gratefully took the drink and thirstily swallowed it down. 'Thanks, Laura. I needed that!'

'What are you up to, George? I don't often see you walking a horse down the road.'

'I don't make a habit of it, that's for sure. Abby Malone has been nothing but trouble since my granddaughter arrived. I don't understand it. Maybe it's jealousy.'

'Trouble?' Laura was alarmed. 'What kind of trouble?'

'First it was telling Lucy to ride before she was ready, now it's horse theft. She somehow got wind that I was selling Moonie, and she kidnapped her right out of my barn.'

'George! I can't believe it!'

'There's no other explanation. The man came to get her first thing this morning, and no Moonie. He left upset and put out. Where does the mare turn up? Abby's farm.'

'But the horse has gone there before, George. Don't forget she headed straight to Abby's farm when Lucy tried to ride her that time.'

'I don't buy it, Laura. A horse can't open a stall door, then the barn door, and go. And isn't it too much of a coincidence that the horse decides to leave the night before she's sold? Come on, Laura. I know you're fond of Abby, but don't be fooled. I'm starting to think she's a clever little so-and-so.'

Laura was distressed. She liked her neighbour very much, but she didn't like him saying bad things about Abby.

'Why are you selling the mare?'

'Lucy's other grandfather, her mother's father, bought her another horse. He knows horses, and it's a good one. A beauty. A little wild at the moment, but he tells me it'll calm down once it gets used to the place. Since Lucy doesn't need two horses, I sold Moonie, or thought I had.' He frowned.

'George, do you think the man will come back and buy her?'

'That's the million-dollar question. If Abby's nixed the sale, I'll be hopping mad. Thanks for the lemonade, Laura, it saved my life.' He handed Laura the glass and started off with Moonie docilely following.

'Anytime, George.' Laura stood with pursed lips, deep in thought. 'Poor little girl,' she thought. 'Pete will know how to help.'

Laura set off to find him. Way off, on the other side of the cow field, she saw Pete repairing a fence rail. She unlatched the gate, walked through and clicked it shut behind her. Laura started off across the field.

'Pete!' she called. She waved when he looked up, and waved again when he responded with both arms. 'That's a hearty greeting,' she thought.

Pete frantically redoubled his efforts. He thrashed his arms forward, and forward again in pushing motions, trying to make her understand to go back.

Laura walked on, waving happily.

Then she got hit. Fifteen hundred pounds of angry cow struck her from behind. Laura was thrown ten feet and landed on her face, thudding hard. The wind was knocked out of her. She lay shocked, unsure of what to do. Her instincts told her to get up and run, but her brain warned her that the cow would chase her, and it could run a whole lot faster.

The cow was right beside her. She could hear it, snorting, pawing. Too close. Adrenalin flooded her body. She gasped for air, struggling to fill her stunned lungs. The cow butted Laura with its sawed-off horns and pawed the small woman's prone body with its front left hoof.

Laura gathered her courage and raised her head to look for Pete. She desperately wanted to send him a message. He was running toward her as fast as he could, holding his bad hip and limping, but moving quickly. She feebly raised her right hand and croaked, 'Bye, Pete.' She thought she was about to die. 'I love you.'

'Laura! Laura!' Pete hollered, breathing hard.

The cow wasn't finished. It butted her hard, again and again, pawing her impatiently. Each stroke of the cow's hoof sent sharp pains through Laura's traumatized body. The enraged cow stepped back, then butted Laura again.

The cow was about to leap on Laura's back, when Pete arrived, screaming. 'GAAAAA! GEDDDUPPP! GET OUT!'

He clapped his hands and yelled and slapped her flanks, and finally got her attention away from Laura. The cow walked backwards a few steps, surprised, then turned and ran to join the herd at the trough.

Pete knelt down, horrified at the attack and alarmed at the damage done to his beloved wife.

'Laura? Can you speak?' No response. He felt the pulse at her neck. A weak but steady beat. He licked his palm and put it to her mouth. He could feel her breath. He had to get help, immediately. He didn't want to leave her with the cows, so first he hurried to shut the gate, to keep them locked in the feed yard.

As he moved rapidly toward the house, he noticed two people riding past on horseback. He urgently called out, 'Hello there!'

They both turned, a young man and a young woman. 'Hello!' the young man called.

'Stay with my wife! She's unconscious here in this field.' He gestured toward Laura, and watched to make sure they saw her. 'I'll call for help.' He disappeared into the kitchen and dialled 911, panting heavily. He tried to collect his wits. He watched through the window as the woman turned her horse to the sturdy wooden fence he'd built to keep his cows safe.

One horse effortlessly jumped over it and cantered the few strides to the helpless form of Laura Pierson. The woman slid off the magnificent chestnut.

'Stay, Dancer.' The horse stood rooted to the spot as the young woman leaned down and spoke soothingly. 'Help is on the way. Don't worry. Relax.' She noted that the older woman was totally unresponsive. She wondered if she was even alive.

The man unlatched the gate and walked his horse into the field. 'Hilary? That was a four-foot plank fence with barbed wire on top!'

'I had to get here quick.'

'How is she?'

'It doesn't look good, Sandy.'

'This is a day for accidents all right,' said Sandy. 'First the Colonel breaks his kneecap on a tree and now this.'

Hilary studied Laura's condition. 'This woman has dirt and grass stains all over her back. I wonder what happened?'

'She was trampled by a cow.' Pete arrived at that moment and answered her question. He carried a blanket over his shoulder.

'Crazy cow must've thought Laura was interfering with her calf. And maybe all the waving got her mad. I can't believe it happened. Her calf wasn't even near. Just shows you, you can never be too careful.' Pete shook his head as he spoke.

Hilary stood as Pete took his post by Laura's side.

'Thanks, folks. There's an ambulance coming. I appreciate your help.'

Sandy said, 'We'd like to wait until it gets here, if that's okay.'

'Thank you very much. That's very kind of you.' Pete gently placed the blanket over his wife and tucked it under her as best he could without moving her.

'We'll feel better knowing it got here all right,' added Hilary James.

Pete nodded agreement as he scanned the road to see if the ambulance was coming. Then his eyes took in the chestnut stallion.

'Your horse is the spitting image of Dancer. Anybody ever tell you that?'

Sandy and Hilary exchanged glances. 'Yes,' she said. 'Often.'

Pete carefully finished tucking the blanket around Laura and checked her pulse. He frowned. He hoped and prayed that she'd come out of this.

Laura's hand reached up and a soft moan came from her throat.

'Laura! My Laura!'

'Pete? Am I alive? Ooh, I hurt all over.' Her voice was weak. 'I'm alive. I love you, Pete.'

'Shh, my darling. I love you, too. An ambulance is coming.' His ear picked up the welcome droning wails. 'Listen. They're here.'

Sandy ran to the road, unlatched the gate and pushed it open as wide as possible. He waved them in.

He and Hilary moved the horses off to the side when the ambulance rolled through the gate. They watched as the paramedics deftly placed Laura on the stretcher, strapped her in, and slid her into the back of the vehicle. Pete climbed in beside her. The doors closed and the ambulance headed north up the road to Orangeville.

'Good thing there's that great new hospital there,' said Sandy.

'Yes. She's probably in her seventies. She's not going to heal as fast as a younger person. I hope she's all right.' Hilary stood watching the swirling dust that followed the ambulance down the gravel road. 'Well, I guess we should shut the gates.'

'You latch the gate by the house,' said Sandy. 'I'll lead the horses out and close the big gate behind me, okay?'

'And not jump it?' Hilary ribbed.

After George Farrow had left her house with his mare, Abby felt empty and desolate. She worried that Moonlight Sonata would be misunderstood in her new home. She hated that Mr Farrow thought she'd stolen his horse. More than anything, though, it was as if she'd lost her best friend.

Fiona finished drinking the coffee that Abby had made for her and stumbled back to her rumpled bed. She couldn't solve all the problems in the world, she thought. Abby would eventually find another horse to ride. Fiona was much more worried about keeping a roof over their heads. Where would they go when the bank evicted them? She felt rotten. Her head throbbed and her mouth tasted awful. She fell asleep.

Downstairs, the stink of rotting food assaulted Abby's nostrils. She couldn't just sit there, she had to do something. The house was a horrible mess.

Abby started cleaning. She needed to do something vigorous to take her mind off Moonie anyway, she thought. Starting with the old food and garbage.

Once the dishes were done, and the kitchen counters, oven and floor scrubbed, she felt she was making headway. Assessing the pile of laundry, Abby was grateful to Mr Pierson for having fixed the washing machine. She sorted the whites from the colours and started a load. She javexed the bathroom and started on the living room. She almost screamed in outrage at the sight of the empty gin bottle on the floor beside the couch. She almost gave up then, but persisted, fuming. As she was vacuuming the dining room, she thought she heard the phone ring. She turned off the machine and listened. The phone rang again.

'Aha! I thought so!' Abby ran for it.

'Hello?'

'My daughter!'

'Dad!'

'How's my favourite little girl?'

'I'm your only little girl!'

Liam laughed. 'It's good to hear your voice, angel.'

'It's good to hear yours, too. I was vacuuming, and I thought I heard the phone ring, but I wasn't sure.'

'Good ears. It's hard to hear over the vacuum. But I didn't call to discuss vacuums, Abby. I've got good news. Is your mother there?'

'Well, yes, but she's asleep. What's the good news? I could sure use some.'

'Anything wrong, Abby?' Liam felt a wave of exhaustion with the information that his wife was sleeping at midday. It meant only one thing.

'Well, Dad … Can I hear your news first? Mine can wait.'

'Listen to this, Abby. The prison has completed my evaluation and I'm being sent to Beaver Creek.'

'Great, Dad! The place with the golf course?'

'Not a complete course, but a few holes for sure.'

'And no glass between us on visiting days? And chalets for you to live in?'

'Yes and yes again, Abby. It's good news.'

'It sure is. When do you go?'

'As soon as they get me there. I'm not part of the planning process around here.'

'How long do you have to stay at Beaver Creek?'

'The rest of my sentence, maybe only another year and a half with parole. I'm very happy about it. I want you to make sure you tell your mother when she wakes up. Okay?'

'Okay. I'm really happy for you, Dad. I can hardly wait to visit you there and get a real hug.' Abby was trying to summon enthusiasm for her father's sake, but she'd rather he was coming home.

'You got it! Now, enough about my news, Abby. What's on your mind?'

Abby explained about Moonie escaping from the Farrows' barn in the night and getting caught in the wire, and Cody bringing Abby to help, and the hounds, and the Colonel, and meeting Mousie and Dancer, and being accused of stealing Moonie, and that Moonie was being sold. She paused to take a breath.

'Whew! All in one day?'

'And it's only noon!'

'Whatever else, Abby Malone, you always have plenty of news.' Liam considered her problem with Moonie, and said, 'I think this is a case for Mr Pierson. What do you say?'

'I always run to Mr Pierson for help, Dad. What can he do, anyway?'

'He can explain it to George Farrow.'

'I tried, and Mr Farrow won't believe me.'

'Abby, sometimes adults have better luck.'

Abby sighed. 'You're right. It's really not fair, though, is it?'

'No, but sometimes life isn't fair.' Liam knew all about that.

Abby felt happier after her father's call. She finished up her work, changed the laundry, and left a note for her mother:

Dear Mom,

I've gone to visit the Piersons. Dad called. He's going to Beaver Creek! Good news, eh? I hope you feel better. Please don't drink until I get home. I need you sober.

love, Abby

Abby looked around briefly, admiring her work. She left the house, intending to go directly to Merry Fields, but a thought crossed her mind. She would examine the fence where Moonie had been stuck the previous night. Maybe there was enough hair and blood on it to prove to Mr Farrow that she'd told the truth.

Abby headed out across the field toward the fence. As she walked through the grass, a motion on the road caught her eye. A person on a bicycle. A tall, dark-haired boy. He turned and pedalled up her lane.

Sam Morris! Leslie's brother. Oh, no, she thought. She blushed, remembering her mouth stuffed with chicken salad sandwiches at the graduation. He must think I'm gross. But he came here, didn't he? To see me. Holy.

How did he find her farm? Leslie must have told him. What was he carrying? Flowers! For her? Abby's stomach rode a roller coaster. She would have hollered 'Yippee!' aloud except he might have heard.

She watched him walk up to the front door and knock. He looked through the glass in the door to see if anyone was home. Abby was extremely glad that he was seeing a tidy, normal house and not a pile of empty liquor bottles.

Abby practised normal breathing while she hurried back to the house to get there before her mother was woken up. He walked around to the kitchen door. Again he knocked. Again he peered through the glass into a clean and shiny room. How horrible if she'd left the mess. What would he have thought of her family?

She was as calm as she'd ever be, so she called out, 'Hello!'

Sam dropped the flowers as he spun around. He smiled at her and waved, then awkwardly bent to scoop them up. Abby realized that Sam was nervous, too, and she felt a little better. She approached him.

'Sam, nice to see you. How'd you find me?'

'Leslie. I picked some flowers on the way.'

'For me?' Abby blushed, regretting the question. What if they weren't for her? Maybe he'd picked them for his mother.

'Yes. Who else?' Sam looked at her shyly.

'Oh, your mother, maybe?'

'No, they're for you.'

'Thank you. They're my favourites. Dandelions, Queen Anne's lace, purple thistles. Thanks.' She hoped she didn't sound as nerdy as she felt.

He stuck out his handful of flowers for her to take. She accepted them too quickly and reminded herself to breathe. She said, 'We should put them in water. Come into the kitchen.'

'Okay.'

They walked in, unsure of each other and of what to say. Abby filled a glass vase with water and made a nice arrangement. She put them in the middle of the kitchen table and stepped back to admire them.

'They're lovely. Thanks for bringing them.'

'Well, I hoped you'd like them, so I'm glad you do.'

'Oh, I do.'

They stood for a long minute of empty air, then both spoke together.

'I was just passing by, so I thought – '

'I was going to look – '

They stopped talking at the same time to listen to the other. Then they began to smile, then laugh at themselves.

Abby started again. 'I was just going to look at the fence where a horse was caught last night. Want to come?'

'Sure.' Sam opened the kitchen door and held it for Abby. She scooted out, being careful not to get too close to him. Once out in the warm summer air, they were more comfortable.

'Do you have baby raccoons?' Sam asked as they walked. 'Leslie told me you do. And a coyote?'

'Yes, that's right. The raccoons are almost grown, now. Their mother was killed when they were little and I adopted them. And maybe you'll see Cody. He's most certainly already seen you.'

Sam looked around, alarmed. 'Cody? Your coyote? What do you mean! He's watching me?'

Abby laughed. 'Yup. Don't worry, he's friendly.'

'Leslie told me all about you. She says you've got a witchy way with animals.'

'Witchy? Leslie called me a witch?' Abby beamed with pleasure.

Sam shook his head. 'No, no, no. She didn't use that word. That was mine. I meant that you're kind of magical with them.'

'I just try to read them, that's all. They can't talk people talk, so I try to understand what they mean by the things they do. And they try to understand me. There's no witchcraft involved. Anyone can learn if they want to.'

'Sounds fair. Like when a dog wags his tail you know he's happy?'

'You got it. There are thousands. Cody's ears, for example.'

He smiled. 'Leslie told me about the day Cody came to school and chased Larry. Wish I'd seen that!'

'It wasn't my favourite day.' Abby rolled her eyes.

'What about Cody's ears?'

'If he's confused or worried, they go straight out from each side of his head, like this.' Abby used her hands to make two low ears. 'When he's alert or curious, they go up together from the top of his head, like this.' Again she illustrated the position of his ears.

'You know a lot about animals.'

'There's a lot more to know. Here's the fence.'

Together they examined the tangled mess of wire. Sure enough, tufts of dark brown horse hair were evident. Dried blood stained the wire, and the torn-up ground around it showed obvious signs of a struggle. There was no doubt that a horse had been caught here.

'He'll have to believe me when I show him this,' said Abby, half to herself. She told Sam about the previous night's adventures and her problem with Mr Farrow.

'It's usually best to clear up misunderstandings right away,' he said, wisely. 'And it wouldn't hurt to explain it here, if he'll come.'

They walked along the fence line toward the back of the farm, and soon they stood beside Abby's tree. She'd never shown anyone her secret hiding place before, but for some reason she wanted Sam to see. 'This is my favourite place to think,' she said softly. 'It's where no one can find me.'

Sam understood how special it was. He gravely studied the grand tree with its low, wide spreading branches. 'Thanks for showing me, Abby. It's ... perfect.'

They walked on through the secret meadow, talking. Abby found her worries fading away, almost as if they'd happened in a different time warp. It seemed to her that she and Sam were encased in a beautiful bubble, oblivious to the rest of the world. She felt giddy and light and pretty.

Abby asked Sam a lot of questions. She wanted to know where he went to school and what he was doing for the summer, and what sports he liked to play. He answered each question, and

Abby admired the way that he made fun of himself in his stories. Abby found out that he'd been sent to a private school because his mother believed he'd get the best education there. Sam liked it and did well at sports, so he was happy. He thought that his sister's education was just as good, and less expensive.

'Teachers can't get worse than Miss Smithers and Mr Edwards and that's a fact.'

'We've got some duds, too. I don't think there's a school on earth with only great teachers. Anyway, whether you pay for private school or go to public school doesn't matter. The quality of the teachers is what makes a good education.'

'Or breaks it. What do you want to be when you grow up?'

'I don't know. Abby, you've asked a lot of questions. You know more about me now than my mother! What about you? You're not normal, you know. Oops, I didn't mean it like that. I've never met a girl like you.' Noticing the admiring look bestowed on her, Abby took it as a compliment. 'I think you're pretty. I like looking at you.'

Abby blushed scarlet and tried to avoid his eyes. 'You're not hard to look at, either,' she replied, trying to make it into a joke.

The two teenagers talked and laughed and teased each other as they walked back to the farmhouse. They both had big smiles on their faces as they appeared over the hill behind where the old barn had stood.

'Sam, I'm going over to Merry Fields to see Mr Pierson. Oh, and thanks again for the flowers.'

'You're welcome. Do you want an escort? I'm going back that way.'

'Sure!'

They jumped on their bikes and rode down the road to Merry Fields.

Cody followed furtively, sneaking from tree to tree. Abby tapped Sam on his arm and pointed him out.

'Is that him?' he asked, awestruck.

'For sure.' Abby enjoyed Sam's response.

'But what if someone takes him for a wild creature, and shoots him?'

[127]

'What an awful thought. Maybe I should put a dog collar on him, or a cowboy scarf. Then people will know he's tame.' Abby shuddered and made a mental note to do just that.

When they got to Merry Fields, Abby turned up the driveway, and Sam waved goodbye. She sighed happily as she waved back. He is really, really wonderful, she thought. And good-looking.

Then she heard the cows and calves lowing loudly. She noticed that they were locked in the small feed-trough area. Strange, she thought.

She knocked on the farmhouse door. No answer. The door was locked. Stranger still. Abby walked around to the barn and sheds, and called for Pete. No answer. The cows were very upset, so Abby opened the gate, after checking that the other gates were closed and the field was secure. The cows barged through the opening and immediately began grazing greedily on the grass.

This was very puzzling. Abby wasn't at all sure what to do. Was there something wrong, or were the Piersons simply away for the afternoon? But the cows wouldn't have been locked up without food, and the car and the truck were both there. Something wasn't right, and Abby was worried.

Just then a taxi drove in the driveway. Abby watched to see who it was, her heart in her mouth. The taxi stopped. Pete stiffly got out and paid the driver. Abby sensed that he was deeply preoccupied. When the taxi had gone, she apprehensively walked up to him and asked, 'Is everything okay, Mr Pierson?'

'"All's well that ends well", Abby, my sweetie. Shakespeare.' He briefly smiled at his young friend and absently walked past her to the house. She followed him.

'Can you answer in English? Modern English? I know something's wrong.' Abby was upset.

Pete stopped walking and looked at her. 'I'm sorry. Of course you don't know. Mrs Pierson got trampled by a cow. She'll be fine in a few weeks. She has a concussion, multiple bruises, and she broke her nose and some ribs.'

'Holy!' Abby was horrified. Her problems seemed very small, now.

'I came home to get her a few things and I'm driving back to

Orangeville.' He unlocked the door, opened it, and turned to Abby. He put his hand on her shoulder. 'Don't look so worried, Abby. She's much better than I feared.'

'Thank heavens for that, Mr Pierson. Trampled by a cow! Can I come with you? If it wouldn't be too much trouble?' Abby blushed when she realized how bold she sounded. He had enough on his mind.

She was about to apologize when he surprised her by answering, 'Nothing would make me happier. I'd love the company, and you'll cheer her up. Jump in the truck while I get what she needs. She gave me a list. Oh, and thank you for letting the cows out to graze.'

After collecting the desired items for Laura, they were on their way. Abby hadn't noticed where Cody went, but assumed he'd gone home to wait for her return.

Chapter Ten

The Hospital

You are my true and honourable wife,
As dear to me as the ruddy drops
That visit my sad heart.
– Shakespeare, *Julius Caesar*, II, i

ABBY DIDN'T LIKE the smells in a hospital. Even a brand new hospital like Orangeville. And the noises seemed hollow and unfamiliar to her. She was glad that she was with Mr Pierson.

They went up the elevator and straight down the hall to Mrs Pierson's room. They opened the door slowly and tip-toed in.

Laura lay quietly on the raised bed, hooked up to machines with transparent tubes full of moving fluids. Abby stared. Laura's pale skin was translucent with large dark bruised patches around her eyes. The tubes in her arms looked like instruments of torture. Her lips were cracked and parched. She opened one eye.

'Pete! You're back. And little Abby, you dear, dear thing.' Her voice was hoarse and whispery. Abby and Pete approached the bed and Pete took her hand. He sat on the chair beside her and motioned to Abby.

'Abby, pull up that other chair next to the bed. Laura can't speak too loudly.'

Abby sat as close as she could, not knowing what to do or say.

'I feel better already, Pete,' whispered Laura. 'Please take me home.'

'Now, now, let's wait to hear what the doctor says.'

'He doesn't know how I feel.'

'Hush, hush. Just get your rest. Abby, what am I going to do with this woman? She's a difficult one.' Pete smiled at her and looked fondly at his wife of over fifty years. 'Did I ever tell you how we met?' he asked Abby.

'Now Pete, you don't have to bore the child,' demurred Laura.

'No, I want to know. How did you two meet?' Abby jumped at this topic. She didn't really want to hear medical details, which seemed the alternative.

'We met in Regina at a teen dance at the church. As soon as I got there, I noticed this giddy girl.'

'Giddy! You always say that but it's not true.' Laura got right into the story, and it seemed to Abby that she had suddenly become the girl that Pete was talking about, intravenous tubes and all.

'You were giddy, dancing and laughing and showing yourself off. I couldn't take my eyes off you. But I was shy and backward, a country boy with little education. I couldn't work up the courage to ask you to dance.'

'You only had to speak up. I noticed you, too, but in those days, girls wouldn't ask boys to dance.'

'A week later a friend asked me over to play cards. It was a cold, cold night. A prairie winter night, thirty degrees below zero. Laura was there. We had a wonderful time.'

'Yes, we did,' Laura reminisced dreamily.

'That night I realized what it was that I mistook for giddiness. It was her joy for life. It captivated me. She had a *joie de vivre* that's never faded.' Pete's eyes shone with love. 'And I walked her home. She had no gloves. So I had to hold her hands in mine, all the way to her house.'

'And your ears got frost-bite because you couldn't cover your ears with your hands!' She began to giggle and then to cough.

'It was worth it,' Pete said as he calmed her. The coughs stopped, and he bent down and kissed her warmly on the cheek.

'That's a great story,' said Abby. 'I hope I have such a romantic story to tell when I'm your age.'

Pete and Laura smiled. Laura cautioned, 'Don't rush it, Abby. Life unfolds in its own time.'

Abby nodded, thinking what wise words were coming out of this bruised face with the bandaged nose. She shuddered, thinking about the tiny woman's encounter with the cow. 'That must have been scary, getting trampled by a cow. They're huge! I can't imagine it.'

[131]

'Good thing Pete was there. He saved my life.' A tear formed in her eye and she grabbed for his hand.

'Don't get all weepy, Laura, you'll hurt your ribs. I wasn't fast enough. Darned hip.'

'You were fast enough to save my life. I couldn't have taken any more from that cow.'

'What were you doing, anyway, coming through the cow field?'

'I wanted to tell you about George Farrow's horse,' she croaked. 'Water, please.' Pete lifted the small paper cup and held the bent straw to her lips while she drank. 'Thanks, Pete. Abby, you tell him.'

'It's not important. Not next to what happened to you.'

'Go ahead, Abby,' said Pete. 'What happened?'

'Oh, Moonie came to my farm in the middle of the night and got caught in the wire at the fence line.' She proceeded to recount her adventures with the Colonel and George Farrow. After she'd told them the whole story, Pete scratched his head.

'I can certainly talk to George about your part in this. It's not going to be easy, though. He was already upset about Lucy's wild ride the other day.' He frowned. 'I can't do a thing about him selling Moonie. If he's sold the horse, it's a done deal and that's that. I wonder why the mare came to you in the first place. Any ideas?'

'None. The only other time was when she was scared by Lucy riding her. She came to me for help that time.'

'Maybe she needed help again.'

'But it was in the middle of the night. Why would she need help? And Mr Farrow said she was in the barn.'

Pete shook his head. 'We'll probably never know.'

Laura asked for more ice water. There was none left in the room, so Abby volunteered to get some from down the hall. She thought that the Piersons could use some time alone.

She had no idea where to go, so she wandered through the halls looking for the nursing station Pete had described. She got to the end of one hall with no luck, so she turned right and followed along the next hall. She found herself peeking in some of the rooms she passed, not meaning to be nosy, but curious for sure. In one room there was a very fat lady with one leg. In the next room was a young man with a leg in traction. At least he has both of them, she thought. A few rooms were empty, but most were inhabited by unfortunate people with substantial injuries and lots of bandages and casts. Abby assumed she was in the accident victim wing.

Finally she spotted the nursing station. She was walking straight for it when she heard a loud, very familiar male voice coming from a room further down.

'I don't want to argue about it. Just get it!'

Another man answered in soft tones that Abby couldn't quite hear.

'That's your problem! Don't bother me with legalities.' Abby knew she'd heard that voice very recently, but couldn't quite ... then it came to her. It was the Colonel! She'd heard his voice just this morning. She came to a stop outside his door. She eavesdropped.

'We need to have it and I want it now. Do what you have to do, and be done with it! Now get out. My knee is killing me, and you're making it worse.'

As Terence Curry stepped out of the room, Abby flattened herself against the wall. His head was lowered and his hands were deep in his pockets.

If I don't breathe, maybe he won't see me, Abby hoped.

Curry walked a few steps in the direction of the nursing station. Abby thought she was safe. She exhaled. Then something made him look back. First it was a glance, then a full double-take. He stopped dead and turned around.

'Abby Malone. What are you doing here?'

Abby couldn't figure out why she was scared. This man was a friend. The Colonel yelled at her this morning, but he probably wouldn't recognize her now. So why was she nervous? Sweaty nervous.

'Getting water for Mrs Pierson. She's here in the other hall. She was trampled by a cow.'

Terence Curry had retraced his footsteps and stood facing her.

'A cow? That's terrible, a woman her age!'

'Yes, she's in a lot of pain.'

'Have you been ... standing here long, Abby?'

'No. I was just walking to the nursing station to get some water for ...'

'Mrs Pierson. So you said. But when I came out you were standing as still as a statue. You didn't move. How long have you been here?'

'Who's out there, Curry?' the Colonel bellowed. 'What's all the racket?'

Terence Curry looked at Abby. She thought she saw great sadness in his eyes. She was puzzled. He motioned to her with a quick turn of his head that she should get out of there. She wasted no time. She shot past him and was at the nursing station before she dared to look back. Mr Curry nodded at her and then stepped into the Colonel's room and closed the door.

Abby was trembling. A nurse gave her a pitcher of ice water and a few paper cups, and with neck stiff and head down she returned to Mrs Pierson's room.

Cody's ruff was up. He started a soft, high-pitched howl. He could take the tension no longer. He knew that his Abby was in trouble. Once he was sure he was alone in the parking lot, he slid out from under the heavy green tarpaulin in the back of the Good Man's pick-up truck and down onto the paved ground. His sensitive nose picked up no threatening odour. His excellent ears heard no suspicious sound. He slunk toward the door through which he'd seen Abby enter and hid under a bush to wait for an opportunity to get inside the building and help her.

He saw a large woman carrying a baby. Cody watched her approach, and timed how long it took the door to close as she walked in. An anxious-looking man went through the door next. Cody didn't try this time, because the man was too alert. A bored delivery man with a trolley of boxes. Now. Cody shot through the door at his heels, unnoticed, and slipped behind a potted palm.

His nose twitched as he tried to pick up Abby's scent, his concern for Abby overriding his natural fear as he peeked out. He picked out a familiar scent. The man that drives too fast. Terence Curry walked past the palm and through the door, oblivious to the watchful grey eyes.

Cody knew that his Abby was near, but he had no idea how to find her in this bustling, hollow place full of echoes and strange smells.

With Terence Curry gone, his ruff flattened to normal. He sensed that his Abby was in danger no more. Now that she didn't need him, it was best to retreat. He noticed a fat man carrying a baby striding quickly for the door. The coast was clear. He prepared to slip through the door with the man. With no warning, two nurses appeared from a room, carrying bags.

'Wolf!' shrieked one, dropping her cargo in horror. Cody was discovered. The fat man flattened himself against the door, shielding his baby from harm. Cody dug in his nails, skidded to a halt and reversed in a flash. He searched for cover, followed by the screams of frantic humans.

'Wolf! Wolf!' Where could he hide? Cody ran, toenails clicking and clawing noisily as he slid on the slippery floor, unable to get a firm grip on the smooth surface. He ducked behind two metal doors as they were closing together. They shut. Cody felt a lurch. The floor was moving. He was being carried up. He shook with fear and his fur stuck up all over his body. He started to drool. The doors opened and no one was there. He was in a different place with different smells. The doors began to close again. He made his decision. He jumped out.

A doctor had been turning the corner when Cody leapt out of the elevator. 'Wolf! There's a wwwolf!' he stammered. 'Call the police!'

Abby and Pete were getting ready to leave Laura for a nap when they heard the excited shouts about a wolf on the floor.

To Abby, it was clear.

'Cody!' she gasped as she dashed down the hall.

'Don't worry, he's my dog!' she yelled to anyone who might hear, and then she bumped headlong into the doctor as they both turned the same corner, going in different directions.

'There's a wolf in the hospital. Go to any room and close yourself in!'

'It's my pet! It's Cody. Where is he?'

[135]

The doctor looked at her with astonishment. He pointed behind him.

Abby raced on. 'Cody, Cody,' she called.

A big voice boomed from a room. 'Is that the coyote brat that chased my hounds? Is there no peace from her anywhere?'

'Sorry, Colonel,' she yelled as she passed. 'Cody, here boy!'

Cody heard Abby's calls, but with all the echoing, he didn't know from which direction her voice was coming. He was too afraid to move from his hiding place. He had wedged himself behind the pipes and the linen carts in the laundry room. He kept as still as a mouse, hardly daring to breathe.

'The police are on their way, doctor,' reported a nurse at the nursing station. 'The wolf was first seen downstairs and the admitting nurses immediately called for help. The Humane Society and Animal Rescue are coming as well.'

'Thank you, nurse. We never ran into this sort of thing at Toronto Hospital.'

Abby overheard the conversation and spoke up. 'If everyone would stop yelling, I'm sure I could find him and take him home.'

'Time to leave, young lady. This is no time for heroics.' The doctor was taking charge. 'Nurse, make an announcement that all visitors must depart in an orderly fashion. And,' he stopped her with another instruction, 'each room must be searched. Close each door when there's no doubt the animal is not hiding there. Give the orders!'

'Yes, doctor!' The nurse ran off to do as he said.

Peter Pierson arrived at the station, panting. 'Abby, there you are.'

'Mr Pierson, tell the doctor about Cody! He thinks I'm making it up!'

The doctor turned to face Pete and looked at him over his glasses.

Pete said, 'This girl owns a coyote named Cody. She believes your "wolf" is her coyote, and if she was given a chance to find him she'd save everyone a lot of trouble.'

'That girl's *name* is trouble!' bellowed the voice in the room.

'Sorry, Colonel,' Abby called back. 'It's true about Cody, you see? So please call off the police and everyone else.'

'Absolutely not,' replied the doctor. 'If it's not your animal, your life will be endangered. Let the authorities handle it. If you want to identify him after they catch him, I have no trouble with that. But until then, I'll ask you both to leave promptly.' The doctor strode away officiously.

'Let's get in the truck, Abby,' said Pete, gently. 'No use arguing with a set mind.'

'Okay, I'll go, but let's take the long way to the elevators.' Abby darted in each room they passed, whispering, 'Cody, here boy,' in each room. No Cody. They got to the elevators, and pushed the button.

The announcement blared over the speakers, 'Emergency! All visitors must leave the hospital immediately! Emergency ...' Abby didn't want to hear the rest of it.

She closed her ears to the noise. Abby's throat felt choked. Her eyes burned. She refused to cry, but that was difficult because she knew how scared Cody would be in this place. It was everything he tried to avoid.

'Mr Pierson, could we wait outside until they find him, just in case?'

Looking down into that beseeching face with those pleading green eyes, Pete said, 'Of course, Abby. We can't leave him here. If it's Cody. It's possibly not Cody, you know. He didn't come with us, remember?'

The elevator arrived, and they stepped on. Abby called for Cody once more and held open the doors. No response. She let the doors go, and watched sadly as they closed together, closing her away from Cody.

'Mr Pierson, Cody can do things you'd never imagine. He might've hopped on your truck and we'd never know. And anyway, what other "wolf" would come into a hospital?'

'I don't know, sweetie.' Pete smiled comfortingly and escorted her past the potted palm, out the door, past the bush by the door, and to his truck.

The parking lot was crowded with curious people, talking excitedly and asking each other what was happening and did they see the wolf? Some cars were leaving, but most people waited, hoping for action.

They didn't have long to wait. Sirens wailed as police cars screamed into the lot and braked noisily at the door. Animal Control trucks and Animal Rescue vans were close behind. Police dogs poured out of the Canine Division vehicle.

Abby watched in horror. 'Cody won't be able to stand it,' she said.

'Don't worry about Cody,' responded Pete. 'He's a smart little guy. Those German shepherds have nothing on him.'

'Except numbers,' Abby worried.

They waited. An hour passed. Now they were alone in the parking lot, except for the emergency vehicles and the staff cars.

Another half-hour went by.

Abby asked, 'Do you think we could find out what's happening?'

Just as she spoke the front door opened and several discouraged-looking men emerged from the building. They got in the Humane Society and Animal Control trucks. The door opened again, and more people appeared. They, too, got into their cars and left. The police with their dogs were next.

Abby jumped down from Pete's truck and ran up to an officer as he was preparing to go.

'Excuse me, officer? What happened in there?'

'Nothing. We found nothing.'

A canine officer had overheard, and corrected him. 'Not quite nothing, Tom. There were wild animal scents all over the place.'

'I meant we didn't find the wild animal the scents belong to, Joe, even with your high-priced help, there.' He gestured to the lovely big shepherd that accompanied Joe. 'Feel like a beer? We're off duty now.'

'Sure. But come over to my place. Freddy's probably already there.' Tom nodded his assent. They prepared to go.

Abby went back to the truck. 'They didn't find him.' A smile started at the corners of her mouth and grew bigger until her whole face was lit up. 'They didn't find him!'

More people came out. Soon all the cars and vans and trucks were gone.

'Let us go visit Mrs Pierson, shall we? And discover where Mister Cody Coyote has hidden himself?' joked Pete in an upper-crust pompous fashion.

'Surely,' responded Abby in the same tone. 'Let us shall.' They laughed at her grammar, and noses up, they walked back through the lobby past the information and admitting desks.

Abby kept expecting someone to stop them, since the hospital had been evacuated and the all-clear had not been given. She thought how much better kids get treated when they're with adults. She knew she'd have been kicked out by now if she had been alone.

They went up the elevator and along the halls undisturbed. It was very quiet. Abby kept her ears open for a sudden soft yip, or any scurrying sounds. They turned the corner and Pete quietly knocked on Laura's door.

'Who's there?' she spoke as loudly as her injured throat could squeak.

'Pete and Abby,' Pete stage-whispered.

'Come in, then! And fast!' she demanded, uncustomarily curt.

Pete opened the door immediately, surprised by her tone.

'Now close the door, and quickly.' Abby had never heard Laura take command before. She wondered what was coming.

A black nose thrust out from under the covers and sniffed. Then a very happy coyote face.

'Cody!' Pete and Abby spoke at the same time.

'Shhh!' remonstrated Laura. 'You don't want him caught now, do you?'

Cody squirmed out of bed and onto Abby's lap. He licked her face and wagged his tail and wiggled all over with happiness. Abby held the small coyote tightly, and finally allowed herself to relax. He was safe.

Laura and Pete exchanged a long, happy glance.

'How did he get here, Mrs Pierson? People looking for him in every square inch of the hospital!' Abby wanted to know.

'I have no idea. He must have smelled me out! Just moments before the police came to my room, the door opened ever so slightly, and Cody seemed to melt through the opening and up under my covers. I feel truly honoured that he trusted me! He stayed still as could be. Kept me toasty and warm!'

'What happened when they searched your room?' Abby asked.

'Not a thing the first time, when it was only people. I thought we were safe until the big dog came in. Oh, he made such a fuss! Jumped at my bed and growled and howled, but Cody never budged. The policeman was terribly embarrassed. He had such trouble calling him off!'

'What did you do?' Abby was fascinated.

'I pretended that I was horrified, which wasn't hard to do because I really was, and I told the young man to control his dog and get out of my room. He tried, you know, but the dog was persistent. Finally another policeman helped him, and they apologized until they were as blue in the face as their uniforms. I tricked them!' she cackled.

'Well done, Laura!' Pete was proud of the way his wife had handled the situation, broken bones and all. 'Well done.'

'It was the least I could do. I'm honoured that he knew I'd help,' she repeated. 'Now, I'm very tired. They'll be in to feed me my dinner, and you'd best get little Cody out of here.'

'How are we going to do that?' asked Pete. They all looked blank.

Abby had an idea. 'Mrs Pierson, can I borrow your fancy pink scarf?' She'd noticed it on the top of the bag that Pete had packed.

'Certainly, dear!'

'And Mr Pierson, can I borrow your belt?'

'What in the blazes will hold up my pants?'

'Pete, just do it,' ordered Laura.

Pete pursed his lips and pulled off his belt. Abby tied the scarf around Cody's neck, giving him a totally different look. Pink chiffon removed the feral quality of his appearance. Now she looped the belt through the scarf to use as a leash.

'We brought Fifi to visit you on your sick bed,' said Abby, 'But now it's time to go.'

Pete laughed out loud at the sight of the coyote in a pink scarf. When Laura started to laugh, her ribs ached and she choked and coughed. Pete rubbed her back and held the water cup for her until it subsided.

'Now scram, all three of you,' she joked, 'before you kill me! Bye, Fifi!'

Abby and Pete and Cody on his belt-leash walked nervously but unnoticed to the elevator. Luck was with them. No one on the elevator. No one watching at the front desk. Just a few more steps to the door.

'Excuse me!' ordered a woman's authoritative voice. They stopped in their tracks. Pete looked around.

'Yes?' he answered pleasantly.

'No dogs allowed! They're very unhealthy and disturbing for the patients. There are signs posted at the door. Didn't you see them?'

'I'm so sorry. I must have missed them. We won't do it again.'

'Thank you.' The woman sniffed dismissively.

Pete turned back to Abby and whispered, 'Let's get out of here!' They opened the door and stepped out into the evening air.

'Hallelujah!' yelled Abby, revelling in their achievement.

'Not so fast, Abby. Get in the truck!' Pete saw police patrolling the parking lot.

They slipped into the cab of his truck with no time to lose. Pete turned the ignition and they were gone.

'Now, Abby, is the time for celebration! We're home free!'

Chapter Eleven

High Hopes

Now my soul hath elbow room.
– Shakespeare, *King John*, V, vii

PETE WATCHED AS Abby and Cody walked toward the house. He'd just dropped them off at their farm on his way home from the hospital. He loved that little girl. He'd invited her for dinner but she'd insisted that her mother had her dinner ready at home. He shook his head. Brave girl. He admired the way she continued to hope for the best. Laura would take Fiona back to AA when she got out. Abby turned back to look, and Pete waved goodbye.

Abby waved back at Mr Pierson and felt good. He was a true friend, a person whom she trusted completely.

'What a day!' she thought. She was exhausted. It was only this morning that she'd awakened to the hounds on her lawn. So much had happened since then. She longed for dinner and her warm bed. But the first thing she'd do was find a red cotton scarf for Cody to wear around his neck, so he wouldn't look like a 'wolf'. If he'd been wearing one today, they could have avoided all the confusion.

As she turned towards her house, she felt uneasy. Dusk had fallen, but there were no lights on. She wondered if her mother had been worrying, waiting for her, not knowing where she was. Had she therefore succumbed to her bottle? Abby sighed. Whatever it was that she was about to face, procrastination wouldn't alter. She gathered her strength and marched into the kitchen.

'Mom! I'm home!' she called.

She heard sounds from upstairs. Scurrying, hurried sounds. Abby was frightened. Had she disturbed burglars?

She ran outside and climbed the oak, scared. She watched the house. A light was on in the spare bedroom that her father had used as an office. Was her mother all right? Were burglars holding her captive? Should she run for help? What should she do?

Cody howled very softly, almost inaudibly. Abby looked for him through the murky dusk.

As she strained to see Cody, she noticed Terence Curry's silver Lincoln parked beside the shed. 'Why is he here?' she wondered.

Abby's attention was redirected to the kitchen door. Curry was leaving the house. Fast.

Abby knew that something was amiss. She watched him get in his car and back it up through a bush. The back tires got stuck in an uneven patch of dirt and spun. He rammed it in second gear and gunned it out. He kept it going forward over shrubs and emerged on the other side of the shed and onto the driveway. He sped away.

Abby stayed in the tree, thinking, 'What's going on?' She was stunned and too confused to get down. A couple of minutes passed before her mother came looking for her.

'Abby!' she called. 'Abby?'

Abby watched her mother from her perch. Fiona was standing outside the kitchen door, looking for her in every direction. Abby climbed down from the tree.

'What is going on, Mom? Mr Curry tore out of here in a big hurry. Is everything all right?'

'Yes, Abby. Everything's fine.'

'Why was Mr Curry here?'

'He dropped by to get some papers or something for a client. Why do you ask? He often stops by.'

Abby's mind raced. She felt numb. 'Mr Curry needs some papers for a client?'

'Yes, Abby.'

'Who's the client?'

'I don't know. He didn't say.'

'Didn't you ask?'

'Why would I? It doesn't concern me.'

Abby tried to unclutter her head. Things were trying to take shape in her brain. Colonel Bradley had told Curry to do something for him in the hospital. Something that he had done before. Something about which he didn't want to think of the legalities.

Could it somehow have something to do with this?

'Abby?' Fiona's voice interrupted Abby's train of thought.

'Did you let him take some papers, Mom?'

'Yes. Actually, he only wanted one.'

'Did you see what it was about?'

'No. Abby, why are you asking all these questions? Mr Curry and your father are law partners. They share their information, they always have. I see nothing wrong in this.'

'Mom, where was Mr Curry going?'

'Abigail! Enough of this questioning!'

'It's important!'

'All right, then! As far as I know, he was going home, but I didn't ask.'

Abby fell silent again. She strained to fit all the pieces together. 'So why was he in such a hurry to leave?'

'I have no idea. Maybe he realized the time and had a meeting.'

'And why were all the lights off?'

'Because it was still light out when we went up to your father's office. What are you getting at?' She was starting to sound impatient.

'I don't know. It was weird, that's all. Coming home, no lights on, hearing sounds upstairs. I thought there were burglars or something.'

Her mother put her arms around Abby and hugged her. 'I'm sorry you were scared, Abby. Everything's fine. Really. Mr Curry needed a paper, that's all. Let's go inside, I'm getting chilly.'

'Okay, Mom.'

They walked toward the kitchen door.

'Aren't you going to congratulate me on being sober?'

'Mom, it's true! You're sober! Yes, I congratulate you.' Abby looked at her mother. She took a deep breath and said, 'And I apologize for asking so many questions.'

'Apology accepted. If you'll accept my apology for scaring you.'

'Mom, it just seemed so weird.'

'I know, honey. I know. But everything's fine.' Fiona kept her arm around her daughter as they walked into the house.

No matter how she tried, Abby could not get to sleep that night. Her body needed it, she yearned for it, but sleep would not come. Her mind was possessed by questions about Terence Curry. Why was he in such a rush to leave the house? Why did he need papers from her dad's files? Why was he so concerned that Abby had overheard something the Colonel had said in the hospital? Why was his glove at the scene of the barn fire? What did the Colonel want him to do? She needed more information. She was determined to clear her dad's name and she felt she was getting somewhere, but couldn't see where it was leading.

Also, she wondered what she and her mother would do if they had to move. Where would they go? What about Cody? She thought that if she could just unravel the mystery of who had stolen the money from the Colonel's trust fund, everything would be all right. She must sleep. She must sleep. She tried to think of happy thoughts, like Sam, their walk through the secret meadow, his dancing eyes.

Just as the early morning sun began to tint the eastern skies with shades of soft purples and pinks and yellows, Abby Malone dropped off to sleep.

Early the following Sunday, Abby woke up to loud knocking at the door. She sat up in bed. That knock again. Concluding that the person was not going to give up, Abby put on her shorts and T-shirt and went downstairs to answer the door.

It was Mr Pierson with a funny, lopsided grin on his face. He looked impishly excited.

'Abby, you'll never guess what I've done.'

Abby's eyes widened. 'You're right. I'll never guess. Please come in.'

'No, thanks. When I got home last night, there was a flyer stuck in the door. It was an announcement from the hunt club about a steeplechase.'

Abby nodded as she rubbed the sleep from her eyes. 'Ah huh?'

'It's on Saturday, August twentieth.'

'Ah huh,' she yawned. 'Excuse me.'

'And there's a big cash prize offered by the Master of the Hunt, Colonel Kenneth Bradley.'

'Cash? How much?'

'Five hundred dollars.'

'Really?' Abby tilted her head with interest.

'*And* a silver trophy. You can't keep it, but your name and the name of your horse will be on it forever.'

'Wow,' she said slowly. She wanted to know more.

'*And* you and Moonie will win it, with me as your coach.'

Abby's mouth dropped open. 'But Moonie's been sold and Mr Farrow wouldn't let me near her if she wasn't. What are you talking about?' Now she was fully awake.

'Step outside. I want to show you something.'

Abby walked out into the cheerful sunshine of the summer morning. At first she couldn't see clearly because of the brightness, but then she noticed the unmistakably graceful figure of Moonie, grazing on the lawn.

'Moonie!' The mare lifted her delicate, pretty head from the grass and shook her glossy black mane. She whinnied a hello, then went back to her munching.

'Mr Pierson,' Abby asked with furrowed brow, 'tell me slowly so I can understand. Why is Moonie here?'

'Abby, sweetie, I bought her this morning.'

'You what?'

'I bought her this morning. The man who'd originally wanted her was so mad that he told George to forget the sale.'

'This is a joke, right? Tell me you're kidding.'

Pete's eyes were twinkling brightly, and his smile had taken over his entire face. 'No. It's a fact. Moonlight Sonata is now my horse, and you are my jockey and I've entered you in the steeplechase Saturday, on August the twentieth.' Pete watched Abby carefully. He was very proud of himself.

'August twentieth? That's only two weeks from now.' Abby's heart beat quickly. Was this really happening?

'More than that. Today is Sunday. Counting today, we have twenty training days. But we have a great advantage. You're a great rider and she's a great horse.

Abby's composure crumpled. She started to say 'Thank you,' but no words came out. Instead, she hugged Mr Pierson tightly.

'Now, now, now. We don't have any time to waste. Get your riding gear, there's work to do!'

Abby regained her composure and started to laugh with joy. This was the best thing that could ever happen. 'Righto, major!' She saluted. 'Actually, I don't have any riding clothes that fit. I'll be fine in jeans and sneakers.'

'And a hard hat?' asked Pete.

'My old one is too small.'

'This is serious. We'll have to borrow what we can and do our best. Get into your jeans, then, and I'll use your phone to rustle up a hat.'

Pete went into the kitchen and picked up the phone. There was a man's voice talking.

Pete said, 'Excuse me,' and hung up.

Fiona called down from upstairs, 'Hello, is that Pete?'

'Yes. I'm sorry, Fiona, I was just going to borrow your telephone.'

'Liam's on the line. He wants to speak with you. Can you pick up the phone?'

Pete picked up the phone. 'Liam! Well, well! How are you doing?'

'Better for hearing your voice, Pete! I'm sorry to hear about Laura. Is she recovering well?'

'I spoke with her this morning, and she tells me she's feeling better already. She'll be home before we know it.'

'Good. And how's my wife?'

'Fiona seems good, Liam. You know how this affliction goes, good days and bad. She's vigilant lately. That's the best you can expect at the moment, Liam, that she's vigilant. She won't always be successful.'

'Good advice. And my little girl?'

'She's great. In fact, let me tell you what we're up to.'

Pete unveiled his scheme to win the Colonel's money, and Liam was very enthusiastic. He'd won steeplechases in Ireland, and he was eager for details. He definitely wanted to be kept up to date. As they spoke of training strategies, Abby entered the room.

'Can I say hi?' she whispered.

'Sure! Liam, our young jockey wants to speak with you.' He passed the receiver to Abby.

'Dad! Did Mr Pierson tell you? ... he did? ... of course we'll win! With Moonie and my coach, how could we fail?' She winked and relayed to Pete, 'Dad said, we'll win because of my superior gene pool!' Then Abby grew more serious. 'Dad, Terence Curry was here last night, and he took a paper he said he needed. Is that okay?'

'I'm sure it is. Do you know which paper?'

'Mom doesn't know and I wasn't here. I saw him at the hospital earlier, visiting the Colonel, and I overheard part of a conversation that Mr Curry didn't want me to hear.' She told her father exactly what she heard and awaited his response.

After a long pause he said, 'Abby, stay away from this. I don't want you thinking any more about it. Promise?'

'Dad, I can't ignore what I heard.'

'Abby, you can't really know what you heard. They might have been talking about anything. Promise me you'll leave all that business alone, and win the steeplechase?'

Abby knew she wouldn't get anywhere by arguing, so she said, 'Dad, I promise I'll try to win, okay?'

'And you'll forget about playing detective?'

Abby sighed. 'And I'll forget about playing detective.'

'I love you, Abby. Can you put your mother back on?'

'I love you, too, Dad. And sure, I'll get Mom.' Abby put her hand over the receiver and called her mother. When she heard Fiona's voice, she hung up.

Pete clapped his hands eagerly, rubbed them together and said, 'Let's get started. We'll think about the proper clothes tomorrow.'

They walked outside filled with great anticipation. Today was day one of the training, and there was no time to lose. Pete had driven his truck to Abby's farm holding a lead shank out the driver's-side window, with Moonie walking along beside him. He'd driven really slowly and prayed that no cars would race past and spook the mare. Many times on the way over he'd berated himself for taking such a chance, but he'd wanted to surprise Abby.

He'd brought his old leather saddle and bridle out of his basement, and cleaned and oiled them before loading them in his truck. Abby could see that they needed a lot more work, but was touched that he'd gone to all that trouble.

Now they tacked up the mare, and with the saddle firmly in place, Pete gave Abby a leg up. She smiled happily.

'Mr Pierson?'

'Yes, Abby?'

'I don't know how to thank you. I mean, really.'

Pete was pleased. He patted her knee affectionately as she sat in the saddle, then, pulling a pad of paper and a pencil out of his pocket, he said, 'Now, to work. I'm writing a list of what we need. We need a saddle pad so the saddle feels comfortable to Moonie, and a hard hat that fits you perfectly. We need the hat before we start jumping. Black boots, breeches, black gloves, and what do you say about a crash vest?'

'They're expensive.'

'Worth every penny if you fall. We'll get one. Now, step one: we're going to trot up to the farrier's barn. I know he's there today, and if we show up, he'll squeeze us in. John's an old friend. Moonie needs her feet trimmed and good shoes on if we're going anywhere with this plan.'

'How far is it?'

'Two concessions. Not far. I'll travel behind you in the truck.'

They trotted along, Abby brimming with hope and confidence. Pete was fully in charge, and Abby could see that he was having as much fun as she was. She looked over her shoulder to smile at him, and sure enough, Cody's happy face popped up from the back of Pete's truck.

They arrived at the farrier's barn. John, a cheerful, hearty redhead, welcomed them into his shop. The fire burned hotly in the small furnace where he formed iron into horse shoes, and the tools of his trade hung on the walls. Pete and John immediately started discussing training methods and regaling each other with stories of horses they'd known. John had trained many horses and offered imaginative and helpful tips as he worked. Abby, fascinated, listened carefully while she watched the shoeing process.

First John cut away the extra growth of horn from Moonie's hooves with large clippers and filed them until they were perfectly shaped. Abby was pleased at their neat, dainty look. Next, John found the right size of shoes and heated them. He pressed the hot iron to her feet, one at a time, causing large puffs of smoke to fill the barn. Moonie took this calmly, to Abby's surprise. Once each shoe was moulded to exactly the right fit, John cooled it down and nailed it onto her foot with eight shoeing nails. Finally, he painted her feet with a special solution to set the nails.

Abby was humming with anticipation. This was fun already.

Pete thanked John and paid him as Abby walked Moonie out on her new shoes. John gave her a lift into the saddle with his strong arms, and wished her good luck. 'I'll be there to cheer you on,' he called as they left the yard.

Shoes on tight, they trotted straight to Merry Fields.

They laid down fence posts in a large circle in the field to practise changing directions over logs. Next to that, they made a line of old oil drums standing on end. The idea was to work on agility and balance by weaving in and out. Pete started Abby on his program and timed each try. After a half-hour's work, Pete called her over.

'Well done, Abby! We're well on our way. We walked and trotted on the roads, and worked on these obstacles. That's enough for today. Let's get our race horse cooled and washed down before we have our lunch.'

Once Moonie was looked after, they ate their lunch, talking of nothing but the steeplechase. Pete rolled out the map of the race that he'd picked up with the entry forms. Until she saw the map, Abby'd had no idea what was involved.

'Sixteen jumps over a three-kilometre course? Can Moonie stand it?'

'No question, Abby! She's young and fit, and she's built for this job. The key is to pace her. She's a quarter horse, and they're good at high speed for just over a quarter mile. And they like to tear away fast from the gate. So if you let her have her way, she'll use up all her gas before you're even halfway through. Keep her steady and she won't let you down.'

Pete keenly unfolded his strategy, jump by jump over the map, advising her where she could conserve energy and where she should make up speed. The fact that all the horses took off together, and raced each other as a pack, increased the difficulty and raised the level of danger. Pete told her always to take the safe way, never risk her neck for the sake of the prize.

After lunch, Abby went to work on the tack at the Piersons' mud room sink. She soaped it all thoroughly, wiped the suds off, and then proceeded to rub the oil liberally into the leather. She polished the stirrups with silver polish until they shone, and she took care that the bit was perfectly clean.

All the time she worked she kept an eye on Moonie from the mud room window. She was a small mare, fifteen hands, two inches tall, just right for Abby and beautifully put together. Her hind end was taller than her front, giving her a coltish appearance. Her legs were long and straight and correct. Her chest was roomy and strong. Lots of power and stamina there, thought Abby. And what a pretty face! Sweet, round, dark brown eyes on a slightly dished nose. Soft little muzzle and a strong jaw. Her fine dark brown coat was shiny and soft, covering a well-muscled frame. I love her to death, she sighed, as she wished for the hundredth time that day that they'd win the race.

Pete drove her home on his way to Orangeville to visit Laura in the hospital. Laura was getting stronger day by day. Happily, her body was healing faster than the doctors had predicted.

Bright and early the next day, Pete picked up Abby to go shopping.

'Monday. Day two,' he announced as Abby climbed into the front seat. He eyed her critically. 'You didn't get much sleep. Too excited?'

Abby nodded. 'I keep thinking the worst will happen. What if I screw up?'

Pete laughed. 'Abby, you won't screw up. And it's only for fun.'

'But you and Dad are so serious about me winning. I've never done this before!'

'We're just reliving our glory days through you, Abby. One of the best moments of my life was winning that race on Carl the Wonder Horse. And your father was without peer in his racing days. Forgive us our vicarious excitement, Abby. Don't pay any attention to two old men.'

'You're two old men I care about. I want you to be proud of me.'

'We're already proud of you, Abby. There's nothing you can do to change that. Your father and I are just getting our competitive natures fired up.'

'And I guess it wouldn't be any fun if we didn't try our hardest.'

'That's the spirit! All things that are, are with more spirit chased than enjoyed. *Merchant of Venice*, I believe. We'll try our best. We'll have a wonderful time making the effort. If we fall on our face and come in last, we're already winners!'

Abby felt much better knowing that she wouldn't be letting them down if she lost. Pete's words had erased her fears.

Minutes later they pulled into the car park of the tack shop on Highway 10 in Caledon. Abby was expertly outfitted in new breeches, gloves, boots, helmet, shirt and padded crash vest. She looked at herself in the mirror and couldn't quite believe what she saw. She looked like a pro, she thought, as she assumed different poses. Stand back, world!

Pete checked out the gifts and chose a tiny porcelain ring-box with a tiny perfect horse standing on top. He asked that it be gift-wrapped. He would give it to Laura that evening when he visited her in the hospital. Abby's heart warmed at the thought of these two people in love for so many years.

The bill must be huge, Abby guessed. 'When we win the money, Mr Pierson, it all goes to you!'

'We'll cross that bridge when we come to it,' he said. 'I got you into this, Abby Malone. You didn't ask for a thing.'

'But this is the best thing that's ever happened to me,' she answered.

Just as they were leaving the shop laden with bags, Lucy came in.

'Lucy!' Abby gasped. She hadn't seen her since she'd been fired.

'Well, hello, Abby. You've been shopping, I see.'

Pete felt the tension between the girls and interjected, 'Lucy, nice to see you again. I've seen your new horse across the road. He looks like a good one.'

'Yes, he is. His name is Diablo. My grandfather bought him for me after he decided that Moonie didn't have enough class.' She tossed her head, and shot a hard look at Abby. 'He hired a professional to give me *proper* training. And before I get to ride him, he's going to win the steeplechase.'

Behind Lucy in the parking lot was a long black limo. Abby stared. Getting out of his car, with great difficulty and obvious pain because of his knee injury, was Colonel Bradley. He stood unsteadily, leaning on a cane.

'There's the Colonel!' said Abby to Pete.

'Yes,' answered Lucy. 'That's my grandfather. We're shopping for my birthday present.'

'I didn't know he was your grandfather,' said Abby, amazed.

'You never asked. And I only recently got to know him, anyway. He's a very busy man.' With an air of importance, Lucy sauntered past them, followed by a hobbling Colonel Bradley. He didn't even look at Abby, to her relief, and before he was through the door he was yelling orders. 'Show us something nice! How does a person get service around here?'

That afternoon, after unpacking their purchases and eating lunch, they went back to work. This was a jumping day. Abby trotted Moonie to the river lands, followed by Pete bumping along in the truck. They took stock of their practice opportunities.

There was a water hazard marked on the map, but it wasn't clear whether they should jump over or in or out or through the water. To be prepared for everything, they practised them all. They galloped through water, jumped in and out of water, jumped over water, all at different places on the river. This was important work, and great fun for Abby and Moonie.

Now Pete prepared to time her running through a wooded trail with five small jumps. She found her way to the far side of the trail, using a different path so Moonie couldn't see the jumps.

Abby wanted Moonie to get used to jumping obstacles she'd never seen before, because that's how it would be on the day of the race. Jumping unknown barriers onto unknown footing required great trust between horse and rider, and Abby took a deep breath before giving Pete the signal that she was ready.

'Okay, get ready, get set, GO!' hollered Pete.

Moonie shot off so fast that Abby was momentarily unbalanced. 'Easy, speedy!' she murmured, getting herself organized for the first hurdle. It was a soggy old tree trunk covered with moss and slime, with mud on both sides. Moonie leapt it with lots of room to spare on the take-off and the landing, and managed to avoid the slippery mud.

On they galloped, following the path to the left and over a wooden coop with a branch hanging dangerously low. Abby ducked to avoid it as they leapt. She felt Moonie's excitement and was thrilled that the mare loved this cross-country ride as much as she did. The third jump was a rubbly pile of rocks, and Moonie soared over it in perfect stride. The path turned now to the right and appeared to end, straight ahead.

Abby couldn't see where the path went. Moonie sensed her apprehension, and slowed. There was a dead end, and a ninety-degree turn to the left. Moonie sat back on her haunches and pivoted left, never missing a beat. The remaining two jumps were within three strides of each other, and no problem for Moonie at all.

As Moonie and Abby streaked past Pete, he pulled his arm straight down and clicked his timer. 'Fabulous, Abby! Great time!' he shouted.

Abby worked at slowing Moonie, see-sawing on her mouth and sitting back. The mare was all wound up and wanted to run and jump some more. Abby turned her in circles until she gave in and began to behave herself.

'Yippee!' Abby called. 'That was fun!' She caught her breath and smiled at Pete. 'Can we do it again? I bet we could beat that time!'

'Not on your life, young lady. We're trying to strengthen her muscles, not bow her tendons! By showing her what to expect, we get her mind ready. By conditioning her carefully, we get her body ready. In the short time we have that's all we can do. The worst possible thing is to push her too fast and break her down.'

'Aye aye, captain!' Abby saluted. Even though she joked, she got the message.

They cooled the mare down on the one-kilometre walk back to Merry Fields, then washed her thoroughly, picked out her feet and fed her Pete's special blend of energy-packed food. He told Abby to keep his recipe secret or else everyone would use it, reducing Abby's chances of winning. Abby was sworn to secrecy.

Once again, she went to work on the leather. It was beginning to feel soft and supple, and it looked dark and rich. She loved this training routine. She was feeling better than she'd ever felt. Mr Pierson, Moonie and Abby shared a common goal and an easy companionship. Best of all, her father was as excited as they were. They gave him a report of their activities every day and he always had good advice to share with them. He seemed altogether happier now that he was involved in an exciting project.

Soaping and oiling the saddle and bridle, Abby sorted her thoughts. She could see that for the next couple of weeks she wouldn't have much time to think about anything but her training. And Sam.

She smiled. That morning she'd found a note from him in the tree. He was helping his uncle on his farm. It was haying time, and Sam said his muscles would be bulging when he got back.

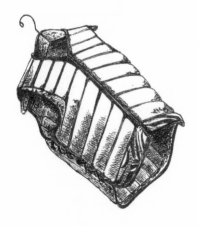

Chapter Twelve

New Information

A friend should bear his friend's infirmities.
– Shakespeare, *Julius Caesar*, IV, iii

ABBY WEARILY GOT on her bike and headed for home after another day of training. Her muscles ached. She waved goodbye to Pete and yelled a reminder to say hello to Mrs Pierson in the hospital. If all went well, she'd be coming home in a couple of days. Somehow, everything seemed different with Mrs Pierson gone. Abby missed her cheerful face, lively personality and generous spirit. Abby knew how lonely Pete was, too, even though he tried his best to remain positive. In fact, the whole neighbourhood seemed to be waiting for her return. Everybody asked about her, hoping for good news, and relating stories of similar accidents that had ended in death or permanent disabilities. Abby shuddered at the thought as she wondered why people needed to tell these things.

Cody loped alongside her bike as they travelled the dusty road. 'We sure need a good rain before the race,' thought Abby.

A white van passed them, raising so much dust that Abby started coughing. 'Slow down!' she yelled at the tail end of the van.

The brake lights went on. It stopped. Abby watched, wondering if they could possibly have heard her. Then it backed up.

Pam, Annie and Pam's younger brother Hugh stared at her through the window. They must have just got home from camp, reflected Abby. Pam's mother was driving. The windows were all up to keep the dust out and the cool air in.

Abby stepped off her bike, unsure of what to expect. The van's front right window came down automatically, and Pam's mother said, in a calm voice, 'We've never met. I'm Mrs Masters,

Pamela's mother. I know you're Abby Malone because my children just pointed you out. This is as good a time as ever to apologize for stealing Pam and Annie's clothes.'

Abby was nonplussed. 'I didn't steal ...' she began, but Pam's window came down and Pam interrupted her.

'You're a liar anyway, no matter what you say.' Pam's chin was up and she looked defensive. 'We were just visiting Lucy and she told us how you lied to her grandfather and even tried to steal her horse.'

'I did not! You're the one who lies, Pam!' Abby was mad. Her face was red and her ears were filled with the sound of blood coursing through her veins. 'You gave me those clothes and you know it! And you, too, Annie! Admit it!'

Mrs Masters turned the engine off and stepped out of her car. 'Pam, Annie, get out of the car. We're going to get to the bottom of this.'

Pam and Annie got out. Mrs Masters walked around the car.

'Pamela, speak up. Tell me what happened.'

'Mom, I already told you!'

'Tell me again.'

Pam rolled her eyes and made a face. 'All right! Abby stole my clothes. When I asked for them she said she didn't have them. Then you went and found them in her room. There!'

'How did I steal them, Pam?' asked Abby. 'When did I have a chance to steal your clothes?'

'All year, you stole one thing at a time ... at gym! And at recess! If I left something at my desk, it was gone.' She crossed her arms over her chest and appeared satisfied.

'All winter?' Abby asked.

'Yes! Fall, winter, spring. All year.'

'So I stole your clothes all fall, winter, and spring, but the clothes your mother got from my room were all summer clothes. Clothes you told me you didn't want because they were so "last year" and you were getting new ones.'

'Pamela,' Mrs Masters said sharply. 'Is this true?'

'No! I swear!'

'But Pamela,' said her mother, 'we argued about this. You

wanted new clothes and I said you had plenty. Then suddenly you didn't have enough of anything, and we had to go shopping. Did you make this whole thing up, including blaming Abby, to get new clothes?'

'No! How can you think that?' Pam was getting ready to cry if necessary.

Annie slowly made patterns in the dirt with the toe of her sneaker, eyes down.

'Annie, what do you have to say?' Mrs Masters asked.

'We didn't mean any harm. We didn't think it would be a big deal, you know. And Abby did need clothes.' She shrugged her shoulders and squirmed, eyes never leaving the ground.

Mrs Masters took a deep breath. 'Pamela Masters, Annie Payne, I want you to apologize to Abby.'

'But Mom! ...'

'But Mrs Masters ...'

'No buts! Apologize this minute or you're walking home.'

'I'm sorry, Abby,' said Annie. 'We just wanted new clothes. We never meant to get you involved like this.'

'It would've worked,' continued Pam, 'except my mother kept at me about where this shirt was and where that pair of shorts were, and finally I told her that you stole them. We never meant to hurt you.'

'And I backed her up. We didn't know what else to do. We're sorry.' Annie looked truly wretched.

'I'm sorry, Abby,' said Pam with a sugary tone. She shot a glance at her mother to see if she was appeased. Abby wasn't fooled. Pam's eyes shifted back to Abby and she smirked. 'But I still wonder why Lucy thinks you stole her horse.'

'Pamela!' hissed Mrs Masters angrily. 'That has nothing to do with you! Get in the car.' She clapped her hands twice and they moved fast.

'Mrs Masters,' Abby said quickly, before they left. 'I want you to know I didn't steal the horse. She came to me in the middle of the night. I don't know why.' She looked intently at Mrs Masters. 'And could you please tell my mother that I didn't steal the clothes? It would mean a lot to her. And to me.'

'Yes, Abby, I certainly will.' She smiled at Abby. 'By the way, George Farrow said you'll be riding Moonlight Sonata in the steeplechase.'

'Yes,' said Abby, surprised. 'I didn't know he knew.'

'No secrets around here, Abby. George tells me that you're a contender. He thinks you're good. Anyway, my money's on you,' she winked. 'That horse the Colonel bought for Lucy is crazy.'

'Crazy? Lucy doesn't need a crazy horse. She had a hard enough time with Moonie.'

'Well, I'd never put her on him. He's just off the track.'

Abby considered this. If he'd been a racehorse, he'd be fast. 'Does he jump?'

'Oh, yes. Like a deer. When he wants to.' She laughed. 'Today he didn't want to. They didn't name him "Diablo" for nothing.' She waved a friendly goodbye, and added, 'I'm sorry about the misunderstanding about the clothes, Abby. My daughter has a lot more explaining to do. I'll tell your Mom the whole story. And see you at the race. We'll be there to watch!'

Abby waved goodbye as the van pulled onto the road. Pam's face popped out her window, tongue sticking out.

Abby got back on her bike and pedalled off, thinking over this remarkable turn of events. She felt much better that the truth was out about the stolen clothes, and she'd tell Pete first thing in the morning what Mrs Masters had said about the Colonel's new racehorse.

Suddenly, she stopped the bike. Lucy is telling everybody that I'm a thief, she thought. Well, that can't go on.

Abby turned the bike around and retraced her route, pedalling quickly to the Farrows' farm. She was angry. Lucy was the liar. Lucy would hear exactly what Abby thought.

She propped her bike against the Farrows' house and walked up to the door. Before she could knock, Lucy's voice rang out behind her.

'Looking for Grandpa Farrow, horse thief?'

She spun around. 'No, liar, I'm looking for you. What right have you to spread stories about me?'

'Those aren't stories, they're facts. Facts are facts, Abby.'

[159]

Abby walked slowly over to Lucy, trying to control the rage she felt pounding in her veins. Lucy sensed it, and shrank back, step for step.

'I'm not going to hurt you, Lucy, so don't cringe. I just want you to stop telling lies about me.'

'What lies? Moonlight Sonata turned up at your house, didn't she? And you were riding her? Is that a lie?'

'I didn't steal her and you know it. Something scared her enough to run to my farm, Lucy, the way she ran to me for help the time before. What scared her, Lucy?'

Suddenly there was a tremendous crash in the barn, followed by a series of sharp thuds and bellowing.

'What's that?' asked Abby, startled.

'Your competition, horse thief. You stole the wrong horse, you know. Diablo's going to win the steeplechase.'

'Maybe he will and maybe he won't. Just stop telling lies, Lucy, or you'll never have any friends.'

'Pam and Annie are my friends,' Lucy gloated.

'Only until you have no more gossip to feed them.'

'That's not true!'

'No? Do you even *know* what's true and what's a lie? I feel sorry for you, Lucy. You're pathetic, and you know it.'

'I'm pathetic? You're pathetic! And a horse thief! I hate you!'

'Oh, I'm so-o hurt!'

Abby hopped on her bike and rode home, feeling worn out and depressed. She'd accomplished nothing by confronting Lucy but to hurt her feelings.

Cody appeared momentarily, and then disappeared again into the bushes. Abby smiled ruefully and thought, at least I'll always have a friend.

When they got home, Abby fed Cody and left food out for the raccoons. She was tired, but pleased at the training progress, and looking forward to seeing Sam when he got back next week. As she opened the kitchen door, the phone was ringing.

'Hello?'

'It's Lucy. We need to talk.'

Abby was surprised. 'About what?'

'About how Moonlight got out. And something else. Important. I can't talk now. I'll meet you in the Piersons' barn tonight at
ten o'clock.'

'Ten o'clock? Are you crazy?'

'It's up to you. Be there or not.'

Abby listened to the dial tone for a few seconds,then hung up.

It was eight minutes past ten, and Abby was wondering if she'd
made a mistake in coming to the Piersons' barn. Lucy probably
wouldn't show up. If this was Lucy's idea of a joke, Abby didn't
think it was funny.

'Abby?' a nervous, high-pitched voice called out in the dark.

'Hello?' Abby answered, startled by the sudden sound.

Lucy's face became visible. 'Geez. It's scary in here,' she whispered. 'Why don't you turn on the lights?'

'And let the Piersons' know we're playing cloak and dagger in
their barn?'

'No! You're right, keep them off. My grandparents think I'm
sleeping.' Lucy said, 'I'm okay now, anyway. It's kind of spooky in
the dark, that's all.' She smiled tentatively. 'I bet you'd like to
know why I called you.'

Abby nodded, and waited for Lucy to speak.

'Abby, I'd like to be your friend.'

'What?' asked Abby, amazed. This was the last thing she'd
expected to hear.

'I've given it a lot of thought since you came over today. You're
right. I'm a liar, and I have no real friends. People only want to be
with me if I've got gossip. Sometimes I make it up. And I've made
trouble for you.'

'Lucy, what's going on?'

Lucy spoke slowly and carefully. 'Abby, I want to prove I can be
a friend, and I want you to be my friend. So. I know two things.'
She shuffled her feet, and paused. 'Things that you should know.'

'What things, Lucy?' Abby felt cautious, but very curious.

'The first is about the night that Moonie ran over to your house
and got caught in the wire. I know why.'

'Why?' Abby was all ears.

'That was the night that Grandfather Bradley brought the black horse to the farm.'

'Diablo.'

'Yes, Diablo. Moonie hates Diablo and Diablo hates her. They kicked their stalls and whinnied and went crazy. Grandfather Bradley said they should go out together and "work it out". Grandpa Farrow said they'd kill each other. Grandfather Bradley laughed and said that Diablo could kill Moonie and not suffer even a scratch. Anyway, we all had dinner together, leaving the horses in the barn where nobody could kill anybody. I went to bed before Grandfather Bradley left.

'He let them out. I saw from my window, but I didn't do anything. I was too scared. In the morning, Diablo was in the field and Moonie was gone without a trace. And Grandpa Farrow was mad, and asked me if I'd let them out of the barn. I told him no, but I didn't want him to be mad at Grandfather Bradley because he'd just bought me this gorgeous big horse, so I told him that probably you'd stolen Moonie so she wouldn't be sold, and then let Diablo out, but he didn't believe me.'

'And then he found Moonie at my house, so he thought you guessed right.'

'Yes. But I saw Grandfather Bradley do it with my own eyes, and anyway, you'd never do that.'

'No, I wouldn't. What made you go to your window that night?'

'The whinnies and the screams. Moonie was scared and Diablo was mad. Then suddenly there was no noise. I hid in my bed and hoped they'd worked it out, like Grandfather Bradley said they would, but I worried all night. I thought we might find Moonie dead or something.'

'Why would your grandfather, the Colonel, do a thing like that?'

'Just to watch them fight. He likes to watch fights, especially when his team wins.'

'Interesting. Lucy, for whatever reason you're telling me, I'm glad to know. So Moonie jumped the fence and came to my house instead of staying around to get the life kicked out of her. Smart choice.'

'Although it deprived my grandfather of a good show.'

'Poor guy,' Abby said sarcastically.

'Yeah. Poor guy,' Lucy repeated, and laughed.

'That was the first thing you were going to tell me, Lucy. What's the second?'

Lucy stared at Abby directly, eye to eye. She wet her lips. 'You can't tell anybody in the world, not even your mother or your best friend. It's a secret that I'll be punished for if anybody knows I told, because I'm not supposed to know.'

'Lucy, what is it?' Abby was nervous now, too. This sounded serious.

'Swear on your life you won't tell?'

'I swear.'

'Last night I stayed at Grandfather Bradley's house in Brampton. Well, mansion. Actually it's more like a castle. And it's not really in Brampton, it's north of Brampton and it feels like it's in the country because there are fields and forests all around it. The land has been in the family forever, I guess, and they kept some of it when the subdivision was built around it.'

'Lucy, can you get to the point?'

'In a minute. I want you to know that I feel disloyal telling you. But my Grandfather Bradley told me he was buying me a horse, but really he bought himself a horse to win the steeplechase. He told the jockey that I was a scared little ninny and laughed. He doesn't know I heard. He also said that there was no use in my taking riding lessons because every time I get near a horse, I break a bone.' Tears welled up in her eyes. 'He said worse things, too, but I'm not going to tell you.'

'I'm sorry, Lucy. And that's not true, anyway. After the steeplechase is over, I'll teach you to ride Moonie, and you'll do great. As long as you don't pull any tricks on me.' She smiled at the miserable girl.

Lucy smiled back. 'You see? That's why I want to be friends. You're always nice to me, even after all the things I've done. Grandfather Bradley isn't nice. At all. Anyway, now that you

[163]

know why I'm telling you, here goes. He had a meeting after dinner with a tall, thin man who was your father's law partner. He drives a silver car. I forget his name.'

'Mr Curry? Terence?'

'Yes! My grandfather calls him Terry. Anyway, it was late and I came down to the kitchen to get some milk, and I passed the study, and they were talking. They'd been there for hours, so I wondered what was so important. And the doors were closed and it was very hush-hush. So I put my ear to the crack between the doors.'

'You did?' asked Abby. 'What did you hear?' She was mesmerized.

'Mr Curry was mumbling something. He'd had enough of it, enough harm was done, or something like that. My grandfather, and he talked louder so I could hear him better, said that the wheels were in motion, and he should've thought of that a long time ago. Then, and this is where you come in, Mr Curry said something mumbly about "Malone going to jail". My grandfather said that Mr Curry knew all along that your father would go to jail and that he deserved it, he was too naive, and if he was worth his salt he would've seen the scam.'

'Just a minute, Lucy,' interrupted Abby, dumbfounded. 'He used the word, *scam?*'

'Yes. Mr Curry was mad, now, and he flatly refused to do whatever. Then my grandfather told him he'd be joining your father in jail if he didn't do it, whatever it was. When Mr Curry still said no, my grandfather told him it was too late because, and this is the important part, he had papers that would prove his part in the whole thing.'

'Papers. Do you know what papers they were talking about? And did he explain what "the whole thing" was?'

'I don't know anything more. In fact I can't figure anything out, only that it concerns your father and I thought you'd want to know. I wasn't going to tell you. Until today when I realized you were right about me being a liar and having no friends. But there's more. After he said he had these important papers, I waited until Mr Curry left and watched my grandfather hide a brown folder in the bookshelves.'

'How could you see? You were hiding outside the door.'

'I went outside the house and looked through the windows.'

'Really? You took quite a chance. Why, Lucy?'

'I don't know. Maybe I wanted to get them later and read them. Maybe because it sounded so secret and detectivish that I was curious. Anyway, now you know.'

Abby stood silent for a long moment, thinking.

'Abby, what are you thinking? Is anything wrong?'

'No, Lucy.'

Then Abby had an inspiration and grabbed Lucy by the arms.

'Abby! Don't hurt me!'

'I won't hurt you, silly. Just take me to your grandfather's house and show me where he put the papers.'

'No! I can't do that. What if he catches me?'

'He won't catch you. We'll be very careful.'

'But there's always a chance, and he'd kill us! He has a shotgun and he'll use it!'

'Really?' Abby asked, momentarily flummoxed.

'Really.' Lucy was serious.

'Well, then, we'll have to think of something clever. I know, why don't you draw me a map of the study, marking the place they're hidden. Then when we go to his house, you don't have to be in the room with me. You can keep him busy and you won't get caught. Okay?'

'How are we going to get there?'

'You can invite me over.'

'But I'm supposed to stay with the Farrows. How can I invite you when I'm not even invited?'

'Good point. I know. Just give me his address and draw me the map of his study. I'll destroy them when I'm finished. This way, you're totally safe and you won't be involved in any way. I promised not to tell, remember?'

Lucy thought for a moment, then nodded. 'I'll do it,' she said. 'If you'll be really, really careful. And you promise to be my friend.'

Abby found Lucy some paper and a pen in the tackroom, and Lucy drew two maps; one of the Colonel's neighbourhood, and one of the study. Abby tucked them securely into her pocket. Lucy made Abby promise for the third time not to tell a living soul. They left the barn together, friends for the first time all summer.

On the bicycle ride home in the dark, Abby tried to put the missing pieces together. It was very confusing, but she vowed that she would leave no stone unturned. She slowly and surely formulated a plan. All she had to do was figure out how to get to the Colonel's mansion.

Chapter Thirteen
The Colonel's Mansion

That what you cannot as you would achieve,
You must perforce accomplish as you may.
– Shakespeare, *Titus Andronicus*, II, i

THERE WAS NO moon. The night sky was totally black and rain
was spitting gently. Abby had her flashlight and her map, and she
was wearing black from head to toe. She'd stuffed her fair hair
under a Chicago Black Hawks tuque turned inside out, and her
mother's black dress gloves encased her hands. She was standing
under the study window of the largest mansion she could imagine,
probably in exactly the same spot that Lucy had stood when she'd
witnessed the Colonel hiding the papers. It did look like a castle,
she thought, with the turrets and stone walls.

Abby wondered if breaking in and stealing papers was such a
good idea. She felt very vulnerable and isolated, back here so far
off the road. She couldn't see any neighbouring houses, and
wondered if anyone would hear her if she cried for help. She
guessed not. And what if the Colonel had moved the papers by
now? Or what if they turned out to be useless? He could have been
hiding the deed to his house, for all Lucy knew.

Coming here had been a spur-of-the-moment decision. A week
had passed since Lucy had talked to Abby in the barn. She'd been
waiting for the right opportunity, and was increasingly frustrated
as day after day passed and the papers remained in the Colonel's
bookshelf. She worked Moonie conscientiously and looked for her
chance.

Her chance came in the form of Terence Curry.

That night, he had dropped by to give them some lawn furniture he didn't want any more. Fiona had insisted he stay for

dinner. Abby said good night immediately after dinner and went up to bed. This was what she'd been waiting for. From Lucy's description she knew that he lived within a kilometre or two of the Colonel.

When Fiona had come up to tuck her in, Abby told her how exhausted she was after another long, hard day of training Moonie. After her mother had gone downstairs, Abby had quickly crept around, finding black clothing and a flashlight. Then she slipped outside and hid herself on the floor of the back seat of Terence Curry's big car. So far, so good.

As Abby lay there, she thought how lucky she was to get a ride to the Colonel's. She'd worry about how to get home later. She could call the police. They'd get her home.

What was that noise? Scratching? Some animal was scratching at the car door. It could only be Cody. Abby scolded herself for being so jumpy as she opened the door to tell him to go away. It was open only a couple of inches, but Cody thrust in his snout and pushed his way into the car, firmly installing himself beside her on the floor of the back seat.

'No, Cody!' she whispered fiercely. 'Go home!'

The coyote disregarded her. He curled himself into a tight ball, becoming as small as he could possibly be, and didn't even look at her.

'Cody...' She could see that he wasn't budging, and time was running out before Curry would appear. She pulled the door shut. 'You win. But you better not get in my way.'

Seconds later, the front door of the car opened. Abby jumped in fright. She remembered herself in time and didn't make a sound. Her nerves were much too tense. She tried to relax. Cody didn't move.

Terence Curry placed his jacket on the passenger seat, then went behind the car and opened the trunk. Abby surmised from the clattering that he was unloading the lawn furniture. She heard him carrying it away and leaning it against the house beside the back door. Then he returned to the car, got in, snapped on his seat belt, and started the engine. He hummed to himself.

They drove for fifteen minutes or so. They were moving fast.

Wind rushed through the open window at Abby's right. Cody's nose never stopped twitching as it recognized and filed the scents of the night. His ears stood alert, and flicked with interest at things that Abby couldn't hear. His eyes registered extreme concentration as they passed intersections and flashing lights. Abby wondered if Cody was charting their course. Nothing would surprise her.

The car began to slow. They turned a corner. Another corner. They came to a stop.

Terence Curry got out of the car and locked it. He stretched and yawned, then went up to the door of his house and put his key in the lock. He was safely inside the house in an instant.

Abby forced herself to count out seven minutes. Then she carefully opened the back door of the car, and crawled out on her hands and knees into the hedge beside the driveway, followed silently by Cody. She pushed the car door closed as quietly as possible. She noticed that it was starting to drizzle with warm rain.

Her heart was pounding so hard she could hear each beat thud in her ears. She feared that the volume of it would wake the neighbours. She took deep breaths until she felt more calm, then opened the map that had been in her pocket. She took a look.

The streets were marked at the corner, and Lucy's map included one of the cross streets. Following Lucy's instructions, Abby found the Colonel's gated and grand house in under ten minutes. Her good luck was holding.

She slipped through an open gate and found herself staring at a towering castle sitting ominously on a hill, at the end of a long lane. She shivered with apprehension, and had to force herself to continue her plan. Thoughts of her incarcerated father gave her the courage to sneak furtively from tree to tree until she was hidden from view around the back of the house. Cody had disappeared.

Now she stood outside the dark mansion in the drizzling rain, frozen with indecision. She heard a scratching noise. She fell flat to the ground. The noise again. Coming from the library window. What was it? Then she heard a distinct meow. She looked up.

A cat? Yes! Pushing the window open to get out! 'Good kitty,' Abby whispered. She got to her feet and examined the window. It was a casement window, the kind that opens out on a crank, and it hadn't been closed properly. The cat, a fat blue-point Himalayan with a snubbed face, watched her intently. Abby was just able to slide her arm into the opening as far as the crank. She turned it once, then twice, and the cat shot out of the house.

Who's the smart one, kitty? she thought. You're getting out while I'm trying to get in. Abby continued to crank the window until it was open wide enough that she could squeeze through. The night was very warm and still, so Abby had no fear that anyone in the house would be alerted by a breeze.

She was in. Now what? She moved forward tentatively. The very first step she took, she tripped over a footstool. She fell with a thud, and lay there motionless, in excruciating anxiety, until she was sure that nobody was coming to check.

While she was on the floor her eyes got accustomed to the dark. Things took on definition, and she had a much better idea of the lay of the room. She looked around and made out the bookshelves and the desk and the large double doors. She noticed the heavy velvet drapes that were pulled back from the large casement windows that she'd crept through. Lucy had marked things well on her map of the library.

Abby had previously memorized the location of the papers. Two cases right from the wall if you're facing away from the desk. Three cases left from the doors, from the same position. Five shelves up. The papers should be right there, behind the never-opened *Complete Works of William Shakespeare*. If I had that book, thought Abby, I'd know it frontwards and backwards, like Mr Pierson.

She got to her feet and quietly moved toward the spot. She reached up and pulled out the book of plays. There, exactly where Lucy had marked, was a brown folder. Abby could see an edge of white. Yes. Papers. She took the folder in her shaking hand, and controlling her nerves as best she could, began to replace the heavy book. All she had to do now was leave the way she'd come, and get back home.

Just then, Abby's alert ears picked up the sound of a long squeak followed by a door closing upstairs. Next she heard an uneven pat, pat, pat, pat, on the stairs. One step heavy, the next step light. Someone large was limping downstairs in slippers.

Abby pushed the leather-bound tome back into place. She slipped silently behind the gathered velvet drapes, folder clutched tightly under her arm. She waited. So intently did she listen that the air around her seemed to take on a high-pitched sonic drone.

The great doors to the study opened. Abby worried that she'd pee her pants. A light went on. Someone was moving around the study, and Abby knew it could only be the Colonel.

Lucy had said that the Colonel would kill them if they were caught. Now Abby hoped it was only a figure of speech. She was terrified. Nobody knew where she was. Nobody could help her now. The best she could hope for was that the Colonel would do what he came to do and then leave without detecting her. As soon as he left, Abby would climb out that window faster than the cat.

She could hear him now over by the casement window. Drats, thought Abby. I left it open. Will he think the servants did it? She hoped so. He closed it tight and locked it.

Now what if he closed the drapes? If he did, the fabric would become unbunched and she would be a visible lump behind the curtain and he would surely find her. She flattened herself against the wall as much as she could.

Abby suddenly tensed. She broke into a cold sweat. If he discovered her, it would be horrible. But if he discovered her with his folder, it would be much worse. Carefully and silently, Abby slid the folder down her leg and onto the floor. With her left foot she slowly pushed it against the wall under the furthest part of the window, where she hoped the folder would remain hidden even if the drapes were fully drawn.

But he walked away.

He unlocked a cabinet and Abby could hear him take down a glass and pour liquid onto ice cubes, the too-familiar sounds of someone pouring a drink. Good, now maybe he'll leave.

No such luck. He sat down on something that squeaked like leather. Then there was a creak, clunk, indicating that he'd opened up a recliner. She'd noticed a leather recliner beside the cabinet directly opposite from where she was hiding.

By now the thick smell of dusty curtain was itching her throat. She swallowed to keep her throat lubricated so she wouldn't cough.

Mentally she pictured his location. If he was where she estimated he was, he'd be facing the drape behind which she was masked. She couldn't see him, but could he see any part of her? She looked at her feet. Mercifully, the drape went right to the floor. She felt safe for the moment.

How long would he sit there? Was he reading? She didn't hear any pages turn or paper rustle. So what was he doing? Contemplating his sins?

Abby's nose quivered. She felt a sneeze coming on. No, no, no, she pleaded. It passed. That was close.

Since she didn't have a watch, she had no idea how much time had passed since she'd hidden behind the drape. It seemed like twenty days and twenty nights. She counted the time by how many drinks the Colonel poured. She estimated a drink every thirty minutes, and he'd had three. Her legs were aching and her head was dizzy and she felt like sneezing and it was hot and stuffy back there. Why wouldn't one of his servants have shaken out these foul drapes? She hoped she wouldn't faint.

Then it happened. She shifted her weight to keep her balance, and the old floor complained. Loudly. She gasped involuntarily then slapped her hand over her mouth. It had been shockingly loud, to Abby's ears. The Colonel was sure to have heard it.

She thought the game was up. She slowly exhaled and waited for the outraged, portly, red-eyed old man to seize her and shake her until her teeth rattled.

Inhale deeply, exhale slowly, inhale, exhale. Slowly, deeply.

Nothing happened. The Colonel didn't make a move.

Abby's hope returned. Was he asleep? Her mother fell asleep after she drank. She must look. Abby edged as far as she could to her left. She found the outside hem of the drape with her fingers, and held it steady while she positioned her face, ready to peek.

She peeked.

What she saw caused her to scream out loud.

She was looking down the barrel of a shotgun. The Colonel sat in the chair facing her, with a shiny hunting gun aimed directly at her head. Beside him on the end table sat his drink.

'Don't shoot! It's me! Abby Malone!'

'Give me one good reason.'

'I didn't mean any harm!'

'Hmph! No harm for who? You're getting a little troublesome, Abby Malone. You've forced me into action.' He cracked open his shotgun and checked his ammunition.

Abby tried to swallow but her mouth was too dry. She remembered Lucy's caution only too well. She couldn't speak.

'What is it you came to get, Miss Malone? Why are you here, in my den?'

'I don't know!'

The Colonel stared hard into her face. 'This is how it is. You're a thief. For all I know, you're a potential murderer. You broke into my house and I shot you. I didn't know that you were only a snoopy busybody until after it was too late. But first, I want you to tell me why you're here.'

'Let me go, Colonel Bradley. I'll never bother you again.'

'No, you won't. I'll let you think for a while. Maybe you'll remember what you came for.'

The next thing Abby knew, the Colonel grabbed her and tied her wrists together tightly with the drape cord. He took off his ascot and gagged her with it. Then he unzipped a cushion, pulled out the bag of feather stuffing and covered her head with the cushion jacket. Once more, Abby was in the dark.

Outside the mansion, two grey eyes glinted. He'd been waiting and watching. The rain had started coming down steadily, but he didn't move to find cover. His Abby was in there. She was worried, he knew that. She was frightened, he sensed that. Now she was terrified, and he could only wait and watch.

Cody had observed his Abby sneaking into the car belonging to the man who drives too fast. He waited for her to come out and go to her den for the night, as always. She didn't. He was bothered by that. Abby didn't want him to come. She told him to stay. But he sensed that she was extremely nervous and might need him. He had to come with her.

A noise. A door at the back of the big house opened. A big human carrying a long shiny stick pushed his Abby down a path toward the woods at the far end of the grounds. Cody followed. He could follow closely because the rain would mask his scent and his noise.

Cody watched as his Abby was thrown into a little shed. He heard her fall hard on the floor. The big man with the shiny stick slammed the door and locked it.

Cody heard Abby cry for help. The big man pounded at the door and yelled something in human. He sounded dangerous. He kicked the door.

Cody's last bit of patience expired. He took action. Growling fiercely, he leapt from his hiding place and lunged at this human. His teeth dug through soft plushy fabric and into the big man's fleshy leg.

The Colonel howled in rage and pain. He lifted the shotgun to his shoulder and took aim at the animal's back.

Abby heard the growls and realized with shock that Cody had placed himself in immediate danger. She couldn't see what was going on outside the shed.

'Home!' cried Abby frantically through the shed door. 'Go home, Cody! Home!'

Cody released his jaw and hesitated. Should he obey? BOOM! BOOM! Shotgun pellets shattered the stillness of the night.

'Cody!' Abby screamed from inside the shed. 'Cody? No! NO! You bastard! You shot Cody!' Abby's nerves had suffered more than they could take in one day. Her best friend Cody had died trying to save her. She fainted on the cold, wet floor.

Chapter Fourteen

Rescue

...'tis true that we are in great danger;
The greater therefore should our courage be.
– Shakespeare, *Henry V*, IV, i

SOMETIME IT'S difficult to sleep, Pete thought, when a person gets older. Hours had passed and he couldn't nod off. He finally decided to get out of bed and have a snack.

As he crept down the kitchen stairs, his thoughts turned to the race. He was getting excited about it. It was only days away. That little Abby Malone is riding like a pro, he thought. I didn't ride any better, even in my prime. She just might have a shot.

Pete turned on the kitchen lights and expectantly opened the fridge. Life is so much better now that Laura's home, he thought happily. He'd brought her home that afternoon, and she'd cheered the place up the moment she stepped into the kitchen. She'd rattled around, getting things back to normal, and had insisted on cooking dinner. She was tired of being a patient, she'd said. Laura had made him a delicious meat loaf, and he loved nothing better than a cold meat-loaf sandwich for a midnight snack.

Sam had showed up at the farm that day to watch Abby practise jumps. Pete chuckled as he thought of the chemistry brewing between Abby and Sam. It will be good for her to have a beau, he thought. And Sam's a good boy.

Pete had stocked the larder before getting Laura from the hospital, and the fridge was full of good things to eat. Pete took out the leftover meat loaf and milk, with apple pie for dessert. He settled himself at the table with a fork.

Laura came in, hair tied up in her bright pink scarf. Her turquoise chiffon dressing gown floated behind her. 'I missed you. May I join you, my love?'

'Of course. I'm always happier for your company. I was just thinking about Abby and Sam.'

'Aren't they cute? I think it's Abby's first romance.'

'Romance? Is it that serious? They only met at graduation.'

'Men! Of course it's serious. Even if it lasts for one day, it's a beautiful thing.' Laura sighed, remembering how intense her emotions were when she was young.

'You're the beautiful thing, Laura, and quite the romantic. Pie?'

There was an other-worldly howl at the back door.

Pete instinctively put his arms around Laura, and she melted into him.

'What the heck is that?' he sputtered.

'I have no idea, but whatever it is, it's right outside our kitchen door.'

Another howl, long and low and mournful. Then a high-pitched yip, yip, yip.

'Cody.' There was no doubt in Laura's mind. She dropped out of Pete's arms and unlocked the door.

'Laura, for heaven's sake!'

'It's Cody, and it must be important.'

'Just look first to make sure it's him, before you let some wild rabid creature into my house.'

Laura drew back the lace curtains on the door window and peered outside. It was too dark to see.

'Yes, it's Cody. I can see him.' she lied, and opened the door.

It was Cody. But covered with blood and soaking wet from the rain. Thick grey mud caked his legs.

'My God,' Pete exclaimed. 'My God.'

'Come in, Cody,' invited Laura, as if to a house guest, then disappeared.

Cody hobbled in, favouring his back left leg. The fur had been torn off his chest, exposing raw flesh. His left hind end was matted with blood and roughened with lacerations. He stood shivering in a puddle of mud and blood. His eyes pleaded with them for help.

'Laura, get some blankets!' ordered Pete.

'I'm way ahead of you,' responded his wife as she dropped a pile of clean towels and a bucket of soapy warm water beside Cody. She wrapped him carefully, warming him but making sure she avoided touching his open wounds with anything but water.

Pete placed a bowl of cold water at his feet but Cody wasn't thirsty. 'Must've been drinking from puddles,' he said.

'He needs a vet,' she said to Pete. 'Can you call young Alan?'

'Alan Masters is a horse vet, Laura. I'll call Colleen Millitch at Cheltenham Vets.'

'Better hurry.' Laura continued drying and cleaning Cody while Pete made the emergency call.

Cody became restless. He turned to face the door and whined.

'Pete, he wants out.'

'Don't let him out. He needs help.' Pete had found the number and was dialling. They still had their old black rotary phone.

Cody lifted his front paw and scratched at the door. He howled.

'Pete, he wants us to do something. Look how he watches us and then scratches to go out.'

'There's a recording with Colleen's home number.' Pete was still on the phone, scribbling down the dictated telephone number.

'Don't call just yet. Pete, there's something very, very wrong when this coyote comes to us for help instead of Abby.'

Pete hung up the phone. 'You're right. Of course. Abby must be in trouble. And from the look of this animal, she could be in grave danger.' He examined Cody's chest and back leg. 'These look like gunshot wounds. He's been hit with bird pellets.'

'Oh, Pete, that's terrible.' Laura paced. 'Let me call her mother. No sense in being alarmed if Abby's safe in her bed.' Laura rose from the floor and dialled the Malones'.

It rang and rang. No answer.

'Fiona doesn't always hear the phone. You know what I mean,' said Laura. 'But Abby would've heard it by now, and picked it up.'

'You stay here, Mother, to answer the phone and be home base.' Pete pulled his work overalls over his striped pyjamas and threw on a raincoat. He grabbed the keys to his truck and his cap off the rack. 'Cody and I will find Abby.'

'Check her house first, Pete, to be sure.'

'You're right, I will.'

'And then where will you go? Do you have any idea?'

Pete shook his head. 'No, I don't. And I don't know how Cody can tell me, but I have to try.'

'Be careful, please. I love you.'

Pete opened the kitchen door and Cody bolted out. Pete hurried to the truck and started it. He opened the passenger door and called Cody to get in, but the coyote was already halfway down the concession.

Cody was heading south, away from Abby's house. Pete made the decision to follow him instead of checking at the Malones'.

The coyote was travelling fairly fast. Pete drove along, keeping him in sight. Cody never paused. He kept a quick, steady pace, occasionally looking back to see if the truck was still there. He turned east. With back leg lagging slightly, Cody continued zigzagging down the side of the road.

How the heck does he know where he's going? thought Pete. He reflected that animals have an uncanny navigating ability. Dogs, cats, horses, even birds have been known to show up after being lost for months. Many times over the years Pete had dropped his reins and let the horse find the path. And a neighbour's dog came home weeks after he'd been left behind on a camping trip. How much more acute would a wild animal's instinct be? He could only assume that Cody had instinctively found his way home and was now retracing his steps. Pete was filled with admiration for this noble animal, and followed him, unsure of their destination.

They turned onto Highway 10, southbound. Pete stayed half on the shoulder with his hazard lights on. His windshield wipers cleared his vision, but sometimes he lost sight of the small grey coyote on this dark, rainy night. There were very few cars, mostly transport trucks. By now it was almost two in the morning.

Pete continued to marvel at Cody's stamina. He'd driven steadily at around fifteen kilometres an hour for twenty minutes, and Cody wasn't letting up. Pete worried about the blood he was losing. He'd get him to the vet as soon as they found Abby. Cody would have run this route the other way, too, speculated Pete. That's a lot of mileage. And Cody certainly seemed to know exactly where he was going. Instinct, he thought, affirming his earlier conclusion. That made sense. Pure, ancient, animal homing instinct. Pete felt awed by nature's ways.

Minutes later, Cody shot in front of Pete's truck and turned east into an exclusive new subdivision. Pete turned left, after letting two trucks pass. Off the highway it was much easier to see him. Pete let out a big sigh of relief. He wouldn't worry as much about Cody getting killed by a truck.

Pete followed Cody as he wound through the beautifully landscaped streets until they got to a hidden cul-de-sac. Right at the end was a monstrous mansion set majestically back from the road. Surrounded by acres of land, it was built to look intimidating and formidable. Although it was new, it had turrets and towers evoking a far earlier era when damsels in distress were rescued by princes.

'I'm no prince,' said Pete aloud. 'But we have a damsel in distress to rescue, or I'm a Dutchman.'

He parked his car off the road out of sight. He got out and stretched his sore legs and hip. Cody was waiting further on.

Pete looked at the mansion as he walked stiffly in Cody's direction. He thought he knew whose castle it might be. Who but the Colonel would design such a place to live? And this subdivision had been built on old Bradley land. Pete had heard that the Colonel had kept a ten-acre parcel and sold the rest. This must be his home. The pieces were falling into place. He was sure now that this night's adventures had something to do with Abby's quest to free her father. 'The crazy kid,' he mumbled.

Cody was extremely tired now. He drank greedily from a pool of rain water at the curb as he waited for Pete to catch up. His body sagged with fatigue, but his job wasn't done.

The two intruders, wounded coyote and determined old man, crept behind the massive iron gates and into the grounds. Cody led Pete up the hill beside the lane and around the back, past the big casement windows of the study, and deep into the wooded area at the far end of the estate.

There stood the shed. Cody sniffed at the door and whined softly.

'Abby,' whispered Pete. 'Abby, are you in there?'

There was no sound from the shed.

Cody dragged himself around the shed sniffing and snuffling at the floor. When he returned to the door after making a complete circumference, he put a paw on it and scratched. He howled a quiet little howl and then two yips. He turned his head and pleaded to Pete with his eyes.

No sound from inside the shed.

Pete watched Cody, and knew that Abby was in the shed. He wondered if she was alive.

'Abby!' Pete said a little louder, right at the crack of the door.

No response.

Cody became very agitated. He whined and wiggled and pointed his nose to the mansion. Pete looked. A light had come on. Now the outside floodlights blazed onto the lawns behind the house.

They were still in the dark, well out of range of the floodlights, but Pete knew he had to move fast. He took his jack-knife out of his overall pocket and began to whittle the lock off the shed door as fast as he could.

Cody whined again.

'Easy, Cody, it'll be just a minute more.'

Pete yanked the metal and the lock came off the wood.

A door slammed at the house. Pete didn't pause, he crept gingerly into the shed and felt a soft body on the floor with his foot. It moved slightly, and groaned.

'Abby, my dear, we're going home.' He scooped her up and carried her out. He pushed the door closed with his elbow to make it appear as if no one had been there.

With Cody at his heels, Pete rapidly walked further into the woods carrying his drooping burden. He was hoping to find a gate somewhere along the six-foot-high chain-link fence.

Cody yipped softly. Pete stopped to listen.

Someone had found the lock on the shed door broken. Whoever it was, he didn't like it. The shed door slammed and slammed again, accompanied by a string of curses.

Pete continued along the fence under cover of the woods. He avoided being exposed by the floodlights and skirted the open areas quickly. His only thought was to get Abby home safely.

There was no gate along the fence. They would have to somehow get out the same way they came in without being noticed.

Pete was grateful for the rain and the black sky. On a clear night with a full moon and stars, they would surely have been caught.

They were now at the front of the property, in the trees near the gate. Checking over his shoulder and seeing nothing to fear, Pete made a lurching run across the lawn toward the opening in the iron fence, Abby hanging limply. He could almost feel freedom. BOOM! BOOMBOOM!

Pete hit the ground, landing on his elbows to protect Abby from his weight. The shotgun pellets had missed their target, but the warning was unmistakable.

Shifting from elbow to elbow and knee to knee, Pete dragged himself with Abby underneath him through the gate to the truck. Cody walked backward behind them, growling and keeping an alert eye on their attacker, ever ready to protect.

Shaking with fear and fatigue, Pete opened the passenger door of his truck under cover of bushes, and heaved Abby onto the seat. He placed her unconscious head in a comfortable position with one hand and straightened her legs with the other. Cody struggled in and flopped onto the floor.

Pete got in the other door and started the engine. Just as he backed up to turn the truck around, more shots were fired. BOOM! BOOM! One blast lodged pellets in the bed of his truck, and one blew out his front right headlight.

'Gotta go, gotta go go go,' muttered Pete distractedly as he gunned the engine. He spun the truck around to face home and sped away.

He finally managed to calm himself down ten minutes later. The windshield wipers slapped rhythmically. He was comforted by Abby's deep breathing. He'd get her home to Laura and then they'd decide what to do. I'm too old for this, he thought. Far too old. But he'd rescued Abby, and he was proud of that.

Cody was asleep on the floor. Pete would get him to Colleen as soon as they'd dealt with Abby.

He wondered what had happened during the night while he was in bed, thinking all was well. How had Abby got herself locked in the Colonel's shed? What the heck was she doing there? The important thing was getting Abby home safe and well. The story would come out, thought Pete. He'd learn about it in good time.

Laura had been watching for headlights. At first she thought a motorcycle was coming up the drive, and wondered if the police had gotten involved. She shuddered, imagining the worst.

Then she realized that it was the truck, with only one headlight working. She threw on her rain slicker, boots, and hat, and hobbled out to help.

'Pete!' she called. 'Pete, what happened? Have you got her?'

Pete climbed down from the truck and said, 'Open the passenger door, Laura.' He was weary, but there was much more to do that night.

Abby lifted her head just as Laura opened the truck door.

'Hello?' she whispered feebly. She cleared her throat. 'Where am I?'

By this time Pete was there and answered, 'Everthing's fine now, Abby. We're home at the farm.' He lifted her over his shoulder and carried her.

Laura hurried ahead and opened the door. She'd put out fresh cookies and coffee and hot chocolate to keep herself busy while she waited, and the warm kitchen smelled delicious. They carefully arranged Abby on the couch by the kitchen fireplace, and covered her with blankets.

Laura lit the fire and soon there was a cheerful glow dancing in the grate. She brought down fresh flannelette pyjamas, and began to help Abby out of her wet clothes.

'Now, Pete, turn your head for a moment, will you?'

Pete had just sunk gratefully into his favourite armchair beside the fire. 'Why, I forgot about Cody!' he said as he hoisted himself onto his feet and strode out the door.

Abby crumpled. She began to sob.

'Abby. Dear, dear, Abby,' soothed Laura. 'It'll be all right.'

'No, it won't,' Abby sputtered. 'It won't be all right. Cody's dead. He tried to protect me and the Colonel shot him.' She was miserable. 'Nothing will ever be all right again. Cody is dead.'

Laura managed to undress her and put her in the warm pyjamas. She wrapped her up in blankets and propped a soft pillow under her head, making a comfortable place for her to sleep.

'Abby, darling, don't think about it now. I'll get you a big mug of cocoa.' Laura wiped away her own tears as she stood at the stove. Oh, my, Cody is dead. Laura felt great distress. She'd become very fond of the little fellow, but what worried her more was Abby's heartache.

The kitchen door swung open and Pete stood at the entrance, arms full of wretched coyote. Cody was shivering badly, and losing blood. Fur fell in tufts to the floor. 'Laura, call Colleen's home number. It's on the pad by the phone. Abby, I've got to get help for Cody.'

'He's alive?' exclaimed Abby.

'He's not dead?' asked Laura hopefully.

'He's alive, but barely,' said Pete grimly. 'Fear alone can kill a wild animal, and Cody is badly stressed. Call Colleen and tell her I'll meet her at her office in ten minutes.'

Abby, who by this time had thrown off her blankets, was hugging Cody in Pete's arms. 'Cody, my Cody. You're alive.' Tears cascaded down her cheeks. 'I thought he was dead,' she told Pete. 'The Colonel shot him and I thought he was dead.'

Cody lifted his head. He tried to wag his tail. The effort was too great, however, and his tail sagged. He gave Abby a lick on her tear-stained cheek, then shuddered and shook. His eyes rolled back and he dropped his head. Abby hugged him tighter.

'He's lost a lot of blood,' feared Pete. 'We've got to get him full of antibiotics, and hope for the best.' He turned for the door.

'I'm coming, too!' Abby cried.

'No, Abby. You won't be able to help. You're too weak yourself. I'll take care of him.'

Laura took the grieving girl by the arm and led her back to the couch. 'Pete, you go now. I'll stay with Abby.'

'Did you call Colleen?'

'Yes. She'll meet you there.'

Pete disappeared into the black, rainy night, coyote in arms. Laura found a clean pair of pyjamas for Abby, to replace the ones bloodied and muddied by Cody, and tucked her back into the warm blankets.

Abby slept fitfully. She awoke with her throat burning. Laura was there waiting at her side with a glass of cool water and two Tylenols.

'Are they back yet?' she asked anxiously.

'Not yet, dear. You sleep.'

Abby took the tablets, drank the water down and dozed off again.

Laura catnapped in the armchair, half awake and ready for action. She kept one ear open for Abby and the other for the phone. She knew that Pete would call if there was a problem. She was unsure about whether they should call Fiona again, but figured that Fiona wouldn't hear the phone. She tried to get a little rest.

Colleen took Cody right into the operating room. The tall, devoted young vet anaesthetized him so she could probe his injuries without causing him pain. He was a wild animal, and she didn't want to be bitten. She gave him a shot of penicillin and a tetanus shot. As Pete fell asleep on the hard bench in the waiting room, Colleen cleaned Cody and stitched him. She wrapped what she could with gauze, and splinted his left hind leg. Two hours later, she awoke Pete.

'Mr Pierson?'

Pete snorted and opened his eyes.

'He's ready to go. I'll give you some pills to give him. I wrote the instructions on the bottle.' She paused and looked at Pete quizzically. 'How was this animal shot?'

'I'll tell you when I find out. I'm not really sure.'

'Okay.' Colleen rubbed her tired eyes. 'But can you tell me why you brought me a coyote? When Mrs Pierson said you'd be bringing in "Cody", I assumed it was a dog. Normally coyotes just go off and die after they've been shot.'

'Oh, this isn't a wild coyote. Cody was raised by my young friend, Abby Malone. Thanks for treating him.'

'I don't do many, that's for sure,' she smiled. 'In fact, he's my first. He was shot twice, you knew that? Gunshot pellets. He got winged by the outside of the pellet spray. Lucky for him he didn't get the full blast. Otherwise it would've been game over.'

'He took those hits protecting Abby from someone, I can't say who. I have to be careful, Colleen, I hope you don't mind.'

'Sure. The important thing is that he'll be as right as rain. Normally, I'd keep him overnight, but I don't think he'd react well to waking in a cage. Just take him home and let him sleep it off. And don't forget to give him his pills. Now we all can go home and get some sleep.'

Pete picked Cody up from the table, still under the anaesthesia. 'Thanks, Colleen. You're good to come in at such an hour.'

'That's my job.' She smiled as she held the door. She was thinking how good he was to bring him in. 'Oh, don't forget. I need to see Cody in a week.'

'Right you are,' said Pete. He carefully placed the sleeping coyote on the truck seat, and drove home.

Dawn broke, and sunlight streamed into the Piersons' kitchen, warming the bed of old blankets that Pete had made for Cody when they got home from the vet's. Cody's eyes opened and blinked. He saw his Abby sleeping soundly on the couch. That reassured him. He hurt all over. He yawned and fell back asleep.

The sun moved slowly across the kitchen floor. Abby awoke with the sun in her eyes a few minutes later. She looked around the room, piecing together why she was here and what'd happened the night before. She noticed a grey furry ball nestled in old blankets on the floor, and felt contentment. Cody was going to be fine. She would never be able to thank Mr Pierson and Colleen Millitch enough.

Abby hoped that Mr and Mrs Pierson would be able to sleep late that day. They'd been up all night.

She considered how she was going to retrieve the papers she'd hidden behind the drape. Judging by the Colonel's reaction, they were very important. Pete would help her think of a way to get them.

She stretched her arms and legs to see what hurt and what didn't. She felt her ribs and head and back. Abby came to the conclusion that the only thing wrong with her was fatigue, and she'd be perfectly fine after one good sleep. The very thought of sleep made her sleepy, so she covered her eyes with a pillow to cut the light and soon she drifted back to dreamland.

Fiona awoke with a horrible hangover. Her head pounded and her mouth tasted disgusting. She lay in bed, feeling too bad to move. After Terence had left the night before, she got lonely and started to drink. She knew that she wasn't strong. She despised herself for needing the comfort of alcohol, especially when she desperately wanted to quit. So many reasons to quit. So many promises broken.

Tears came unbidden. Fiona felt deeply sorry for herself. She allowed herself to ache with self-pity. Her husband was in jail, leaving her to keep their lives intact. She just couldn't do it, and that was that. They were going to be evicted the first of September, no two ways about it. There was no money left after the trial. They'd have nowhere to go, unless she accepted Terence Curry's offer. She yawned and rubbed her sore eyes. Unless she could come up with an alternative, the day was coming soon when she and Abby would be moving into an apartment paid for by Terence. She'd find a way to pay him back, of course. She'd get a job. It would really be a loan, which she greatly appreciated. Fiona wanted to make sure that Abby would be settled in somewhere before the school year started, so she would have to start the arduous process of packing. Tomorrow, she thought. I can't, today.

She knew that Terence wanted more than friendship. He'd made that clear the night he'd come for the papers from Liam's files. Fiona had tried to move on to other subjects, but Terence had persisted. Fiona loved Liam with all her heart and would remain loyal to him, she'd told him. Terence had tried to kiss her, and she'd pushed him away. That's when they'd heard Abby calling from downstairs. Terence had grabbed the papers and fled. Abby was right when she'd said something felt weird, Fiona thought. It was. Totally weird. Thankfully, Terence hadn't mentioned it since. Neither had she. But it made the prospect of taking up his offer of lodging fraught with possible problems.

She was broken in spirit, and grasping at straws. Terence Curry would at least give them a place to live until she found something else.

She was expecting him around noon to take her to out for lunch. They'd look at apartments and discuss school enrolment for Abby. However nervous she was about his intentions, she was still extremely grateful that he was prepared to help them out. How to inform Abby that they'd be leaving the farm was another matter. Her head pounded.

She looked at the clock beside her bed. It was early. She needed sleep. She turned over and closed her eyes. Worrying wouldn't solve anything, she thought, as she drifted into a fitful slumber.

Abby awoke later in the morning. The big kitchen clock read eleven o'clock. She could hear Pete in the next room, on the telephone.

'Thanks, Milo, I'd appreciate it. So, we'll see you for lunch?... No, we insist. Laura will be hurt if you won't eat with us, and it's the least we can do when we ask a favour.... Right, then, twelve or so.'

He put down the receiver with a click, then tiptoed into the kitchen. He quietly opened the fridge door and took the orange juice out with his left hand.

'Is that Milo, as in Inspector Milo?' Abby asked.

'Aah! You scared me, Abby,' gasped Pete. Luckily the juice stayed upright. 'Yes, it's Milo Murski. He's coming to chat about last night.'

Abby pondered this information. 'Do you think he'll believe me?'

'About what?'

'About anything. You know how it is. The Colonel is a rich, powerful businessman, and I did break in, you know.'

'Now, Abby. The man fired on us. He locked you up. He

wounded your pet. We all might have been killed. Don't you think the police should know?'

'But I broke in to find some papers that I don't even have because I had to leave them there. And he can say he defended himself by grabbing me and locking me up. He shot Cody because he attacked him. I heard the growls. And you trespassed, and he could say he was defending his property.'

'Abby, you're right. That's exactly what he will say, I have no doubt. But, and this is the big but, he had no legal right to hold you prisoner. If he wanted to lock you up until the police got there, that would've been fine. But he didn't call the police. You see?'

'Okay, but I'm still nervous.'

'"True nobility is exempt from fear." *Henry VI*.'

'Shakespeare didn't help much last night. That book weighed a ton.'

'What book?'

'The Colonel's papers were hidden behind *The Complete Works of William Shakespeare*. On the shelf.'

'Oh, I see.'

'I was shaking so hard, I could hardly get it back in time.'

'Just don't worry. All you have to do is tell Milo the truth.'

'The whole truth?'

'And nothing but the truth, so help you God.'

Abby grinned weakly. 'Okay, I will. I'll tell him everything. I might have to break a confidence, though.'

'You better do it. This is no time to protect your source. What confidence?'

'You can't break me so easily, Mr Pierson,' Abby teased. 'It's the person who told me about the papers. I promised never to tell how I knew.'

'Why not wait to see if it's important. It might not matter to the police who told you. If it matters, you better tell. If it doesn't, then your promise can keep.'

Abby nodded. 'Sounds like a plan.' She sat up straight. 'Oh, what about Moonie? Has she been fed?'

'I fed her. Look. There she is, out in the front field. With fresh water, so don't worry.'

Abby looked out the kitchen window at the quarter-horse mare. Moonie lifted her graceful neck and shook her satiny black mane. The sun glistened off her healthy dark coat.

'Great. Thanks a lot.' Abby was relieved. Moonie had worked hard the day before, but she looked ready to go again. 'Isn't she gorgeous? She's a great horse, Mr Pierson.'

'Sure is. And you're a great rider. The race is in two days, Abby. We better get you rested up.' Pete got back to the business at hand. 'Now, let's call and tell your mother where you are.' He picked up the phone.

'I think it's too early.'

'It's after eleven.'

'I know. I don't want to wake her up. And even if she is awake, which I doubt, she'll think I'm out riding or something. Most mornings I'm gone before she's up.'

'But what if she missed you last night?'

'She probably didn't.' Abby looked at the floor, avoiding his eyes.

Pete guessed what that meant and was saddened by it. He knew that she wasn't going to AA meetings, but he hadn't known how badly things had deteriorated at the Malones'. He remembered well the happier days when the family was busy and active together in the community. They were upstanding citizens. Now, Liam was in jail and Fiona was drinking and Abby was left fending for herself, trying to prove her father's innocence and taking big risks doing so.

He gave her a little hug. 'What can your loyal slave prepare her royal highness for brekkies?'

'Pancakes!' exclaimed Laura before Abby could answer. 'Pancakes and syrup and bacon for our princess!'

Laura made her entrance. She wore a bright red skirt, brilliant blue blouse with matching hair ribbon, vibrant green shoes and belt. 'This should cheer everybody up,' she said as she twirled her skirt. Laura filled the kitchen with life, and even Cody, still drugged, cocked his ears.

After lunch, which the adults ate while Abby devoured her huge delicious breakfast, Inspector Murski sat back and considered what he'd heard. 'So you say, Abby, that you broke into the Colonel's house to look for some papers that might be new evidence of such magnitude that a new trial could result?'

'Yes, that's right. I know I shouldn't have, but it seemed the right thing to do at the time.'

'Well. I can't condone it, that's for sure.' Milo rocked his chair. 'What's peculiar is that Kenneth Bradley hasn't called in a break-in. He's on the phone to us if a neighbour's cat meows or a tree branch is encroaching on his property. That makes me wonder. And two neighbours called to report gunshot sounds last night.' He wiped his chin with the napkin. 'John Bains and I will pay him a visit.'

Abby blurted out, 'Do you think you could look behind the drape beside the bookshelves, opposite the reclining chair? That's where I hid the folder. I had to leave it and we'll be lucky if it's still there. Oh, and make sure you don't let him see it. It might be evidence that Dad is innocent.'

Milo looked fondly at Abby, and smiled at her kindly, 'Abby, I will. But don't get your hopes up. There's likely nothing in that file that affects you at all. We will look, though, I promise.' It was obvious to Abby that he thought she was hoping for miracles.

Milo stood. He reached over to rumple Abby's hair. He shook Pete's hand and thanked Laura for lunch.

'Your cooking would get me over here any old day,' he said, causing Laura to smile broadly.

Pete walked him out to his car. They passed the truck and Abby watched while they examined the gunshot holes. Milo nodded at something Pete said and then got in his car and drove off.

When Pete came back into the kitchen, he said, 'Milo says that the pellets are all flattened, but they'll gather the cartridge cases to try to get a ballistics match with the Colonel's shotgun.'

Abby lay down with Cody and rubbed his ears, careful not to touch him anywhere it hurt. Which was everywhere. He was groggy and sore, but happy for her attention. She wondered how this would turn out. How would the Colonel react to the police questioning him? Would the police find the papers? Would they be proof of her father's innocence? It was a real long shot, Abby knew. She had to do something, get busy, find a way to pass the time until she heard what papers were in the folder. She stood up.

'I think I'd better go home and check in. Mom will be up and about by now. Can Cody stay here for a while, until he's fully awake?'

'Sure he can,' answered Pete. 'I'll drive you over, but why not phone? Don't you want to wait and see what Milo finds out?'

'Well, it could take all day. I'd like to have a shower and change, so if you don't mind I'd rather go home for a while.'

'No problem,' answered Laura. 'You go ahead. If there's any news, we'll call or come over.'

'Thanks. For everything.' Abby smiled at these two remarkable people. They'd saved her and Cody from the fate that had awaited them.

Chapter Fifteen

The Crash

Mine honour is my life; both grow in one;
Take honour from me, and my life is done.
— Shakespeare, *Richard II*, I, i

PETE DROPPED ABBY off at her door and insisted she call him whenever she was ready to come back. She walked into an empty house. Fiona wasn't home. Abby had no idea where she was.

As she trudged toward the stairs she wondered where her mother's zest for life had gone. Abby remembered the mother of her childhood as a happy, energetic woman, involved in causes and charities, always willing to pitch in when a friend or neighbour needed help. Now Fiona was a sad, lonely, idle woman. She had no hobbies, she'd lost interest in gardening, and she had nothing to do all day. She certainly didn't cook or clean.

They didn't talk together any more. Neither Fiona nor Abby knew much about what the other was doing or thinking or feeling.

It occurred to Abby that if her mother knew how close they were to solving the mystery, maybe she'd get renewed strength. She must be worried about losing the farm. Abby certainly was. And that strain alone would be enough to wear her down. Knowledge of Abby's progress might give Fiona enough hope to hang on a little longer. Abby resolved to tell her mother everything; the break-in, the papers, the Colonel, everything.

A foul aroma caught her attention. She couldn't bear the smell in the kitchen. Abby intended only to take out the garbage, and ended up polishing the whole room like new. Then she looked into the bathroom. Ugh. Okay, just this once, she thought. Never again. She disinfected and shined up the bathroom, then walked into the living room. There were empty bottles and garbage and food and crumbs all over the couch and rug.

'I hate housework!' she yelled at the top of her lungs.

She grabbed a garbage bag and shoved everything into it. 'To heck with sorting paper from glass today,' she said aloud. 'I have absolutely no patience left.'

Grumbling and cursing aloud, Abby tidied, cleaned and vacuumed the living room and gave the dining room a thorough going-over.

She stormed up the stairs to take a shower, indulging herself in a black mood. Her mother could pull herself together if she wanted to, Abby was certain, and Abby was mad that she chose not to.

She had her shower and changed into fresh clean clothes. She noted that it was she who did the laundry, too.

Knowing there was nothing in the house to eat, Abby was thinking of biking back to Merry Fields. She wanted tell her mother about the papers and fill her in. But where was she? It was after three o'clock and there was no sign of her.

She decided to wait for her mother. To pass the time, she thought she'd go up to the secret meadow and look around for the raccoons. She hadn't seen them lately. They've probably decided they've outgrown me, Abby thought. Just as well. Summer was drawing to a close and they should be firmly established in the wild by the time winter comes around.

As she left the house, she bumped squarely into Sam.

'Oh! I'm sorry! I wasn't ...'

'Hey! I haven't even knocked, yet!'

They laughed at their clumsiness, holding on to one another in the doorway. Abby was very happy to stand there with Sam's arms around her. She realized that they'd both stopped laughing. She looked up at him. His eyes were full of emotion.

'Abby, do you mind me holding you like this?'

'No, Sam, it feels nice. Very nice.'

She rested her head on his shoulder and hugged him tighter.

Sam bent his head and kissed her cheek. 'I like you, Abby Malone. I like you a lot.' He moved her face toward him, and kissed her lips.

Abby's knees buckled, and Sam caught her.

'Whoa, there. Are you all right?'

'Fine. Fine.' Abby felt wonderfully weak all over, and her head was spinning. That was very, very, very, nice, she thought.

She pulled away. 'Come with me, Sam. I was just going to look for my raccoons.'

'Sure.'

Sam's face looked flushed to Abby, and she wondered if hers was, too. She began to chat about the raccoons and Reddy and the barn fire, anything she could think of, until she felt normal again.

Sam looked at her oddly. 'I never took you for a chatterbox.'

'Until now,' finished Abby. 'Give me a break. I've never been kissed before.'

'Until now,' said Sam, reaching for her hand.

'Don't you touch me,' Abby laughed, walking faster. 'I can't think straight when you touch me.'

'Neither can I, but I won't let that stop me,' said Sam, smiling, as he walked faster, too.

Abby broke into a run, and Sam grabbed her hand. Together they ran, laughing, all the way to the secret meadow.

'Now, we have to be very quiet if we want the raccoons to come out,' Abby instructed him.

'I'll follow your every order,' Sam answered.

'Shhh.' Abby put her forefinger up to her lips. 'I hear something.'

'What's that?' asked Sam. 'It sounds like an animal crying.'

Abby listened. The sound got louder.

'It's not an animal, Sam.'

'You're right. It's a police car, and it's coming this way. I wonder where it's going.'

The sirens wailed loudly, then stopped.

'It sounds like they're here, at your farm,' Sam said, concern on his face. 'Let's go.'

The teenagers held hands as they ran back the way they'd come. As they crested the hill by the ashes of the barn, they saw two police cars in the driveway.

'Oh! The papers! I forgot all about the papers,' sputtered Abby. She dropped Sam's hand and started running toward the house.

Sam was puzzled, but right on her heels. Abby hoped they had good news after speaking with the Colonel.

As she arrived at the cruisers, Pete's truck came up the drive. Abby waved. Pete raised his hand and made a motion with his forefinger that seemed to mean 'just a moment'. She could see that Laura was with him, and they both looked upset.

Suddenly it all felt wrong. Something was wrong and she had no idea what it was. She only knew there was a hole growing in her stomach the size of Canada.

Abby ran past the cruisers to the Piersons' truck.

'Mr Pierson! Mrs Pierson! What's going on?'

Pete opened his door and climbed down. He looked older and stiffer than usual, probably due to all his exercise at the Colonel's. His faced wore a worried frown.

'Abby, there's been an accident. I haven't heard the whole story, but the officers will fill us in.' Pete put his arm around the frightened girl.

'It's Mom, isn't it,' Abby said, dully. She couldn't think.

'Your mother is fine. She's in the hospital, and she's conscious. She was in a car accident. I don't know the whole story yet.'

Laura hugged Abby and said softly, 'Dear, dear, dear Abby. We'll go to see her right away, but first we have to hear what the officers have to say.'

Abby stood, numbly.

Sam was standing slightly off to the side, unsure of what do. He stepped closer. 'Is there anything I can do to help?'

Pete turned to face him. 'Sam, my boy, thanks for the offer, but it's best if you leave Abby with us. She'll call you when she gets home from the hospital.'

Sam nodded. 'Sure, if you think it's best.' Now he spoke to Abby, 'I'll call later. I hope your mother's all right. I'm sorry, Abby. I want to help, so if there's anything ... I mean it.'

Abby watched the tall, good-looking boy walk over to his bike and pick it up. She vaguely noticed that some soot from the barn ashes had soiled the cuffs of his pants. He looked back, kindness and goodness filling his soft brown eyes. Abby nodded goodbye. Sam pressed his lips together grimly and rode away.

They were seated in the living room. Abby thought vaguely that she was glad she'd cleaned the house. She sat on the sofa between the Piersons, staring straight ahead. Waiting for the news.

Inspector Milo Murski sat in the wing chair to the right of the fireplace, and Detective John Bains sat on the left. Another two police officers stood by the window.

Milo spoke. 'Abby, your mother was in an accident. She has minor injuries, but she's in good shape and is resting comfortably in the hospital. The driver of the car, Terence Curry, was not so lucky.'

'What do you mean? Not so lucky?' asked Laura.

'Unfortunately, he died at the scene.'

Abby's hands shot to her mouth. 'Mr Curry is dead?'

Milo responded, 'I'm afraid so.'

Laura put her arm around Abby, but Abby shrugged it off. She wanted to know everything. 'How did it happen?' she asked.

'Detective Bains and I went to the house of Kenneth Bradley early this afternoon to inquire about the events of last night. He was unhelpful, to put it mildly. He told us to speak to his lawyer, Terence Curry. I called in to headquarters for a search warrant so we could link the cartridge cases found on the ground with Bradley's shotgun, and legally retrieve any evidence relevant to your father's case. Headquarters got the warrant from the judge, and Detective Bains and I drove over to Mr Curry's house, which isn't far from the Colonel's.

'These two officers,' he said as he indicated the two standing men, 'left for the Colonel's place with the warrant. John Bains and I arrived at Curry's to find your mother in his car and Curry locking his house. We asked if we could speak to him, and he complied. His cell phone rang in his pocket. He answered it, listened for a few seconds, then jumped in the car and started it. Detective John Bains ordered him to stop. He refused. Bains called to him again, but Curry ignored him, backed out of his driveway and raced off.

'John and I got in our cruiser and followed. We were very curious about where he was going and why he was avoiding a police interview.

'He drove recklessly through the subdivision in an apparent

effort to lose us. He attained a speed of ninety kilometres an hour in a forty zone. It appeared that your mother was frightened, because she sank down deep in her seat. Curry turned north onto Highway 10 without looking, and a northbound truck hit his car broadside. He was probably dead on impact. The truck driver was shaken but uninjured.'

Milo looked at Abby, Laura and Pete. 'Have you followed me so far?'

They nodded, as one.

'Ambulances arrived immediately and took your mother to the Brampton General. On arrival she was conscious with no serious injuries. There's no need to go into detail about Mr Curry at this time.'

Abby spoke up, her voice uneven. 'Has anybody told Dad about the accident?'

'Don't worry about that, Abby. I'll look after it.'

'Thank you,' Abby said, concerned about her father's reaction to the news. 'Can I see my mother, now?' She stood up, anxious to go.

'Sit down for another minute, Abby. We have an update on another subject.' Milo's face lost its serious expression. 'Abby, you'll be happy to hear this. While we were occupied with the crash, the two officers searched the Colonel's house and found the folder you described.' He smiled. 'It was exactly where you said it might be.'

Abby's eyes widened. 'Have you looked at the papers?'

'Yes, we've looked at them. And you were quite correct. They are critical to this case.'

Abby jumped out of her seat again. She was agitated. 'What do they say? What are they about? Is Dad going to get out of jail?'

'Hold on, Abby,' said Milo. 'The Crown attorney's staff are looking at them right this minute. I'm not at liberty to discuss it, but you'll be kept informed.'

'But, I really want to know. Is my dad innocent?'

Milo took a breath and said, 'Abby. It looks good. That's all I will say, and I shouldn't have said even that.'

'But I.... Can't you.... Why does the law make things so

complicated? All I want to know is, will my dad be freed?'

'I understand how you feel, Abby, believe me. I'll tell you everything I can as soon as I can. I don't want to jeopardize the case in any way.' Milo stood up and motioned for his men to follow. 'Pete, will you take Abby to the hospital to see her mother? I'm going to headquarters to follow this up.'

'Yes, Milo. Laura and I will take her right now.'

'Good. Abby, I promise to wrap this up as fast as possible. Can you trust that I will?' He put out his hand for Abby to shake.

She took it. 'Yes. But please, will you tell me as much as you can as soon as you can?'

'Absolutely.' They shook hands and the men turned to go.

'Oh, Abby,' said Milo. 'Good work. But next time, call us. That's our job.' He winked and left the room.

Abby was silent for most of the drive to the hospital. Laura tried to cheer her up, but Abby was too absorbed with the recent events to respond. Her mother was fine, they'd told her, but Abby wanted to see with her own eyes. And she couldn't stop thinking about her father. What would happen? Were the papers going to prove his innocence? She worried about Cody, too, suffering from his gunshot wounds.

They asked for Fiona's room number at the front desk and rode up the elevator. Her room was down the hall to the left. Abby wasn't sure what she'd see when they got there, and her hands were cold and sweaty with nervousness.

Pete knocked gently on the door.

'Come in,' answered Fiona.

Abby hesitantly opened the door. She looked at her mother, so pale and small in the tall hospital bed, and her eyes filled with tears.

Fiona opened her arms and whispered, 'Abby.'

Abby fell into her mother's embrace. They hugged each other tightly, Abby fervently grateful that her mother was alive, and Fiona praying silently that she could make her life count for something. She was blessed to be alive and to have a daughter like Abby.

The two Malones stayed in their embrace for a few minutes,

eyes closed and emotion strong. Pete and Laura stood to one side, respectfully.

When they pulled apart, Fiona wiped her tear-stained face and said to Abby, 'We have so much to be thankful for, my wonderful child. I saw today how fragile life is. I won't waste any more of it. When they let me out of here, I promise you Abby, I'll be a real mother to you. I've had a close call. I've been given another chance.'

Abby thought she heard a new strength in her mother's resolve. 'Mom, I know you can do it this time.' She wanted to believe it.

'Oh, I will. Just watch me.' Fiona smiled, and in her smile was determination. 'I'll do it, all right. We'll be a real family again. You, me, and Dad. We'll make it, Abby, somehow, until your father's back at home.' Her tears started again. 'I've been selfish and foolish. It took a car crash to shake some sense into me.'

Fiona struggled to sit up in bed. Pete helped her, and Laura stuffed pillows behind her back for support.

Laura approached the bed. 'Tell me about your injuries, dear. Is anything broken?'

'A few ribs, nothing more. They're tender. I have a concussion and general bruising. All in all I'm very lucky. Wearing a seat belt saved my life, they told me, and I was down low in the seat when we crashed.'

'Amazing,' said Pete. 'You were hardly touched.'

'They haven't told me how Terence is,' Fiona said. 'Have you seen him yet?'

Abby caught her breath. Pete and Laura glanced at each other. Laura nodded briefly at him. Pete cleared his throat and said, 'Did you see him after the crash?'

'No. I was knocked out. They put me in the ambulance and brought me here.'

Laura spoke. 'And you don't know anything about his condition?'

'No.' Fiona looked from face to face. She knew there was bad news. 'How bad is he? Please be honest.'

'We know his condition, Fiona,' said Pete. 'It can't get worse.'

'He's paralysed,' stated Fiona, steadily.

'No, Mom,' Abby said softly. 'He died in the crash.'

'He what? He what?'

'He died in the crash.'

Fiona fell silent. Her face showed nothing. Then she wept. 'The truck ... we turned onto 10 ... hit hard.... Why did he run from the police? Why?... He raced, swerved around corners ... no need to speed ... scared the wits out of me ... don't understand ... what was he thinking?'

The others in the room let her weep. They could answer none of her questions, so they didn't try.

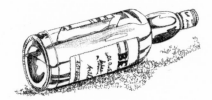

Chapter Sixteen
Abby's Outburst

Like a red morn, that ever yet betoken'd,
Wrack to the seaman, tempest to the field.
– Shakespeare, *Venus and Adonis*, line 453

ABBY CAME HOME from the hospital with the Piersons later that day. It was after six o'clock. Cody seemed much better after his restful day. He'd come out of the anaesthesia well, and was eating and drinking normally. Abby took him outside. He happily sniffed around every tree, slowly wagging his bushy tail. At first he hopped on three legs, but soon started testing his weight on his wounded leg. They walked out into the field to visit Moonie, Abby carrying her grooming kit.

Abby brought a carrot as a treat, which Moonie quickly accepted. With a hoof-pick Abby picked her feet clean, then proceeded to curry the mare from head to foot. The rubber teeth on the round flat brush felt good to Moonie, and she stood quietly while Abby massaged her skin and scratched her itches. She relaxed and enjoyed the sensation. Once Abby finished currying, she took her soft brush and cleaned Moonie's fine, silky coat, flicking out all the dust and dirt. Then she took the towel and polished Moonie until her coat reflected the late-afternoon sunshine. As a last touch, she combed her jet-black mane and tail completely free of tangles.

'If you were a cat, you'd be purring,' Abby said affectionately. The little mare looked beautiful, all shined up and fit and healthy. Moonie thought so herself, and she strutted proudly around the field with her neck arched and her knees high. Abby watched with pride. Every movement that Moonie made was musical and elegant. Every line of her body was sleek and correct. She was built for speed and agility, and was beautiful, too.

Suddenly Moonie snaked her head around and pulled the rubber curry-comb out of Abby's pocket. With glinting eyes, she challenged Abby to get it back. She took off with the curry in her mouth, tossing her combed-out mane and flicking her flowing black tail. Abby laughed at her antics, and started to pursue her. Cody tried to join in the play, but tired very soon and decided to provide the music. He howled happily. They played a game of darting and dodging, weaving and leaping. Moonie would almost allow Abby to grab the brush, then she'd leap away, spinning on her back legs.

From the kitchen window, Laura watched this game. It was a game between two healthy, youthful animals, played with vigour and abandon. Laura admired the two agile figures as they twisted and spun in this carefree dance. That one was a horse and one was a girl made the dance more unusual and watchable. She felt both a part of it, drawn to it by her own enthusiasm, and a spectator. Laura watched until the dance was done, when the beautiful bay mare placed the curry in Abby's outstretched hand.

Laura rang the dinner bell.

Abby looked over at the Piersons' farmhouse and saw Laura standing outside wearing her bright pink scarf and ringing the chime. Abby felt a tug at her heart. Laura was very important to her, always ready to console, advise, help and feed her. She'd taken it in stride when Pete had brought Abby home, wet and in shock, in the middle of the night. She'd accepted Cody into her home and tended his injuries. And now, with Fiona in the hospital, Laura simply expected Abby to move in, and she made her feel so welcome that Abby didn't worry about being a burden. In fact, she was made to feel that her presence was a bonus, an unexpected pleasure for the Piersons'.

And Laura never asked anything in return. Abby hoped that one day she could repay her. She ran toward the house, flushed, happy and at peace with the world. Cody followed at his own speed and found a perfect spot for himself under the steps.

After they'd finished a hot dinner of chicken and dumplings with carrots and peas, the phone rang.

Liam Malone was calling. He wanted to hear the details from

Pete about Fiona's accident and Terence Curry's death. It was very difficult for him, being far away and out of touch. He and Pete talked for a while, then he asked to speak to Abby.

'Are you all right, sweetheart?'

'Yes, Dad. I'm fine. Really.' It was good to hear his strong familiar voice. Abby clutched the phone to her ear.

'How's your mother?'

'Mom looks good. She'll be out tomorrow or the day after.'

'Are you okay about Mr Curry?' Liam asked this question gently.

'I think so, but I'm not sure it's sunk in yet. It doesn't seem real.'

'No. Not to me, either.'

'I'm sad he died, and so is Mom. He drove too fast. He always drove too fast. Why do you think he was running from the police?'

'I don't know, Abby. I can't get a handle on it. I'm just terribly glad that your mother's all right.'

'Yes.' Abby and Liam didn't speak for a moment, both subdued by the thought of Fiona's close call.

'Are you all ready for the big race?'

'Sure am. Moonie's fit and muscled up. I don't think we could be readier. Dad?' asked Abby, as a new thought occurred to her. 'Where are you calling from? Weren't you going to be transferred to Beaver Creek?'

'Yes, but apparently that's been changed. Something's going on, I don't know what.'

'Maybe they'll let you come home.' Abby was sorely tempted to tell about him the papers, but stopped herself. She didn't want his hopes raised, then dashed if it didn't work out.

'Stop dreaming, my darling. It'll be just a little longer. The months are flying by.'

'Time flies when you're having fun,' said Abby wryly.

'Smart alec. Oops, I've been informed by the guard that my call is finished. Now, Abby, I don't want you stewing and fretting over all this. I'll call you when I can. Look after your mother, now.'

'Okay, Dad. I love you.'

'I love you, too, Abby, I never stop thinking about you.' It was true. He worried about the weight of burden that his young daughter carried. He anguished that he couldn't lighten it.

Sam had left an envelope addressed to Abby in the Piersons' mailbox late that afternoon. Inside was a short note, written on a sheet of white paper.

> Dear Abby,
>
> I hope your mother recovers soon. I'm sorry about Mr Curry. I know you have a lot on your mind, but I'd like to see you so call me when you can.
>
> I'm thinking of you, Sam

It thrilled her that he'd written her a note and brought it over. She tucked it under the pillow on the couch in the Piersons' kitchen when she went to bed that night. She envisioned his liquid brown eyes and his shy, charming smile. She remembered the sensation of holding his hand and imagined his kiss on her lips and the thrilling strength of his arms holding her. She replayed the conversation they'd had as they walked through the secret meadow, embellishing it as she wished. She made up scenarios where he rescued her from evil, or she saved his life. She would drift into a delightful sleep. But she never slept long. She'd awaken wondering about the Colonel, the papers, Terence Curry, her mother, where they'd live if they were evicted. She was curious about what the police had found in the folder, and impatient to know the results.

Then she'd turn her thoughts to Sam and feel peaceful again, drift back to sleep, only to reawaken with her fears and worries.

Morning finally came. At five o'clock the day was just beginning to dawn. The sky was red over the horizon, and the air was still.

Abby climbed into her jeans and T-shirt. She gulped down a glass of orange juice, stuffed a piece of bread into her pocket, left a quickly scrawled note, and headed out the door, Cody trotting at her heels, a little slower than usual.

Abby carried the saddle and bridle into the meadow. She

tacked up Moonie and swung her leg over the saddle.

'Cody, are you up for this? Is your leg okay?'

Cody lovingly gazed up at her, trying to tell Abby that he'd follow her anywhere.

She didn't know where she was going, only that she couldn't stay in bed one more minute and that she needed to clear her head. The best place she knew for head-clearing was in the saddle, and Moonie needed a gentle tune-up today. Tomorrow they would race. Tomorrow they would test their speed and agility against all comers. Abby's stomach flipped.

It looked as if it was going to rain later, too, so it was a good time to ride.

They headed down the road toward home, out of habit. Abby kept a close eye on Cody as he limped gamely along. They'd only travelled a short distance but he was already lagging farther and farther behind. She stopped Moonie and dismounted. Gently, she picked up the skinny little coyote, avoiding his many sore spots. Very carefully she placed him at the front of the saddle, and climbed up behind him. She wiggled her bottom to the back of the saddle to give him room.

Moonie rolled her eyes back to see what foolishness was happening on her back. She snorted and threw her head to register disapproval.

'Easy, Moonie. This is no time to get opinionated.' Moonie snorted again, but she stopped pawing the ground.

Cody was shaking with fear at this new arrangement, and blinked his eyes at her beseechingly. 'Cody? You okay?' she asked. 'Let's go a little way like this, and if you don't get used to it, I'll put you back down on the ground.'

Abby nudged Moonie forward into a slow walk. At first, the mare was nervous and Cody was scared, but after a few minutes, this strange experience became acceptable. Cody stopped shaking. He thumped his tail on Moonie's side and gave Abby a quick lick on her hand.

'Good boy. We won't go fast. When you want down, you tell me.'

Cody thumped his tail in agreement. Moonie didn't seem to

mind now, either, and Abby patted her neck in praise.

'Thanks, Moonie, you're a sport.'

She really was a sport, thought Abby, fondly. There weren't many horses that would allow a dog or coyote on their backs. Moonie was strong-willed but sensible, and enthusiastic once she understood why something was being asked of her. Like in the steeplechase. She'd have to win the race with speed and determination. There was great trust between them, and as they walked along the road Abby realized that trust was the essence of their relationship. Moonie knew that Abby wouldn't ask her to do anything dangerous, or take a jump that she couldn't handle. Abby gave Moonie confidence by riding intelligently, just as Moonie made Abby brave by wholeheartedly doing Abby's bidding. It was as if Abby was giving Moonie her brain, while Moonie gave Abby her strength and speed. Abby smiled at this revelation, and patted Moonie's neck again.

They arrived at the dark, empty Malone house. A shiver went through Abby's body as she compared the warm and cosy Pierson farmhouse to her own. There were always delicious cooking smells and friendly welcomes for her at Merry Fields. How she wished for the same feeling in her own home.

A white piece of paper attracted Abby's attention in her secret mail hole. 'Hey, a note from Leslie. Maybe she's home early from camp.' Abby hoped so. She walked Moonie over to the big tree and reached into the old squirrel's nest in the hollow. She pulled out the note and read:

Abby –

I hope you're okay. Sam told me about your Mom when I called last night. I hope she'll be all better soon. I'm thinking of you. I'll see you when I get back. (I'm dictating this note to Sam on the phone and I told him to drop it off for me.) Mom still doesn't know that Sam has a crush on you.

Oops! Did I tell a secret? – Leslie

Abby's spirits soared. The note was written in Sam's

handwriting. Sam wanted her to know that he liked her! Holy. And she was glad to know that Leslie was thinking of her. Leslie always made Abby happy. It was good to have a friend like her.

Moonie, Abby and Cody walked back through the secret meadow. Abby's head was full of thoughts of Sam. She sighed, as she always sighed when she thought of Sam. She couldn't help it.

They continued back along the ridge and made their way toward the Farrow farm. It was close to seven, now, and Abby was getting hungry. She breathed in the early morning air and enjoyed her ride. She felt more peaceful about waiting for the results from the police.

They used the path past the Farrows' barn on the way to the road. George was out doing chores.

'Hi, Mr Farrow,' called Abby. She hadn't spoken to him since the day he'd accused her of stealing Moonie. She worried that she might not be welcome on his property. 'Is it all right to use this path? I don't know any other way to get back to the Piersons' from my house.'

'No problem, Abby. Use it any time you like. Abby,' he stopped her from going further, and walked toward her. 'I want to apologize for thinking you took Moonie out of the barn that night.'

'It's okay, Mr Farrow. Lucy told me what happened.'

'She did?' He was obviously surprised.

'Yes. We're friends, now.'

'Well, I'll be. That makes me very happy, Abby.' He stood on the path smiling and scratching his head. 'I hope you come by real often.'

'Thanks, Mr Farrow.' A weight lifted off Abby's shoulders. She hadn't even known that it was there. She liked Mr Farrow and was glad to put past misunderstandings to rest.

'That's a strange way to transport a coyote,' he noted, jovially.

'It's the only way I know,' Abby answered, smiling. 'He was injured, but he's healing well.' She patted Cody to calm his fears. He'd tensed up when George Farrow got close.

Just then a face appeared in the upstairs window of the farmhouse.

'Abby!' Lucy hollered. 'Stay right there! I'll be right down!'

Cody was getting very nervous now. There were too many people around for his comfort level. Abby swung down, lifted Cody off the saddle and put him on the ground. In a flash he disappeared into the bushes.

'That's more like the Cody I know,' said George Farrow. 'I'm glad to have a chance to talk to you, Abby. I've been feeling badly about the way I fired you.'

Abby started to tell him that it was all right, but he wanted to finish. 'No, Abby, let me say my piece. I didn't treat you right, and I'm sorry. I hope we can be friends again.'

'For sure. I understand how it happened. If I were you, I probably would've thought the same.'

'That's very generous of you, Abby. Oh, and good luck tomorrow in the steeplechase. You sure can ride, and I know Moonlight Sonata will try her hardest.' He looked at the pretty mare with fondness, and stroked her neck, then stepped back and looked up at the cloudy sky. 'I'd better finish the chores before the rain starts,' he said. 'See you soon.'

'For sure.' Abby waved goodbye as he disappeared into the barn.

'Well?' whispered Lucy.

'Well, what?' responded Abby.

'The papers! What happened? Did you get them?'

'Lucy, I'd like to tell you, but I'm not supposed to say anything at all about this.'

'I'm the one who told you about them! I even drew the maps!'

'I know, I know. All right. I'll tell you this, and only this. The police have the papers.'

'The police? How did the police get them?'

'I said I'd tell you only that one thing, Lucy. When I can tell you more, I will.'

'Well, don't we sound important!'

'Lucy, this isn't a game. It's serious stuff. The police won't even tell me what's in them! I promise I'll tell you when I can, okay?'

Lucy grudgingly agreed. She wasn't happy about it, but she realized it was a losing battle.

'Abby, when can I start riding lessons again?'

Abby groaned. 'Lucy, you're going to drive me crazy.'

'You said I'd be great, remember? And I already promised not to pull any stunts.'

'How do I know you won't?'

'I promise. Scout's honour.'

'Lucy, you're not a scout.'

'So?'

'Oh, all right. We'll start after the steeplechase and when I hear about the papers. Until then, I won't be able to concentrate on anything else.'

'Fair. Thanks, Abby! See you later!'

Lucy ran back to the house, pyjamas flapping and slippers covered in mud. Abby chuckled as she remounted Moonie. She couldn't help liking Lucy.

As she and Moonie crossed the road, a police cruiser pulled into the Piersons' driveway. It was seven-thirty, and the lights were on in the kitchen. Through the window, Abby could see Laura bustling around preparing breakfast.

Milo Murski got out of the car and walked to the kitchen door in his deliberate, unhurried way.

'Hello, Mr Murski!' called Abby from Moonie's back.

Milo turned. 'Abby. Just the person I wanted to see. I've got news about the folder. Can we talk?'

Abby had been waiting for this minute impatiently, but now a cold fear gripped her heart and sweat trickled down her arm. She badly wanted to know, but if the news was disappointing she wasn't sure she could bear it. She called to him. 'Why don't you get a coffee while I untack Moonie. I'll be right there.'

Not waiting for his response, Abby trotted off to the barn.

She watched from the stable window and saw him enter the farmhouse. She slipped off the saddle and bridle, brushed Moonie and picked out her feet. She walked her out to the front field and removed her halter, watching as Moonie rolled and shook herself off. Moonie threw her head at Abby and nickered.

'You think I should go in now, little girl?'

Moonie snorted.

'Okay. But I think I know what I'll hear. "There's nothing we can do. We have to wait and see. We need more proof." Adults!'

Abby took a deep breath and walked into the house. They were all at the table with coffee and toast.

Pete had a strange look on his face.

Laura was at the stove with her back to Abby. She turned. Tears streamed down Laura's face.

Abby's heart sank. She knew it. It was all for nothing. The burglary, getting shot at, Cody almost killed, being locked up, Pete's rescue. It was all a charade. Abby could feel her own tears coming.

'Abby!' Laura ran to her and hugged her tightly. 'Abby! You did it!'

'What?' Still clasped in Laura's embrace, Abby turned her head to look at Pete. He was wiping a tear and nodding at her.

'You did it, Abby. The papers.'

'What about the papers? What's going on? Someone tell me!'

Laura finally released her iron grip. Abby earnestly looked from one face to the next.

Milo spoke. 'Abby, you'd better sit down.'

Abby sat. If Laura hadn't pushed a chair under her, she would have fallen to the floor.

'The papers are very significant. The Crown lawyers have gone over them with a fine-toothed comb, and have verified the contents.'

'What's in them? How do they change things? Will Dad be let out?'

'Hang on, Abby,' chuckled Milo. 'Let me explain. These papers contain such vital information that the Crown has made an application to the Court of Appeal. It's being presented by our top Crown counsel. Since this is new evidence, it obviously wasn't considered at the first trial. That's why it's called new evidence.'

'What do the papers say? Who committed the crime? Who did this to Dad?' Abby's fingers clenched the bottom of her chair tightly. She sat rigid, listening intently. The only thing that moved were her toes, wiggling nervously on the bottom rung.

Milo Murski pursed his lips. He wanted Abby to understand the procedure perfectly without telling her details that he wasn't at liberty to discuss. Abby sat in the kitchen chair, waiting, willing herself to be still.

'Let me explain,' he repeated. 'The Court of Appeal has three choices. One, they can disregard this new evidence if they consider it irrelevant, and sustain the guilty conviction. Two, they can order a new trial. Three, they can overturn the conviction by substituting a finding of not guilty.'

'Right on the spot?'

'Right on the spot.'

'And Dad would go free?'

'And your dad would go free.'

'So if they think the new evidence proves his innocence, they'll let Dad out today?'

'Yes. In fact, they'd have to release him immediately. Otherwise they'd be holding him unlawfully.'

Abby could sit still no longer. She jumped out of her chair and paced the length of the kitchen. She stopped and faced Milo Murski. 'Inspector Murski?'

'Yes, Abby?'

'Do you think this evidence is powerful enough to do that?'

'To have him released? I personally think it is.'

Abby whirled around to face the window. She stumbled over to the sill, and stared outside. She was trying to come to terms with this information. It was so amazing that she wasn't sure she should allow herself to believe it. Absent-mindedly she watched Moonie graze. The mare lifted her head and looked directly at Abby through the window. Somehow, that action helped give Abby strength. She knew what she had to do.

Abby addressed Milo directly, in a quiet but determined tone. 'Then, there'd be a new trial to convict the real thief, wouldn't there? So everyone would finally know that Dad has always been innocent.'

Milo answered thoughtfully. 'Yes, Abby. Your father would be exonerated.'

'Good. Does Dad know about any of this?' Her voice was very quiet, wavering with contained emotion.

'Not yet. The warden, Jim Price, was told to hold on to him, pending new instructions, so your father probably wonders if something might be happening. He'll be informed promptly when the judgement comes down.'

'And when will that happen?'

'Could be within hours.'

Abby nodded and looked out the window again. Moonie was still looking at her. Abby tried to stay calm, but it was increasingly difficult. She wanted to cry, to scream, to laugh hysterically, to run around the world. She took a deep breath and turned to speak to Pete. She was trying hard to control her emotions. Her voice was a little louder now.

'We should go now. To Kingston. To be with him when the judgement comes down.'

Pete and Laura were caught off guard. They looked startled. Before either one could speak, Milo jumped in. 'Abby, I wouldn't do that.'

'Why not?'

'We don't know when it's coming down, Abby. Or what it'll be. Maybe they'll throw the whole thing out.'

'But you don't think so.'

'No, I don't think they'll throw it out, but nothing is guaranteed.'

'And when would the judgement likely come down?'

'I can only guess. I really can't say.'

'I know that. If we go to Kingston for nothing, at least we can visit him. If we go and he's released, we can drive him home! Don't you see? There's no down side. Let's go!'

'Abby, let's think this out,' Milo said with authority.

Abby wasn't listening. She looked for an ally. 'Mrs Pierson? Don't you think we should go to Kingston?'

Laura was flustered. She didn't know what to say. She wanted to support Abby but she didn't want to contradict Milo. 'Abby, maybe we should wait. Your mother is coming home today. She shouldn't come home to an empty house.'

That was the breaking point.

Abby leapt forward, startling everyone in the room with her fierceness. 'Why not? Why can't she come home to an empty house? I come home every day to an empty house! Empty of love, of food, of happiness. Empty of everything. I come home to a stinking, filthy, empty house with empty liquor bottles and rotting garbage, and a drunken, smelly, drooling, rotten mother unconscious on the couch!'

She was yelling, red in the face with emotion and unable to stem the flood of words. Tears gushed from her eyes, her face contorted and her hands clenched and unclenched as she swung her arms around helplessly. 'My dad has been sitting in a stupid cell for something he didn't do, and he shouldn't be there one more minute! We should be there when he gets let out and you all know it! We should be there to drive him home! He shouldn't stay in there one damned minute longer than he has to. Why can't anybody understand that?'

Pete said, 'Abby, he might not be released for days, if at all.'

'Abby, dear, try to understa – ' Laura started to say.

Abby cut her off. 'No! You try to understand! I've tried to do everything everybody wants me to do and now I want one thing and nobody lets me do it! I'd drive myself if I could, and then you could all sit by the phone and wait until hell freezes over! And don't use my mother as an excuse! My mother can sit in an empty house for one day! She *should* sit in an empty house! Maybe she'd figure out what's is like for me! At least it's a clean house because I cleaned it!'

Abby suddenly stopped yelling. She looked at the stricken faces of her most precious friends, the Piersons. She registered Milo Murski's shock. Horrified at the things she'd said, Abby clamped her hands to her mouth. She felt horrible.

'I'm so sorry,' she mumbled as she flung open the kitchen door and ran. Cody was right on her heels.

Chapter Seventeen

Trouble

I am amazed, methinks, and lose my way
Among the thorns and dangers of this world.
– Shakespeare, *King John*, IV, iii

ABBY STUMBLED down the road to Highway 10. She wiped her eyes and tried to sort her thoughts. She'd embarrassed herself beyond belief. She'd said nasty, irretrievable things about her mother, things that her mother would never forgive. The Piersons must think she was the most despicable girl on earth. And they'd been so kind to her. She could never face them again. She had nowhere to go but to her father. Maybe he'd understand. And even if he didn't understand, he'd still love her. Abby was certain of that.

Why was she so certain he'd understand? she wondered. She herself didn't understand why she'd said what she said. Abby was deeply ashamed of herself.

The morning skies darkened. It was starting to rain. Clouds had blown in quickly from the northwest. Earlier that morning it had been so different from now. Riding Moonie with Cody on the saddle seemed light years ago.

Abby calculated that it was nine o'clock or so. She had no money, nothing in her pockets, no raincoat and nowhere to turn. She felt she had no alternative but to hitchhike to Kingston.

In the pit of her stomach, Abby wasn't sure how good an idea hitchhiking was. Cody would present a problem getting a ride, injured or not. She'd have to send him home. He was smart. He'd find his way back to her house or to the Piersons'. She looked down at her trusted friend, limping beside her with bandages on his leg and chest. She hoped he'd forgive her.

Cody knew something bad was happening. He knew that his

Abby was deeply unhappy. He also suspected that she was going to get herself in trouble. She should go back now. He wasn't sure she'd listen, but he had to try.

Cody gently grabbed her hand in his mouth and pulled it.

'No, Cody. I can't go back. It's that simple.'

Cody darted in front of her and tripped her. 'Cody! Why did you do that?' Abby regained her balance.

'Here comes a car. Watch this.'

Abby turned to face the car, and stuck her thumb out. The car whizzed by, not even slowing.

Better luck next time, she told herself.

Cody had no idea what she was doing, but he knew it wasn't right. He grabbed her hand again.

'No! Go home, Cody! Go home!'

Cody stiffened. He must disobey.

'Now! Go home!' Abby ordered. She was upset. Frustrated, angry and ashamed. She screamed at Cody, 'Go home!'

Cody didn't move. Abby ran at him, waving her arms. She chased him into the woods at the edge of the road, crying and screaming at him. She'd never done anything like this before. She knew that she'd lost control of herself even as she was doing it . But Cody couldn't come with her. Nobody would give a ride to a girl with a coyote She must get to Kingston!

The police cruiser passed while she was chasing Cody into the woods. The men didn't see her.

Abby walked back to the road and stuck out her thumb again. Cody lurked in the bushes, watching. He must get help for his Abby. She was in a new kind of danger. Danger from herself. He turned and ran. He would bring the Good Man.

The rain came down hard. The wind was picking up, sending sheets of rain landing in rows on the black highway. Abby stood with feet planted on the ground, soaking hair and clothes plastered to her body, jaw clenched, and thumb firmly pointing toward Kingston and her father.

Back in the Piersons' kitchen, Laura and Pete argued.

'I tell you we should look for her, Pete.' Laura peered anxiously out the window. All she could see was rain. 'She'll catch her death of cold.'

'For the tenth time, Milo's out there looking, Laura. He told us to sit tight, and that's what we'll do.' Pete's lips were pursed stubbornly, but inside he was as worried as Laura.

'He told us to sit tight because he thinks we're too old.'

'Too old for what?'

'For anything. I could see it in the way he looked at us. He might as well have said, "There, there, old folks, it'll be all right. Just put your shrivelled old feet up and rest by the fire while us real men go to work."'

'Stop it, Laura. He said no such thing.'

'Might as well have.'

'He's out there now, looking for her.'

'And what good is that? He can't see three feet in front of him with this rain.' Laura wasn't about to give up.

'So how could we see any better?'

'We love her more. We'd look harder.' Laura began to cry softly. Abby was out there somewhere, horribly upset, and Laura feared the worst.

'Now, now, Laura sweetie.' Pete relented. He hated to see her so sad, and he wanted to find Abby every bit as much. He stood up and took her in his arms. 'I'll go look, if you'll feel better.'

'I want to come, too. You drive, I'll look.' Without waiting another second, Laura threw on her rain slicker and tossed Pete his jacket and cap. She slid into her boots, and then began to pack food in a cardboard box.

'Pete, honey, get some blankets and sweaters. She'll be cold and wet when we find her.'

'Right. I'll leave the door unlocked and a note for Murski in case he finds her and comes back here.' He stopped in mid-flight. 'How will we know if she's here, if we're out driving?'

'We'll call from pay phones or restaurants every so often.'

Pete nodded. Action was far preferable to sitting and waiting, he thought, even if they were disobeying police orders.

The windshield wipers worked steadily, but the rain came down faster than they could wipe. Pete drove slowly while Laura squinted and craned her neck in every direction. She saw where they were going.

'I don't think she'd have gone home, Pete. I have a hunch that she's headed to Kingston.'

'I feel the same, Laura, but Milo's checking the roads to the highway. We'll go to her house first, to be sure, then double back. We'll stop and see if she's come back to our place, and then we'll keep on going.'

'If that's what you think, Pete.'

'That's what I think. Do you have a better idea?'

'No. I just want to find her.'

The Malone farm looked deserted, but Pete got out of the car to look anyway. He checked the doors. They were all locked. There was no sign of life in any of the rooms he could see from the windows, and there was no water or mud on the floors by the doors. Abby hadn't come home. He got back into the car and drove out.

'Now we'll see if she's back at Merry Fields.' Pete tried to appear calm for Laura, and he thought he was doing a fine job.

'Pete, you can stop grinding your teeth. It's driving me crazy.'

There was no sign of Milo's cruiser, but a bicycle was propped up at the Piersons' door. A tall young man stood under the stoop, dripping wet. It wasn't until they were up the drive that the Piersons' realized who it was.

'Sam!' called Laura. 'Go in and get out of the rain. The door's unlocked.'

Sam didn't hear her. He ran out to the car and opened Laura's door.

Pete leaned across Laura and said, 'Sam, Abby's not here, is she?'

'No. I've been knocking, and there's no answer.'

'Do you think you could help us out?'

'Yes, of course. Anything.' Sam sensed their concern.

'Could you wait for Abby? She's gone missing. If she comes back, tell her we're out looking for her. We'll phone every hour to check in with you.'

'She's missing?' Sam's brow was furrowed.

'She's upset, that's all,' responded Laura. 'You'll get the whole story later.' Laura eyed the soaking, puzzled boy. 'It'll be fine, Sam. Don't worry. Now get in the house and dry yourself off. There are clean clothes in the dryer. And make yourself a hot lunch.' She closed the car door as Sam ran to the house through the rain.

'We'd better get going, Laura. No telling how far she's got.'

'We should've followed her as soon as she left.'

Pete couldn't disagree.

Cody ran along the side of the road toward Merry Fields, aching all over. He hated leaving his Abby alone. He must find the Good Man. The Good Man helped him before. Finally the rain was easing off. It wasn't hurting his eyes any more. Every time a car or truck came along, Cody looked at it hard, and sniffed the air thoroughly. Not many vehicles had passed. One truck had had a familiar shape and smelled like cows. Cody had run out to stop it, and had narrowly missed being killed. He would be more careful.

Abby felt drained and unhappy. She was wet through to her skin, and the wind was chilling her. Nobody was stopping to pick her up. One family had slowed down. Abby had been hopeful and relieved, but when the car window came down, a woman wearing a tiny, flowery hat had scolded her harshly. 'God will punish you for your sins!' she'd screamed. 'Go home where you belong!' The window had closed and the car drove on.

Abby was left standing at the side of the road with her mouth hanging open. Was she committing a sin? Against whom? And where was home, anyway? With her mother or her father? The woman's condemnation cut her deeply. Abby's confidence seeped out of her like air from a balloon.

But wait. Here was another car. She stuck out her thumb and looked eagerly at the driver. He slowed down and came to a stop at the side of the road. Abby's heart soared. She'd get to Kingston after all.

'Where are you heading?' the driver shouted, after he reached over and opened the passenger door for her.

'Kingston!' Abby called as she ran to his car.

'Kingston? That's quite a way.'

'I know. Where are you going?' She leaned in to talk to him.

'Toronto.'

'Could you drive me to the 401?'

'Sure. Hell, I'll drive you all the way to Kingston.'

Something stopped her from getting in. Something wasn't right. Abby was confused. She looked at the man closely. He appeared normal. He was dressed normally. But there was an air about him that wasn't normal.

'Get in! What are you waiting for?'

'Why would you drive me all the way to Kingston, when you're going only as far as Toronto?'

'Why all the questions? I feel like being a good Samaritan. Get in, it's wet out there. You'll be nice and dry in here with me.'

The little doubt flickered again in Abby's gut. She needed to get to Kingston and away from here. But her instincts told her to wait for the next ride.

'You know, I just remembered, it's my friend's birthday and I have to go to her party.' Even as the lie came out of Abby's mouth, she could hear how lame it sounded. She cringed.

'You had your thumb out. I stopped. Now, don't be silly. Get in the car.' The man smiled reassuringly.

'I have to go.'

'Get in the car!' His smile abruptly disappeared. He opened the driver's-side door. Abby turned and ran.

'Pete! Look! Is that Cody?' Laura had been watching a small dark dot getting bigger and bigger until it began to take the shape of a dog. Something about its lopsided action had gotten her attention, and now she was certain. The rain was subsiding and the sun was trying to come out from behind the clouds. She was able to get a really good look at him.

'Pete! Stop the car! It's Cody!'

'By George, you're right.' He pulled off the road and stopped the car. Cody, gasping for air and in pain, ran right up to them.

Laura jumped out and opened the back door for him.

'Pete, look at his bandages. They're soaked with blood!'

'He must've re-opened the wounds by running.'

Cody scrambled onto the back seat as best he could. Laura got in again and closed her door.

Immediately, Cody slid onto the front seat and put his paws on the dashboard. His nose flattened on the windshield and his eyes glared straight ahead. He howled urgently.

Pete had no doubts. 'He's telling us that Abby's down the road this way. Let's go!'

'I hope the poor girl's all right.' Laura's mouth pressed into a worried frown.

Cody didn't move from his post at the windshield. Quiet howls involuntarily emanated from his throat. They drove quickly and silently, scanning both sides of the road for signs of Abby.

Cody's quiet howls got louder. At the sight of a car at the side of the road up ahead, he growled and wailed.

'Lord a'mighty, Pete! I'll go deaf!'

Pete didn't respond. There were two people struggling beside the parked car, and one of them had a wet blond ponytail. His heart beat faster. His knuckles showed white on the steering wheel. He swerved off the road leaning on the horn, and bumped into the rear of the car. They came to an abrupt halt.

'Stay in the car, Laura,' he ordered firmly as he opened his door. Cody jumped over him and out of the car before Pete could get one leg on the ground.

Suddenly the air was filled with human screams and horrible wild yips and howls. By the time Pete got around his car, the struggle was over. Cody, snarling, was keeping the horror-stricken man down on the ground, motionless.

Abby flew into Pete's steady arms as soon as she saw him. 'Thank you, thank you,' she whispered, trying to catch her breath.

Pete hugged her tightly. 'Now you get right into the car.'

Laura was behind them. She pried Abby away from Pete and helped her to the passenger seat of the car. Once they were safely inside, she locked all the doors, and put her arms around the frightened girl.

Pete's eyes had never lost contact with the man on the ground, who was now white with fear and making whimpering sounds. Cody held firm.

'What did you do to her?' Pete barked.

'Nothing, I swear!'

'You're a liar. I saw you fighting with her.'

'That's not true!'

'Then you tell me, mister. What happened?'

'She was hitchhiking. I stopped to give her a ride.'

'And?'

'And nothing! I swear!'

Pete was enraged. He pushed Cody off the prone man and grabbed his shirt. The trembling man staggered to his feet and made a desperate dash to his car. Pete took hold of the man's arm and spun him around, landing a blow square in the man's startled face.

The surprised look was replaced by a nasty, hateful leer. 'You think you're tough, old man? You're just a stupid, doddering old fool.' He pushed Pete hard, throwing him off-balance. Pete stumbled and fell backward onto the muddy bank.

Cody, quick as lightning, sprang at the man, ripping his shirt and tearing into the flesh of his chest with his claws. Taken by surprise, the man was once again on the soggy ground, a captive of the angry coyote.

Pete struggled to get back on his feet. As he regained his bearings, he heard the sound of a car pulling onto the gravel shoulder.

'Milo!' he called. It was a police cruiser driven by his young friend. 'I've never been happier to see your face.'

Milo leapt out of the cruiser and took a good look. 'Seems Cody's got things under control here.' He waved to his partner, John Bains. 'Bring the cuffs!' he ordered.

In the front seat of the car, Laura held Abby close to her and turned on the heat to dry her clothes. Abby was grateful. Together they watched as the policemen took the licence plate number and checked the man's driver's licence. John Bains got in the cruiser and made a call. When he emerged, his face was stern. He immediately slipped the handcuffs onto the man's wrists and shoved him into the back seat of the cruiser.

After a private consultation with Milo Murski, John returned to the cruiser and made another call.

Milo and Pete approached their car. Milo said to Abby, 'We need to talk.' They got into the car, Pete in the front and Milo in the back. Abby and Laura turned to face them.

'Were you hitchhiking, Abby?'

Abby studied the stitching on the seat cover. 'Yes.'

'Do you know how lucky you are that we found you?'

Abby, embarrassed, looked up and briefly met his eyes. 'Yes.'

'Let me tell you who stopped to pick you up. That man has been wanted for six months. He stalks the high schools. Did you hear me, Abby?'

She whispered, 'Yes.' Laura held her tighter.

Milo rubbed his temples with his hands. He was sickened by perverts like this man. 'Had he got you into his car, Abby, there would've been an unhappy ending.'

'I'm sorry. I'm really sorry. I've never done it before.'

'And she'll never do it again, will you, dear?' intoned Laura with her soothing voice.

'No. I never will.' Abby fought back the tears. 'I wanted to be with my father, and I said awful things about my mother ... and I ... and everybody looked at me weird and ... That's why I....'

'No matter, Abby,' said Milo, kindly. He realized that she was suffering enough without his standard lecture. 'It's over and done with. We have our man, and you've learned a valuable lesson. When you stick out your thumb on the highway, you invite any creep that's passing by to help himself.'

'Thank you, Milo,' said Pete, 'It was lucky you came by when you did. I don't know how long we could have held on to him.'

'I'd already passed this way once. Don't know how I missed her.' He took off his hat, scratched his head and smiled grimly. 'I'm glad we've got you safe with us, Abby.'

'Thank you. I'm glad I'm safe, too. I'm sorry.'

'What's past is past,' said Pete.

There was silence in the car.

'Let's get home and dry off,' said Laura firmly, trying to lighten the air, 'before we all catch a chill.'

Pete nodded agreement. 'Abby, my dear, we've got work to do. Don't forget, tomorrow's the big day. Tomorrow we run the steeplechase.'

Chapter Eighteen

The Steeplechase

When I bestride him, I soar, I am a hawk:
he trots the air; the earth sings when he touches it ...
– Shakespeare, *Henry V*, III, vii

THE DAY OF the steeplechase dawned sunny and hot. It had
rained hard all the day and night before, turning the dry dusty
ground to slippery mud. The air was heavy with moisture and the
greenery looked brighter after the showers, and slightly blurred by
a hazy film of mist. Abby listened to the buzzing and humming
and chirping all around her and marvelled at the new life the
downpour had given to mosquitoes and birds alike.

Abby sat quietly on Moonie, thinking about the hitch-hiking
fiasco. She was still embarrassed, even though the Piersons had
been very understanding about it.

She looked around the grounds of the hunt club. The large
parking lot was full of mud-splashed cars and trucks and horse-
trailers, and the latecomers parked on both sides of the lane.

'What a crowd,' she said to Moonie, thinking how people love
an event to celebrate the end of summer. The summer had flown
by, she realized, and soon school would start again. Abby pushed
that thought out of her head, knowing that her next thought
would be about where they'd be living and what school she'd be
starting, and she wanted to concentrate on the race. She wanted to
know what had happened with the new evidence, too, but she
couldn't do anything about it now. She had a race to run.

Moonie flicked her tail constantly, ridding herself of flies. She
stomped her front foot impatiently. She was sweaty already with
the humidity. Abby nudged her forward with her heel. 'Let's find
a cool spot,' she said. 'We've got time.'

A festive crowd was forming by the starting line, happily

anticipating the race. This was the first steeplechase to be held in Caledon in ten years. There had been nasty accidents in the past.

The most shocking had been when the Master of the London Hunt, a beautiful young woman, had broken her neck in a dramatic fall in full sight of the crowd. She was winning the race, going hell for leather, when her horse misjudged a jump and hit it at full speed. She was thrown forward out of the saddle and onto the horse's left shoulder, where she clung with great determination and the athletic prowess of an acrobat. The horse managed to find its feet, and in its panic ran faster and faster. She was unable to slow it down, hanging on but sliding down under the chest of the horse. She'd lost the reins and the empty stirrups flapped at the horse's sides, urging him on. She knew she had to jump off before they came to the next large hurdle. She pushed herself away as hard as she could to avoid the thundering hooves. She hit hard, rolled many times, and then didn't move. Bleeding and unconscious, she'd been put on a stretcher and taken away in an ambulance. She eventually recovered from the fall, to everyone's relief, but the accident unnerved a lot of riders. Abby'd heard the gruesome story so many times from people who'd been there that she could picture it vividly. That year had been the last year it was run. Until today.

Today, with the Colonel's large prize offering and human nature's bloodthirsty enjoyment of danger, there was an excited buzz in the air. Cars were still coming in. Abby guessed that the club would make a huge profit once the betting money was added to the price of admission.

Separate from the crowd, they walked quietly through the adjoining glen into a small pond where Moonie cooled her legs and took a long welcome drink. She pawed the water and splashed herself all over. Abby knew she wanted to roll.

'And why not?' she asked Moonie. 'We've got a little time.' Abby moved her out of the pond and slid out of the saddle. She swiftly removed the tack and placed it on a dry area of ground. 'Go on, Moonie, have a quick dip.' Abby pushed her flank to encourage her into the pond. The hot, sweaty mare hesitated for only a moment, then plunged into the deepest part. She swam a few strokes and then returned to the shallow side. Moonie pawed the water and snorted, shaking her head up and down happily. She thrust her nose into the water and blew bubbles. Abby laughed aloud. Then Moonie dropped to her front knees and lay down in the shallowest water and rolled. Up she came, all excited, and bounded out of the pond. She shook herself off like a dog, not concerned at all that she soaked Abby from head to toe.

'Holy, Moonie! Thanks a lot!'

A worried-looking Pete appeared at the edge of the pond. 'Abby! What are you doing? I've been looking everywhere for you! We've no time to lose. They're gathering at the gate. I've got you registered, and here's your number. Let's get Moonie tacked up and over there right away!'

As he talked, Abby threw the saddle over Moonie's soaking back. She slipped the bridle onto her head, and Pete tied the number over Abby's crash vest. It was number 73.

Before her feet were in the stirrups they were moving toward the gate.

'Abby!' called Pete as he hurried behind her. 'Have fun, and keep her steady. Don't worry about the competition, just run your own race. No more rehearsals, this is show time!'

'You bet, coach!' Abby yelled, and trotted on ahead toward the ever-growing crowd. A bright pink chiffon scarf caught her eye. Mrs Pierson was here to watch the race. Abby was very happy that her good friend had come. She cheerfully rode to the starting area.

There were more horses entered in the race than Abby had reckoned. A couple of them looked unfit to Abby, and some of the people looked out of shape, too. One stout woman was suffering with the heat already and breathed heavily. But mostly the horses appeared fast and keen, and the riders seemed focused and competitive. Thoroughbreds outnumbered any other breed. They have the speed and the stamina for racing, and they keep their speed over jumps. Moonie was the smallest horse there by far, and Abby the youngest rider.

Abby started feeling nervous. Next to these hot, tall, powerful thoroughbreds, her little quarter horse seemed inadequate. And this was her first race, while some of these riders looked almost bored, they'd raced so many times.

There were over twenty entrants, and they'd all be vying for the best position over sixteen jumps and three kilometres. She began to think about how dangerous it could be, and her confidence flagged badly. Not only could she not possibly win, but they could possibly get hurt. She started to feel as if she'd been foolish and anxiously wondered if they should race at all.

'Moonie, Mr Pierson said we were here to have fun. Does this look like fun to you? Me neither, so let's get out of here. Let's stay out of trouble and live longer, okay?'

Just then there was a hush over the crowd. Moonie's sensitive ears pricked up and Abby turned to view the object of all the attention.

Diablo. The Colonel stood proudly with the sleek black racehorse, the likes of which Abby had never seen. So this was Diablo. He was fiery and lean, stomach tucked up in racing condition. Muscled and aggressive, he jumped and snorted and reared and shook his head. Lucy, Pam and Annie, carefully keeping out of kicking range, looked pleased to be part of the entourage. People gave him a wide berth as he turned and twisted and tried to get free of the jockey's grip. The jockey was small, perched up on the horse's withers, wearing a racing cap with orange and lime green racing colours. The Colonel arrogantly accepted slaps on his back and congratulations. He puffed greedily on his cigar and gloated.

Abby felt even more demoralized. She was to race against this team of professional jockey and high-bred speed machine?

She intently watched the reaction around her. The heavy-breathing woman pulled out of the race. Just as well, thought Abby, I'll be joining her. Others looked concerned. One man told another that he was going to complain to the authorities. This was an amateur race. The other man told him there were no rules, so if he didn't like the competition he should leave.

Abby looked for Pete to tell him she was going to bow out. She hoped he wouldn't mind too much, after all the anticipation. There he was, sitting with Laura in lawn chairs they'd brought from home. They waved when they saw her looking at them, and Pete gave her a thumbs-up. Abby grinned weakly at him and nodded. She had to go tell him about her change of heart.

Then she remembered what her mother had said from her hospital bed that morning. Her voice on the phone had been steady and clear. 'Abby, I'm so proud of you. Good luck, and stay out of danger. I love you. You're a brave girl, Abby. You have the heart of a lion.'

And her father had told her from the prison, 'I'll be riding with you every step of the way. Let your spirit soar, Abby, and your little horse will soar with you.'

Abby had no choice. She couldn't pull out of the race after those words of support. She'd have to at least try to make those words come true.

'Good luck, Abby!' called Laura, blowing kisses. The colour had returned to her cheeks and the bruises were fading, and her ribs and nose were healing well. Abby blew kisses back. She dearly loved this sympathetic lady with her bright pink headscarf.

'Abby! Abby! Over here!' Abby looked around. Who was calling her?

'Abby! It's me! Leslie!' Suddenly Abby saw a pretty face and curly dark hair. Her best friend was running toward her as fast as she could.

'Leslie! You're here!'

'Yes, I just got back from camp last night! I left a good luck note in the tree, but I guess you didn't look. I bet all my allowance on you, so you better win!'

'You better believe it!' Abby's heart thrilled at her friend's confidence in her.

'Abby! Good luck!' It was Sam, pushing through the crowd. He grabbed her outstretched hand and squeezed it hard. He kissed it, and said, 'Come back safe, Abby!'

'I will, Sam!' Abby was going to run the race the best she could. She had a cheering section she couldn't let down. Moonie couldn't stand still any longer. The mare danced on the spot in her eagerness to be off.

'Get over to the gate, Abby!' urged Pete. 'Showtime!'

Without another word, Abby and Moonie cantered to the gate. They stood, tense. The contestants were all bunched up waiting for the starting shot. Moonie, cooled by her dip in the pond, was ready to go. Her delicate ears were pointed rigidly forward in anticipation of whatever lay ahead. She was eager but restrained. Moonlight Sonata wasn't plagued by any self-doubt. Abby stroked the brave mare's neck and felt reassured by her composure. 'Let's give it a whirl, sweet little Moonie,' she whispered.

The black horse was to their left, apart from the rest. No other horse risked getting near him. He dripped with sweat, and snorted and pawed the ground. His nostrils flared and showed bright red veins, a sure sign of agitation. Better stay clear of Diablo, thought Abby.

The starting gun went off. The black horse reared high, thrashed his front legs and whinnied. Without delay, Moonie gathered her weight onto her hocks and lunged forward, joining the stream of horses leaving the gate. They dashed past the black, and the race was on.

Moonie eagerly tore into the woods at great speed, then almost immediately had to put on the brakes. There was a pile-up of horses in the woods straight ahead. Four horses were already jammed together on the path, each rider determined to be the first through. A fifth horse slid to a halt behind them, worsening the situation. This is lunatic, Abby thought. She didn't know whose fault it was, but the accusations and swearing indicated that a slow horse had hogged the path and wouldn't allow others to pass. Coolly and skilfully, Moonie picked another route around the horse-jam and quickly threaded back to the path. Once out of the woods, she shifted to high gear with a great burst of speed. Moonie had cleverly gained the lead and Abby wanted to stay there.

'Pace yourself, Moonie,' cautioned Abby. The little mare was running full speed ahead toward a three-and-a-half-foot wooden coop. To avoid a crash at the fence, Abby gave her a half-halt, a quick, firm tug on the reins, to get her attention. Moonie listened and settled in for the take-off. Just as she lifted off the ground, the black racehorse sailed out of thin air and over the jump with them, grazing Abby's shoulder sharply with his rear hoof. He landed lengths away from the coup and disappeared into the next grove.

He had talent, and lots of it, but he was dangerous to be around.

'Bye-bye, Diablo,' said Abby aloud. 'Good riddance!' She was much happier having him out of her riding space, even if it meant that he was ahead of her. She'd love to beat him. She'd enjoy watching that self-satisfied leer drop off the Colonel's smug face.

Abby didn't dwell on it. She wiped her mind clear of everything but the business of racing and the sheer thrill of it all. The warm, moist wind hummed and whistled in her ears as she sped across the fields. The landscape zoomed by on either side as Moonie galloped in large, ground-eating strides. This is pure, she thought. Pure, uncomplicated, intense. At this moment there was no room for anything else in her heart or her mind. Abby felt that together she and Moonie were something huge and powerful, a formidable combination.

She heard the rhythmic thudding of hooves behind her. They were getting louder. Moonie kept her pace as two long-legged thoroughbred horses passed her on either side. Abby got a quick look at them before she ducked her head, narrowly avoiding the clumps of mud that were flung at her by eight racing hooves. One of the thoroughbreds had a white face and the other was a dark brown. They ran in tandem, and disappeared around the bend.

Moonie galloped steadily. She'd found her perfect speed; fast but maintainable. Her ears pricked forward as she smoothly sailed over a solid ski jump and dealt with the mud on the other side. The coffin jump was coming up fast and Abby was concerned about that. Moonie had never seen one before, and because of the wide ditch underneath, most horses find them frightening. Abby looked over the jump, not down into the ditch, and pushed her on. Moonie never missed a beat.

Abby was riding well. Her muscles were toned, her mind was focused, her attention was complete. She was relaxed but alert, confident in Moonie and enjoying herself. She felt one with the horse.

Now she studied the difficult task that they faced next: a tall, narrow, free-standing gate. It stood alone with lots of room on both sides for a horse to run out. Abby knew that it was up to her. Given a choice in the matter, any horse would go around it. Abby positioned her reins low, hands together and maintaining a good contact with Moonie's mouth. She tightened her legs evenly and securely to give the little mare confidence that her rider was in control. Abby steered her in perfectly, straight and true, and asked her to take her jump. Moonie jumped. She never paused or balked. She took it like she'd taken everything so far; in stride, with speed and power. Abby grinned and praised her, 'You're a superstar, girl!'

They'd now passed the quarter point, were safely over four jumps and coming up to the water hazard.

Moonie dashed through the little grove of trees and turned the corner to the pond. There stood the black horse, lathered and looking mean. He was refusing to put his hoof into the water. It was far too wide to jump, and he'd be eliminated if he went around, so the jockey was whipping him and kicking him, and cursing at him. The jump judge stood with his check list in hand, watching. Abby suspected that if he hadn't been there, the jockey might have cheated.

Abby thought that the two thoroughbreds who'd passed her had gone through already, until she saw one of the riders struggling to get out of the pond.

'All right?' she called as they splashed through.

'Okay!'

Moonie leapt out the other side and powered along. She might not be the fastest horse here, thought Abby, but she's steady and honest. While the others falter and refuse, Moonie makes up time.

By Abby's reckoning they were running second. Then the black horse shot past like greased lightning. 'I hate seeing that horse's back end!' she said to Moonie. Diablo must have either decided to jump the pond or finally waded in. Either way, he was past them now. His speed was undeniable.

Moonie's pace had slowed a little, indicating fatigue. Abby pulled her in a bit more. She felt it was a good time to conserve energy. A big bay passed them at the next jump, a wide hedge, and a grey sped by just beyond.

There were four horses ahead of them now, and Moonie didn't seem to have a lot more to give. Abby decided to ease her into a slow canter and be satisfied to safely complete the course. Moonie dropped her head and relaxed her whole body. She breathed deeply, gathering her strength.

As they cantered along, a big chestnut horse powered past. 'Five, and counting,' Abby noted.

They were now halfway through the race. Heavy humidity, high temperatures, and tricky footing on the muddy ground conspired against all the contestants equally. Abby wondered how many had dropped out. She looked back to see where the other horses were, something her dad had warned her never to do. 'It doesn't change anything, it only slows you down. Just run your race,' he'd said.

His words came true as a sweaty, heaving bay clumped past, breathing noisily. Now Moonie geared into action. Abby could feel her renewed energy. Without seeming to exert herself, Moonie quickly outdistanced the bay and kept her speed over the next hurdle, a solid square box.

They now faced a deep, mucky field. The rains had come so hard after the drought that the ground hadn't yet absorbed all the water. Shiny patches on the surface indicated swampy conditions.

The chestnut hadn't made it. He limped horribly, lurching in great pain as his rider led him out of the mud. From the look of him, Abby assumed he'd bowed a tendon, an injury that could take at least six months to heal if it ever came right again. She felt sorry for them. It could happen to anyone.

To avoid that mischance, she steered Moonie along the edge of the field where the mud wasn't as deep. It cost time, but Abby knew it was the wisest choice.

Shouts of 'Loose horse!' suddenly came from behind. Abby could imagine the kind of trouble someone was having, but she'd learned her lesson last time she'd looked back and was passed by the bay. She must keep her concentration. There were lots of spectators and jump judges who would help. She didn't look back. They carried on, intent on their race.

Up ahead, there was a drop jump and then a large stone wall with only two strides between. The drop jump was a wide, earth-covered rise; the horses were expected to jump up onto it, then down off the far side. Moonie cantered to it calmly, sprang up and leapt off perfectly. 'Well done!' praised Abby, impressed again at her mount's courage.

Now they were facing the stone wall. Three, two, one, lift-off. Brilliant.

Danger.

At the same instant that they soared over the jump, Moonie and Abby saw the rider scrambling for safety on the other side of the wall. Moonie couldn't stop in midair, but she valiantly strained to alter her direction by twisting her body. However she accomplished it, her hooves managed to avoid the terrified man by a hair.

'I'll call the medics!' Abby assured him.

'Overtake the black!' he hollered. 'Son of a bitch! He ran us over!' He was clear of danger now, and very angry.

His horse wasn't so lucky. The big, strong grey stood with a drooping head and a dangling leg. Abby gasped as she realized that there was no cure but peaceful death from lethal injection. She couldn't leave an injured horse like this. It was horrible. She slowed.

'Get going! There's nothing you can do for him!' The man had tears running down his face. He shook his fist in the air. He was racked with grief. 'Get the black! Win the race for Silver Dollar!'

Abby was galvanized. She clenched her teeth and cried out to him, 'I will!' She dug her heels hard into Moonie's sides.

That made Moonie mad. Abby had never done that before. Moonie gave an angry little buck, and grabbed the bit in her teeth. She'd show Abby. If Abby wanted speed, Moonie'd give her speed. She raced faster than Abby ever suspected she could go.

Nose pushed straight out, ears flat back, legs flying, the valiant, defiant little horse ran. The jump ahead was large and solid, sturdily constructed of oak planks. Moonie didn't check her pace one bit, she simply took it in stride. It was scary but they made it, and Abby was amazed at her finesse.

The marker on the tree indicated a turn to the right, so Abby muscled her now-wilful charger into the turn. They were so close to a tree that they risked knocking Abby's knee-cap off. 'I'd hate to share an injury with the Colonel, Moonie,' Abby muttered. 'Give us some room.'

Coming out of the woods she could see the end of the course ahead. The rolling green hills of the hunt club lay at their feet as they jumped down the rocky bank for the final stretch. Four jumps left, three-quarters of a kilometre to go, and three horses to pass.

Moonlight Sonata tore on, her equine mind set firmly on winning. Every cell of her small body was intent on home. Abby, equally intense, let her run, thrilling at her speed. The next obstacle looked like a doghouse, and sat up on a rise between two trees. They careered over the dog-house jump without slowing and overtook the bay gelding on the other side. The bay didn't like that one bit. He sped up after her and came up to challenge with his ears flat back on his head. Moonie thrust out her neck and showed her teeth, telling him that he'd have to fight to win. She was confident and unfazed and pulled ahead of the confused gelding.

Abby could hear the crowd now, cheering and screaming them home. For a split second she imagined her own little cheering section, how joyful they'd be to see her so close to the front. She kept her concentration on the hedge ahead.

The bay gelding challenged again, and was neck and neck with Moonie as they leapt the vertical hedge, landing together at exactly the same instant. Moonie increased her speed, trying to outrun him. The bay caught up and passed her. Moonie flew faster, and was exactly even with him as they approached and challenged the white-faced thoroughbred that had passed Moonie before the pond. Now the three horses ran together, Moonie taking a stride and a half to every one the tall thoroughbreds took. Their legs were long but Moonie's heart was big.

The black was suddenly within reach. Abby could taste victory. She could feel Moonie's energy and there was lots to spare. Two jumps and three horses and a hill remained between them and the finish line.

The orange-and-green-silked jockey looked behind him, faltering and losing a costly stride. He suddenly realized that he couldn't dally. He cracked Diablo with his whip. The jockey had a look of desperation that made Abby wonder briefly if there was a penalty for losing.

Diablo didn't like being whipped, and understandably sidestepped to avoid another blow. The jockey momentarily lost his balance with the sudden shift, but corrected it quickly. Coming up to the second-last jump, an old wooden cart, he cracked the black again.

The black recoiled and reared. He'd had enough.

The two thoroughbreds that were running with Moonie were alarmed. They fell back. Moonie kept her speed. She was suddenly alone.

Taking her chance, she darted past Diablo, leaping the old cart jump and heading fast for the threaded tires. Abby could see the finish beyond. The bay recovered and joined her on her left. White-face came up on her right. They were all determined to win.

They were approaching the tire jump quickly, three abreast. Old tires had been strung together like beads on a necklace and piled three deep and two high. The jump was wide enough for two horses, but not three. It was a game of chicken now. Nobody wanted to give. Moonie kept pace with the others, and Abby made her decision. She was in the middle and she refused to be squeezed out. Somebody else would have to fall back. It wouldn't be her.

The black, with jockey perched forward and arms thrust front, was closing on them now, snorting heavily and sounding like a train.

The tire jump loomed. The bay, Moonie, and white-face leapt as one. Shoulder to shoulder, stirrup iron to stirrup iron, flank to flank. They safely landed in harmony, to the hysterical cheers of the crowd.

The black landed a millisecond behind them. He began to stride out. With his superior breeding and race-course fitness, he overcame them easily. He was sailing to the finish line, eating up the scenery as he galloped up the hill.

The jockey punched his fist high, proclaiming victory. He swung his whip grandly in the air and landed one last triumphant and unnecessary whack on the black's flank. The indignant horse bucked and twisted in the air, diving straight down to the ground. This buck was intended to remove the rider. It did.

The stunned jockey landed hard and rolled in front of Moonie as she galloped into the home stretch. She gathered her wits and jumped big to avoid the man. The leap propelled her across the finish line first. The bay and white-face tied for second, a head behind.

Moonie ran on, spooked by the fallen jockey and unaware that the race was over. People scattered out of her way, and Abby wrestled to get her under control. She dropped the left rein and hauled on the right with all her strength, pulling Moonie into a circle and bringing her to a stop.

She had the uncanny feeling that her father was watching.

Chapter Nineteen

Victory

My crown is in my heart, not on my head.
– Shakespeare, *Henry VI*, Part Three, III, i

PETE GRABBED her rein. 'Abby! Abby! We won! You were incredible. What a great race!' His youthful, intelligent eyes sparkled and danced in his handsome old face. His whole being radiated elation.

Abby slid down from Moonie, and hugged the mare's sweat-soaked head and neck. Pete hugged Abby and Moonie together, and the three of them buried their faces and clung together. When Pete pulled out of their joyful huddle, he had tears on his cheeks.

'You're crying, Mr Pierson!' exclaimed Abby.

'You should talk!' retorted Pete, and they laughed at each other and hugged again.

Leslie rushed up and shook Abby hard by the shoulders, jumping up and down with joy. 'Hooray, hooray, hooray!' Abby laughed delightedly at her friend's pleasure in her success, then her eyes fell on Sam, standing beside Leslie.

Abby couldn't say anything. She could only look. His beautiful dark brown eyes shone with pride. She knew she was blushing.

Sam smiled and stepped toward her. He pulled her to him and hugged her tightly. He said, 'Abby. You were terrific. I've never seen anything like the race you just won. I... I think you're great.' Then he shyly moved away to let all the other well-wishers get a chance to talk to her. Abby's heart swelled.

Now Laura pressed up to Abby, smiling and congratulating her. She beamed with unmasked delight, proud and pleased for her. Annie and Pam stood back, unsure of how to behave. Abby could see that they were reluctantly impressed.

Abby smiled a greeting and said, 'Hi, guys! Wasn't that wild?'

Annie recovered first, and said, 'Abby, you actually were fantastic. I wish I'd bet on you!'

'What were the odds?' Abby asked Pete.

'Fifty to one,' Pete answered jubilantly.

'No!' gasped Leslie. 'I put five dollars down. I just made two hundred and fifty dollars!' She ran to cash in her stub.

'And I made a thousand,' exclaimed Laura, 'by putting twenty dollars from the piggy on you.'

'Laura! You've never bet a penny before in your life,' Pete chided.

Laura winked at him. 'And I never will again, sweetie. I'll leave well enough alone.' She hugged Abby and whispered, 'I only bet on sure things.'

Pam grudgingly complimented Abby on her victory, a tribute that Abby graciously accepted.

Lucy stared at Moonie, then turned to Abby. 'I can't believe she won the race. I can't believe it. Little Moonlight. I really underestimated her. And you, too. I really thought Diablo would win, but I'm really, really glad you and Moonie did.' With that, Lucy gave Abby a big hug. 'Friends?'

'Friends,' responded Abby, smiling broadly.

Pete raised his hands and quieted the crowd around Abby. 'Moonlight Sonata needs walking out now, so would you please excuse us.' He gave Abby a leg up and cleared a path through the onlookers. Pete kept them back to let Abby walk away on Moonie. 'Keep her walking,' he instructed.

Abby kept an eye out for Sam as they threaded their way through the people walking toward their cars. 'Where is that guy?' she asked Moonie, hoping he'd appear to walk along with them.

Moonie didn't care at all about Sam and was happy to get away from all the people. She wanted to head straight for the pond. Since she was still too hot to drink, Abby steered her away. 'I promise I'll let you drink your fill and roll in the water in a few minutes, Moonie. You'll blow up like a balloon if you drink now.'

They walked past Pete's truck. The tarpaulin moved. Moonie shied away, and Abby held on tight.

'What's your problem, Moonie?' Abby asked. The tarp moved

again, revealing a very hot coyote, tongue out and ears at half mast.

'Cody! You could die under there on a day like today. Come on out, we'll go to the woods where there's shade.'

Cody suspiciously eyed the surrounding area. When he was convinced that there were no humans around he slipped out of the tarp and slithered down the side of the truck as best he could with his bandaged leg. Not waiting for Abby, he disappeared into the bushes beside the lane.

They strolled along a shady path and followed it as it twisted around toward the road and back. Walking along the cool paths, she replayed the race in her mind and felt amazed all over again that she'd won.

She'd call her father the minute she could get to a phone. She could hardly wait to tell him that they'd won the steeplechase. Remembering how she'd had a feeling that her father was watching the race, she smiled at herself and wished it could have been true. He would've loved it. Her adrenalin supply was slowing down, and fatigue was taking its place.

Then she thought of Silver Dollar, the grey gelding who'd broken his leg. She wondered if he'd been put out of his pain yet. At least the owner would know that Diablo and his jockey didn't win. There was some kind of justice in that, since their reckless quest for victory had caused such wasteful destruction.

By the time the path had circled to the pond, Abby felt that the mare was cool enough to drink. While she untacked Moonie, Cody slid into the refreshing water, lapping up the cool water. His bandages needed changing later, anyway, Abby thought. She released Moonie and sat on the ground to watch.

Moonie waded in. She splashed herself with her front right hoof then drank her fill standing knee-deep in the water. With no warning, she went down on her knees and flopped her rump down and rolled. Cody lunged at her and she shot to her feet and lunged back at him. They played for a few minutes, until Abby decided to cool herself off, too. She was hot and sweaty, and the sight of water was too inviting to resist. She pulled off her hat, gloves, number, crash vest, boots and socks, and dove in. Heaven, she thought.

Sheer heaven.

Leslie came running. 'Abby! Come quick. And ride Moonie. They're saying that you're disqualified because you rode away before giving back your number, or something weird like that. And the Colonel is saying that his granddaughter should get the prize money anyway because Moonie is still legally hers! Or her other grandfather's or somebody else's. Is that true? The papers haven't been processed yet, or something.'

Abby stood up in the pond, water pouring off her in sheets. 'What?' She called Moonie out and slapped the tack on the soaked horse. 'I don't know anything about the rules, Leslie. I hope Mr Pierson can straighten it out. Where's Sam?'

'Abby got a crush on Sammy?' Leslie teased.

'Oh, shut up, Les!' Abby didn't mind the ribbing.

Leslie laughed her joyful, bubbling laugh and said, 'Your secret's safe with me. Now get mo-oving!'

Cody had vanished. As Abby cantered past Pete's truck she assumed he'd be hiding under the tarp again. After his swim and a good drink of water, he'd be fine until they left the grounds. They went straight back to the starting point to defend their victory and find out what was going on.

As she got closer, she could see the Colonel standing on the judge's podium, gesturing largely. Pete was standing toe to toe with him, gesturing as well. The two judges, a man and a woman, looked as if they'd rather be anywhere else, and Lucy was trying to pull the Colonel away.

Abby slowed Moonie to a stop beside the podium. She didn't want to interrupt, so she sat quietly until Pete spied her.

'Abby,' he called. 'We may have a small problem here.'

'Small problem?' spat Colonel Bradley. 'That horse should be disqualified. It isn't registered to the proper owner!'

'I bought Moonie from George Farrow almost three weeks ago,' said Pete, obviously not for the first time.

'I know, I know, and you paid cash on the barrel. But you didn't bother to change the papers!' The Colonel was purple in the face. Abby wondered if he might have a heart attack.

Abby spoke up. 'May I ask the judges something?'

The female judge, grateful for the distraction, said, 'Yes, of course.'

'Did Moonie and I win the race?'

'Are you number 73?'

'Yes. Here's my number.' She handed the folded cardboard to the nearest judge, the man. He unfolded it and held it up.

The woman loudly declared, 'Number 73 fairly won the race. I see absolutely no problem.'

The male judge agreed. 'I concur. Number 73 is the official winner of the steeplechase. The ownership of the horse isn't our problem.'

The Colonel blew up in a rage. 'This is unconscionable! This is outrageous! And what of the registered owner? These people shouldn't receive the prize money! I should!'

Lucy interrupted. 'But, Grandfather, you've never been the owner. Grandpa Farrow owned her before he sold her to Mr Pierson.'

'Shut up, Lucy! Keep out of this!' he spat at her with horrifying venom.

Lucy turned pale, then hung her head and stepped down from the podium. She was shocked and humiliated.

George Farrow stepped up. He was furious. 'What kind of operation are you running here?' he asked the two astonished judges. 'My name is George Farrow. I owned Moonlight Sonata until I sold her to Mr Peter Pierson, standing right here, who is an honourable gentleman. He paid me in full. I have it here in writing that the horse has changed owners. Is that not sufficient?' He waved a piece of paper.

The two judges nodded their heads in unison, but the Colonel bellowed, 'Corruption!'

The male judge took a deep breath and said to the Colonel, 'I will have to ask you to leave. Your complaints have been considered and dismissed. If you have further complaints, we'll sit down later to discuss them.' He lifted his arm and summoned three men who'd been waiting for his signal. They were members of the club who'd gathered for support. Now they took the Colonel's arms and prepared to hoist him down from the podium.

Just then, police sirens blared as two cruisers and an armoured van drove straight across the field to the stand, through the crowds. Curious people scattered in every direction. They were definitely getting their money's worth today.

Milo Murski and John Bains got out of the first cruiser, and two officers got out of the second. A third and a fourth descended from the van. They all converged on the Colonel.

'I am here to arrest you, Kenneth Barrymore Bradley, on charges of fraud, obstruction of justice, perjury, unlawful confinement, and aggravated assault. Caution him, Officer Bains.'

'I'm the senior master of the gawddammed fox-hounds! You can't just arrest me like this! Like a common criminal! You'll regret it!' Bradley continued to yell, to the mortification of Lucy. 'And I want the prize money back! I withdraw my offer! I will not give one cent to that girl!'

John Bains read the Colonel his rights as he continued to rant and rail. When the legalities were finished, Milo raised his hand, signalling to the other officers to come and take the Colonel away.

'You don't know who you're dealing with! I'll get my lawyers on this case and every goddammed one of you will be in serious trouble! I want to call my lawyer! Someone get Curry on the phone! Terence Curry! Damn! He's dead. Get me a lawyer! I demand a lawyer!'

While the fuss continued, Abby sat quietly on Moonie, taking everything in. She watched as the Colonel was unwillingly escorted to a cruiser and forced to sit in the back.

Hope was slowly growing in her heart. If the police were arresting the Colonel, what exactly did that mean? Was her father exonerated? Was he a free man? They wouldn't arrest the Colonel otherwise, would they?

Pete grabbed her foot in the stirrup. 'Abby. Look. The van.'

Abby turned her head in the direction of the armoured police van. Her heart stopped.

'Dad!' she screamed. 'Dad!'

Abby slid off Moonie's back and stumbled across the grass to where Liam was emerging from the van, tears streaming down his face.

'Abby, my little love!' he called, and started to run to her.

They met. The overjoyed father picked up his daughter in his arms and hugged her tightly. He was overcome with emotion.

Abby clung to him.

'Dad! I can't believe you're here. I can't believe it.'

'Because of you, Abby. I'm here because of you. Thank you.'

Pete and Laura waited for the right moment, then approached them. Laura said, 'Come back to Merry Fields for a celebration after the award ceremony.' She clasped Liam to her, lips trembling and tears of joy in her eyes.

Pete just reached out his hand. Liam took it, and they shook hands in a manly fashion. Then they embraced each other with great affection. 'It's good to see you, Liam,' said Pete.

'It's great to see you,' answered Liam. His eyes took in his daughter. 'You won the steeplechase, Abby! I saw the finish. Boy, was it dramatic! You rode brilliantly, tenacious to the end! I want to hear every little detail. I kept telling the driver to go faster, but he said it wasn't him that was running a race. We got to the top of that hill just as you stormed the last jump and nailed the finish. I couldn't believe it. And I couldn't be prouder.'

'Oh, Dad,' said Abby as they hugged again. 'I'm so glad you saw it. I'm so glad you're home.'

There was a huge crackle of static from the podium. The speakers had been turned on, but the judges didn't know it.

'Is there a hold-up?' the male judge asked.

'Let's get on with the presentation before everybody goes home.'

The second judge nodded, turned to the microphone and tested it. It worked. He put his hand over it, and mouthed, 'It's on.'

The loudspeaker squawked again and the woman judge's voice echoed through the grounds. 'Attention! Please gather for the prize ceremony!'

Pete, Laura, Liam and Abby walked back, arms linked. Liam took Moonie from Lucy, who'd been holding her, and nodded his thanks. He hoisted Abby into Moonie's saddle, and gave her the thumbs up. 'I'm so proud, I'm fit to burst,' he said, eyes glowing.

People came from the food tent and the washrooms and the horse trailers, and eagerly assembled. There had been rumours of a dispute, and everyone wanted to know the decision.

'Thank you for your patience. We have a big surprise. Two celebrities are presenting the cup today. While our surprise guests come forward, I'm pleased to announce today's champion. Against all odds, the winner of the hunt club's first steeplechase in ten years is Abby Malone on Moonlight Sonata!'

The crowd had gathered around the podium, and when Abby's name was called, people broke into wild applause, hooting and stamping their concurrence. They'd seen the stupendous finish. There would've been a big problem if the Colonel had succeeded in disqualifying the plucky little girl on her quicksilver mare.

Abby's ears were ringing with the cheers, but her eyes returned again and again to her father. She was so happy. He'd been there, after all, to see the finish. She seemed to be on automatic pilot. There was too much to absorb.

Then, Abby heard gasps and oohs and ahhs. She turned to look. There, striding lightly on his long athletic legs, trotted Dancer. His shiny chestnut coat flashed in the sunlight, highlighting his well-defined muscles. Hilary James, graceful and confident, rode him out of the woods where they'd been waiting for the decision. She had a happy grin on her face, and was obviously delighted to be presenting the cup.

Abby's jaw dropped. She'd daydreamed about this moment. Hilary and Dancer presenting her with a prize. She'd never, ever, really believed it would come true. It was just a daydream.

But it was true. Dancer drew up beside them. Hilary dropped out of the saddle and jumped up onto the podium to gather the awards. She clipped the large, red, first-place ribbon on Moonie's bridle.

Moonie tossed her head proudly and nickered. Hilary laughed, and said, 'You're welcome!' She looked up at Abby, sitting on Moonie.

'Abby Malone, I knew you that had courage the day that I met you, when you rode the hounds off Cody. I am truly thrilled to have the honour of presenting you with the prize money.' She handed the long, white envelope to Abby.

Abby accepted the thick envelope containing five hundred dollars in cash, and murmured, 'Thank you.'

'I watched the race, Abby. You were great. My heart was in my mouth as you came out of the woods and took on the thoroughbreds. You rode like a professional, fast and safe. I hope you had fun, too.' Hilary smiled warmly.

Abby was overwhelmed with the high praise from her idol. She tried to return the smile but her lip trembled. 'Yes, I did have fun. I sure did.'

Hilary now lifted the silver cup up to Abby. Moonie sidestepped as the late summer sun reflected off the silver and momentarily startled her. Abby patted her neck and talked reassuringly to her. She reached down, took the cup from Hilary and held it in her hands. She and little Moonie had won this silver cup. It was large and round with two handles, one on each side, and an attached pedestal. On it were engraved the names of the winners of all the steeplechases dating back one hundred and fifty years.

'Wow. It's beautiful. Thanks so much.' The flashing silver reminded her of Silver Dollar, the horse with the broken leg. 'We won it for you, Silver Dollar,' she yelled loudly. She hoped the owner of the doomed horse would hear her tribute. 'And for my dad! Liam Malone!'

The crowd roared its approval.

Hilary 'Mousie' James spoke. 'You won it well, Abby Malone, fair and square. Get your name engraved on it, and it will remain there forever.'

'But I bring the cup back next year, right?'

'Next *steeplechase*,' corrected Hilary, laughing. 'And you'll notice the last winner kept it for ten years!'

Abby laughed with her. She could hardly believe that this was happening. What happened next made her wonder if she was dreaming.

Dancer reared up on his hind legs. People stepped back. He stood for many seconds like a bronze statue, then dropped his front feet down. His nose touched the ground as he bent his front legs and stretched his long neck down into his famous bow at

Moonie's feet. Moonie pricked her ears toward him and sniffed his neck. She was intrigued. Dancer nickered to her and lifted his upper lip and sniffed long and loud.

The crowd broke into cheers and hoots and applause. Abby would remember this day for the rest of her life.

Abby needed some time alone. So much had happened today . Her dad was out of jail. She'd won the steeplechase. Sam had been proud of her.

She was thankful for the quiet walk back to Merry Fields, just to let everything sink in. Cody happily limped along behind. Abby led Moonie into the Piersons' barn and took off the tack. She washed her down and rubbed her dry. She combed out her mane and tail and picked out her feet. She soaped and oiled the saddle and bridle and hung the saddle pad out to dry. Finally, Moonie was safely tucked her into her stall for a well-earned dinner and rest. Abby quietly patted her head and whispered, 'Thank you, Moonie. You ran a great race.'

By the time Abby arrived at the farmhouse, the victory party was in full swing. As the kitchen door opened and Abby stepped in, a big cheer went up. 'Hip, hip, Hooray! Hip, hip, Hooray!'

Laura had organized the celebration for Abby the day before, to be held whether she won or not. She had streamers hanging all over the house and plates were piled high with salmon and egg and ham sandwiches. There was steaming coffee, hot chocolate, cookies and brownies.

Laura and Pete had invited Mr and Mrs Morris and Leslie and Sam, Mr and Mrs Masters and Pam, Mr and Mrs Payne and Annie, Lucy and George Farrow. And Liam Malone. Abby looked around at the friendly, smiling people who stood in the kitchen.

'Hooray, hooray!' sang Laura, dancing stiffly after her episode with the cow. Pete rushed to Abby and gave her a big hug. 'Well done, jockey!'

Liam hugged Abby and told her again how extremely proud he was. 'Don't forget, I want details,' he chuckled.

Leslie laughed proudly as she hugged her best friend. Leslie's mother, Mrs Morris, looked at Abby with a new respect. Abby wondered if this day might change her mind about the suitability of her being friends with her daughter, and possibly her son.

Lucy shot through the kitchen and gave her a high five. 'Friends?'

'Friends!'

Sam came up to congratulate her. He reached out to shake her hand. When Abby's hand touched his, she felt like she never wanted to let it go. Sam held it tight, and stared at her. Mindful of the onlookers, Abby said, 'Later.'

Everybody had good wishes for her, even Pam and Annie. Laura brought them over to Abby, one girl on each arm. At first Abby was waiting for sarcasm, especially from Pam, but she very sincerely told Abby that she'd been 'awesome'. When Pam and Annie turned away to get some lunch, Abby gave Laura a questioning look.

'You wonder why I invited your worst enemies to your party?' Laura asked. 'Because with a little coddling and praise, we can drown their meanness with kindness. Don't sink to their level, make them rise to yours. Believe me, Abby, you'd rather have them as friends than foes when you start your new school.' Laura winked, and Abby understood again the wisdom of this wonderful woman. She thanked Laura and gave her a kiss on the cheek.

'I also invited Hilary James, but she had a date with Sandy in Toronto and she didn't want to be late. They're going to dinner and the theatre.'

Abby sighed. That's so romantic, she thought.

'She said to tell you how sorry she was to miss it. She said to congratulate you again for her. Oh! Did you know it was Sandy and Hilary that helped Pete the day the cow trampled me? He recognized her and Dancer today!'

Liam came up behind Abby and tapped her on the shoulder.

'Hi, Dad!'

'My little love! I'd give anything to have seen the whole race. Pete was just telling me about how you came out of the woods and challenged the thoroughbreds! My heavens, you gave the people a show!'

'Dad, I listened to all the things you told me, but in the end, I just let Moonie run her race. She was brilliant, like Carl the Wonder horse.'

'Mr Pierson's horse?'

'Yes, when he was a kid. He told me that story. It was almost the same, Dad. We both were the youngest, riding the smallest horse.'

'With the longest odds.'

'You're right. We made everybody rich!'

'Only those who were smart enough to bet on you. Tell me, was it fun or scary?'

'Both. At the start it was pretty scary, then, when I settled down it became fun. I don't know if I'll ever have as much fun again in my life.'

'That's called adrenalin, Abby, and it's why I kept on racing.'

'But Dad, one horse broke his leg. Silver Dollar. The Colonel's black horse pushed him at a jump, and the horse fell wrong.'

'Abby, I'm sorry you had to see that. It's very sad. But the only way for a horse to stay perfectly safe is to stand in a stall and do nothing. And that's dangerous too, because their intestines cramp and they colic. Most horses would rather die running, given the choice.'

'I guess you're right.'

'I can't really believe I'm here,' he said, looking around. 'Just this morning, I was sitting in my cell.'

Abby studied his face. 'Are you happy, Dad?'

'Oh, yes, I'm happy. But I want to see your mother. Laura said she was coming home this afternoon. I'd like to get the place ready for her.'

'I'm ready to go, anytime. I'll just check on Moonie.' She looked at him closely. 'Tell me Dad, was prison awful?'

Liam's face got serious. 'It wasn't great. But it was better for me than for many others. The warden looked out for me. He still laughs about the time you broke in to see me. He asks that I send his best.'

'He's a nice man.'

'He certainly is.' Liam changed the subject. 'So, find me after you check on Moonie, and I'll see if I can borrow Pete's truck to get us home.'

Abby slipped outside with some scraps and a big prime rib bone that Pete had saved. 'Cody!' she called. The coyote appeared from the bushes. He gingerly lifted the meat from Abby's hands, took it away to one side and gobbled it up. Then he returned for the bone. Opening his mouth carefully, he put the bone between his teeth and disappeared. Abby sighed with contentment and smiled as she wiped her hands on the grass.

She counted her blessings. All was more than right in her world. She thought of Sam and sighed. Just the sight of his melting eyes put her in a dreamy state. She floated to the barn to check on Moonie. Moonie was cool and dry. She'd finished all her oats and still had lots of hay. Abby walked her outside and released her in the field. She gave Moonie an apple and rubbed her forehead as the mare crunched her treat.

Someone came up behind her and put his arms around her waist. She jumped with surprise, and looked around. When she saw that it was Sam, she threw her arms around him. They held each other close. Abby felt happy from the top of her head to the bottom of her feet.

Chapter Twenty
The Homecoming

Wife and child, those precious motives,
those strong knots of love.
– Shakespeare, *Macbeth*, IV, iii

PETE INSISTED that he and Laura drive them home. The guests were on their way anyway, each congratulating Abby again on her ride, and heartily welcoming Liam back.

As they were driving out the lane of Merry Fields, Liam yelled, 'Stop the car! Look!'

Out in the front field stood Moonlight Sonata. With her was a tall stallion with a rich chestnut coat that glistened with the last rays of the setting sun. He lazily nuzzled her neck, and she groomed his withers with her teeth. The people in the stopped car watched spellbound as the two horses showed their affection for one another.

'It's Dancer,' gasped Abby.

'It can't be!' exclaimed Laura.

'But it is,' responded Liam. 'There's not another like him.'

'He's come to call,' said Pete approvingly. 'Well, I'll be.'

Dancer turned to face them. His delicately pointed ears swung forward on his handsome head. His neck arched.

'Wow,' said Abby. 'He's gorgeous.'

He bumped Moonie playfully with his nose, then trotted straight to the four-foot rail fence. He hopped over it like a deer, then cantered nonchalantly down the road toward his home. Beautiful, doe-eyed Moonie watched him until he was out of sight, then resumed grazing on the grass, which was already damp with evening condensation.

Before long they were driving up their winding gravel road. There was a red glow on the western horizon. Liam's heart thrilled at the familiar, fondly remembered sights. He had dreamed many times of these very landmarks in the rolling hills of Caledon.

There was lots to talk about on the short drive home. Cody, Abby and Liam rode in the back, Laura and Pete in the front. There was non-stop chatter and laughter while Liam got filled in about the local gossip he'd missed and heard colourful details about adventures that had occurred while he was in prison.

Abby felt alternately elated and disbelieving. She found herself studying her father's face, reaccustoming herself to his presence, pinching herself. Her dreams had come true, and she'd made them happen. She was filled with joy.

Cody slept in Abby's arms. He had a lot of recovering to do before he'd be healthy again. That he'd be content to ride in a car with people, even these special people, meant that he was in a weakened state.

Pete's car came to a stop outside the Malones' door. The house was blazing with light, and through the windows Abby could see her mother bustling from kitchen to dining room preparing the return feast. Fiona's face looked radiant. She was a beautiful woman, Abby thought, a new woman, a happy woman. She'd taken care with her make-up to cover her bruises and was wearing Liam's favourite dress, a birthday present he'd given her of soft green cotton with a crisp white underblouse. Abby stole a glance at her father. Liam's eyes were devouring his wife as he watched the same scene from inside the car.

Liam ran to his door and flung it open. Fiona threw herself into his arms and they clung together, holding each other in a passion-ate, loving, almost desperate embrace. Tears cascaded down both their faces. Fiona sobbed.

Pete, Laura and Abby waited. Not one of them would break this joyous reunion. Each one understood the sanctity of the moment.

Fiona laughed and wiped the tears from her cheeks. 'Now I've run my mascara! You can't see me like this!'

'You're the most beautiful woman in the world to me, my Fiona girl, with or without mascara. Let me look at you.' He gently cupped her face with his hands and kissed her mouth. He smudged away the mascara with a finger and kissed both of her eyes. 'You're perfect.'

Abby would never forget this picture. It would be a little snapshot in her mind forever. Proof of the love between her mother and father, and confirmation that she was part of a strong and lasting family. A solid rock that she could count on and grow from.

They held eye contact for a lingering moment before Liam stepped away, his arm around Fiona's waist, and motioned to the door.

'Come in, come in, everybody!' he said, loudly, covering his emotion.

They all stepped into the Malone house. Fiona couldn't take her eyes off Liam.

'We'd hoped to get here ahead of you, to get the house ready,' said Abby. 'Are you feeling okay?'

'Don't worry about me, Abby. I'm the happiest woman on the face of the earth.'

'Fiona, how did you get home?' asked Laura. 'Ambulance?'

'Oh! I almost forgot!' Fiona threw her hands to her mouth. 'I'm so excited to see Liam that I'm losing my mind! Come into the living room. There's someone here. A very special guest.'

Pete and Laura hung back to let Liam and Abby go first, followed by Fiona.

Standing in front of a pleasantly burning fire stood Jim Price, the warden of the Millhaven Penitentiary.

'Warden!' Liam Malone was shocked.

'Call me Jim. Please. And may I shake your hand.'

Abby looked at her mother. Fiona was smiling like she hadn't smiled since Liam's arrest.

'Abby, my friend,' said Jim Price, jovially. 'It's good to see you.'

'It's good to see you, too. This is Mr and Mrs Pierson, our friends.'

'People call me Pete, and this is Laura, my wife.'

'Well, it's indeed a pleasure.' Jim Price looked around the room. 'I know my presence here is a mystery to you. Let me explain. Shall we take a seat?'

'Oh, please,' exclaimed Fiona. 'Please, everyone sit down.'

People found places to sit while Jim Price took a folder out of his briefcase and set it on the coffee table. He removed his glasses from their case and set them down beside the folder.

'Liam was released this morning, and special arrangements were made to deliver him home. Normally, a person is given a train ticket and a boot out the door, but I decided that Liam deserved to be driven home. I do that very rarely.' Jim smiled at Liam, then went on. 'I didn't have a chance to talk with Liam before he left, so I thought I'd drop in to explain the reasons he was released. I wanted, in this case, to do it in person. Since it was convenient, I picked up Fiona from the hospital and drove her home this afternoon. My sister doesn't live far away, and she's invited me for the weekend.'

'You drove me home, but you didn't answer any of my questions,' Fiona complained.

Jim smiled. 'That's because I wanted to tell it only once, and don't you think your husband should hear it first, anyway?'

'Please,' said Abby. 'Everyone wants to hear.'

'Right you are. Let's not waste any more time.' Jim Price looked from face to face, then spoke directly to Liam. 'Your conviction was overturned by the Court of Appeal based on new evidence that was discovered by your daughter, Abby Malone.'

Liam nodded. 'That's all I was told. What did Abby find? What happened? Who did it? Can you enlighten us?'

Jim nodded, beaming. 'Of course. That's why I'm here. This is what was sent to me. Stop me anytime if any of you have questions.' He placed his reading glasses on his nose and cleared his throat.

'Abby located, er, by unconfirmed methods, ahem,' he winked at Abby, 'some papers in a folder in Kenneth Bradley's study. They were legally removed by the OPP and sent by the Crown to the Court of Appeal as new and pertinent evidence. I was faxed copies of the contents of the folder. Indeed, the papers illustrate how it was done.'

'How what was done?' asked Liam.

'The crime.'

Liam shook his head, flabbergasted. He prompted, 'And what papers were these?'

'There was a photocopy of a cheque signed by you, Liam, for five thousand dollars made out to "A.B.C." Here is a copy.' Jim Price set it on the table where they all could see it.

'And here's a second photocopy of a cheque signed by you for five million, five thousand dollars, made out to Mr Al B. Chalmers.' He placed the second paper on the table beside the first.

'But I never signed a cheque for that much money to anyone,' stated Liam firmly. 'I said so in court under oath. I don't know anyone of that name and I wasn't in the office the day it was issued!'

Jim Price smiled. 'Have patience and it will all come clear. If you look closely, you will see how the cheque has been altered. Your signature is authentic, but the date, the amount and the recipient have all been falsified. Look.

'The date on the original was October the second. It was altered to read October twenty-seventh by typing in a seven after the two.' Jim Price pointed to the dates on each photocopy, and continued.

'On the "pay to the order of" line, A.B.C. was changed to Mr Al B. Chalmers by putting "Mr" in front, typing "l" over the period after the "A", and adding "halmers" after the C.

'On the original cheque, "five thousand" was typed in the middle of this line. Which left room,' he said, indicating the amount line, 'to add "five million" in front of it. The same technique was used in the box where the dollar amount is written numerically. "5,000.00" was originally typed leaving room for "5,00" to be added to the front of it, changing the amount to 5,005,000.00. Do you follow, so far?'

Nobody answered. They were all staring at the photocopies on the coffee table. He resumed his explanation.

'The falsified amount was to be withdrawn from the Colonel's children's trust fund. That was added to the bottom left section entitled, "memo". All these changes were made on the same typewriter as the original, but at a different time. This has been substantiated by the forensic people in Toronto. The alterations were less than one-thousandth of a centimetre off. Undetectable unless you were specifically looking for them with a microscope.'

Everyone continued to study the photocopies. 'Now, here is a memo to you from Terence Curry, requesting you to sign a five-thousand-dollar cheque made out to the A.B.C. office equipment people, in payment for services.'

'Which was unusual, but Terence said the person who does the office bookkeeping was sick, and I never questioned it.' Liam's brows furrowed. 'I remember. I just signed it.'

'Then there's this.' Jim pulled out another page. 'This letter is to Al Chalmers from the Bank of the Bahamas. It confirms that the sum of five million dollars was received from the Banque de Guerre in Switzerland. This letter, which is new evidence, states that the Bank of the Bahamas had fulfilled their instructions to purchase a condominium on behalf of Mr Al B. Chalmers. The letter also states that a money order was made out to a Terence Curry on behalf of the same party. The remainder was put in a numbered company owned by Mr Al B. Chalmers. That left nothing in the account and it was immediately closed. This is a photocopy of the money order.' Jim Price looked up. 'So far so good?'

Bewildered faces looked back at him.

'How much of the money did Curry get?' asked Pete, frowning.

'One million, plus the five thousand, which he used for travelling expenses.'

'Travelling expenses,' pondered Liam aloud. 'So he doctored the cheque and took it to Switzerland and deposited it himself. With fake I.D.? He must have presented himself as "Al Chalmers". Am I correct?'

Jim nodded. 'You are correct. Once it was safely in an account in Switzerland, where they protect information by law, he knew it would never be traced back to him. The trail ends there. But, just to be doubly sure, he had it moved electronically once more, and had it in the Bahamian bank in an account he'd opened earlier, before the Toronto banks opened Monday morning. Very tidy.'

Abby jumped up, enraged. 'So, they'd been planning this? And he had another identity ready to use at a moment's notice?'

'Yes, Abby,' answered Jim. 'Passport, driver's licence, health card, social insurance, the works. The real story has been uncovered, thanks to your finding this file, Abby. At the first trial, the jury had only the altered cheque that had been returned to the firm, signed by Liam, and dead-ending in Switzerland. The Al Chalmers name was assumed to be Liam's alias, and it looked as if the money was hidden, waiting for Liam to recover it at his leisure. But with the photocopy of the original pre-doctored cheque, the memo and the letter from the Bank of the Bahamas, the Crown knew what to look for and they wasted no time. Oh, and there's more.' Jim pulled a sheet out of the file. 'The autopsy report. Terence Curry's fingerprints correspond exactly to the fingerprints all over the papers in this file, linking him physically to the new evidence. No doubts remain.'

Pete and Laura and Liam all responded at once with various noises of disbelief.

'It's sick,' exclaimed Laura. 'You can't sell loyalty and friendship for money. And to think that he sat mute throughout the whole trial and allowed his best friend and law partner to go to jail!' Laura shook her head angrily. Pete patted her hand. He loved her feisty defence of integrity.

'Well, he's far from earthly justice, now. He'll be dealing with the ultimate court.' Liam's weariness caused him to sink down further into the couch.

'I think he was sorry in the end about what he'd done,' said Abby thoughtfully. 'Remember the barn fire and how he tried to get insurance money for us so we could keep the farm?'

Pete nodded. 'Those things make sense now, don't they? Maybe he thought he'd make it up to your family somehow. It's too late now, of course.'

'Not really.' Jim pulled a paper out and waved it. 'Says here that he willed all his possessions to your family, Liam. I gather he had no relatives.'

'Except his wife, but she'd left him for another man. They had no children,' answered Liam, nodding.

'That means you'll be financially secure,' continued Jim. 'With the house and stock options and his investments and assets, minus the million that will go back into the trust, you're looking at a nice little bundle.'

'He's saved the farm,' stated Liam. 'I have to thank him for that.'

'It's only right!' exclaimed Laura. 'After all, he put it in jeopardy in the first place. He ruined your reputation and sent you to jail in the name of greed!'

'Dad's reputation will be better than ever,' responded Abby loyally. 'Once people know the real story, I bet he'll have more clients than ever.'

'My girl,' said Liam as he gave her arm a squeeze. 'It's never easy to rebuild a life, but I'll give it my best shot. I won't waste any time worrying about the past.'

'Wait a minute,' mused Abby aloud, thinking hard. 'We had a piece of the evidence all along. Remember how Mr Curry needed a paper from Dad's files? You know, that Mom let him take the night that Mrs Pierson went to the hospital after being trampled by the cow?'

Liam looked thoughtful. 'It must have been the photocopy of the original cheque I signed for five thousand dollars. I always photocopied cheques for my records, and he knew that.' Liam shook his head, trying to understand. 'I can't believe it. I never thought to look for a cheque that could be falsified. I never imagined anything like this ... I trusted him. But why would he want it? Especially when it would prove his guilt?'

'Better in his possession than yours, Liam,' nodded Pete wisely.

'But why keep it? Why not destroy it?' asked Liam.

'Lucy overheard the Colonel telling Mr Curry that he had documents that would put him in jail,' Abby offered. 'And I heard the Colonel telling Mr Curry to get something when I was at the hospital. Maybe the Colonel ordered him to get the photocopy to create a blackmail file.'

'If Terence knew it would be used against him, he obviously wouldn't have given it to the Colonel,' said Pete. 'The Colonel likely told him that he'd destroy it so nobody could ever track them down.'

Jim Price spoke up. 'This is all speculation. However this folder was put together, whoever did it and for whatever reasons doesn't matter. We have it in our hands. And it proves the innocence of Liam Malone. The police are now investigating Colonel Kenneth Bradley, who is going to try to pin the whole thing on Terence Curry, of course. The old saying goes, "Always blame a dead man." Of course, now the Colonel is referred to as Mr Kenneth Bradley. The Canadian forces are looking into his false use of a military title. They might press their own charges.' This news pleased everyone.

Liam remained sombre. 'The Colonel stole money from his own children. Kenneth Bradley's father didn't trust his own son to manage the family money, so he bypassed Kenneth in favour of the following generation.'

'Smart father, to recognize larceny in his son and admit it,' said Pete.

'So Kenneth Bradley stole over five million dollars from his children and put you in jail to cover it up. It's despicable.' Laura couldn't imagine the deceit.

'And paid Mr Curry to do it for him,' said Abby with agitation. 'He shot Cody and locked me in his shed. He's a horrible man. I hope they put him in jail and throw away the key!'

'What I find ironic,' said Pete, 'is that he has hoist himself with his own petard.'

'Shakespeare again?' guessed Abby.

'*Hamlet*, Act III,' nodded Pete. 'Bradley collected evidence to blackmail Curry into further service, and ended up condemning himself.'

'What goes around comes around, my dear,' said Laura. ''Twas ever thus. That could be Shakespeare, too, but I'd have to look it up.'

'If any questions arise, I'll be at my sister's. I'll leave her number with you.' Jim Price stood up. 'I must be off. I don't want to be late for dinner.'

'Thank you, Jim,' said Liam, standing. 'It's beyond the call of duty for you to come to talk to us. And I really appreciate your picking up Fiona today.'

'It was my pleasure. As I said, my sister doesn't live far from here. Liam, I wouldn't do this for just anyone. You were a model prisoner, and a gentleman from day one. I'm delighted that justice was finally done, thanks to your daughter. It was my privilege to carry it out.'

Jim Price headed for the door. Fiona and Liam followed him.

'I appreciate your taking the time to tell us personally,' said Liam.

'Thank you, Jim,' Fiona said as she opened the door for him.

Jim Price shook their hands and he was gone. Fiona and Liam stood watching his car drive away, Liam's arm around Fiona's shoulder.

Then Liam turned to Pete and Laura, who were standing in the living room. 'Please, everyone, come into the dining room. From the delicious aromas I would say that dinner is served! Am I right, my love?'

'You're absolutely right. It's so good to have you home.' Fiona led the way through the front hall.

Abby noticed how much work her mother had done since coming home from the hospital that day. The house was orderly and clean. Colourful, fragrant flower arrangements adorned the living room, the dining room, the kitchen and the hall. A roaring fire crackled cheerfully in the fireplace. Their best white Irish linen was draped over the dining table, which was set for five with sparkling crystal wine glasses and all their best silver and china. Tall candles sat in the centre of the table, glowing softly, reflected again and again in the silver spoons and the china.

Pete wasn't sure they should stay. He didn't want to intrude. 'We'll say our good nights, Liam. Laura and I have had a long day.'

'Dinner's ready, Pete! We'd be disappointed if you left now.'

Laura said, 'Your family's together again. You should have some time alone, to reaquaint yourselves.' She took Pete's arm, ready to leave.

'Please, Laura,' said Fiona, stopping them. 'We have all our lives together to do that. Tonight, we'd be honoured if you'd stay. You've done so much for us, and especially for Abby. It would mean a lot to me.'

Pete saw the sincerity in her eyes and checked with Laura. She smiled and nodded. 'Smells good,' he said. 'What's for dinner?'

Everyone laughed at the mischievous expression on Pete's face. While Laura and Fiona clattered in the kitchen, Abby made a soft bed of old wool blankets for Cody. She put it out of the way of kitchen traffic, but where he could keep an eye on things. Cody wasn't usually allowed in the house, but Fiona was too busy preparing dinner to notice.

A crispy green salad, broccoli in creamy cheese sauce, hot dinner rolls, and a perfectly browned steak and kidney pie were carried in. Once everyone had washed up and the steaming food was on the table, they all sat down.

They held hands around the table and sang the Johnny Appleseed grace. It had long been a tradition in the Pierson home, and Abby liked it so much that the Malones adopted it for themselves.

Oh, the Lord is good to me,
And so I thank the Lord,
For giving me the things I need,
The sun and the rain and the apple seed.
The Lord is good to me.
Amen!

There was ice water in the crystal wine glasses, and no wine bottles in sight. Abby lifted her glass and said, 'Before we eat, I'd like to make a toast, please.' She had everyone's attention. She stood, awkwardly wiping a stray strand of hair from her eyes.

'I want to say welcome home, Dad. I missed you.' Liam nodded encouragement. 'And Mom, thank you for making home so perfect tonight. You went to a lot of trouble, even though you're just out of the hospital.' Fiona looked touched and pleased. 'And here's to the Piersons, who are my friends. You helped me when I was in big trouble.' Laura took Pete's hand and squeezed it. 'I'm not sure I'd be alive if Mr Pierson hadn't rescued me from the shed, and I'm not sure I've ever really thanked Mrs Pierson for all the kind things she's done for me. I love you all. Cheers.' Abby blushed and sat down.

They drank the toast, then Laura took the floor. 'Anything I do for you, dearest Abby, makes me happy, so I'm the winner. I thank you for being the wonderful girl that you are.' Her voice became hoarse. 'It's so nice to be sitting here with your family all together … Pete? … can you …' Laura had become emotional and couldn't speak further. Pete took her arm, helped her into her seat and kissed her cheek.

He raised his glass. "I count myself in nothing else so happy, as in a soul remembering my good friends." *Richard II*. I propose a toast to the Malone family. Strong and true. You've been through the fire, each of you, and you're tougher for it. May the next years bear the fruit you so richly deserve.' As they drank to this, Abby noticed on Pete's kind, strong face the drop of a tear, glittering for only a second in the candlelight.

Fiona began to speak. She faltered, and cleared her throat. 'I'm deeply grateful to everyone at this table. You all know my personal struggles. I'm sorry for how I've let you down. I pledge to change all that, with your help and understanding, and I want each one of you to know how much I love you.' She seemed about to cry, and Abby wanted to hug her, but she went on, 'And my husband, my love has no bounds. To see you at the end of the table once more …' again she could barely continue, so deep was her gratitude at having him home '… brings me untold joy.'

By now there was such an outflowing of emotion at the Malones' dining room table that they needed a diversion. Liam shot to his feet. 'The dinner's getting cold!' he declared cheerfully. 'And it's steak and kidney pie! My favourite food in all the world. I'll serve, and you'd better be nice to me or you won't get seconds.

'But just before I dig the spoon into this perfect crust, I have to speak. My Irish heart is bursting. Abby, you got me my freedom; the most precious gift of all, after love and health. You're truly a brave girl, and I'm proud of you.' Abby blushed again. 'Fiona, the future starts today, and I'm blessed to have the honour of sharing it with you.' He bowed to her, and she nodded. 'Pete, Laura, your friendship is treasured by all the Malones, but maybe especially by me. You looked out for my family when I was locked away. Let's raise our glasses to life, to love, to health, to friendship. And to freedom.'

After Liam's toast, no more were needed. It seemed the very air around them was saturated with pleasure and a warm, hopeful vision of whatever was to come. Abby sat back in her chair, listening to the cheerful conversation, smelling the hot, wholesome food, and feeling the love in the room. She wrapped it around her like a blanket, and stored it away in her heart.

She felt a cold nose on her leg. Mysterious grey eyes looked up at her, asking to be included in the emotion. She gently and lovingly patted his rough fur. Now satisfied, Cody lay down at her feet.

Epilogue
One Year Later

I know a bank where the wild thyme blows,
Where oxlips and the nodding violet grows.
– Shakespeare, *A Midsummer Night's Dream*, ii, i

It was late August. A full year to the day had passed since Liam had been released from prison. The air was warm, ripe with the delightful aromas of summer. Abby inhaled the scents of fragrant flowers, damp rich earth, and her own sun-warmed skin. She listened contentedly to the whirring sounds of busy insects interspersed with the symphony created by various species of birds singing out to each other. She languidly watched the fluttering shadow patterns that crossed her arm as the soft breeze caressed the leaves above her. With her trusted Cody at her side, Abby sat in her favourite tree lazily remembering that day one year ago. How happy it had been. She contemplated all the changes that the year had brought since then.

They had paid the bank in time to save their farm. It was September first, the day of the deadline, that Liam Malone had slapped the payment on the manager's desk.

The 'Colonel', Kenneth Bradley, had gone to jail. He'd tried to put all the blame on Terence Curry, but it wouldn't stick. He had profited too much himself, and there was evidence that he was about to attempt another raid on that same trust fund, a raid that Terence Curry had been opposing. The folder Abby had found in his den not only freed her father, but it definitively put the guilt where it belonged. Abby was pleased and proud at the part she'd played in proving her father's innocence, but still shuddered at the memory of that dark rainy night when she'd broken into the Bradley mansion. She rubbed Cody's head and scratched his ears, thinking again how brave he'd been, and how close to death. Cody looked back at her, adoration shining in his gentle grey eyes.

After much discussion, the family had concluded that Terence Curry had fallen prey to the temptation of greed in a time of weakness. His divorce had been very costly, giving him the choice of selling his half of the law firm and his house, or taking the option presented by the Colonel. Once into the dirty deal, it was too late to turn back. However, his guilty conscience nagged at him. He visited Liam in jail many times. He started the barn fire to get insurance money so the Malones could keep the farm. When that plan failed, he offered to pay for an apartment for Fiona and Abby. But no matter how remorseful he felt, he didn't have the courage to come clean and take his punishment. Instead, he let Liam take it for him. Even so, at one time he'd been a friend and a partner, and his downfall and death were mourned.

Her father's conviction had been stricken from the record, which meant that officially it was as if it had never happened. He wouldn't be interrogated at airports, or have the prison sentence come up on police computers when he was stopped for a speeding ticket.

Liam had stepped back into his practice and never missed a beat. As Abby had predicted, people were eager to use his legal services. Liam was looking for a good horse to buy for himself, so that he and Abby could ride together. He wanted to ride, to travel, to ski, to sail. He wanted to live his life to the fullest. He often said that prison teaches you a greater appreciation for freedom. He looked healthy and happy and Abby felt grateful each day that he was home. She admired his ability to look forward, not to cast blame or demand retribution for the past.

Her mother had worked hard reclaiming the gardens around the house, and the painters had smartened up the trim. Their lovely red-brick farmhouse looked cared-for and attractive again. She'd joined a club and enrolled in a credit course to finish her university degree. So far, with Liam's strong presence, she'd been able to resist the temptation of alcohol. Home had become a loving, thriving place once more. Her mother was disciplined and determined to succeed, but knew that it would be a lifetime addiction. The relationship between Abby and her mother was growing steadily. They were replacing the dark memories. They laughed together, and talked to each other about almost everything. It doesn't get better than this, Abby concluded.

Abby loved her new school. As Mrs Pierson had predicted, her old enemies Pam and Annie had become neutralized. They'd never be friends, Abby considered, but at least they said hello in the halls. Leslie, loyal, kind, and trustworthy, would always be her best friend. They were inseparable. Lucy, who'd moved in with the Farrows, was turning out to be as good as her word; she never made any more trouble for Abby. In fact, Abby and Lucy had become friends. Lucy was the class clown, with her caustic wit and quick retorts making her popular with everyone. Abby would always remember that Lucy had told her where the incriminating papers were hidden.

Abby had been dating Sam since last summer. She couldn't imagine a more decent and humorous person. Sitting in her tree hideout, she smiled broadly, thinking about him. They always had fun and they never ran out of things to talk about. He'd started riding, too. Abby was teaching him. Abby knew the other girls envied her having such a good-looking boyfriend.

The Piersons were in good health and remained dear friends of the Malones. They were like family, thought Abby, always ready and willing to help. Their kindness and good humour prevailed, no matter what happened. Abby would be forever thankful about how supportive they were all through her troubles.

So quietly had Abby sat as her mind meandered, that a little red squirrel had climbed the entire length of the tree trunk and was now looking her square in the eye. It reminded her of Reddy, the ill-fated baby killed in the barn fire. She felt sad as she remembered the sight of his charred little body. The red squirrel continued to stare at her, unsure of what large creature it had come upon. Abby averted her eyes subtly, and remained motionless and unthreatening. After sixty seconds of hesitation, it continued its climb, satisfied that it was in no danger. Abby watched in covert fascination as tiny paws grasped the bark and plumed tail twitched. It disappeared around the trunk and Abby continued her reverie.

Moonie's belly had begun to get larger around Christmas. Alan Masters had been called in through the deep snow to determine the cause. There was much celebration and speculation when the vet proclaimed her to be in foal, due in late July, eleven months after Dancer had been seen visiting. A horse's gestation period is eleven months. It was the best Christmas present possible.

Right on schedule, a perfect filly had been born at Merry Fields. Moonie delivered her at midnight behind the shed in the pouring rain. For the week before the birth, Pete and Abby had been taking turns checking on her at two-hour intervals. That night, it was Abby's turn. Taking her flashlight with her, she looked everywhere for Moonie, but the night was so dark that she could see nothing. Finally the beam caught something white. She trained the light on the white object, and saw that it was growing. Then she realized that it was coming out of Moonie's hindquarters. It was the amniotic sac! A foal was being born while Moonie was still standing. Abby ran to the house and got Pete.

He came running, but by the time they got there, the foal was already out and Moonie was licking the sac away from its nose to let it breathe. Pete and Abby had stood in awe, watching innate maternal instincts at work.

The rain that night had continued to fall. Pete worried that the baby might catch cold, so he and Abby put her into the wheel barrow and rolled her into the barn where a warm, dry stall had been prepared. Moonie followed the barrow, making low, reassuring noises to her baby.

Before long, the baby girl was up on long wobbly legs looking for nourishment. Pete helped her find her mother's teats. They laughed at the loud sucking noises she made until she was firmly on the teat and drinking the vital first milk that would immunize her against disease.

It was when the filly was a week old that the last remaining doubt as to her parentage was dispelled. Already, they knew she was going to grow up to be an exceptional mare. She was extra tall, clean-limbed and leggy, with a perfect head carriage and a springy step. Her coat was coming in a dark chestnut, and her face was handsome and intelligent. But when she was only seven days old,

Dancer made another visit.

Pete and Laura had watched, transfixed, through the kitchen window. The gracefully athletic Dancer hopped the fence and strolled over to where Moonie and the filly were grazing. Pete had concerns about what the stallion might do, but they proved needless. Dancer greeted Moonie like an old friend and sniffed his daughter all over. Once satisfied that all was well, he hopped back out. He reared up on his back legs and whinnied a deep, long bellow that echoed for miles. He dropped back down, nickered to his woman, and was on his way. Pete and Laura stood at the window long after Dancer had gone.

When Hilary James first heard the news, she'd been bewildered and quite concerned. He'd never jumped into a field and impregnated a mare before, at least to her knowledge. But when she'd been convinced that neither Abby nor the Piersons were upset, she was relieved. She'd been as excited as Abby when she saw the filly, and had proclaimed that she'd never seen a more perfect foal.

Abby named the filly 'Moon Dancer'. No other name seemed as right.

Abby stretched her legs. She'd been sitting in her tree for some time. She prepared to climb down, thinking she'd bicycle over to Merry Fields and play with Moonie and Moon Dancer. She loved grooming the little filly and picking up her feet. She groomed every part of her strong little body, to get her used to human handling.

Sam got off work from his summer job at the Valu-Mart at five, so they'd meet for a hamburger and take in the seven o'clock show.

Just then, she heard a noise. 'Che che che che.' Abby looked up into branches and all around. 'Che che che che.' Where was it coming from?

A large masked raccoon head came into view below her on the ground. Then another. Elated, she slid down the trunk and sat on the ground. 'Well, hello, boys. Long time no see. Have you two ever got big!'

The raccoons kept their distance, but wriggled their noses happily and made welcoming noises. Then they waddled off. Abby watched them go, delighted to see them alive and healthy, but wistful that they weren't pets any more.

Rook turned to look at her. 'Che che che che.' Around the base of a big old weeping willow popped another masked face. A small, pretty female face. Then three furry little baby faces, curiously peeking out behind their mother.

'Rook! You're a father! Congratulations!' Abby was thrilled.

Rascal, not to be outdone, called Abby. 'Che che che che!' She looked where he had hidden himself behind a bush. A second later out came Rascal, followed by a lovely female and four cute babies.

'Rascal, you rascal!'

Abby sat on the ground watching in awe as the raccoon families sauntered proudly away. With their tiny round ears and bouncing behinds, the little ones reminded her achingly of Rook and Rascal as they'd been when she'd first found them, motherless and hungry and scared. She found that tears were coming down her face in torrents.

'This is crazy! I'm happy, not sad,' she told Cody. He'd been sitting quietly with her the whole time, and now, one front paw consolingly placed on her lap, he busied himself licking away her tears.

'I'm happy my family is together again in our own house. I'm happy my life is good. I'm happy about Sam and all my friends and the wonderful Piersons and Moonie and Moon Dancer and you. So why am I crying?'

Cry she did. Abby Malone sat on the ground under her favourite tree with her brave Cody and cried all the tears she could not cry when she'd needed to cry the most.

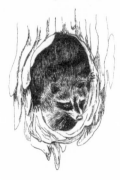

Acknowledgements

To my great love, David, thank you. To Ben, to Chloe, and to Adam: you enrich my life on a daily basis and bring me joy.

I thank all my family, Matthews and Petersons, for support and encouragement. Many of you read and commented on early drafts, giving me immeasurable assistance. I thank my mother, Joyce Mathews, and my niece, Robin Spano, in particular.

Our good friends the McGraths cheerfully helped throughout. Judge Ted McGrath expertly advised me on legal matters in Abby's world (any errors are my own), and Nancy contributed her grammarian skills.

Once again, I'm indebted to my dear multitalented friend and riding companion Marybeth Drake for the exquisite and masterful illustrations that enhance these pages.

Katie Harris graces the cover on her wonderful mount, Starman.

Super-editor John Metcalf cleverly made me think his insights were my own, which is only a small part of his genius. Doris Cowan (a.k.a. the Grammar Girl) polished the final copy with precision and sensitivity.

My heartfelt thanks to Tim and Elke Inkster of The Porcupine's Quill, who produce the finest-looking books in Canada. They bring *Abby Malone* to my readers in a form of which I'm very proud.

Born in London, Ontario, Shelley Peterson is the second of six children of Don and Joyce Matthews. She was trained in Theatre Arts at the Banff School of Performing Arts, Dalhousie University, and University of Western Ontario. Her first theatrical appearance was in a production of *Pinocchio* at the Grand Theatre at the age of ten. Her professional career began with *A Midsummer Night's Dream* at the Neptune Theatre in Halifax when she was nineteen. Since then she has played over one hundred roles in television, film and on stage. She starred in two television series, 'Not My Department' and 'Doghouse'.

Shelley has had a lifelong love of animals, big and small, with a particular interest in horses. She has ridden since she was a girl, and currently holds the trophy for the Caledon Steeplechase Team Event.

Shelley divides her time between Toronto and Fox Ridge, a horse farm in the Caledon hills, which she shares with her husband, their two sons and daughter, and the family dog, Wile E. Coyote.